ALSO BY JOYCE CAROL OATES

A
GARDEN
OF EARTHLY
DELIGHTS

JOYCE CAROL OATES

A
GARDEN
OF EARTHLY
DELIGHTS

Afterword by the author

THE MODERN LIBRARY

NEW YORK

2003 Modern Library Paperback Edition

Copyright © 1966, 1967 by Joyce Carol Oates
Copyright © 2003 by Ontario Review, Inc.
Biographical note copyright © 2000 by Random House, Inc.
All rights reserved under International and Pan-American Copyright
Conventions. Published in the United States by Modern Library, an imprint
of The Random House Ballantine Publishing Group, a division of
Random House, Inc., New York, and simultaneously in Canada by
Random House of Canada Limited, Toronto.

MODERN LIBRARY and the TORCHBEARER Design are registered trademarks
of Random House, Inc.

This work was originally published, in substantially different form, in 1967 by
Vanguard Books. This edition is published by arrangement with the author.

LIBRARY OF CONGRESS CATALOGING-IN-PUBLICATION DATA
Oates, Joyce Carol, 1938–
A garden of earthly delights / Joyce Carol Oates.—Modern Library pbk. ed.
p.   cm.
ISBN 0-8129-6834-4
1. Children of migrant laborers—Fiction. 2. Fathers and daughters—
Fiction. 3. Illegitimate children—Fiction. 4. Mothers and sons—
Fiction. 5. Poor women—Fiction. I. Title.
PS3565.A8 G3 2003
813'.54—dc21   2002038012

Modern Library website address: www.modernlibrary.com

Printed in the United States of America

2 4 6 8 9 7 5 3 1

JOYCE CAROL OATES

Joyce Carol Oates, one of America's most versatile and prolific contemporary writers, was born in the small town of Lockport, New York, on June 16, 1938. She grew up on a farm in nearby Erie County and began writing stories while still in elementary school. As a teenager she devoured works by Faulkner, Dostoyevsky, Thoreau, Hemingway, and the Brontës, and soon moved on to D. H. Lawrence, Flannery O'Connor, Thomas Mann, and Franz Kafka. Oates graduated Phi Beta Kappa from Syracuse University in 1960 and was awarded an M.A. from the University of Wisconsin in 1961. During the 1960s and 1970s she taught English at the University of Detroit and the University of Windsor in Ontario, Canada. In 1974 she cofounded the *Ontario Review* with her husband, Raymond Smith. Oates was named a member of the American Academy and Institute of Arts and Letters in 1978, the same year she became writer-in-residence at Princeton University, where she is currently the Roger S. Berlind Distinguished Professor in the Humanities.

Oates's first novel, *With Shuddering Fall* (1964), the story of a destructive romance between a teenage girl and a thirty-year-old race car driver, foreshadowed her preoccupation with violence and darkness. Her next novel, *A Garden of Earthly Delights* (1967), is the opening volume in a trilogy about different socioeconomic groups in America that incorporates *Expensive People* (1968) and *them* (1969), for which she won the National Book Award. Throughout the 1970s Oates pursued her exploration of American people and institutions in a series of novels that fuse social analysis with vivid psychological portrayals. *Wonderland* (1971) exposes the shortcomings of the medical world; *Do With Me What You Will* (1973) centers on the legal profession; *The Assassins* (1975) attacks political corruption; *Son of the Morning* (1978) tracks the rise and fall of a religious zealot; and *Unholy Loves* (1979) looks at pettiness and hypocrisy within the academic community. "Like the most important modern writers— Joyce, Proust, Mann—Oates has an absolute identification with her material: the spirit of a society at a crucial point in its history," noted *Newsweek*. Novels such as *Childwold* (1976) and *Cybele* (1979) showcase what Alfred Kazin called "her sweetly brutal sense of what American experience is really like."

"Joyce Carol Oates is a fearless writer . . . [with] impossibly lush and dead-on imaginative powers," noted the *Los Angeles Times Book Review*. During this same period she secured her reputation as a virtuoso of the short story with eight acclaimed collections: *By the North Gate* (1963), *Upon the Sweeping Flood* (1966), *The Wheel of Love* (1970), *Marriages and Infidelities* (1972), *The Goddess and Other Women* (1974), *The Poisoned Kiss and Other Stories from the Portuguese* (1975), *Crossing the Border* (1976), *Night-Side* (1977). "In the landscape of the contemporary American short story Miss Oates stands out as a master, occupying a preeminent category of her own," said the *Saturday Review*. "[Oates] intuitively seems to know that the short story is for a different type of material from the novel: a brief and dazzling plunge into another state of consciousness," remarked Erica Jong. "Miss Oates [is] our poet laureate of schizophrenia, of blasted childhoods, of random acts of violence." Her stories have been widely anthologized, and she is a three-time winner of the O. Henry Continuing Achievement Award as well as the recipient of the PEN/ Malamud Award for Lifetime Achievement in the Short Story.

"Joyce Carol Oates is that rarity in American fiction, a writer who seems to grow with each new book," said *Time*. She set out in new directions in the 1980s with an acclaimed series of bestselling novels that exploit the conventions of Gothic literature: *Bellefleur*

(1980), *A Bloodsmoor Romance* (1982), and *Mysteries of Winterthurn* (1984). In addition she wrote *Angel of Light* (1981), *Solstice* (1985), *Marya: A Life* (1986), *You Must Remember This* (1987), and *American Appetites* (1989): a succession of works that make it clear why *Commonweal* deemed her "the most relentless chronicler of America and its nightmares since Poe." "Oates's best novels are strongly reminiscent of Faulkner's, especially in their uncompromised vision of the violence her characters visit upon one another and themselves," said *The Washington Post Book World.* "Even her humor—and she can be hilariously funny—is mordantly ironical." Using the pseudonym Rosamond Smith she began writing a series of psychological suspense novels: *Lives of the Twins* (1987), *Soul/Mate* (1989), *Nemesis* (1990), *Snake Eyes* (1992), *You Can't Catch Me* (1995), *Double Delight* (1997), and *Starr Bright Will Be with You Soon* (1999). Her compilations of short stories continued with *A Sentimental Education* (1980), *Last Days* (1984), *Raven's Wing* (1986), and *The Assignation* (1988). In addition she enjoyed great success with *On Boxing* (1987), an eloquent meditation on prizefighting.

"Oates's unblinking curiosity about human nature is one of the great artistic forces of our time," observed *The Nation* as her output proliferated throughout the 1990s. Her novels further examined the violence underlying many realities of American culture: racism (*Because It Is Bitter, and Because It Is My Heart,* 1990), alienation (*I Lock My Door upon Myself,* 1990), poverty (*The Rise of Life on Earth,* 1991), the interplay of politics and sex (*Black Water,* 1992), feminism (*Foxfire: Confessions of a Girl Gang,* 1993), success (*What I Lived For,* 1994), serial killers (*Zombie,* 1995), family disintegration (*We Were the Mulvaneys,* 1996), outlaw cults (*Man Crazy,* 1997), criminality and greed (*My Heart Laid Bare,* 1998), and fame and celebrity (*Broke Heart Blues,* 1999, and *Blonde,* 2000). "A future archaeologist equipped only with her *oeuvre* could easily piece together the whole of postwar America," said Henry Louis Gates, Jr. "No one knows the darkness of our age, of our own natures, the prison of our narcissism, better than Joyce Carol Oates," wrote *The Washington Post Book World.* Her volumes of short stories dating from this period include *Heat* (1991), *Where Is Here?* (1992), *Haunted: Tales of the Grotesque* (1994), *"Will You Always Love Me?"* (1996), and *The Collector of Hearts: New Tales of the Grotesque*

(1998). "Oates has imbued the American short story with an edgy vitality and raw social surfaces," stated the *Chicago Tribune,* and Alice Adams deemed her short fiction "immensely exhilarating, deeply exciting." In 1994 she received the Bram Stoker Lifetime Achievement Award in Horror Fiction.

"Joyce Carol Oates belongs to that small group of writers who keep alive the central ambitions and energies of literature," said *Newsweek.* Though best known for short stories and novels, she has also won acclaim for her poetry, essays, and plays. "The best of Miss Oates's poems create a feeling of controlled delirium, verging on nightmare, which is a lyrical counterpart of the rich violence of her novels," wrote *The New York Times Book Review.* Her volumes of poetry include *Anonymous Sins and Other Poems* (1969), *Love and Its Derangements* (1970), *Angel Fire* (1973), *The Fabulous Beasts* (1975), *Women Whose Lives Are Food, Men Whose Lives Are Money* (1978), *Invisible Woman: New and Selected Poems* (1982), and *The Time Traveler* (1989). As George Garrett noted: "The bright center of all Joyce Carol Oates's art and craft has always been her poetry." Her several collections of essays—*The Edge of Impossibility: Tragic Forms in Literature* (1972), *New Heaven, New Earth: The Visionary Experience in Literature* (1974), *Contraries* (1981), *The Profane Art: Essays and Reviews* (1983), *(Woman) Writer: Occasions and Opportunities* (1988), and *Where I've Been, and Where I'm Going: Essays, Reviews, and Prose* (1999)— display a range of knowledge and interests that explain why she numbers among America's most respected literary and social critics. Oates made a name for herself as a dramatist early in her career with plays such as *The Sweet Enemy* (1965), *Sunday Dinner* (1970), *Ontological Proof of My Existence* (1972), and *Miracle Play* (1974). During the 1990s she resumed writing plays and turned out *In Darkest America* (1991), *I Stand Before You Naked* (1991), *Gulf War* (1992), *The Secret Mirror* (1992), *The Perfectionist* (1993), and *The Truth-Teller* (1993), which have been performed Off-Broadway and at regional theaters across the country.

"Joyce Carol Oates is one of our most audaciously talented writers," judged Erica Jong. "Her gift is so large, her fluency in different genres—poems, short stories, novels, essays—so great, that at times she seems to challenge the ability of readers to keep up with her. In an age of specialization she is that rarest of generalists, a woman of letters. She gives her gifts with such abundance and generosity that we may pick and choose, preferring this Oates to that, quibbling about which of her many talents we like best." John Updike concurred: "Joyce Carol Oates was perhaps born a hundred years too late. She needs a lustier audience, a race of Victorian word-eaters, to be worthy of her astounding productivity, her tireless gift of self-enthrallment. Not since Faulkner has an American writer seemed so mesmerized by a field of imaginary material, and so headstrong in the cultivation of that field." *The New York Times Book Review* concluded: "What keeps us coming back to Oates Country is her uncanny gift of making the page a window, with something happening on the other side that we'd swear was life itself."

CONTENTS

FOR MY HUSBAND, RAYMOND

A
Garden
of Earthly
Delights

I.

CARLETON

1

Arkansas. On that day many years ago a rattling Ford truck carrying twenty-nine farmworkers and their children sideswiped a local truck carrying hogs to Little Rock on a rain-slick country highway. It was a shimmering-green day in late May, the Ford truck ended up on its side in a three-foot drainage ditch, and in the hazy rain everyone milled about in the road amid broken glass, a familiar stink of gasoline and a spillage of hog excrement. Yet, among those who hadn't been hurt, the predominant mood was jocular.

Carleton Walpole would long remember: the skidding on the wet blacktop, the noise of brakes like a guinea hen's shrieking, the sick weightless sensation before impact. The terrified screams of children and women, then the angry shouts of the men. By the time the truck overturned into the ditch most of the younger and more agile of the farmworkers had leapt clear, while the older, the slower, most of the women and younger children, struggled with the tarpaulin roof and had to crawl out on their hands and knees like beasts onto the soft red clay shoulder. Another goddamned "accident": this wasn't the first since they'd left Breathitt County, Kentucky, a few weeks ago, but it wasn't the worst, either. No one appeared to be seriously injured, bleeding or unconscious.

"Pearl? Where the hell are you?"—Carleton had been one of the first to jump from the truck, but he was anxious about his wife; she was pregnant, with their third child, and the baby was due soon. "Pearl! Pearl!" Carleton yelled. His heart was beating like something trapped in his rib cage. He was angry, excited. Always you feel that mean little thrill of relief, *you* aren't hurt. . . . Though once Carleton had been hurt, the first season he'd gone out on the road, his nose broken in a similar crash and the truck driver who was also the recruiter had set it for Carleton with his fingers—"See, a nose will begin healing right away it's broke. It ain't bone it's cart'lige. If you don't make it straight it will grow in crooked like a boxer's nose." Carleton had laughed to see his new nose grown in just slightly crooked at the bridge, but in a way to give his face more character, he thought, like something carved; otherwise, he thought he looked like everybody else, half the Walpole men, long narrow faces with light lank hair and stubbly bearded chins and squinting bleached-blue eyes that looked as if they reflected the sky, forever. When Carleton moved quickly and jerkily his face seemed sharp as a jack-knife, but he could move slowly too; he had inherited someone's grace—though in him it was an opaque resistance, like a man moving with effort through water. Not that Carleton Walpole gave much of a damn how he looked. He was thirty, not a kid. He had responsibilities. With his broke nose, people joked that Carleton's looks had improved, he had a swagger now like his hero Jack Dempsey.

This time, Carleton hadn't been hurt at all. A little shaken, and pissed as hell, his dignity ruffled like a rooster that's been kicked. He'd been squatting on his heels with other men at the rear of the truck chewing tobacco and spitting out onto the blacktop road that stretched behind them like a grimy tongue. Where were they bound for?—Texarkana. That was just a word, a sound. A place on a map Carleton might've seen, but could not recall. How many days exactly they'd been on the road, he could not recall. How many weeks ahead, he'd have to ask. (Not Pearl. Used to, Pearl had kept track of such details, now she was letting things slide as bad as the other women.) Well, there was paperwork—somewhere. A contract.

Carleton wasn't going to think about it, not now. It was enough to console himself *I have a contract, I can't be cheated* because there'd been a season when he had not had a contract, and he had been cheated. Enough to think *I have a savings account* because it was true, alone of the sorry bunch of bastards in this truck Carleton was certain he was the only one with a bankbook, issued from the First Savings & Loan Bank of Breathitt, Kentucky. Not that Carleton needed to speak of it, he did not. He was not a man to boast, none of the Walpoles were. But there the fact was, like an underground stream.

Waiting for local law enforcement, waiting for a tow truck to haul the truck out of the ditch, goddamn. Everybody was excited, talking loudly. Where the hell was Pearl? Carleton was helping women climb up out of the truck. A woman looking young as a girl herself handed him her two-year-old; with a laugh and a grunt he swung the kid over the side like she weighed no more than a cat. Carleton's upper arm muscles were ropey, and strong; his shoulders were narrow, but strong; his back and his neck were starting to give him trouble, from stoop-picking, but he wasn't going to give in to moaning and groaning like an old man. "Pa, hey." There were Carleton's kids, banged up but O.K. Sharleen, shoving and giggling. Mike, only three, was bawling as usual, but he didn't look as if he'd been hurt—his face wasn't bleeding. Carleton picked him up and swung him around kicking, set him down out of harm's way by some women who could tend to him. There was a smell of spilled whiskey mixed with the smells of gasoline and hog shit and mud and it was like you could get drunk just breathing, feeling your heart beat hard. Carleton touched his face, Christ he was bleeding, some. Was he? He clambered down into the drainage ditch to wash his hands, and wet his face. Maybe he'd banged his lower lip. Bit his lower lip. Most likely that's what he had done, when the brakes began to squeal, and the truck went into its skid, those seconds when you don't know what the hell will happen next.

Up front, the driver of the old Ford truck with Kentucky license plates was shouting at the driver of the hog truck with Arkansas license plates. Carleton laughed to see, both these guys had fat bellies. Their driver had a cut eye. Carleton checked to see was anybody dead up front, lying in the road in the rain, sometimes you saw newspaper photos like that, and he'd seen one of a Negro man lying flat on his back in some place in Mississippi and white men banded around the body grinning and waving at the camera, and it made you sick-feeling but excited too, but the driver's kid brother, a smart-ass bastard who rode up front sucking Colas like a baby at a teat, was walking around unharmed, Carleton was disappointed to see. This kid started saying to Carleton, like Carleton had come to accuse him, "It wasn't our fault! It was that sonuvabitch's fault! He come around the turn in the fuckin middle of the road, ask Franklin, go ask him, don't look at me, it ain't none of our fault." Carleton pushed the kid aside. He was taller than this kid, and taller than fat-ass Franklin, and the less friendly he was with them, the more they were respectful of him, and maybe scared. For they seemed to see something in Carleton Walpole's face. The other driver was cursing at Franklin. He was a squat fattish man with a bald head and eyes like suet and he talked funny like there was mush in his mouth. The cab of his truck was smashed inward but the rear looked unharmed. Too bad, Carleton was thinking, the hogs hadn't got loose. Not a one of them had got loose. Christ he'd have liked to see that, hogs piling out of a broke truck and landing hard on their delicate-looking hooves (that were not delicate in fact but hard and treacherous as a horse's hooves) and squealing in crazed outrage as a hog will do then running off into the countryside. And some of those hogs weighing two hundred pounds which was a nice lot of hog. Carleton smiled to think of how that would've been, hogs running away squealing not taken to the slaughterhouse where the poor beasts were awaited. The hog driver was cursing and whining and half-sobbing holding his belly with his elbows like a pregnant woman clutching herself. This driver was alone with his truck: they could gang up on him, and he knew it, and there was the thrill of antici-pation that they might, but it would maybe be a mistake, they were in Arkansas and not Kentucky and the local law enforcement was Arkansas, and you had to know it, you had to acknowledge it. So nothing would come of the possibility like a match that didn't get lit and dropped into hay. Not this time.

Carleton saw with satisfaction that the hog truck's motor was steaming beneath the wrecked hood, the left front fender twisted against the tire so you'd need a corkscrew to untwist it. How bad off their truck was nobody could see since it was lying on its side like a stunned beetle in the ditch.

The last time they'd had trouble like this, it had been raining too: outside Owensboro, Kentucky. Whenever there was an accident or motor trouble everyone was disgusted and angry and threatening to quit but a few hours later they forgot. It was hard to remember anything overnight. And if you moved on, after a few hours on the road you forgot what happened behind you in some other county or state or time. Franklin was promising now he'd make the pur-chase of a new truck, if they could get to Texarkana he would get the money *by wire* he was saying, louder and more sincere than he'd made the promise last time, and Carleton shook his head, Jesus! you wanted to believe him even if you knew better.

There was a philosophy that said: The more accidents you had, the less in store for you.

Like the philosophy credited to Jack Dempsey: The more punches a man takes, the closer he is to the end. Because a man has only a fixed number of punches he can take in his lifetime.

"Pa? Momma wants you."

It was Sharleen pulling at his arm. Carleton went with her to the back of the truck, worried now. What about Pearl? But there was Pearl squatting at the side of the road, on her haunches so she looked like something ready to spring, even with that watermelon belly. An older woman she was friends with was holding her arm. Women's faces lifting to his like this, Carleton steeled himself for reproach. Goddamn, he wasn't going to be blamed for this was he? This and every other goddamned thing? *Hadn't never wanted to marry. Not anybody. Hadn't never wanted to be anybody's daddy how the fuck did all this happen?*

"Honey, you all right? I thought—I saw you—you were lookin all right." Carleton didn't want to show any anxious concern for his wife in front of the other women gaping at him.

"Hell of a lot you care."

Pearl spoke sullenly. Her face was a pale pretty moon-face: or would've been pretty if it wasn't that bulldog look Carleton hated. When he wasn't standing in front of her, Carleton could recall how pretty she'd been, and not that long ago. Pregnant with Sharleen, and her skin rosy like a peach. And she'd been loving with him then, even with her belly starting to swell. Not like now.

Pearl was younger than Carleton by three years. Fifteen when they'd gotten married, and Carleton had been eighteen. She'd been shy of him, and shivery in love if just he touched her sometimes, or rubbed his stubbly jaw against her skin. He'd been crazy for her too, he seemed to remember. Whoever he'd been.

Strange how Carleton couldn't see the change in Pearl day following day. A pregnant woman, her belly swelling up. Until by the eighth and ninth month it's a size you'd need a wheelbarrow practically to transport. How their legs supported them, Carleton was stymied to think. Made him sickish and faint to think. Where Pearl Brody had been a hard-breasted hard-assed little girl he'd liked to wrestle with, the two of them shrieking and panting, there was now this sallow-faced sullen woman with hair she never washed, and her underarms stale and sour, body soft as a rotted watermelon and a mouth that was set to jeering.

"Hell of a lot *you care*." It was like Pearl to say things twice, the second time with some emphasis meaning he hadn't comprehended it the first time. Trying to make him look stupid before others.

Before Carleton could mumble he was sorry, or better yet tell Pearl to shut her mouth, there she was pushing past him—"Bastard just takes our money, don't give a damn if he kills us." She was on her way to yell at Franklin, a look in her eyes wet and shining like gasoline. "You men ought to do something, what the hell's wrong with you? All you do is drink, get *drunk*."

Drunk?—Carleton hadn't had a drink that day.

Pearl was a head shorter than Carleton and her lower body was swollen to twice its size, but damn if he didn't have to walk fast to keep up with her. Damn!—Carleton was embarrassed of her, his young wife, carrying on like this in public. Lately Pearl was flying into rages at the least provocation. Sharleen, who was five, had sometimes to plead with her—"Mamma? Mam*ma* no." Pearl was wearing shapeless bib overalls some fat woman friend had given her, and over top of these a pink cotton smock printed with flamingos that would have been pretty except it was soiled, and on her feet frayed tennis shoes. She was furious, glowing hot. She cast off Carleton's hand on her left, and on her right little Mike who was whining and sniveling for her. "You men don't give a damn! Call yourselves men! Cowards!" Pushing her way through a band of observers, Pearl clambered up to Franklin, grabbed his arm, and continued to yell in a high-pitched quavering voice: "Why in hell don't you look where you're going? Who gave you a license to drive? You let my husband drive and pay him, he's better than you any day. 'Carleton Walpole'—he's a better driver than you. And you're cheatin us, too. What about my baby? Where'm I gonna have my baby?" Franklin tried to appease the indignant woman, you could see he was frightened of her, and the blood trickling down from his cut eyebrow made him appear more frightened; and Franklin's kid brother trying to intervene, and Pearl threw off their hands with a look of contempt, and turned to the Arkansas man, the hog driver, standing there in the middle of the glass-strewn road gaping at her—"*You!* You hit us on purpose! Trying to kill us! I'm gonna have you arrested! What about my baby? Look here, you bastard," Pearl was pleading now, lifting the pink smock to show her pregnant belly, "what about this? Think I got this on purpose? Not some man? One of you's fault? Fuck you all lookin at me, thinking you got a right to kill us like vermin."

Other women joined in. The fat woman friend of Pearl's put her arm protectively around Pearl's shoulders and yelled at Franklin and his brother. When women began yelling like that, there was nothing to do but back off, exchange glances with other men, smile, try not to laugh out loud. 'Cause that only combusts them more. Any public display of female rage was exciting and scary: it was comical, but you had to admire it, too. A man flying off the handle like that, he'd be shamed, but a woman like Pearl, and almost-pretty with her widened blue eyes like a startled doll's, flailing her hands about like that, you felt different. Still, Carleton felt the sting, being called a coward, though he knew for damned sure he was no coward, and Pearl would regret her accusation later, when they were alone. For now, Carleton wasn't going to intervene. Pearl was winding down, another woman was yelling, louder. Louder and uglier. The mood of the crowd was becoming festive. Carleton smelled fresh-opened whiskey. And there was his little girl Sharleen nudging his knee—"Pa? Pa, look." Sharleen was proud of a bump on her forehead the size of a crab apple. She took her father's stained fingers to feel it, and Carleton teased, "Know what that is, sweetie? A billy goat horn coming out." Sharleen giggled, "Is *not*." A little-girl friend of Sharleen's felt Sharleen's bump and showed her a flame-like rash on her own neck, that was like some rashes Carleton had on his neck, and on his sides, bad as poison ivy but it was some insects, or maybe pesticides, itched like hell. "Don't you go touchin that," Carleton scolded Sharleen, but she didn't listen, running off with her friends squealing bad as the hogs. Too many kids in the truck, his own and the others' and the shock of it was, damned if you could tell them apart sometimes. Especially the small ones like little Mike runny-nosed and sniveling for his Momma all the time.

Hadn't wanted to be anybody's daddy how the fuck did all this happen?

That was not true of course. Carleton Walpole was crazy about his kids, and his wife. All a man has is his family, when you get right down to it.

Carleton spat. His mouth was dried out from the tobacco he'd been chewing. Christ, he was bored!

Drifted to the side of the road where some guys were passing a flask of home brew. They included him, and he thanked them. These were men who liked Carleton Walpole, and he liked them. They were his age mostly. They were young fathers, too. They had his young-old face. His ropey-muscled arms, and fair skin that burnt faster than it tanned, and his bad teeth, that were mossy-green and crooked. They had his quick laugh, and his hopeful way of glancing up, squinting, to see what was coming next. Some of these guys, "Red" from Cumberland, for instance, were alone on the truck, they'd left their families back home. Like Carleton, Red was working to pay off debts. Not that Carleton didn't have money saved, too: his mother had told him, always have a few dollars in the bank no matter what. And so Carleton had, forty-three dollars that Pearl knew nothing of, and would not know of, though maybe when they got back he'd buy her a little present from it, her and the baby, to surprise her as sometimes he did. Red was saying he sent money home to his family, and he missed them. When they'd been drinking together once Red had confided in Carleton, he was eleven hundred fifteen dollars in debt to a Cumberland bank, and Carleton bit his lip not knowing what to say—*he* was only eight hundred some odd dollars in the hole, not that he was proud of such a fact but—well, it wasn't eleven hundred, that sum made you swallow hard. Of course, trouble is, Red and Carleton had to laugh, you can't pay off a debt more than a few dollars since you have got to eat, and your family has got to eat, right now. So Carleton and Red, they got along like brothers. Better than Carleton got along with his own brothers in fact. But like brothers they were cagey not to tread on each other's toes. Red respected Carleton who looked and behaved older. It had required a couple of weeks of groping around before they discovered the "facts" about each other. The way they pronounced their *a*'s and *i*'s, the way words slurred out into an extra syllable, turned out their father's families—Walpoles, Pickerings—were both from North England, the countryside around Newcastle—but a long time ago, neither could have said how long. And Pearl's people, Brodys, they were from Wigtownshire, that was in Scotland. Carleton didn't know or care much about these old places—"Have to figure people left for a good reason."

Carleton was telling Red this was going to be his last season on the road. The money he owed was mostly to one of Pearl's uncles and that would be paid off, or nearly. Two wet springs in a row back in Breathitt County, wiping them out. Small farms, less than fifty acres. And the soil hilly, thin. He and Red were standing beneath a tall scrubby willow tree where the smell of hogs wasn't so bad. Inside the truck, you ceased smelling the truck; but when you climbed back in, it hit you. Like the camps they stayed in picking lettuce, onions, radishes. Carleton was chewing a plug of tobacco, and spat in the direction of the truck. "Yeah. I'm settling what I owe. Going back."

They talked of *going back*. At the moment neither could have said which direction Kentucky was in, the sky was hazy and overcast like mucus so you couldn't see any sun to know which side it was slanting down on, that would be *west*. Anyway, on the road, the road's always curving so you get confused. What Carleton meant by *Kentucky* was just where he lived, a circumference of perhaps thirty miles at the most, though there was Hazard he'd been to a few times, and Pikeville. He didn't try to add up how long he and Pearl had hired out for farmwork, how many seasons. It was like cards in a deck: shuffled together, in no order. There was no point in trying to remember because there was nothing to remember. Like squatting at the edge of the truck watching the road roll out. Seeing where you'd been, not where you were going. There was a comfort in that. If you could live your life backward, Carleton thought, you wouldn't make so many mistakes.

Aloud he said to Red, "Ever thought how, like a mirror you could look in over your shoulder, you'd see where you were going, but backward? And not mess up."

Red laughed, spitting tobacco juice. Whatever the hell Carleton Walpole was speaking of, he'd agree.

Red spoke of quitting, too. Going back to work construction. There was a dam going to be built, somewhere near Cumberland. Carleton was silent, jealous of Red: not the thought that Red would get a good job but the thought that Red believed he might, at least for the moment. Carleton himself had been hired for highway construction in east Kentucky but with that kind of work he was the only person in the family to work and they needed more money than that—in the fields his wife could work, and she'd used to have been a good picker, especially of difficult things like strawberries where you can't grab and clutch with a big hand, you need smaller fingers to avoid the leaves, and some places even kids could work: Sharleen who was five could make herself useful somehow. This was against the law in some states but nobody gave much of a damn. Local law enforcement did not. Very rarely did *law* intervene except if you got drunk and caused a ruckus in some local place which was dangerous anyway. Turned out, the sheriff's men were guys looking like Carleton, same lean severe face and a look of being cheated, it was their bosses with the bald heads and fat faces like Herbert Hoover. Carleton sneered, and spat.

A cry went up: a tow truck had appeared. Carleton and Red went to watch. Carleton felt a stab of envy, Christ he'd have liked to own such a truck, and to drive it like that guy was driving like it was just something he did, a *job.* Like it wasn't anything all that unusual or special. Though you could see the driver knew he was important. Carleton caught this guy's eye as he backed the truck around, and a young kid jumped out of the cab to assist. Franklin was standing there wiping his hurt face with a rag and looking worried. Thank God, Pearl had shut up; the other women were quiet, too. Carleton was aware of kids playing in the drainage ditch but damned if he was going to look for his, if Pearl wasn't.

Carleton wished the tow-truck man would ask him to help. Invite him to ride into town with him. Carleton was good with his hands, good at repairing farm equipment. Not trucks or tractors but wagon wheels. Carleton, Sr., was a blacksmith and also did farm equipment repair. But there was no money in it, you could rely on.

There came Pearl clutching at Carleton's sleeve, her face pinched. "Carleton, I don't feel right."

Except she was poking at him, with her fists. Like trying to wake him. Carleton stared at her. She'd been crying, had she? He felt his underarms break out in a sweat. That damn rash up and down his sides like fire ants stinging. Was she going to have the baby here? So soon? Carleton wanted to protest it was early, wasn't it? Pearl had not gone to any doctor but had counted the months and this baby was not due until next month.

"Carleton, I told you *I don't feel right*."

Carleton yelled, " 'Melda, Lorene? Hey—Pearl's gonna need you."

Carleton was holding Pearl, who'd begun to lose strength in her legs. She gave a sudden high scream like a kicked dog, and clutched at her belly. Contractions? Carleton knew what that meant. But it meant you had time, too. Last time, with Mike, Pearl had been in labor through a day and most of a night, Carleton hadn't been present and had been spared.

Now, women hurried to Pearl, to claim her. That animal glisten in their eyes a man found fearful to behold.

Carleton and Red backed off. White-faced, and needing a drink.

There came Franklin bellying up to them, the cut on his face still fresh. "You, Walpole. She's having that baby right now, you and her are *out*. We can't wait for you. We got a contract, we're not waiting."

When Carleton ignored him, Franklin said, appealing to the others, "If that woman dies it ain't my fault! I don't want no pregnant women on my truck! I don't want no nursing babies! I got troubles bad enough!"

It was just blustery bawling, Carleton thought. The truck wasn't going anywhere except to a garage. Nobody was going anywhere for overnight at least. Carleton wanted to slam the fat bastard's face, bloody his nose like his eye was bloodied, but knew he had better not, his quick temper had got him fired in the past. He wasn't young like Jack Dempsey had been getting started at sixteen, seventeen fighting in saloons out west, Christ he was thirty, and losing his teeth. Get on a recruiter's blacklist, you were dead meat.

"Hell, Franklin. Your old mother had got to have *you*, hadn't she?"

This wasn't Carleton talking, it was somebody else. Carleton was drifting back toward the truck. The women had torn off the tarpaulin, and were making a kind of tent there. It was raining harder now. And the red clay shoulder of the highway getting softer. Kids liked to run in the rain like dogs, but not adults. Carleton was shivering. Carleton heard another high-pitched scream. That was Pearl, was it? He said, "It's my fault. I shouldn't of let her come with me. I told her to stay home but she didn't listen." By *home* he meant not his and Pearl's own home because they didn't have one, he meant his in-laws, but nobody would know. Carleton was fearful of crying. His lips were moving—"Jesus Christ. Jesus Christ." First time Pearl had had a baby, he'd broke down like a kid. So scared. He was a coward, that was so. He knew, there was danger of infection when a woman had a baby in such filth, everyone knew of babies that had died, and mothers burning up with fever, or hemorrhaging to death. "Carleton, she'll be all right. They're taking care of her. Carleton?" It was a woman named Annie: freckle-faced Irish: big motherly girl, in her late thirties but still a girl, breasts soft against Carleton's arm like they were loose inside her shirt. In the rain Annie looked like a wax doll, smiling at him with her mouth shut so he could not see her teeth. Red was smiling, too. Smiling hard and ghastly. And thumping Carleton's shoulder. Telling him it didn't make any difference to any baby that ever got born, whether it's a hospital or anywhere.

Carleton tried to say yes.

"Them hospitals are treacherous," a man was saying. "Sometimes they cut open the wrong people. Put you to sleep and you don't wake up. Ever been in a hospital?"

"Never was, and never will be," Annie said. "They do things to women, you can bet. When they're doped up and laying there."

Carleton heard the dog cries again. He was grateful for people close around him, talking to him and about him as if to create a wall of talk to protect him. There was Franklin looking repentant. Handing him a bottle. "Jesus, Walpole. You look like you need this more'n me."

Carleton thanked him. Carleton raised the bottle to his mouth, and drank. Swallowing the sweet liquid fire he didn't hear Pearl's screams, so he drank more. Jerking his head to one side and then to the other like a horse trying to shake free his collar. "Naw, keep it," Franklin said. "You need it more'n me."

Kids were running wild, poking sticks through the slats of the hogs' truck. Hog squeals, and a stink of hog panic. Nothing smelled worse than hog shit, not even skunk. For skunk, at a distance, is not a bad smell at all. Only just close up.

Franklin was saying, "She oughtn't said those hurtful things to me. She oughtn't gotten herself riled up." But he was sounding repentant, and Carleton could figure he wouldn't drive away and leave them at the side of a country highway in wherever this godforsaken place was. Arkansas? *Aw-kan-saw* they pronounced it?

Carleton busied himself with the tow truck after all. Helping with other men to lift the truck out of the ditch, so the tow-truck man could position the hook better, and secure it. Behind, out of sight from this position, where Pearl was lying beneath the tented tarpaulin, thank God there was silence for a while.

And what if she died? And what if, and back home they would say of him *He's the one who let his wife die. Died having a baby in a drainage ditch in Aw-kan-saw. Him.* He wanted to protest, he had not meant for Pearl to come along with him this time; it was just something that had happened. If she died, he would die, too: he would get hold of a shotgun. Both barrels, you don't know a thing of what hits you. In the mouth, painless. If so he wouldn't have this terrible pressure on him like a tire being pumped up too high. He couldn't remember why he'd had to marry Pearl so bad. Crazy with love for her and she hadn't let him touch her, hardly. That was how she'd been brought up, and Carleton respected it. Vir-gin-ity. He was sure he loved her but love was—it was hard to say what love was—when you were so scared, and your teeth chattering. Maybe he had killed her, pumping himself into her so hard. Like hot molten wax, the stuff that leapt from him. It was an agony to hold it back, he could not hold it back. If God helped them this one more time, Carleton vowed he would quit this job he'd hired on for and return home, maybe not at once because they needed the money but by August possibly, they could return by Greyhound bus. He would work every minute of every day, do anything, he would get them all back home—Pearl, Sharleen, Mike, the new baby—before it was too late and they never knew they had a home.

"Carleton? It's a girl! Baby girl."

"Carleton, come look!"

"Carle-ton!"

The women rushed at him. He was on his knees bawling. The baby born that day in red-clay Arkansas was a girl: they called her Clara, after Carleton's little sister who had died of scarlet fever at the age of four.

2

Back home in Breathitt County there was a wedding portrait of Carleton Walpole and his bride Pearl: Carleton tall, gangly-limbed yet handsome in his dark serge suit and stiff-collar white shirt, and Pearl standing barely to his shoulder, china-doll-pretty in her white silk-and-lace wedding dress and veil twined about her curled blond hair; both young people gazing intently at the camera as they'd been commanded by the photographer, eyes widened in the effort not to blink. They'd tried so hard, they'd forgotten to smile! The photograph had been taken just after the wedding service, in the anteroom of the church; a harsh winter sunlight had poured through a window, casting them in such clarity Carleton wanted to shield his eyes, looking at it afterward. He was self-conscious about pictures of himself but Pearl was so pretty, he'd liked to look at her. Until one day his mother remarked *Butter wouldn't melt in that one's mouth* and Carleton felt the sting, his mother hinting he'd married a too-young girl, an immature girl who detracted from his (and the Walpole family's?) dignity.

Carleton had turned on his heel and walked out of the room. You can love and honor your mother, but goddamn if you're going to tolerate any insult to your wife.

The photograph that was framed in a gilt sunburst pattern was still on the wall back home, but Pearl had brought along with them a dozen smaller photos from the wedding, hauled from place to place, month after month and eventually year after year amid her things. She liked to look at these on rainy days, and show them to the kids, telling of how beautiful the wedding had been, her sister and her cousins who were bridesmaids, how Brody relatives had driven from Nitro and West Hamlin, in West Virginia, and her mother's relatives from as far away as Portsmouth, Virginia—"On the Atlantic seaboard." Pearl pronounced *Atlantic seaboard* reverently as if she were speaking of someplace far as the Milky Way.

Carleton, thumbing through Pearl's things when she wasn't around, stared at these old photos with scorn. Jesus! Him in a monkey suit. And not knowing better than to open his mouth when he smiled, showing those damn teeth. Yet he'd looked pretty good, considering he was only eighteen at the time and hadn't known his ass from a hole in the ground. Like he was staring into the future down one of those blacktop highways into the distance, and not flinching. But Pearl beside him was leaning into him as the photographer directed, her arm linked through his in a formal way nobody ever stood in real life. "Goddamn bastard." Carleton meant the photographer, who had his so-called studio in Hazard. Acted like he was a big deal, charging a low fee for hillbillies that couldn't afford "premier" paper stock.

Hell, Carleton wasn't going to cry. Maybe it was sad that the young people in the picture no longer existed, but what really hurt was him, Carleton, not being able to get back to that place: a few miles from his father's farm that was hundreds of miles away from where Carleton was now. At night before he sank into an exhausted sleep like a stone sinking through murky water he had to endure the flash of rows of beans or strawberries or sweet corn that made his fingers twitch before he'd be surprised by a circle of warmly smiling faces, adult faces of his family and relatives when he'd been a boy; and his dream might open up (the walls melting away like in a motion picture) to show him the vegetable garden, and the pear orchard, the barnyard with its old rotting rich-smelling haystack, and the hay barn itself—everything! All he'd lost. And his eyes would ache with the knowledge that he could not push through the density of sleep to get to this place.

He was too shamed to return. He had never repaid the money he owed, only just sending a few dollars at some time like Christmas, then ceasing. For a terrible time—a long season of drought, crops withered in the fields and fruit never matured in the orchards—Carleton and Pearl and the kids had to live in a derelict old hotel in Cincinnati, till at last their luck changed, and the "picking" trucks came in again, and they were saved. For another season at least.

It was a way to get by. You didn't save anything except pennies doing farm-hire work but there it was, and there was a comfort in it, in a way. Like eating the same food each day is a comfort, not only you don't have to think but your teeth, chewing, don't have to think nor your stomach digesting it. And the more kids you had old enough to make themselves useful, the better; not like factory work where some kind of child-labor laws ruled against you.

Early on, when they'd talked all the time of going back home, it was harder. Everything is harder if you compare *what is* with *what was*. That first summer in New Jersey they'd had Sharleen, put the infant down at the end of each row wrapped in a blanket in a box, so Pearl could check her and nurse her as they worked. Dusty and hot and the baby had cried in a thin rasping way like a sick cat. The foreman told Pearl to keep that baby in the cabin out of the sun so she'd done so, and one day had a premonition and ran a half-mile out of the tomato field and there was the baby sleeping and fretting in her cardboard box on the bed, and peering right in at her a rat sniffing at the baby's face! Pearl screamed so hard, the rat was out of there in a shot. When Carleton came in, there was Pearl just standing over the box, blinking and biting at her fingers. The baby was awake now, and crying. All Pearl could say was how stiff and pink the rat's tail had been. And its whiskers, so stiff. Carleton tried to suggest there had not been any rat, that was what you did with a high-strung female, but Pearl never forgot.

What Carleton knew of rats, they bred faster than rabbits and they had to tear and chew and grind their teeth because their teeth were growing continuously and would grow into their jaws if they didn't wear them down. Carleton shook his head, wondering. If

God made things, He made them strange. It was proof that God was different from man because man would have made things sensible.

All this time Carleton Walpole was a young man. Seemed like being young just went on and on forever. Hard to believe you'd ever get *old*. (One day Carleton had word that his father, Carleton, Sr., was dead. Another day, that the farm had been sold piecemeal. Another day, the First Bank & Trust of Breathitt had shut its doors, gone bankrupt so none of its customers could collect a penny of their savings. After that Carleton never telephoned any relatives, sick to hear pity in their voices.) Young as he was, and one of the best farmworkers you could ask for, yet there was ever a crop of men younger and more willing. In taverns he fought them, barefisted or wrestling or both, except if Carleton was too drunk and had to be shielded by his friends. Wherever it was, he wouldn't recall afterward except they'd crossed the Mississippi River that day, he'd swung at some mush-mouthed southerner with a fox face that wanted breaking, and the guy shoved Carleton back stumbling against his friends saying, "Shit, I ain't gonna hit no old man. Hold that old drunk off me."

3

Florida. On the day of that night that forever afterward he would think *I have blood on my hands, Jesus has shook me off* there was little Clara he loved like crazy, his best girl, his little-doll-girl coming up behind him and so carefully placing her cool just-washed hands over his eyes whispering, "Dad-dy got a head-ache?"

And he'd placed his big calloused hands over hers and pretended he was a blind man saying he was blind as a bat, and knocking things over until Clara's giggling was becoming scared, and Pearl grunted at them what sounded like *Damn fools* and slammed down plates on the table for supper.

Five years after *Aw-kan-saw.* Five years and six days: Clara's fifth birthday, her daddy was mortified he'd forgotten.

Making up for it later, as Carleton Walpole would do.

Christ, was he tired! Hunched at the table spooning whatever it was into his mouth. Couldn't chew too well on the left side of his mouth anymore. Couldn't sit for long on any chair except if it had a pillow, goddamned hemorrhoids driving him crazy. The kids were bickering, Mike was banging his elbows on the table and Pearl was sullen and silent meaning getting ready to explode. Sharleen, his ten-year-old, was passing saucepans and platters. "Honey, thanks. Now set it down." Steaming mashed potatoes, his favorite kind of potatoes. Never minded the lumps in them, it was a kind of chewing he could do, and enjoy. Pearl objected as Carleton brought a jug of hard cider to the table, not on the table but set on the floor at his feet. "Hell with you. A man has got to live." Carleton wasn't sure if he'd said this aloud, but it struck him as funny like a wisecrack on the radio.

"Dad-dy forgot to wash!"—they were laughing at the rings of dirt around his neck.

Actually he missed the fields. You got into a rhythm, a way of moving. Mind gone dead. Peppers, cucumbers, squash. Snatch 'em off the vine, place 'em in the basket. Not fussing with getting under the leaves like fucking bush beans, pole beans, wax beans. Fuck onions that were worse, the stems breaking off in your hand if you got impatient.

"Sit still. Sit up. Mind your milk." Pearl spoke with deceptive quiet to Clara. "Hear me, Clara: *Mind your milk.*"

For sure, Clara was going to overturn her milk glass. It was a matter of waiting.

Carleton eyed Pearl warning *Don't you touch my daughter, I'll break your ass.* Trouble was, Pearl didn't catch these signals like she'd used to. Pearl ground her jaws, and picked at the scabs on her face and neck, hummed to herself and even rocked back and forth like some kind of mental case, in such a state she wasn't fearful of Carleton, Christ he was fearful of *her.*

Five children now, and one of them a seven-month baby. What you call an infant. Nursing, and fretting and crying half through the night. Driving their neighbors crazy, and Carleton couldn't blame them for banging the walls. With each baby Pearl was getting stranger, sometimes Carleton swore her eyes hadn't any pupils, all iris, like a cat's. All she seemed to like were the new babies, but only when she nursed them. Humming and rocking and stroking the baby's soft thin-haired head in a way that repelled Carleton, like something sick and disgusting he couldn't give a name to.

How Pearl got pregnant, damned if he knew. She'd keep him off her with both feet, the soles of her hot little feet, if she caught him in time.

Pale blond hair stiff with grease, and the back of her head balding in patches from the damn ringworm. Still, if she fixed herself up she looked pretty, or almost. In the fields, on the bus (they traveled now by bus, and it wasn't bad), people looked at Pearl in a certain way that drove Carleton wild. *Don't you feel sorry for me you assholes.* Carleton had his women friends to console him, also he consoled himself, a woman gets a little crazy every time she has a baby and Pearl has had five babies so maybe she will grow out of it.

There's a philosophy that says: No point in preparing for trouble because unexpected things will happen instead.

There's a philosophy credited to Charles Lindbergh that says: No point in preparing for disaster (like a crashed plane) because another kind of disaster (your baby kidnapped) will happen instead.

Carleton lifted his cider jug, and drank.

Sometimes, Pearl was extra-vigilant watching the kids at the table, almost hoping (you could see!) for one of them to knock a glass over, or drop their food from their mouths. Other times, and these were maybe worse times, Pearl was dreamy and not-hearing in their midst. The kids could kick one another under the table and Pearl didn't give a damn so it was left to Carleton, and he had a temper.

"Next month, we're going to Jersey by ourselves." Carleton was picking his teeth. Making his announcement to Sharleen and Clara, now that Mike had run outside and Pearl was staring at something on the floor. (What? A rat? No rat. Nothing.) Carleton spoke carefully, quietly. It was his Daddy voice. It was not a voice you contested. At night when he was done for the day and he was free of them, spending an hour or two in a tavern or with a woman, his voice was normal as anybody's: he liked to joke, and he liked to laugh. It was a hard youngish harsh voice that nonetheless liked to laugh. But here in the cabin, so hot sweat ran in rivulets down his naked sides, he never spoke in that voice.

"Up there there's no spic bastards. 'Wetbacks.' "

Clara was reaching for her milk glass. Carleton caught it just in time.

"Dad-dy? Where is 'Jer-sey'?"

"Up north. Way north. Where there's snow."

"Hell, we ain't gonna see no *snow*." Sharleen made her lips swell outward in a way Carleton hated, reminded him of a baboon.

Sharleen was a thin, nervous, sallow child with scabs on her arms and legs. Pesticide burns, Carleton thought they were, or fleabites, except they were hard and thick and she was always picking them off making them bleed to form new scars. She had a rat-quick face, narrow little eyes you couldn't judge were mischievous or malicious.

"Hey, there: that ain't nice, contradictin your daddy."

Carleton spoke pleasantly. But Sharleen took warning.

Clara was trying to feed two-year-old Rodwell. (Where the hell was Pearl's mind? The woman was just sitting there, damp-mouthed and dreamy at her own table.) The little boy, cornsilk hair the color of Carleton's as it had used to be, and pale blue wide-open eyes, snapped anxiously at the spoon and it fell clattering to the floor.

"Piggy-pig-pig," Sharleen sniggered.

"He can't help it," Clara protested. "He's just a baby."

"*You're* a baby. Baby asshole."

"Both of you, button them mouths." Carleton lifted the jug to drink in that way he'd perfected: the hefty crockery jug you hook your thumb through the handle, heave it up behind your left shoulder so the mouth of the jug rests on your shoulder, bring your own mouth to it, lean to the right so the liquid runs into your mouth, and drink. And wipe your mouth afterward on the back of your hand.

Sharleen and Clara giggled, watching their daddy do his cider-jug trick.

Sharleen said, "How are we gonna go north? Some damn old bus? There's niggers and trash on them buses. I ain't goin."

Carleton was pissed, seeing the look in the kid's face. Without so much as snapping his fingers to warn her, he swung his arm around and cracked her sneering face with the back of his hand, sent her backward onto the floor. Rodwell shrieked, but it was a happy-baby shriek. Pearl turned languidly to look at them as if she'd been dozing with her eyes open.

Sharleen began to bawl. Clara pressed her hands against her mouth trying not to giggle. Carleton caught Clara's eye and winked, she was her daddy's ally. Clara was five years younger than Sharleen but you'd never know it. More reliable, sharper-witted than any of them.

The new baby, in his cardboard-box crib, was bawling.

And Rodwell, fretting in his high chair, was sucking in air getting ready to bawl.

"You, you caused this. Get the hell out."

Carleton poked Sharleen on the floor with the point of his shoe. Sharleen scrambled up sniveling and limped out of the cabin and Pearl looked after her with a vague frown. Carleton was waiting for the woman to start bitching, goddamned useless mother she was getting to be, but Pearl said nothing. Her mouth worked, wordless. On her plate tiny portions of mashed potatoes, boiled pork scraps, green beans lay congealing in a soupy gravy.

Fuckin flies in the kitchen, buzzing Carleton's plate!

Christ he couldn't wait to get clear of here. This supper that tasted like sawdust in his mouth, damn wobbly chair made the crack of his asshole ache, his wife he'd used to be proud of she was so sweet-faced and pretty as a doll, getting to be a mental case, and not a fit mother. And the kids driving him bats. Even Clara sometimes, looking at her daddy like she loved him so, she believed he was going to do something special for her, protect her or—what the hell she was expecting, he didn't know, and it drove him bats. "Goddamn zoo in here. Flies in the food, and nobody fuckin cares." Carleton nudged Pearl, who looked, not at him, but at her pudgy forearm he'd nudged, where the impress of his hard fingers had made a mark. "It's dirty in here. Smells like burnt grease in here. Why's that screen got a rip? Fuckin flies comin in."

But Pearl wouldn't reply. Clara had ceased giggling. In mute appeal she pointed to something in her partly drunk glass of milk, something for her daddy to see not her momma, and Carleton saw to his disgust a fly was floating in the milk. The exchange between them was immediate and wordless *Daddy I don't need to drink my milk do I?* and Daddy signaled *No, honey* but Pearl blinked and wakened and intervened which was just like that woman, eyes in the back of her head when you didn't want it. "Clara, drink your milk. That's whole milk. That's expensive milk. You kids," Pearl said, her voice rising dangerously, "have got to drink your milk you're going to get polio." So Clara was sniveling, and Carleton said to leave the girl alone, and Pearl said, "They told us and told us, they told us 'Give your children whole milk, they're going to get polio if you don't, going to be crippled if you don't,' *they told us.*"

Carleton settled it by fishing the fly out of Clara's glass of milk with a spoon. Now, Clara could drink it, though making a sour face bad as Sharleen.

The baby was crying louder. Rodwell was kicking up a storm.

Carleton rose from the table. Crack in his ass like fire, and pinching pains in his back, between his shoulders, every damn joint in his legs. "Goin out for a while. Don't wait up."

Christ he needed fresh air: anywhere, to get out of here.

His good friend Rafe, Rafe that was like a brother to Carleton Walpole, he'd be waiting for him. The two men deserved a few drinks in town, Rafe had a bitchy wife and kids, too.

At the sink Carleton washed his hands. A lukewarm rust-tinged water emerged from the hand pump, he worked up a meager lather out of the gritty-gray 20 Mule Team bar of soap. Wiped his hands on his thighs, his work pants. Still a little wet, he wiped them on his hair, smoothing it straight back from his forehead, caught a glimpse of himself in a mirror Pearl had taped to the wall: except for his stubbly jaws, and a corkscrew-twist kind of look in the eyes like he was wanting to break somebody's ass, Carleton was surprised he looked so young, still. Women coming up to him in the tavern saying *You ain't from here, are you? You look like some mountain man.*

Carleton hugged Clara saying he'd bring her a bag of pretzels from town, be a good girl and clean up the dishes, and Clara hugged her daddy hard around the neck begging him to take her with him, and now Pearl was scolding, muttering it would be a cold day in Hell he'd bring them anywhere except the fields or the bus to make them work like niggers in a chain gang, and Carleton raised his fist to quiet her, and Pearl laughed at him, and Carleton set Clara aside to deal with Pearl, and Pearl snatched up the bawling baby out of the cardboard crib saying, "Go ahead! Hit us! Hit your flesh and blood, go ahead, coward!" But Carleton would not, and hastily departed the cabin, and Clara was in the doorway calling after him, "Dad-dy! Dad-dy!" like her little heart would break.

———

It was almost twilight. So far south, this godforsaken white-trash-and-spic state, the sun was big and bloody like a spoilt egg yolk leaking down into the flat scrub horizon, seemed like it would never get night. Every day was like every other day like for Christ sake somebody'd torn out his eyelids. Couldn't shut his eyes. Sunlight slanting off the packing sheds and piercing his brain. Pounding sun on his head through the crappy straw hat. Gabble of spics—Mexicans—dark-skinned as Indians, but not like niggers, their hair wasn't nigger-hair and their lips and nose, not. Carleton felt how he and his kind were the freaks here, pale-haired, fair-skinned so they burnt instead of darkened, had to wear long sleeves in the field and long fuckin pants stiff with dirt. Still, this camp at Ocala was a damn lot better than the previous one outside Jacksonville where they'd lived in tents. When it rained the tents bunched up with water, leaked and caved in. Mud everywhere. Mud, flies, fleas and them flying roaches big as bats: palmetto bugs. In the Sunshine State, that was your major crop.

Anyway here they lived in tar-paper shanties, that got hot but not so wet. Heat you get used to. The other day Carleton had been questioned by some Jew-looking man with glasses and a white shirt and tie, a half-dozen of 'em at the camp asking damn-fool questions writing answers on a clipboard, how long had Carleton been working on the season as it's called, how much did he make hourly, how much did his employer deduct for expenses, did his wife work in the field with him and if so did his wife make the same wage as he did, where'd he come from "originally" and how (this in an undertone, with an embarrassed smile) could he work in such heat—

a nosy son of a bitch, trying to pass himself off as your friend but nobody's taken in. Not long afterward, all of 'em were chased out of the camp by the foreman and his men. Had to laugh, the Jew-looking guy was scared shitless they were going to unleash the German shepherd barking like crazy and growling for blood. But it made Carleton think, he didn't mind the heat anywhere like he'd minded it at first, in fact he hoped for sunny days better than cloudy because if it rained too hard they lost money; if there was a storm, like a hurricane, the growers lost their crops and you could starve. Carleton had mumbled some of this to the man taking notes on his clipboard then he'd added: "See, mister, the major crop is palmettos, here. We catch 'em with hand nets like fish, in the air. Pack 'em and can 'em and they're shipped up north." Almost he'd wanted to say to Jew York City but had not.

In Breathitt County, Kentucky, there hadn't been any Jews. Carleton was sure he'd never seen a one of them yet somehow he knew what they looked like and how they operated. It was like a Jew to ask questions nobody else would ask. A Jew is smarter than you because a Jew comes from an ancient race. Back in the time of Abraham, Isaac. Back in biblical times when the sun could stand still in the sky and the Red Sea part. This Jew who'd asked Carleton questions was edgy-seeming though, even before the foreman came charging out after him. Carleton was feeling bad he hadn't talked better to that man, more intelligent like he was capable; he'd gone to school to sixth grade, and he was no fool. Might've got written up in some newspaper or *Life* magazine they did articles like that sometimes, and ran photos. Feeling bad his mind got switched on by that bastard and later he couldn't switch it off. He'd told his friend Rafe, the questions that guy asked him made him realize there were people who didn't know the answers to them, people who didn't do what he did. Thousands, millions of people who didn't hire out for crop picking and didn't know if you were paid five cents a bushel or thirty-five cents or a dollar or fuckin ten dollars! People no different and no better than them who didn't kneel in the dirt picking beans, tomatoes, lettuce, fuckin onions breaking off in your hand if you grabbed them too hard. Rafe laughed to see Carleton riled up saying, "Hell, so what?"

Damned if Carleton could think of an answer.

At Rafe's, there was his wife Helen nursing the baby. New baby, little boy like Carleton's own. Cutest damn things at that age, if they're not bawling, or puking, or soaking their diapers. Seeing Carleton in the doorway Helen made a coy gesture to close her shirt over her fat floppy white breast, then just giggled. A blush rose into her face. "You, Carl'ton Walpole! Rafe says I c'n come with you two tonight."

"Oh, yeah?"

"Think a woman can't tomcat, too? Some women, try 'em."

Carleton laughed. He liked a good-natured woman, somebody you could joke with. Between him and Helen there were some secrets Rafe never needed to know about.

"That you, Walpole? Right there!" Rafe was at the sink slicking back his ripply hair. Same thing Carleton had been doing, and frowning at himself in a dime-store mirror. You had to like Rafe, a heavyset old boy from the mountains like Carleton except east Tennessee. One of those ruddy faces and eyes lighting up with jokes in the right company, like Carleton Walpole. Losing his red-brown hair he was vain of, and younger than Carleton by three-four years.

Carleton was impatient to get out of here but had to be polite with Helen teasing and flirting like a dog desperate to have its head stroked, asking how's the family, how's Pearl, and when Carleton shrugged not taking the hint he didn't want to speak of such things saying with a pulled-down mouth how pretty Pearl's hair was if she'd fix it up more and Carleton muttered something inaudible not rude exactly, but Helen persisted, "You know, Carl'ton, I try real hard to be friendly with that wife of yours but she don't give me the time of day, why's that?" And Carleton said, "My wife ain't got the time of day, honey. What's going on in her head, it ain't got a thing to do with the time of day or what month or year on the calendar. Got it?" Carleton was speaking in almost his pleasant-Daddy voice, and the bitch caught on like he'd reached out and pinched that floppy white breast on the nipple.

There came Rafe to join him with a yodel—"Whoooeee!"

Rafe was in a damn good mood, Carleton saw.

Seeing too that his friend's living quarters weren't much cleaner than his own. Kids running wild, and flies—a sticky ribbon of fly-catcher hanging down from the light above the kitchen table like a Christmas tree decoration, must've been twenty fat black flies stuck in the thing and some of 'em buzzing and wriggling their wings. Enough to make you sick, you had to eat supper there. And Helen wasn't a mental case. Beneath the cabin that was propped up on concrete blocks was a shadowy space where bits of garbage and trash lay strewn, a scuttling of palmetto bugs you would not want to investigate.

The men walked through the camp to the highway. Just each other's company, it was like oxygen pumped in the lungs.

For a man requires a good friend like a soldier requires a buddy he can trust. Closer than a brother, even. 'Cause you can't trust your brother. Can't trust any woman for sure.

They were almost at the highway when there came a thin little cry—"Dad-*dy*!"

Carleton whipped around: it was Clara.

The little blond girl with fingers stuck in her mouth, smiling at her daddy who was shaking a forefinger at her. It hurt Carleton's heart to see how small she was, there in the rutted lane. "You, Clara! What the hell you doin followin me? Get the hell back home."

"Daddy take me with you? Dad-dy?"

"Damn little brat, you are not going anywhere tonight with your *dad-dy*."

Carleton hot-faced and riled up. Always embarrassed of some kid of his acting up in public. Clara wavered in the lane, then ran to hide behind the corner of a tar-paper shanty, peeking out. Rafe said with seeming sincerity, "That's Clara? Pretty little girl."

Carleton said, "Pretty little ass is gonna get warmed, I warn you." He was worrying, if he kept on walking out of the camp, along the shoulder of the highway, his daughter would follow him; there was a bold streak in Clara, small as she was. Daddy tried sweet talk: "Be a good girl, kitten. Said I'd bring you something, didn't I? You can have it tomorrow." His fingers twitched with wanting to grab on to her and break the brat's neck.

Clara giggled, hid behind a straggly tree and peeked out at her daddy through her fingers. Rafe was trying to be polite, which burned Carleton's ass: "What's she, four? Three?"

"Five."

Carleton chucked some dried mud toward Clara, not to hit her but scare her like you'd scare a damn dog, and finally Clara lit out running back toward home. It was unspoken between the men that Clara was young to be wandering through the camp this time of early evening.

The men walked on. Carleton said, "The other day some nigger kids were teasing my girls."

Rafe cursed. His words were hissing, scintillant.

Carleton said, "If anybody gets hurt, it ain't going to be my fault. But a man will protect his children." He was conscious of making a statement, like to the man with the clipboard who'd asked him questions. Something that Rafe might repeat. Possibly the incident had been more play than teasing, and not mean-spirited, but Carleton hadn't liked the sound of it, his kids squealing and carrying on with nigger kids like there was no difference between them. "Now I know, them families have got to live down by the crick, not up here with us, but the fact is they're in the camp and acting like they got a right and that's the first step. Course they're no more dangerous than spics that're worse 'cause they speak their own language not like niggers who are leastways Americans." Carleton spoke vehemently, and Rafe nodded. Anything Carleton said in such a mood, Rafe was going to agree.

"I know by Jesus what I'd do," Rafe said. "Any one of 'em touched my kids."

"There's some white women saying white men are getting to be cowards." Carleton spoke tentatively.

Rafe cursed, and Carleton drew his switchblade out of his pocket, that had a six-inch spring blade and a discolored mother-of-pearl handle. A spic knife, you had to know. Carleton had found it in the men's latrine, back in Jacksonville. He punched it open and the men admired it. Rafe had seen it before but always whistled at that blade.

Carleton said quietly, "You can trust a blade better'n a twenty-two, know why?"

"A blade don't make no sound going in."

"A blade don't leave no evidence behind."

Rafe laughed. "A blade don't need no fuckin ammunition to re-load."

They had to walk at the edge of the highway for maybe two miles before they entered a crossroads town with no name Carleton knew. A shut-down sawmill, and a coal yard. Boys were hanging out on the bridge over the creek tossing stones into the water, talking loud and laughing. They weren't from the camp, you could tell by their accents. Ahead there was a blare of radio music. Carleton felt a rush of hunger, like a stab in the belly, Christ he was hungry, starving, for that kind of music, and lanky teenaged boys tossing stones into a creek, laughing in the summer twilight.

When Carleton had first seen this town, on the bus going through to the camp, the place had been empty with noon heat. Now, at the tavern, there were cars, pickups, loud-talking people. You had to push through the open doorway to get inside, and push your way to the bar. Carleton looked straight ahead as he walked; he wasn't the kind to look around in any new situation, for that showed weakness. Yet he had a sense that there was hardly anybody from the camp here, the patrons were locals. Farmworkers, hired men, day laborers maybe. Not looking too different from Carleton and Rafe, he was thinking. It was a dense, noisy atmosphere. The air was smoky and congenial. You wouldn't be judged here, maybe. If you minded your own business.

Carleton and Rafe ordered beers at the bar and the bartender took his time waiting on them, took their money without smiling though he hadn't eyed them suspiciously, either. Which was a good thing. Carleton was thinking of these dollar bills he'd saved out for tonight, carefully folded in his pants pocket: how many hours in the hot sun had been required to earn them. Which made his thirst more hurtful. Which made the first swallows of lukewarm bitter beer more delicious. Which made Carleton laugh at some damn-fool thing Rafe was saying. In a tavern Rafe was the kind of companion you wanted, the guy lighted up like a Christmas tree needing to have a good time. You could laugh with Rafe not hearing half the words he was saying except you knew they were meant to be funny.

A large mud-spangled hound lay wheezing-sleeping beneath a table. Even in the smoke and din there were flies: big fat horseflies. And fuckin mosquitoes, biting Carleton's neck. Another picker from the camp, a white man like themselves they'd befriended since Valdosta, Georgia, came to join them, and later two others. These guys were all right: Carleton had nothing against them. But the bar area was getting seriously crowded. You had to stand sideways at the bar, and you were always being jostled, and it took a long time to get waited on unless the bartender knew you. Carleton had seen that the men the bartender knew and was friendly with, who had to be locals, were sitting at the bar, a long line of them, on stools, at the curve of the bar by the opened windows where the air was cooler, you could smell a breeze now and then from the creek. Carleton was thinking if he lived here, had his own place here, he'd be sitting with those men and not standing with these farm pickers, though they were all white men and that should mean something at least. *Cowards, fuckin cowards* a voice sneered. Not Pearl's voice exactly, and not Carleton's own. He signaled for another beer, and drained the glass he had. You come to a no-name place in some godforsaken white-trash countryside for a purpose. Turn off your mind from everything. Like shutting off a car ignition. Younger men were pushing in, guys who knew one another, muscle-guys in their early twenties looks like. And now Carleton saw with a stab of irritation a half-dozen swarthy-skinned workers from the camp. These jabbering bastards, Carleton despised. Not spics exactly, but maybe they were. Some spics and mexes were dark like Indians. The breeds were all mixed, Carleton supposed. Only the Caucasian was not mixed, but that could be a disadvantage in certain climates where you stood out like a goiter on some poor bastard's neck.

"Sumbitches. Can't speak English they should go the fuck back where they came from." Carleton made this pronouncement in a loud aggrieved voice. Half-hoping the bartender would hear him, and the guys at the far end of the bar, but the damn noise. Too many goddamn people. A few women, he'd noticed. Indian-looking women, with that straight crow-black hair, coarse faces. They were with the swarthy-skinned men and didn't give a damn how people stared at them. The jabber they talked, it was all *ssss*'s and *ii*'s and *a*'s and they spoke so fast you couldn't hear 'em almost. Carleton believed this was Spanish. *Sí* he knew and *buena* he knew and *gracias* he guessed he knew and there was *por favor?* and *como?* he'd figured out. What riled him were certain *zzzz* sounds unnatural to his east Kentucky ear and those *a, o* endings to their words that had an air of deliberate mockery. *Adónde va?* he heard in his presence and *me entiendes?* more than once provoking muffled laughter and he had known with certainty that it was of him the sons of bitches were speaking and his heart was filled with rage but he had been alone at the time. Only just the switchblade in his pocket he had not dared touch.

Out back of the tavern to take a leak in some bushes already stinking of piss and when he returned his place at the bar was taken. Goddamn: Carleton made like somebody was pushing him so he could push back against a stocky fat-assed spic of about his age.

Words were exchanged. Carleton was shoved, and Carleton shoved back. Rafe and his friends crowded in.

Fat-faced spic bastard backed off. The moment passed.

Loud voices. There was a dispute at a table: someone had brought a girl of about eleven into the tavern. "It's the law, you. Get her out of here." Somehow, Carleton didn't know how this was, he and Rafe were involved. "See, it's the law. Translate for your friends." They protested: "They're not our friends. We're Americans."

Carleton's heart was beating pleasantly hard. Like he'd been running. Christ, he was feeling good: that good hard cider, and now the beers, a warm buzz at the back of his skull. Thinking he'd like to break some spic bastard's face for him. Or anybody, who insulted him. You don't insult a Walpole, a Walpole does not walk away from a fight. Hadn't hit a man since, where was it—Carolina. Damn near broke his fist. "Gimme a shot. Whiskey." Rafe was drinking whiskey. Carleton unfolded dollar bills to count out. The noise was louder, you got used to it. Drum-sounding noise making you want to laugh. Standing up like this, Carleton couldn't feel those damn boil-like things in his ass: hemorrhoids. His face was good and sweaty, that kept the mosquitoes off. A strong smell in his armpits and crotch.

"Hey, mister: gonna buy me a drink?"

Two young girls, white-skinned girls in shirts open to practically their boobs, were laughing with Rafe, eyes sliding onto Carleton but he knew to play it crafty. Girls from towns: you had to be damn careful.

"Bet he's married. Bet he's got kids."

"Five kids, at least. Six, seven! All of 'em real young."

The girls giggled together. They were young, maybe eighteen.

Couldn't remember Pearl at that age. Couldn't remember himself at that age.

The men Carleton was drinking with were laughing so hard tears gathered in their eyes. Hard to say what was funny, but Carleton laughed, too. Another time he was shoved, and shoved back. The girls squealed sighting friends just coming into the tavern and without a word hurried to join them. And Carleton and Rafe had just bought them beers! "Fuckin bitches." Carleton was seriously pissed seeing the girls making up to some hulking guys, especially the long-haired cat-faced one who'd been giving him the eye, now she's practically shoving her boobs against this six-foot boy in just overalls, no shirt or undershirt, gap-toothed and grinning like he'd won him a prize.

"Better wash your cock, it's gonna fall off you mess with her. Turn gang'rous, know what that is? Rotting-black. Falls off in your hand."

Carleton yelled this warning to the boy in overalls but the noise in the barroom was such, nobody heard except Carleton's friends who near to broke up with laughing. Walpole was shit-faced drunk and still on his feet, had to hand it to him. He could see himself from a little distance and liked what he saw, long as he didn't have to see his actual face close up. Couldn't say where the fuck he was. Georgia, Florida. One of the Carolinas. His ass hurt from the bus seats. His ass hurt from having to take a crap, in the latrine so smelly you near to puked just approaching it. Or the stink of lye, so strong your eyes watered. On the bus, the kids squabbling and Pearl rocking holding the baby against her floppy cow-breasts and her own mouth agape, glistening with saliva, Carleton chewed tobacco until his aching teeth were numbed and consoled himself thinking if the bus crashed, slid down a ravine into a river, maybe that would be for the best. He saw himself setting Clara aside, " 'Scuse me, kitten." Walk to the front of the bus and knock the driver aside with a single blow of his fist and turn the steering wheel sharply, and—

Next month he was going to Jersey. A new recruiter, and a new job. New contract. This wasn't work for a man here. Stoop-picking, out in the fields. Nigger work, and spics. You had to pay the five cents and you had to pay for fuckin water that tasted like piss. Christ he wanted so badly to get back home to Breathitt County except: owed Pearl's uncle.

Except: the farm was gone. Sold piecemeal.

That's him. Walpole. Trash that sends his wife and kids out into the fields to pick like niggers.

Him and Rafe, arm wrestling at the bar. Straining so the sweat ran in rivulets down their faces. Mostly Carleton could beat Rafe except if Rafe cheated. A trick he had. Except if Carleton was shitfaced. Rafe's eyes bulged in their sockets.

The first time, Carleton won but not so easy as he'd have wanted.

The second time, on a bet (one dollar each) Rafe near-to won, and the girls were back to cheer him on which pissed Carleton, he'd been thinking the long-haired one with the cat face had favored *him.*

Carleton took up the two dollar bills, feeling good. Like Rafe was his brother, he'd allowed him, Carleton, to demonstrate how strong he was. "Naw, I don't want your money. Take it."

"Take it yourself. Shove it."

Was Rafe joking? Carleton wanted to think so. Teasing in that way he had. Carleton said, "Hell, man, you're improvin. Sometime soon Helen's gonna have to let you win." To the small circle of onlookers Carleton explained, "Helen is Rafe's big ol' woman. And I do mean *big.*" Carleton made motions with his hands, that Rafe glared at without laughing.

"You mean you don't practice none with your wife?" the long-haired girl said to Carleton, cutting her eyes at him in a way he liked, he hadn't seen a girl so young and pretty do in a while.

There was a third girl, older and heavier in the bust. Black curly hair like a wig. Fat crimson lips. Eyeing Carleton like she knew him from somewhere before. "Gonna buy me a beer, Popeye?"

Carleton was Popeye 'cause of his arm muscles. He took pride in his arm muscles. "Sure, honey. C'mere."

Rafe intervened, sullen and pushy. Carleton had been trying to give him the dollar bill back, but Rafe was acting like an asshole refusing. "C'mon, let's try again. Two bucks." Carleton waved him aside, like you'd wave aside a damn fly. The black-haired girl smelled of some sweet strong perfume. Down between her breasts, that you could almost see in the V of a silky green blouse. Rafe was saying hotly, "C'mon, Walpole! Don't you insult me."

When Carleton ignored him Rafe said, louder, "Look here, I got lots of money saved. More'n you. You and them five kids—" Now Carleton was hearing his friend, and not liking what he heard; Rafe was talking loud so the girls would hear. "Now look here," Carleton said, "I bring in more money than you and your fat wife any day, and you know it."

"Walpole, take care. You're shit-faced."

"*You're* shit-faced. Get the hell away."

"Fuckin white trash. Hillbilly asshole."

Rafe was pushing at Carleton, looking like he'd like to kill him. Rafe's face all sweaty, bulgy-eyed. Carleton felt a rush of excitement like liquid flame through his veins. "Oh, yeah? Yeah? *Yeah?*" Suddenly he could see so clearly—like looking through a telescope. At the edges of things, he could not see; but he could see through the scope, and he saw his friend's oily face, and those damp pig eyes. "C'mon! One more time, and winner take all." Rafe set his elbow hard on the bar and opened his hand to grip Carleton's hand and Carleton had no choice, had to follow suit. Smiling hard to get past the sensation in his mouth that seemed to be oozing up from his guts. Both their hands were wet. Rafe was grunting, and Carleton heard himself grunt, Christ he knew better than to breathe through his mouth like a dog. Slowly, Carleton was forcing Rafe's arm back, the men's arms, shoulders, necks trembling with the strain. Everybody was watching. The bartender was watching, with a frowning kind of smile. The girls were shrieking with excitement like children. It was pissing Carleton, that he couldn't seem to force Rafe's arm down; he was stronger, he was winning, yet he couldn't seem to force Rafe's arm down all the way to the bar; that sweaty oily face so ugly to him, so jeering and hateful he'd been wanting to kill for a long time. Like creatures on the bottom of the sea, sinking beneath the pressure of the murky water. He wondered did his own eyes bulge like Rafe's. Then Rafe weakened, and with a yodeling sound of triumph Carleton slammed his arm flat down onto the bar, and the girls clapped and cheered. The black-haired one with the boobs stood on tiptoe to wipe Carleton's sweaty face with a tissue.

"Oh, man. Are you somethin!"

"Ain't he cute? He's strong."

"He's a mountain man. No mistakin."

Carleton said to Rafe magnanimously, "Give it up, buddy. You had enough for one night. And I don't want your fuckin money you can't afford to throw away."

Carleton paused to give his pumping heart time to recover.

Christ he was tired. . . . But Rafe was saying in a mean way, with that look of a wounded dog that wants you to come near enough so he can sink his teeth around your wrist, "This is fuckin puling stuff."

"What?"

"Maybe could try something else. Out back."

"Hell, you had enough for one night, buddy. Save some for your fat ol' wife."

Why was he calling Helen fat, Carleton didn't know. It was making these drunk girls laugh. The black-haired one with the boobs.

"Hillbilly bastard. Cocksucker." Rafe muttered these words you had to stoop to listen to, and to believe. Carleton could not believe what he was hearing.

Rafe struck Carleton a blow to the chest. A fist to the bony place called the solar plexus. A boxer can kill you hitting you there. Carleton was thrown back against the bar, and bottles and glasses went flying, and the bartender was shouting, and then Carleton was puking, or almost puking, bent over like a crippled man.

"Now—you had enough? Huh?"

Carleton hugged himself, waiting to recover. His heart was pumping like crazy. He saw a smear of blood on his hand.

Goddamn he was afraid, his bowels were fearful and he knew the symptoms. Fearful of Rafe but he couldn't let it go: by morning everybody in the camp would know, and laugh at him. And Pearl would know. *Coward.*

Carleton snapped his fingers in Rafe's face. It was a gesture he'd seen a man do, in a similar situation in a tavern. Carleton hooted the pig-calling sound—*Soooooooeeee!* Anybody who didn't know what *soooooooeeee!* was was going to laugh like hell it sounded so comical, and anybody who did know was going to laugh even harder. Except Rafe, Rafe was not laughing. Grunting, he tried to get Carleton in a headlock, but Carleton squirmed free, and struck Rafe on the throat, a frantic blow. The men staggered away from each other panting and staring like they'd never seen each other before.

"Get those hillbilly assholes out of here."

"C'mon, you two. Out."

They were being hustled somewhere. Carleton was conscious of swaying on his feet, and his head heavy as a crock of cider. And his nose bleeding. Rafe was just behind him and kicking at him like a kid would do, out of spite and frustration, and sniveling from some hurt to his pride. And outside, where the air was swirling with bugs by the bare-bulb-lighted entrance, and loud-voiced kids were drinking beer in the cinder parking lot, there Carleton felt a sharp blow to the back of his head behind his left ear, and something exploded in his brain, and the girls (who'd followed them outside?) were screaming *Watch out! watch out!* so Carleton knew he was being attacked though in his confusion not knowing who it was, only he had to defend himself, and it was his friend from the camp sobbing and pounding at him, and Carleton shouted and ducked away, and when he turned there was Rafe rushing him like some crazed animal—a black bear, that somebody had roused to a fury. Rafe was coming at Carleton with something long and thin in his fist, maybe a rod; a whiplike rod, that Carleton, wiping at his eyes, could not name.

A narrow strip of metal, he'd ripped off a pickup. That would be identified later.

"Hillbilly bastard—fucker—"

"Stinkin sonuvabitch—"

There was a circle of alert excited faces. Strangers' faces. And all of them white. These faces, and nobody moving nor even seeming to breathe except the two struggling men, sweat-slick, hair in their faces, shirts torn. Carleton felt how far away and flat he looked in the eyes of these strangers who might have been watching from a distance as you'd watch the furious antics of insects. He wanted to break through that picture: wanted to come alive to these strangers who were judging him. The girls who were squealing and whimpering like dogs being tickled were not the ones who mattered. Just females, and it was men who mattered. There were men watching, too. And more men coming out of the tavern. A fight! Knife fight! It was the men who mattered. Rafe was lumbering drunkenly toward Carleton whipping the wirelike rod in his hand, his face smeared with dirt and blood like the face of a man about to die; Carleton ducked, and stumbled away, terrified of the silence he and Rafe were caught in and by the fact that Rafe did not seem to understand what it meant. That whirring, whipping thing! Carleton had his knife out, and as Rafe moved at him Carleton ducked beneath his arm like Dempsey bending his knees to crouch and spring at the giant Jess Willard sinking the blade high into his chest, where it skidded against bone.

"Now you lemme alone! Fucker."

Carleton's voice was raw and pleading. Make a man plead like this, with strangers to witness, you'd be making a man goddamned mad and that could be a mistake.

Carleton's heels made crunching noises in the cinders. Gnats were stuck to his forehead, eyelids. His lips. The blade had gone in, Carleton knew that, but Rafe did not yet know it. Eyes watching them closely and the silence sharper than before even the females' tittering had ceased. Rafe moaned, turned and swung, whatever-it-was he'd gripped with both hands struck Carleton's shoulder and numbed him but in the same instant Carleton turned, switched his knife to his other hand bringing it up from his knee, frantic to make a hit, catching Rafe in the thigh in a long tearing cut. This time Rafe yelped with pain. "Now you stop! Fucker"—Carleton heard himself panting, begging. The thing in Rafe's hand fell to the ground. Rafe rushed at Carleton and seized him in his arms. Muttering in Carleton's ear like he was trying to explain something to his friend not wanting the others to hear. Yet gripping Carleton hard, staggering against him so Carleton had no choice but to slash at him with the knife. He felt the sharp slender blade cutting in, catching cloth and tearing, rising, sinking, and still Rafe didn't release him. Rafe clutched at him drawing breath in long languorous-sounding shudders and Carleton began to sob trying to work himself loose, he slashed the slippery blade now across the back of Rafe's neck where the flesh is tender, where his own flesh burned and pulsed with a mysterious skin rash, and Rafe grabbed Carleton's head with both his hands, his thumbs in Carleton's eyes wanting to gouge out his eyes and Carleton was the one yelping now *Stop, stop!* and the groping knife blade plunged and sank another time striking bone, and striking through bone, stabbing, plunging, meeting no resistance now against the falling man's broad, bent back so it appeared that Carleton might be striking his friend with only his hand, his fist, in a gesture of brotherly affection. And at last Rafe released him, and fell.

Carleton jumped craftily back. His muscles thrummed with energy. He saw his friend writhing on the cinders, bleeding from a dozen wounds Carleton would believe to be flesh wounds, glancing blows he'd made in self-defense like you'd slash at a vicious dog with a tree limb whipping the limb back and forth, only just flesh wounds yet the man was making a high-pitched moaning sound hugging his bleeding belly, his belly Carleton would swear he'd never touched. Carleton cried in triumph, "Call me a hillbilly! Nobody better call me a hillbilly, a Walpole ain't no hillbilly white trash!" It pissed him how Rafe was pretending to be hurt bad, swaying the judgment of witnesses, Carleton slammed his fist down hard on the top of Rafe's head the way you'd pound a table, and Rafe's head thudded against the ground, and Carleton was crouched over him shouting up at the faces, "See? Y'all see how a Walpole exacts justice." And there came a roaring in Carleton's ears like a sudden wind blowing south and east out of the Cumberlands blowing up a fierce hail-spitting storm so in even this moment of triumph

Carleton Walpole is being made to wonder will he ever get to where it's quiet, ever again.

4

South Carolina: spring. A woman in a dark dress stood in the entranceway and waited until everyone passed by and settled inside. It was hot. The schoolroom smelled of something nice—wood and chalk and something Clara did not recognize. The woman had broad shoulders and a heavy, solid body that reminded Clara of a tree trunk: the way she stood there waiting, her face hard as the children hurried by sometimes slowing one down by grabbing the back of his neck, you'd never think she could come to life and walk to the front of the room. Her hands were big and veined and her neck was veined too, but she had a winter kind of paleness that set her off from the people Clara was used to seeing. There was no telling how old she was. Clara's last teacher, a few weeks ago in another state, had been like that too—different from the women at camp. She used her words more cautiously. Clara had never heard anybody talk as much as schoolteachers talked and she thought this was wonderful.

But people on the outside always talked more. When you met someone from camp outside, in town, you could tell they were from camp; there was just something about them, people as far apart as Clara's father and Nancy and Clara's best friend Rosalie and Rosalie's whole family.

"Stop that! I said stop that!"

The teacher was after someone. Clara and Rosalie giggled, pressing their hands against their mouths. They heard a scuffle, and choked sounds of laughter. Their spines tingled but they didn't turn around to look even though everyone else did—they were new here and kept themselves tamed.

"He hit me first, goddamit," a boy said.

"Get over here—sit down!"

After a moment the teacher came to the front of the room. Clara saw her eyes flick over her and Rosalie and the other new kids from the camp; they were all together, sitting up near the front with the little kids. Rosalie was a year older than Clara; she was eleven; but both she and Clara and the boy with the splotches on his neck were with the little kids. They giggled and hid their faces in their books when the teacher was with the other grades. Clara's knees were hard against the bottom of the desk. She was getting big. She could feel herself growing. She was as tall as Rosalie and would be taller, and as tall as some of the girls from the farms. Being with the six- and seven-year-olds made her want to baby them, the way she babied her two little brothers. But they didn't like her. She wondered why the teacher had put her and Rosalie and that boy up front with such little kids.

On the first day, the teacher had held a book up too close to Clara's face and said, "Read this." Clara had blinked at the type nervously. Rosalie had her own book and held it hard against her stomach, her head bowed, but she did no better than Clara. "You're both slow. Far behind," the teacher said, not looking at them. And then Rosalie had started to giggle and Clara joined in, and the teacher had gotten mad at them both. Rosalie's mother, who had brought them over, had hollered at them and said it was a fine beginning for them, what the hell was the matter . . . ? Rosalie's mother had worn shoes with black bows on them that day, just to take them over to the school.

Now the teacher was approaching the first-grade group. It was only nine o'clock and already hot. Clara liked the heat, she could feel it get inside her and make her sleepy; she liked to close her eyes in the sunlight and fall asleep like one of those happy clean cats you saw sometimes around farms. She'd looked out the bus or out the back of the truck many times to catch sight of those cats— sometimes they'd be sleeping on a stone wall right out by the road, their fur ruffling in the wind. A patch of sunlight fell through the window and onto the teacher's arm. Clara watched it. The teacher's arm was lard-pale but had dark hairs on it like men's arms. The teacher had a solid, thick waist. Her belt was thin and had begun to turn over on one side, showing a cardboard lining. Clara watched her dreamily through her lashes. Everyone hated the teacher but Clara didn't; she liked that kind of skin and she liked the big round pin on the woman's collar, a round gold pin that looked like the sun.

She would buy a pin like that someday, she thought, with her own money, and maybe she would be teaching school too—

"Hello. I am a boy. My name is . . . Jack," one of the six-year-olds read. He was from a farm. He sat across from Clara and up one, and Rosalie sat right behind him. Rosalie had long stringy red hair and surprised eyes. If she was caught doing something bad she turned those eyes on you and you had to laugh—once at recess, in the last school they'd been at, Clara had seen her opening up a handkerchief and when she snatched it away a little tin whistle fell to the ground. The whistle had been someone else's, a girl's, but Clara would never tell; she thought it was funny. Things came into Rosalie's hands as if they were just lying there waiting for her. She never stole things but only "found" them.

"I live in a white house. This is my house. . . . This is my dog. My dog is black."

The boy read slowly, emphasizing each word the same way. He was the best reader and Clara kept hoping he would make a mistake. She followed the words with her eyes, memorizing them. She knew where the sound "house" was because there was the picture of a house over it. The house was white with three big trees in the front lawn. Clara loved the pictures in the book and had stared at them many times. Her favorite was the one of the mother and the baby sitting in the kitchen. It was toward the end of the book, so probably they wouldn't get to it; they'd be moved to another state by then. This picture showed a woman with nice short yellow hair holding a baby on her lap. The black dog was sitting and looking up at them and it looked as if it were smiling. Behind the woman was a big window with white curtains with red polka dots on them, and plants in flowerpots on the windowsills, and a clock. But the clock was fake; if you looked close there was no time on it. To make Rosalie jealous, Clara told her that she had been in a real house once, up in Kentucky.

"Next, Bobbie," said the teacher.

Behind them something was going on. Clara heard a book fall but she didn't dare look around. One day the teacher had shaken her and she hadn't even done anything—someone else had been laughing. So she sat with her mouth frozen into a polite little smile while the teacher's face reddened with that look all adults had that showed they wanted to kill. Behind Clara there was quiet.

"Pick up that book," said the teacher.

A desk squeaked as someone bent to pick it up.

The teacher stood staring for a while. The red backed out of her face unevenly. Then she woke up again and said, in a sharp, vicious voice: "I saw that! You—get out in the entry! Get out, you little pig!"

She began to yell. She threw down her book and rushed up the aisle. Clara and Rosalie looked around, their fists pressed against their mouths to keep from laughing. They laughed at everything here in school—what else could they do? Everything was so strange here! Kids as big as they were sat at desks and read haltingly out of books instead of working out in the fields to make money—why was that? If the people from town hadn't come out to the camp in cars and talked with someone, she and the other kids would not be here. It was all so different, so strange. She laughed at everything. People who picked fruit laughed to give themselves time to think. Clara was maybe doing the same thing. She looked around and saw the teacher shake one of the boys—he was big, about twelve. A farm boy. His name was Jimmy and he had done something nasty in the girls' outhouse once, on the floor. The teacher shook him and knocked him back against his seat. The desks were attached at the bottom and so the whole row rocked.

"Stand out in the entry—you filthy little pig!"

He went out, his shoulders hunched with laughing. The teacher wiped her face. Clara saw her eyes move over the room jerkingly, and something twitched in her cheek. It was a little twitch like a blink. Clara thought that when she was a teacher she wouldn't yell so much. She would smile more. But she would shake up the bad boys and scare them. She would be nice to the girls because the girls were afraid; even the big girl with the braids wound around her head, who was thirteen or fourteen, was quiet and afraid. Clara would be nice to all the girls but hard on the boys, the way her father was. He whipped Rodwell all the time but never Clara. . . .

"Read. Start reading!"

She was pointing at Clara. Clara's face tried to ward this off by smiling the way Rosalie's mother had smiled, but it did no good.

She bent over the book. Silence. She could feel something itching up high on her legs but she could not scratch it. The words danced.

"I live in a white house. . . ."

"He just read that! We're on the next page."

The teacher walked heavily toward them. Rosalie was hunched over her book, not looking at Clara. Everything was quiet except the flies.

Clara stared over at the next page. Her breath was coming fast. There was a picture of a strange man on that page, dressed in a strange way. He had a white shirt on but it was half covered up by a kind of coat, a short coat, that didn't come closed all the way up in front but left part of his chest to get cold. A red thing was tied around his neck. The strange coat was blue and the man's trousers were blue too. Clara wondered what kind of man this was supposed to be. He was smiling but she had no idea what he was smiling at; it looked as if he was just smiling, by itself.

"Go on and read. We're waiting."

Clara gripped the book harder.

"You can't be that stupid!" the teacher cried. "Go on and read!"

"My . . . My . . ."

The teacher leaned over Clara. With one long impatient finger she tapped at Clara's book. The baby had spilled something on this page and Clara's face burned with shame.

"Begin with this word. This word!"

She was tapping at a word. Clara knew it was a word, it was letters put together, it was like the letters up at the top of the blackboard that went all the way across the front of the room. . . .

"Say it, come on! Say it!"

"My . . ."

Clara felt waves of heat rise about her. She and the teacher were both breathing hard.

"*Father.* Say it—say *father.*"

"Oh, father. Father. Father," Clara whispered. "My father . . . My father . . ."

There was silence when Clara's voice ran out. Someone giggled. The teacher's finger did not move. Clara could feel heat from the teacher and she could hear her breathing—she wanted to get away from here, get far away and sleep for a long time. That way no one would be mad at her.

"How am I supposed to teach you anything? What do they expect? My God!" the teacher said bitterly. Clara remained sitting as straight as possible, the way Rosalie's mother had sat. It was the way to be. After a hot, ugly moment, the teacher said: "How long are you people going to be here?"

She leaned around so that she could look at Rosalie too. But Rosalie sat the way Clara was sitting, with her own finger on the page, pretending not to notice. "How long are your parents going to be living here?" the teacher said. "Do you have any idea?"

This frightened Clara more than anger, because she did not know what to do with it. She could hear something nice in the teacher's voice. She smiled, then stopped smiling, then looked over at Rosalie in panic. Rosalie turned and caught Clara's eye and both girls giggled suddenly. Their giggles were like something nasty.

The teacher made an angry noise and straightened up.

"All right, next. Bobbie. You read," she said. Clara could tell that the teacher's voice was now going high over her head and that it could not hurt her.

At recess they ran outside together. The teacher stood in the entry and made them pass one by one. If a boy pushed anybody she grabbed him and he had to wait until everyone else was out.

Clara and Rosalie approached the other girls. The girls did not pay any attention to them. There was a high concrete step in front of the school, cracked and crumbling, and a walk that led out to the road. Clara and Rosalie sat on the edge of the big step, by themselves but close enough to the other girls to hear what they said.

The boys played games, running hard. Cinders were tossed up when they skidded. They threw cinders and bits of mud at one another and at the girls. The girl with the braids cried when she couldn't get flaky pieces of mud out of her hair; the pieces were caught. The boys ran by Rosalie and Clara and said, "Let's see your nits! You got nits in your hair!" One of them grabbed Rosalie's long hair and jerked her off the concrete step. Rosalie screamed and kicked at him. "You fucking little bastard!" Rosalie screamed. The boys giggled and ran around the schoolhouse.

Clara shrank back. She heard the teacher's footsteps in the entry. The teacher ran out and grabbed Rosalie's arm and shook her. "What are you saying!" she cried. Rosalie tried to get away. "What did I hear you say?"

"They pulled her hair," said Clara.

"Don't you ever talk like that again around here!" the teacher said. She was very angry. Her face was red in splotches. Clara, crouched back against the wall, stared up at the teacher's face and couldn't figure out what she saw: the big, hard, bulging eyes, the stiffening skin, the mouth that looked as if it had just tasted something ugly.

Rosalie jerked away and ran out to the road. "You come back!" the teacher cried. Rosalie kept running. She was running back toward the camp; it was about a mile down one road and a little ways down another. Clara pressed her damp back against the wall and wanted to take hold of the teacher's hand, to make it stop trembling like that. Her mother's hands had been nervous too. If you touched them and were nice, sometimes they stopped, but sometimes not; sometimes they were like little animals all by themselves. When her mother was dead and in that box, her hands had been quiet up on her chest and Clara had kept peeking and watching for them to shake.

The teacher turned around. "She's a filthy little pig," she said. "She shouldn't be in school with— You tell her mother that she can't come back if she behaves that way. You tell her!"

Ned, the boy from camp, was squatting nearby. He began to giggle slyly.

"What's wrong with you?" said the teacher.

He stopped. He was maybe thirteen but runty for his age; his nose was always running; he was "strange." His parents let him come to school because he was too stupid to pick beans right. He bruised them or pulled the plants out or overturned his hamper.

"Tell her mother that— I don't know—" The teacher's face was heavy and sad. She was talking only to Clara. Clara wanted to cringe back from those sharp demanding eyes, she wanted to protect herself by making a face or swearing or giggling—anything to stop the tension, the seriousness. The teacher said, "What are you going to do with yourself?"

"What?" said Clara brightly.

"What are you going to do? You?"

It was like a question in arithmetic: how much is this and that put together? If the things were called beans Clara could add them together fast, but if they were squirrels or bottles of milk she could do nothing with them.

"You mean me?" Clara whispered.

"Oh, you're all—white trash," the teacher said, her mouth hard and bitter. She hurried by Clara and into the entry. Her footsteps were loud.

"White trash," said the girl with the braids.

"White trash," said Ned, smirking at Clara.

"You shut up—you're the same thing!" Clara snarled in his face. She hated him because they were together and there was nothing she could do about it. When the other kids laughed at them they made no difference between Clara and Ned—and Rosalie—and the twenty or so bigger kids from the camp who had come to school on the first day, then never showed up again.

Inside, the teacher was ringing the bell. It was a loose, rusty bell the teacher shook angrily by hand.

They ran back in. Clara's head had begun to ache. She sat at her desk and picked up her book and looked again at the white house and the man who was a father but who did not look like her own father or any father she knew, and kept looking at it as if trying to figure it out, until the teacher told her to put it away and do her writing. Penmanship. Clara felt heavy and hot and sad, imagining already school over in the afternoon and the way she would have to run to get away from the stones and mud balls. She and Ned would both have to run, cutting across muddy fields, with the boys laughing behind them. . . . "White trash!" They were white trash, everybody knew that, and what it meant was that people were going to throw stones: you had to get hit sooner or later.

5

New Jersey: tomato season. They came up together in a rickety old school bus. Carleton sat with Nancy, and across the aisle Clara sat with Rodwell and the baby, Roosevelt, on her lap. The bus was noisy and everyone was eating or smoking; Carleton took a bottle out of a canvas bag on the floor now and then, and he and Nancy drank from it.

"I never been this far north before," Nancy said.

"Well, I been here before," said Carleton.

His voice was flatter than it used to be; sometimes it surprised him. When Nancy acted like a young girl and made her eyes get big, he wanted to grab the back of her neck and shake her. He knew she was pretending and he hated people who pretended anything.

"You been everywhere, the whole world over. I never knew anybody like you," she said.

In the other seat Clara was holding Rodwell and Roosevelt apart. Rodwell must have been teasing the baby. "She's a real cute kid," Nancy always said of Clara. "I never seen any kid nice like her, her age." Clara was nice because she made supper if Nancy didn't feel up to it: she could make macaroni with melted cheese, and hot dogs fried in the pan, and rice with tomatoes and chopped field corn. She could sweep out the single room they'd be living in, place after place, and if she was fearful of Nancy she gave no sign. "She's done real well considerin her ma," Nancy said.

"Her mother taught her a lot," Carleton said sharply.

He stared out the window. In patches life came to him now. More and more in tattered patches like clouds—every time you looked, clouds were different-shaped, some of them weird and beautiful to knock your eye out, laced with sunlight like veins, but all of them swift-changing, forgettable. Christ, it was getting hard to stay sober: to want to stay sober. *Carleton! Help me.* Pearl had called for him like a woman waking from a dream but too late.

Nancy: a pretty oily-faced girl with a stale, sweet odor that Carleton liked all right, made him feel jumpy and sexy and almost-young, but shit she chattered all the time, wore a man out. In a group she was her best: when everyone was drinking, she could make them all laugh and men liked her, and Carleton felt a thrill of possession he hadn't felt in years, since Pearl had begun letting herself go.

When a woman does, that's the end. Like letting a garden go to weeds. Overnight it happens. Till you can't see what there had ever been in the garden to make it special, choked with weeds.

Carleton leaned his head against the window, that was cloudy with a light film of grease from where somebody else had been leaning his head. Outside there was nothing: countryside. Farmland, scrubby woods, hills in the distance. Carleton imagined a horse thundering along outside, keeping pace with the bus but oblivious of it. A high-stepping Kentucky Thoroughbred. The kind you never saw up close, only in pictures. A white star on his forehead, a long streaming shiny-black tail. Three white stockings, and the rest purely black. Carleton smiled feeling the horse's muscles plunge and jerk, admiring the ease of his galloping, the remarkably thin shinbones, ankles; he could feel the soft earth give way beneath the stallion's hooves. That way a horse had of frolicking in an open field, making nick-nick-nicking noises to his friends grazing in another pasture but ignoring any human being trying to call him over . . . All this while, the girl beside him was talking. Nudging her hot skin against his. Carleton was trying not to listen because behind such female chatter he could sometimes hear Pearl, the way she'd been before—

Carleton! Help me. I don't want to die.

Months Pearl had hardly spoken to him, or to anyone. All she could rouse herself for was nursing the baby. Then pushing the baby from her, to Clara. No more! No more! Carleton must've been drunk, goddamn he must've been, hadn't meant to get Pearl pregnant one more time he'd vowed, yet somehow it had happened. Those last months she'd worked in the fields slow and clumsy and indifferent as any mental case you'd see and sometimes she would lie down in the dirt and shut her eyes and nobody could rouse her, Carleton would have to haul her back to the cabin like a sack of seed. So shameful! Christ, he'd hated her. Pearl had ceased to know him, so that she need not despise him, Carleton believed. Until at the end, when the hemorrhaging began, she had called for him in a panic clear-minded and her eyes alert with pain *Carleton! Help me* and he'd been shit-faced drunk and slow to be roused and later there was a doctor who'd been so disgusted with Carleton he refused to look at him. Carleton had been humbled, stone-cold sober. Three-day drunk, and three days' whiskers, and he hadn't eaten a morsel in those days and so shaky on his feet he near-about fainted, yet had to endure the doctor's scorn like he was a filthy concrete floor being hosed down. "This should never have happened," the doctor was saying in a low, rapid voice, not meeting Carleton's eye, "this poor woman, in her condition, how many pregnancies did you say she'd had? And these living conditions." Carleton had but a vague sense of the room that was smelling of blood, buzzing with flies; he was grateful that the kids had been taken to the foreman's cabin, and kept from seeing their mother in such a state. The doctor was a youngish man, he'd shoved his mended glasses against the bridge of his nose, furious, frustrated; for of course Carleton could not speak, would not speak, out of Walpole shame and humility. "What's wrong with you people? Don't you know about birth control? Don't you ever—" Carleton stood mute and repentant and his face shut up tight as a fist. He had not believed even then that Pearl would die, or could die; he had no capacity to imagine the world of what-might-be, there was so damn much to worry about in the world that was. So he tried to grasp what was happening: the baby in Pearl's belly was twisted wrong, or something was wrong with Pearl's blood, and there was an infection, or—

All you can tell yourself, Carleton, it was Pearl's time. God took her back to Him. This consolation one of Carleton's women friends gave him, Carleton cherished in his heart.

Nancy was about eighteen. She was the daughter of a man Carleton knew and she wanted to leave Florida, so she just ran away with Carleton and his kids. She had dark hair cut very short and jagged about her face, exposing the tips of her soft ears, and when she laughed she squinted with hilarity—everything was so funny, she made you want to laugh along with her. That was one thing about the bus and the camps, Carleton thought; everyone was quick to laugh. They were good people. Right now they were laughing on the bus, carrying on. Just behind him was a family from Texas, Bert something and his wife, both of their faces tanned and round, and across the way were two of their children, Rosalie and Sylvia Anne, and behind them two more children—two boys. Carleton didn't like so many kids but he liked Bert and his wife because nothing got them down. Rosalie was Clara's best friend, but Carleton didn't like her quick clever eyes. They all liked to laugh. Carleton didn't mind hearing them, but he was different and thought of himself as different: he was better than these people, whose parents had traveled on the season too, because his family owned land and were farmers and he was about ready to go back there himself. The problem was that in 1933 everyone had it bad.

"I sure do like New Jersey. We're in it now," Nancy said. She was talking with Bert and his wife. "I s'pose you been up here too?"

"Look, I been all over," Bert said.

They laughed at this or at some comical twitching of his face. Bert always made everyone laugh, especially women. Carleton stared out the window at his leaping figures and saw that they jumped and twisted with a freedom that was almost desperate—there he was himself, free, able to glide along inches above the ground, easily outdistancing this old bus. A young Carleton, running along, letting his arms swing— The Texas couple started talking about something that had happened back home, a hurricane, and Carleton tried to shut his mind off since he'd heard this four or five times already. He concentrated on his running figures but Bert's voice kept coming through.

Bert was a thin, earnest man of about forty, with a meek bald head shining through his hair. But his earnestness and his meekness kept giving way to big mocking good-natured grins; he couldn't stop grinning. His wife had no face that Carleton could remember. It was just a woman's face.

"Somebody with no head?" Nancy shrieked.

"It was a nigger. We all seen it ourselves," Bert said.

Nancy giggled. "You're kiddin me!"

"Honey, I ain't kiddin you. Why for would I kid you?"

"Seen worse things than that," his wife said, pushing forward. "Don't you believe me? That was one real hard storm in Galveston."

"What's Galveston?" said Nancy.

"Yeah, we seen some sights," said the woman enthusiastically. Her voice slowed as she raked through debris and peeked into darkened ruins of houses. "A funnel come right down out of the sky—"

Carleton squirmed in his seat. The harder he stared at the figures the less clear they became, as if they were afraid of a funnel sweeping down out of the sky and destroying them. It was like a dream: when you tried to keep it going, it faded away. He heard the Texas couple's friendly drawling voices beating against him and felt a sudden violent hatred for them, even for Nancy: they were stupid, they didn't understand! They belonged in this life because their families hadn't been any better. They could see that Carleton was different and when they talked to him they were serious; they didn't fool around with him. But he didn't care about what they thought. It was other people he wanted to take him seriously, men who hired day labor on the roads or for digging trenches and pole holes. Those men had different, shrewd faces. They talked faster and didn't bother to joke and laugh apologetically during every pause. They always said to Carleton, "There's men of our own that ain't got work. . . . Nobody's building right now. . . . My brother wants a job too, but. . . . You're from the camp outside town, huh . . . ?"

Carleton still tried to stand straight and tall before witnesses. For always witnesses are judging you. Conscious of his muscled arms, shoulders, legs. But Christ, it was getting to be hard work keeping his shoulders straight when they were wanting all the time to bend like a bow, from stooping over in the fields. And Carleton's face—now he was missing front teeth, and his damn nose more crooked-seeming for some reason God only knew, gave him a cockeyed look sometimes like a mental case, lines in his forehead like cuts made by a knife, he had to practice making his face like the faces of men outside. Outside the farmworkers' camps. Bastards eyed you like expecting you to steal from their pockets or stink up the fuckin air they own. Some of 'em knew: a man like Carleton Walpole would wish to tear out their throats with his teeth if nobody knew, if he would never be caught.

In the fields, people let their faces go, mostly. Nobody's watching or gives a damn so maybe you talk to yourself, squinch up your eyes replaying old quarrels and fights and sometimes old good times too, if you can recall the good times, spit into the dust, all the time thoughts buzzing through your skull like fat black flies over coils of human shit out back of the fields in the scrub pinewoods where, if you got to go, you go there. And the foreman watching you leave the field, to see you don't linger. And the people in town, they seem to know all this. Even the women, with powdered faces and white high-heeled shoes, eyes sliding on you in pity and revulsion. Even the young ones. So in town you must walk in a certain way, or god-damn you try. There Carleton Walpole carried himself straight as he could and his face reserved and dignified like a soldier who would fight to the death if you challenged his honor. Or the honor of his family. No: you would not wish to do that.

Yet alone sometimes his shoulders sagged with the hurt of what he'd done he had not meant to do, Christ as his witness.

At that tavern outside Ocala. Far away in the fuckin Sunshine State.

"It wasn't. It was never. Not my fault. *It was not.*"

They'd believed him. No: they'd believed the witnesses, not him.

They'd believed the witnesses speaking carefully yet with contempt as you would speak of two dogs fighting in the dirt. The one, going for the jugular; so the other had no choice but to go for the jugular, too. That was all it was. Two dogs.

Something had gone out of Carleton since that night. And the terrible days and nights following.

Like losing teeth. Your jaws feel better in time. But there's the emptiness, dead nerves. Like dead wires. No current going through them. His mind worked slower now. His flaring-up times were maybe more frequent but did not require thought. He talked slower, and heard words slower. Like coming at him slow through murky water. So he'd wake in some godforsaken place like the middle of a potato field having seen the circle of faces smiling at him like welcoming him back and for a confused moment he'd think *I was back home* and almost he would think *It's a place I can get to, from here*.

Except they would stare at him in astonishment demanding to know what he had done with his little blond wife that sweet little Brody girl hardly came to his shoulder.

"Not my fault. Christ as my witness."

A woman's hand prodded his side. Nancy giggled he was talking in his sleep again. Twitching, kicking.

Damn bus was bouncing on a dirt road. Must've left the highway so Carleton pretended to know this. Something hot and hungry in his gut like a ball of baby snakes. He fumbled for the whiskey. What was left of it.

It burned as it went down, and then it stopped burning.

A warm numb sensation. Baby snakes settling to sleep.

"Hon, you gonna share? Sure!"

Nancy pried the bottle from his fingers and lifted it to her mouth drinking quick and practiced wiping her mouth with the back of her hand as a man would do, and her eyes glowing warm and amber like the whiskey. You weren't supposed to drink on the bus but the driver himself sometimes drank. Some way to get through the long hours, the fuckin heat. Nancy was passing the bottle to the Texas couple behind them, these two she'd struck up a friendship with as Nancy had a way of doing, quick to make friends and quick to make enemies that was Nancy's way. Now she was acting like it was Carleton's idea to pass the whiskey to them, boastful of her man she saw as good-looking and a real man, Christ it pissed him hearing her bragging on him like he was somebody special. Stroking his upper arm, his ropey muscles like it thrilled her. "This man of mine he's been all over the map, comes from Kentucky, lived in a hotel in Cincinnati for a while, he crossed the Mississippi how many times, hon?—" and Carleton only just shrugged. He knew sometimes when she was drunk and feeling sexy she would hint to people that Carleton had hurt—her words were *hurt, hurt bad, had to hurt*—a man back in Florida, but she never spoke of this to Carleton's face, she knew she had better not.

Carleton supposed the Texas couple was wondering why he didn't turn around and be friendly with them well fuck 'em let 'em wonder: Carleton Walpole wasn't any old trained bear. Let them go to hell: he hated them. Not as bad as spics and niggers that you hated on principle, these types you hated soon as you laid eyes on them for what they were. Fuckin losers, deadbeats and assholes and drunks. And the women loud, worse than the men. Mostly everybody on the bus Carleton was feeling savage about except his kids and maybe Nancy if she didn't gab so fuckin much, like to tie a sack over her head to shut her up. His kids he would spare, though Rodwell was pissing him off with his smart-ass mouth, hee-hawing at the back of the bus with some boys, and Roosevelt was the homeliest kid you ever saw like a retard with that glaze in his eyes and a stammer if his pa looked at him crossways. Carleton took back the bottle and drank and shut his eyes to the fiery blur of the sun thinking if this busload all died in a crash it'd be no loss to the world. Except the fuckin bus was not going fast enough on this dirt road to crash hard. Turn over into a ditch? A creek? Might not be deep enough, a creek. Over the side of a bridge into the Mississippi River, that would do the trick: maybe a hundred feet deep, and a mile wide, and a fast-moving current and undertow.

Except: say the bus careened off a bridge and into the river and everybody on the bus drowned except Carleton Walpole and his family for God had spared them.

Know why I spared you, Carleton Walpole?

And he would bow his head in meekness. For he would not know.

Seek and ye shall find was God's reply. *All the corners of the world shall ye seek and one day ye shall find.*

The camp was just off the dirt road, hidden by a scrubby orchard. When they climbed out of the school bus everyone felt the ground wobble. Carleton looked suspiciously about to see what it was like. Nancy helped Roosevelt down, scolding to Clara, "He shouldn't ought to do that in his pants, old as he is. You got to teach him better, honey. You're his sister."

Clara bit at her thumbnail. "I thought he was O.K."

Before them the grassless space was strewn with junk. The remains of a trash fire. On both sides were shacks that had been whitewashed years ago. At the far end was a tomato field. Carleton shielded his eyes looking that way: heat waves glimmered there like gasoline fumes. "They painted these places up nice, that was nice of them," Nancy said. She was carrying her clothes and things rolled into a soiled quilt. "What do you think, honey?"

Carleton frowned. Being called *honey* didn't always ring right with him. He grunted, "Looks all right."

They were assigned to their cabins. Carleton never looked at the crew recruiter, who spoke in the same loud bossy way to everyone—Carleton Walpole as well as old deaf cripples who could hardly walk—and who liked to pretend that Carleton wasn't as good a man as he was. This recruiter also drove the bus to make a little more money.

"This'll suit us fine. Ain't this fine?" Nancy said.

"Somebody left some clothes for us." Carleton kicked at a pile of soiled clothes on the floor of the cabin. Bloodstained underpants.

They were always happy on the first day. Even Carleton would feel some hope. This shanty, that the recruiter called a cabin, wasn't too bad, bigger than the previous one, and not so smelly. There were cobwebs and dead insects and more trash on the floor, but Nancy and Clara would take care of that. Carleton said nothing and let them unpack. His underarms and sides were slick with sweat. Damn crack in his ass burning-hot. He was damn thirsty but would have to wait on that, he knew. That whiskey-dryness in his throat like he'd been sleeping. Carleton tested the lightbulb over the kitchen table and it worked. That was good. He plugged in the hot plate and that worked too. With his knee he prodded the mattresses; they were all right. When he was finished he jumped down from the doorstep and stood in front of the shack with his hands on his hips.

Each of the shacks was numbered. Theirs was ∂. Carleton stared at this figure in disgust, to think that he would have to live in a shanty with a six painted backward on it, as if he himself had been stupid enough to do that! Children were already out playing around the shacks. The shacks were propped up off the ground on concrete blocks and some of them did not look very stable. Carleton walked slowly along, his hands still on his hips as if he owned everything. Back between the shacks were old cardboard boxes and washtubs. Some were turned over, others were right side up and filled with rainwater. He knew that if he went over to look he'd see long thin worms swimming gracefully in the tubs. Out in front of some of the shacks were big packing crates filled with trash. Some kids were already picking through them.

"Roosevelt, get the hell out of that crap!" Carleton said.

He cuffed the boy on the face. Roosevelt had a narrow head and light brown hair that grew out too thin, so that he looked like a little old man at times. There were hard circular things on his head, crusty rings that had come from nowhere, and two of his front teeth had been kicked out in a fight with some other kids. He shrank away from Carleton and ran off. "You stay out of other people's goddamn garbage," Carleton said. The other children waited for him to get past. They were afraid of him.

The rest of the men were outside now, waiting. They spent their time working or drinking; when they had nothing to do, their arms were idle and uneasy. Two of them squatted down in the shade of a scrawny tree and took out a deck of cards. "Want to try it, Walpole?" one said.

"You don't have no money," Carleton said sullenly.

"Do you?"

"I don't play for fun. You don't have no money, it's a waste of my time."

"You got lots of money yourself?"

The Texas man, Bert, appeared in the doorway of a shanty, stretching his arms. He had taken off his shirt. His chest was sunken and bluish white, but he looked happy, as if he'd just come home.

"C'mon play with us, Walpole," he said.

Carleton made a contemptuous gesture. He had some money saved and maybe he could double it if he played with them, but he had come to despise their odors and stained teeth and constant, repetitious talk; they were just trash.

"I got no heart for it," he said.

He walked by. He could hear them shuffling cards. "We don't go out till the mornin," someone said. Carleton did not glance around. His eyes were taken up by other things, drawn back and forth along the rows of cabins as if looking for something familiar. Some sign, some indication of promise. There were a number of sparrows and blackbirds picking at something on the ground; Carleton tried not to look at it, but saw it anyway—a small animal, rotted. It made him angry to think that the farmer who owned this camp didn't bother to bury something like that. It was dirty, it was filthy. The whole camp ought to be burned down. . . . And the junk from last year, last year's garbage still lying around. Carleton spat in disgust.

He had left the packed-down area between the shacks and was looking now out over a field. The tomato plants were pale green, dusty, healthy. Carleton could see in his mind's eye the dull red tomatoes, rising and falling as if in a dream, and his own hands reaching out to snatch them. Out and down and around and back, in a mechanical, graceful, endless movement. Out and down, tugging at the stem, and then around and back, putting the tomato gently in the container—then inching ahead on his heels to get the next plant. And on and on. He would squat for a while and then kneel; the women and kids and old men knelt right away.

It used to be that he would dream about picking after he had worked all day, but now he dreamed about it even before he worked. And the dreams were not just night dreams either, but ghostly visions that could come to him in the brightest sunlight.

"Son of a bitch," Carleton muttered.

He turned and shaded his eyes to look back over the camp. He saw now that it was the same camp they'd been coming to for years. Even the smells were the same. Off to the right, down an incline, were two outhouses as always; it would smell violently down there, but the smell would be no surprise. That was the safe thing about these camps: there were no surprises. Carleton took a deep breath and looked out over the campsite, where the sun poured brilliantly down on the clutter: rain-rotted posts with drooping gray clotheslines, abandoned shoes, bottles of glinting red and green, tin cans all washed clean by the rain of many months, boards, rags, broken glass, wire, parts of barrels, and, at either side of the camp, rusted iron pipes rising up out of the ground and topped by faucets.

A slow constant drip fell from the faucets and had eaten holes into the ground. Alongside one of the shanties was an old stove; maybe it was for everyone's use.

It was another bad year, Carleton thought, but it would get better. Things had been bad for a long time for everyone—they talked about rich men killing themselves, even. The kind of work Carleton did was sure, steady work. Up on high levels you can open a newspaper or get a telephone call and find out you're finished, and then you have to kill yourself; with people like Carleton it was possible just to laugh. It was the times themselves that were bad, Carleton thought. It was keeping him down, sitting on him. But he would never give up. When things began to get better—it would start up in New York City—then men who were smarter than others could work themselves up again, swimming upward through all the mobs of stupid, stinking people like the ones Carleton had to work with. They were just trash, the men squatting there and tossing cards around, and the fat women hanging in doorways and grinning out at one another: Well, we come a long way! Ain't we come a long way? Some of these people had been doing fieldwork now for twenty, thirty, even forty years, and none of them had any more to show for it than the clothes they were wearing and the junk they'd brought rolled up in quilts.... This was true of Carleton but he had a family to keep going; if he didn't have that family he would have saved lots of money by now.

He did have about ten dollars, wadded up carefully in his pocket. Nancy knew nothing about it and what she didn't know wouldn't hurt her. It struck Carleton sometimes that he should spend this money on Clara—get her a little plastic purse or a necklace. He did not feel that way about his other children. Mike had run off a while ago and nobody missed him; he'd been trouble at the end. Carleton had had to give it to him so hard that the kid's mouth had welled with blood, he'd almost choked on his own blood, and that taught him who was boss. Sharleen was back in Florida, married. She had married a boy who worked at a garage; she liked to brag he had a steady job and he could work indoors. But she never brought the boy home for Carleton to see. So he had said to her: "You're a whore, just like your mother." He hadn't meant anything by that.

He hadn't thought about what it meant. But after that he had never seen Sharleen again. He was glad to get rid of her and her darting nervous eyes.

The fear he saw in his children's faces did not make him like them. Even Clara showed it at times. That wincing, cautious look only provoked him and made him careless with his blows; Nancy had enough sense to know that. What Carleton liked was peace, quiet, calm, the way Clara would crawl up on his knee and tell him about school or her girlfriends or things she thought were funny, or the way Nancy embraced him and stroked his back.

Carleton was hungry. He headed back toward the cabin. The square now was filled with children and women airing out quilts and blankets on the clotheslines. Bert's wife was flapping something out the doorway. She had a beet-red face and surprised, tufted hair. "Nice day!" she said. Carleton nodded. Two boys ran shrieking in front of him. He saw Clara and Rosalie by the men who were playing cards. Clara ran out to him and took his hand. He thought how strange that was: a girl runs out and takes his hand, he is her father, she is his daughter. He felt warm. "Rosalie's pa won somethin an's goin to give it to her!" Clara cried. Carleton let himself be led over reluctantly to the cardplayers. Bert was making whopping noises as he tossed down his cards. He chortled, he hooted, he tapped another man's chest with the back of his fingers, daintily. Carleton's shadow fell on his head and shoulders and he grinned up at Carleton. Behind Bert were the rest of his kids. The girl's hair was a frantic redbrown, like her father's, and she had her father's friendly, amazed, mocking eyes. "Here y'are, honey," he said. He dropped some things in her opened hands. Everyone laughed at her excitement.

"What's this here?" Rosalie said. She held up a small metallic object. Clara ran over and stared at it.

"That's a charm," said Bert.

One of the men said: "Don't you know nothin? That ain't a charm!"

"What is it, then?"

"A medal," the man said. He was a little defensive. "A holy medal, you put it somewheres and it helps you."

"Helps you with what?"

Rosalie and Clara were examining it. Carleton bent to see that it was a cheap religious medal, in the shape of a coin, with the raised figure of some saint or Christ or God Himself. Carleton didn't know much about these things; they made him feel a little embarrassed.

"It's nice, I like it," Rosalie said. The other things her father had given her were a pencil with a broken point and a broken key chain.

"How does it work?" said Clara.

"You put it in your pocket or somethin, I don't know. It don't always work," the man said.

"Are you Cathlic or somethin?" Bert said, raising his eyebrows.

"Shit—"

"Isn't that a Cathlic thing?"

"It's just some medal I found laying around."

Carleton cut through their bickering by saying something that surprised all of them, even him. "You got any more of them?"

"No."

"What're they for?"

"Jesus, I don't know. . . . S'post to help a little," the man said, looking away.

Carleton went back to the shanty, where Nancy was sitting in the doorway. She wore tight faded slacks and a shirt carelessly buttoned, and Carleton always liked the way she smoked cigarettes. That was something Pearl hadn't done. "Y'all moved in?" Carleton said. He rubbed the back of her neck and she smiled, closing her eyes. The sunlight made her hair glint in thousands of places so that it looked as if it were a secret place, a secret forest you might enter and get lost in. Carleton stared at her without really seeing her. He saw the gleaming points of light and her smooth pinkish ear.

Finally he said, "Don't think you made no mistake, huh, comin up here with me? All this ways?"

She laughed to show how wrong he was. "Like hell," she said.

"You think New Jersey looks good, huh?"

"Better than any place I ever was before."

"Don't never count on nothing," Carleton said wisely.

———

Which turned out to be good advice: that evening the crew leader, a puffy-faced, lumpy man Carleton had always hated, came to the camp to tell them it was all off.

"Come all the way here an' the fuckin bastard changed his mind, says he's gonna let them rot out there," the man shouted. Flecks of saliva flew from his angry mouth. "Gonna let them rot! Don't want them picked! He says the price ain't high enough an's gonna let them rot an' the hell with us!"

Carleton had heard announcements like this before and just stood back, resting on his heels to absorb the surprise. Around him people were making angry wailing noises.

"What the hell is it?" Nancy said faintly.

"It's his tomatoes, he can let them rot if he wants," Carleton said, his face stiff as if he wanted to let everyone know he was miles away from this, miles and years away. It did not touch him.

It turned out finally that they got a contract to pick at another farm the next morning, so they had to ride there in the school bus, an hour each way, and could still stay at the campsite—it was the only one around—if they paid that farmer rent (a dollar a day for a cabin); and out at the second farm they had to pay that farmer for a lunch of rice and spaghetti out of the can and beans out of the can and bread (fifty cents for each lunch, thirty cents for kids); and they had to pay the crew leader who was also the recruiter and the bus driver for the ride (ten cents each way, including kids), and then had to pay the recruiter twenty cents on each basket for finding them this other job, because he was their recruiter, and, when that job ended, they had to pitch in to give him fifty cents apiece so that he could ride around the country looking for another farm, which he did locate in a day or two, some fifty miles away, a ride that would cost them fifteen cents each way. At the end of the first day, when they were paid, Carleton won five dollars in a poker game and felt his heart pound with a fierce, certain joy. The rest of these people were like mud on the bottom of a crick, that soft heavy mud where snakes and turtles slept. But he, Carleton, could rise up out of that mud and leave them far behind.

6

Tom's River was the name of the town: Clara smiled wondering if there was a boy named Tom, and it was his river.

People talked of the *Pine Barrens,* too. Clara whispered "Pine Barrens." No idea what it was except cranberry farmers lived there. And sometimes they hauled in day-pickers, and sometimes they did not.

Tom's River was seven miles from their camp. Always they were being driven through it on their way out, on their way back from where they were day-hauled. Whenever they rode through Tom's River, Clara and her friend gazed hungrily out the grimy window hoping to catch somebody's eye. *Hi! Hello!* they would wave and giggle like little kids being tickled.

Clara believed that towns were special places with their grids of streets, some of them paved and some not; stores built so close together they were in a row; and some of them double-decked on the others so your eye lifted up to the second story, surprised. Clara had never set foot above any first-floor place. She wondered what it was to live so high, like it was nothing special to look out a window and see where you were like in a tree!

"Don't you get lost in Tom's River. Nobody is goin to come fetch you, miss."

Nancy was moping, it wasn't right for Clara who was her daddy's damn favorite to take an afternoon off. A damn big hungry girl always eating more than her share. But if Nancy voiced such an opinion, Carleton told her shut up. Like that: "Shut up." In front of the kids disrespecting her.

So Clara had permission to go. It was Rosalie's birthday: that day Rosalie was thirteen. Rosalie's father gave her fifty cents saying it was her special day, and Carleton winked (so Nancy wouldn't see) and gave Clara a dime. A coin so small it grew moist and hot in your hand right away and would be easy to lose, if you weren't careful.

They were going to hitch a ride, walking along the edge of the road toward Tom's River and waiting for a car to come along, or a pickup. It was what all the kids did and nobody got in trouble except if a sheriff's car came cruising by, then you might. A deputy in dark glasses staring at you like he'd like to run you off the road. But mostly people were friendly. People tended to feel sorry for you, and were friendly. The girls were excited and uneasy, walking in the road, waiting, and when their eyes met they laughed together breathlessly.

"What's it feel like to be thirteen?"

Rosalie shrugged. A blush rose into her face. "You'll find out." And right away she changed the subject saying with a snigger, "Guess you showed that bitch back there."

"The hell with her." Clara liked how her daddy uttered these words like passing pronouncement from a high throne.

"Thinks she's so special hookin up with you people," Rosalie said. "I wouldn't let no nasty bitch like that in my house if my ma died."

Clara didn't like such talk. *Ma died.* Nobody in their family talked like that ever, they'd have got their mouths slapped hard.

"Oh, Nancy is—" Clara paused. She was going to say *Nancy is nice, sometimes.* She wanted to say *Without Nancy we'd be lonely!* But it was a mistake to argue with Rosalie on this special day.

They fell silent not knowing where to look: a car was fast approaching.

"What if it's some guy tries to get smart?" Rosalie muttered.

Clara gritted her teeth as the car came closer. She hoped it would go past.

The car went past. A man's face behind the wheel and in the passenger's seat some prune-faced old woman with eyeglasses.

"Sonsabitches." Rosalie stooped to pick up a handful of pebbles and tossed them after the car, not hard enough to hit. A cloud of dust rose in the car's wake.

Another car passed, more slowly. And then a pickup, its back loaded with tomatoes in bushel baskets. The front seat was crowded with a driver, a teenaged shirtless boy, a yellow Lab sitting up like a person. "No room, girlies." The driver grinned at them and wagged his hand out the window.

"Fuck you, mister." Rosalie mouthed this after the pickup, not loud enough to be heard.

Yet each time a car approached the girls straightened their faces to looking polite, serious. Like at school. Rosalie had washed her hair in the sink and her ma had brushed it so it didn't look halfway so stringy as usual. Clara had washed her hair too and brushed it herself so it hung down past her shoulders and it was a gleaming ash-blond, like her father's hair. Except Clara's hair was growing in thick and Carleton's was thinning out so sometimes you could see his scalp at the crown of his head like something you hadn't ought to see.

The girls' faces, lost inside their long hair, were furtive and hopeful at the same time. Rosalie had all kinds of faces, Clara admired how her friend could switch from one to another. Like somebody turning the dial on a radio. Sometimes Rosalie could look halfway pretty, and sometimes Rosalie looked like a rat with darting eyes and a nervous mouth. At school Rosalie had one kind of face for when the teacher was looking at her, and another kind of face for when the teacher had turned her back; Rosalie had one kind of face when she and Clara had to walk past the kids who called them white trash, and another kind of face when Rosalie was with her own kind. And still another, kind of sly-comical, when she was with just Clara alone.

Everybody said how Clara had her daddy's eyes—that frank, perplexed blue—but a nice-looking blue, like the sky on a clear day—and her cheekbones were high like his, so people said she'd be real good-looking someday, more than just cute. But also like Carleton she could look haughty, and suspicious.

"Kind of make your mouth smile, Clara," Rosalie said, annoyed. "You got to act like you deserve a ride not just want one."

So Clara tried. Clara watched how Rosalie made her mouth smile, and tried. It should have helped that both girls were wearing their best dresses, cotton floral prints, with short sleeves and sashes that tied behind, and both dresses were just a little tight for them, uncomfortable under the arms. Rosalie kept shrugging her chest, where the cotton made her itch from being tight.

Finally they got a ride with a man who didn't look like a farmer. "Room for both of you up front," he said kindly. They slid in. The man drove along slowly as if not wanting to jar them. The girls stared out at the familiar road; it looked different, seen from a car window instead of from the bus. From time to time the man glanced over at them. He was about forty, with slow eyes. "You girls from the camp back there?" he said. Clara, who was in the middle, nodded without bothering to look at him. She was inhaling carefully the odors of an automobile. It was the first time she had ever been in one; she sat with her scraped legs stuck out, her feet flat on the floor. Rosalie was investigating a dirty ashtray attached to the door, poking around with her fingers.

"Where are you girls from?" the man said.

"Not from nowhere," Clara said politely. She spoke the way she spoke to schoolteachers, who only asked questions for a few minutes and then moved on to someone else.

"Not from nowhere?" the man laughed. "What about you, Red? Where you from?"

"Texas," said Rosalie in the same voice Clara had used.

"Texas? You're real far from home then. But ain't you sisters?"

"Yeah, we're sisters," Clara said quickly. "I'm from Texas too."

"You people travel all over, huh. Must be lots of fun."

When the girls did not reply he went on, "You must work hard, huh? Your pa makes you work hard for him, don't he?" He tapped on Clara's leg. "You got yourself some scratches on your nice little legs. That's from out in the fields, huh?"

Clara glanced at her legs in surprise.

"Them cuts don't hurt, do they?" said the man.

"No."

"Ought to have some bandages or somethin on them. Iodine. You know what that is?"

Clara was staring out at the houses they passed. Small frame farmhouses, set back from the road at the end of long narrow lanes. She squinted to see if there were any cats or dogs around. In a field there were several horses, their heads drooping to the grass and their bodies gaunt and fragile.

"Pa had a horse once," she said to Rosalie.

"What was that?" said the man.

Clara said nothing. The man said, "Did you say they hurt?"

Clara looked at him. He had skin like skin on a potato pulled out of the ground. His smile looked as if it had been stretched on his mouth by someone else.

"I mean the scratches on your legs. Do they hurt?"

"No," said Clara. She paused. "I got a dime, I'm gonna buy somethin in town."

"Is that so?" said the man. He squirmed with pleasure at being told this. "What are you gonna buy?"

"Some nice things."

"Can't get much with a dime, little girl."

Clara frowned.

"Your pa only gave you a dime?"

Clara said nothing. The man leaned over and waved a finger in front of Rosalie. "Your pa ought to be nicer to two nice little girls like you." They were approaching a gas station. The road had turned from dirt to blacktop, getting ready for town. "Could be there's some soda pop at this garage," the man said. "Anybody like some?"

Clara and Rosalie both said yes at once.

The man stopped and an old man came out to wait on him, wearing a cowboy hat made of straw. Clara watched every part of the ceremony; she was fascinated by the moving dials on the gas pump. The driver, standing outside with his foot on the running board to show he owned the car, bent down once in a while to smile in at the girls. "Wouldn't mind some pop myself," he said. They said nothing. His foot disappeared after a moment and he went into the gas station. It was a small wooden building, once painted white. As soon as the screen door flopped closed behind him, Rosalie opened the glove compartment and looked through the things in there— some rags, a flashlight, keys. "Goddamn junk," Rosalie said. She put the keys in her pocket. "Never can tell what keys might open," she said vaguely. Clara was looking in the backseat. One brown glove lay on the floor, stiff with dirt. She lunged over and got it, then sat on it because there was nowhere to hide it.

The man came back carrying three bottles of pop, all orange. As he drove he drank his, making loud satisfied noises. The girls drank theirs down as fast as they could.

"Ain't this good for a hot day?" he said, sighing.

They were nearing the town now. To Clara and Rosalie this town was very big. It was ringed with houses that were not farmhouses and buildings that did not seem to have anything for sale in them. There were areas of wild land, then more houses, a gas station, a railroad crossing, and then before them on an incline was the main street—lined with old red-brown brick buildings that reared up to face each other.

"You girls never said where you were goin. I bet you're goin to the show."

"Yeah," said Rosalie.

"You like them shows?"

He had slowed the car. It came to a stop. Clara was surprised to see nothing much about them. They had just crossed the railroad tracks and now there was a great field with old automobiles parked in it.

"The show don't begin till five o'clock, so you got lots of time till then. Two cute little girls like you. You want to come visit at my house?"

They sat in silence. Finally Rosalie said cautiously, "We got to be home again fast."

"How fast is fast?" the man said loudly, trying to make a joke. He was pressing against Clara while he talked. "Only this minute got into town; you ain't already goin back, are you?"

"I need to get somethin for my leg, my leg hurts," Clara said. She was leaning over against Rosalie to get away from him.

"Does your leg hurt?" the man said in surprise.

"Stings real bad," said Clara. She could sense Rosalie listening to her, puzzled. Clara did not know what she was saying but her voice seemed to know. It was not nervous and it went on by itself. "It hurt when I fell down yesterday and made me cry."

"Did it make you cry?" the man said. He put his hand on her knee, cupping it gently. She stared at his hand. It had small black hairs on its back, and fingernails that were ragged and edged with dirt; but it was a hand she felt sorry for. "A little girl like you oughtn't to be workin in the fields. There's a law against it, you know. They can put your pa in jail for it."

"Nobody's gonna put my pa in jail," Clara said fiercely. "He'd kill them. He killed a man anyway, one time." She looked at the man to see how he would take this. "He killed him with a knife but I'm not s'post to tell."

The man smiled to show he did not quite believe this.

"I ain't s'post to tell," Clara said. "They let him go 'cause the other man started it an' my pa was only doin right."

She looked at the man. A strange dizzy sensation overcame her, a sense of daring and excitement. She met his gaze with her own and smiled slowly, feeling her lips part slowly to show her teeth. She and the man looked at each other for a moment. He took his hand away from her knee. Something strange seemed to be happening but Clara did not know what it was. She seemed to be doing something, keeping something going. The sun was warm and dazzling. Then she forgot what she was doing, lost control, and her smile went away. She was a child again. She leaned against Rosalie to get away from the man's smell.

"We got to get out now," she said.

Rosalie tried the door handle.

"That door opens hard. It's tricky," the man said. His face was damp and he kept looking at Clara. "You got to be smart to open it. . . ."

"It don't come open," Rosalie muttered.

"It's a little tricky. . . ."

Clara held her breath because she didn't want to smell him. He leaned over to tug at the door handle, pretending to have trouble with it.

"Open it up!" Rosalie said. Clara's heart was pounding so hard she could not say anything. The man grinned apologetically at her, his face right up against hers, and finally he got the door open. Rosalie jumped out. Clara started to slide out but he took hold of her arm.

"Listen, little girl," he said, "how old are you?"

Clara slashed at his hand with her nails. He winced and released her. "Goddamn old asshole!" Clara cried, jumping out. "Go fuck yourself! Take this—it ain't no good!" She threw the glove at his face and ran away. She and Rosalie jumped the ditch and ran into the field, laughing. She could hear Rosalie laughing ahead of her.

They hid behind one of the junked cars. The man was still parked by the road. Clara peered through a yellowed, cracked old windshield and watched him. He leaned around, looking outside like a lost dog. Clara pressed her knuckles against her mouth to keep from laughing.

"Think he's gonna tell the police?" said Rosalie.

"My pa will kill him if he does."

Finally he closed the door and drove away.

It was a warm, bright afternoon. Both girls forgot about the man in the car and looked around, ready to be surprised and pleased. The junked automobiles all around them looked as if they had crawled here and died; their grilles were like teeth lowered into the earth. The girls walked along, bending to look inside at the tattered seats and the torn upholstery. Once Clara slid into an old car and turned the steering wheel, making a noise with her mouth that was supposed to be the sound of an engine. She tapped at the horn but it did not work.

"I'm gonna have a car like this, only a real one," she said.

They kept smiling, they didn't know why. Nothing smelled bad here. There was only a faint metallic odor, and the odor from occasional pools of oil. No smell of garbage or sewage. A few dragonflies flew about, but no flies. And every car was something new to look at. There were old convertibles with the tops half ripped off, as if someone had attacked them with knives. There were old trucks that looked saddest of all, like tough strong men who couldn't keep going. There were red cars, yellow cars, black cars, the paint peeling and rusty or overlaid with another color so that the two colors together made a third strange color that was like a wound. Clara could not examine anything close enough. They had come to town and already they were seeing things they'd never seen before. Windows everywhere were cracked as if jerking back from something in astonishment; the cracks were like spiderwebs, like frozen ripples in water. Clara stared and stared, and what she saw got transformed into new, strange things. A piece of rubber was a snake, sleeping in the sun. A scraped mark on a car was a flower, ready to fall into pieces. In a yellowed car window was a face that might have been under water, so blocked out by the sun behind it that she could not make it out—it was her own face. Clara and Rosalie stared at everything. They kept smoothing their dresses down, wiping their hands on them, as if they'd been invited to visit and were ashamed of the way they looked.

"This one here—lookit. What's wrong with this?" Clara said sadly. The car was a dull, dark blue and looked new to her. She tried to imagine her father sitting in the driver's seat, one arm hanging loosely out the window. They looked under the hood and saw some weeds: no engine. "My father used to have a car like this, in Florida," Clara said.

They climbed up on the hood of one old truck, then up on the roof of the cab. The metal surface was hot and smelled hot. On the roof of the truck was an old tire. Clara sat on it and hugged her knees.

"Why'd you act so funny with that bastard back there?" Rosalie said. Her freckles gave her a sandy, quizzical look. "You acted real funny."

"I didn't either."

"Yes you did."

"Like hell I did."

"You talked different—like Nancy or somebody."

"I never talked like Nancy!"

"I was scared, I thought you an' him were gonna leave me," Rosalie sneered. "Thought you were gonna run off with him."

Clara laughed contemptuously, but she felt nervous. She knew what Rosalie meant but was just as puzzled over it as Rosalie was.

After a while they jumped down. Rosalie lost her balance and had to push herself up off the ground with one hand. She made a face as if she'd hurt herself. "You all right?" Clara said. But Rosalie straightened up and was all right in the next instant. The religious medal her father had given her showed now at the throat of her dress, catching the sunlight.

They made their way through the cars and came out to the road.

"Clara, you afraid?"

"No."

They came into town on the main street, heading right in. Both felt their knees tremble a little. Their eyes grabbed at people's faces as if looking for someone they knew. Once in a while people stared back at them. A boy of about sixteen, leaning against a car, watched them go by and grinned at them.

"Thinks he's so smart," Rosalie muttered.

They lingered in front of store windows, pressing their hands and noses against the glass. When they moved on there were spots where they'd touched the glass. They stared at the bottles and boxes and pictures of handsome people smiling out at them in the drug-store window, and at the old dead flies at the bottom, and at the strange green thing made of glass with water in it that hung down from a gold chain. The smell of food made their mouths water vio-lently. They moved on slowly, fascinated by the great confused dis-play in the five-and-ten window. Clara tried to look at everything, every mysterious object, by itself. There were skirts and dresses laid out, and socks, and lamps, and spools of thread, and purses, toys with wheels, pencils, book bags like the kind they had noticed other children bringing to school in the past. Pearl necklaces, silver bracelets, jars of perfume, lipstick in gleaming gold tubes. And bags of candy, cellophane bags so that you could see the chocolate can-dies inside. Clara's eyes ached.

"C'mon, let's go in," Rosalie said. She pulled at Clara and Clara hung back. "What's wrong, you afraid?"

"I don't want to go in."

"What? Why not?"

She stared at Clara contemptuously, then turned to go in. Clara watched her push the door open and walk right inside as if she had been doing things like this all her life. After a second she hurried in behind Rosalie. Rosalie said, "I been in stores like this lots of times."

There were a few other people browsing through the store, all women. Clara and Rosalie followed one young woman who carried a baby, anxious to imitate her. She paused to examine a pair of scis-sors. Clara came up to the counter after the woman left and looked at the scissors, wishing she could buy them. Nancy would like her better if she brought her back a present like that.

She felt the dime in her pocket again. Her fingers were begin-ning to smell from it. Rosalie had her mother's black change purse out. She counted the coins inside. "I guess I'm gonna buy somethin," she said. Clara looked around shyly. A salesgirl was leaning across a counter to talk to another salesgirl. Both wore cotton dresses and looked quite young. Clara stared at them, trying to make out their conversation; she could not imagine what it would be like to be one of those girls.

"I'm gonna work in one of these places someday," she said to Rosalie.

"Yeah, lots of luck."

Rosalie was examining tubes of lipstick. She handled them carefully and with respect. The salesgirl, a woman of about twenty-five, watched them without much interest. She had glamorous red lips and arched eyebrows. Clara stared at her until the girl's expression changed to let her know that she should look at something else. "These are all nice," Rosalie said, loud enough for the salesgirl to hear. Clara stood behind her, a few feet from the counter. She was fascinated by the way everything gleamed. The lipstick tubes were made of gold. There were some small plastic combs for sale, all colors; they cost only ten cents. Clara wanted one of the combs suddenly, but she had intended to buy Roosevelt a present with part of her dime.

"I wish I could get one of them," she muttered in Rosalie's ear.

"Go on, buy one."

"I can't. . . ."

"I'm gonna buy this one," Rosalie said. She handed the tube of lipstick and the fifty-cent piece to the girl. Clara watched each part of the procedure, so that when she was a salesgirl she would know what to do. She thought she could do it as well as this salesgirl, who was a little slow.

"Thanks an' y'all come back," the girl said tonelessly.

Rosalie walked over to another aisle and Clara followed her. Rosalie took the lipstick out of the bag and dabbed some on her mouth, then she rubbed her lips together. "You want some?" she said to Clara. Clara liked the way the lipstick smelled. It was a smell she could not place, something new and glamorous. "I better not, Pa might get mad," she said sadly.

"Hey, why didn't you buy one of them combs?"

"I only got a dime."

"What're you gonna buy, then?"

"Some toy for Roosevelt . . ."

"Hell, get something for yourself."

They came to the toy counter. A fat blond woman with cheerful pink cheeks was in charge. "Can I help you little ladies?" she said. Clara and Rosalie did not look at her. Their faces were warm.

"How much is that there?" Clara said. It was the first time she had talked to a salesgirl and her words came all in a rush.

"That airplane? Honey, that's twelve cents."

Clara stared at the airplane. Then she realized she could not afford it. "I can give you the two cents," Rosalie said, nudging her.

"No, never mind."

"Oh, Christ . . ."

Clara could feel the salesgirl and Rosalie watching her. She pointed to a bag of marbles. "How much is this?"

"Honey, that's a quarter. That's expensive."

"Go on and buy the airplane, what the hell," Rosalie said. She was leaning against the counter in a way that surprised Clara; she looked as if she'd been shopping in stores like this all her life.

"How much is this?" Clara said, pointing at something blindly.

"Honey, that's got real rubber tires, you see them? That's expensive."

Clara swallowed. Her face was hot. She would remember this moment all her life, she thought—the colorful toys, her sweaty fingers closed about the dime, the saleswoman's pity, Rosalie's contempt. "This one," she said, "what about this?"

"That's just a dime, honey."

It was an ugly little doll without clothes. Clara did not want it but had to buy it. "Here," she said, thrusting the dime at the woman. "I'll buy this."

She stared at the saleswoman's pudgy hands, waiting. The saleswoman did everything quickly and dropped the doll in a bag. "Here y'are, sweetie," she said, stooping so that her smile would be in Clara's range of vision. "You come back again real soon, huh?"

Clara took the bag from her and hurried away.

Outside, she discovered she was trembling. Rosalie ran out behind her. "You act crazy or somethin," she said. "What's wrong with you?"

"Nothin."

"Why the hell'd you buy that crappy old thing?"

"Shut up."

"Shut up yourself—"

"You shut up first!"

Clara walked stiffly ahead of Rosalie. Her lips shaped the words she would have liked to say to Rosalie, except she and Rosalie had fought already and she knew Rosalie could beat her.

"Act like goddamn stupid white trash," Rosalie hissed.

"You know what you can do."

"I got fifteen cents left, all for myself."

"You know what you can do with it, too."

"Go to hell."

Clara stopped at a curb. There were no cars on the street. She held the paper bag up near her chest so that if anyone looked, they would know she had bought something. Rosalie waited behind her for a few seconds, then Clara turned. The girls looked shyly at each other.

"Let's go up this way," Rosalie said.

She was pointing up a side street. They walked along together as if they hadn't argued. The street was bounded on both sides by a dirt walk and by buildings that looked empty. One of them was an old church; its windows were boarded up and weeds grew everywhere. "I want to go to church sometime," Clara said.

"We went once, it was lousy. Pa was snorin."

"Did he fall asleep?"

"He can fall asleep anywhere—out in the field if he wanted to."

"My pa—" Clara thought of what to say, wanting to say something, but she knew she hadn't better say it: that her father sometimes did not even sleep at night, but stumbled outside to walk around and smoke, all by himself. He was like a stranger then, when he woke her up at night, stumbling over her and her brothers on his way out. He would never say anything.

They were passing old frame houses. On a porch two withered

little women watched them. Clara and Rosalie lowered their eyes as if in shame at being so young. They walked faster. It was hot in the sunlight but they did not mind. Clara saw that there was a smear of lipstick on Rosalie's lower lip and she felt a tinge of jealousy.

"O.K., kid," Rosalie said, "want to see something?"

She took a comb out of her pocket—a red plastic comb like the ones Clara had seen. "What's that?" Clara said.

"It's for you, stupid."

She held out the comb for Clara.

"Where'd you get that from?"

"From the bean field, stupid."

Clara took it wonderingly. But Rosalie had more to show: another tube of lipstick, this one with flashy pink jewels on it, and a spool of gold thread, and the celluloid airplane, and some tiny limp colored things that Clara could not identify.

"What's that?" she asked breathlessly.

Rosalie pulled them apart. They were made of rubber, blue and red and green. She put the end of one to her mouth and blew. It was a balloon.

Clara clapped her hands over her mouth to stop her laughter. "How'd you get all them things?"

Rosalie held out the airplane to her. "I told you—from the bean field. Ain't you seen things like this out in the bean field?"

"You givin this to me?"

"For your little brat brother. Go on, take it."

"It's awful nice. . . ."

Rosalie shrugged her shoulders. Clara looked at the things, biting her lip. They were such a surprise, such gifts. She tried to run the comb through her hair but it caught right away on some snarls.

She and Rosalie walked along with their arms linked. "You're awful nice, Rosalie," Clara said. Rosalie laughed like a boy. "I shouldn't of been mean, back there," Clara said. "Hey, what if you get caught?"

"So what?"

"What if they put you in jail?"

"I'm gonna get in trouble anyway, so what's the difference?" Rosalie said. Her mouth was twisted down.

"Huh? What kind of trouble?"

"You'll find out."

Their arms fell loose of each other, as if by accident. Rosalie said in a sneering voice, "Bet you'd be afraid to take things." Her face was slightly flushed, as if she had just said something she regretted. "You're a little baby sometimes."

"I don't want no police after me."

"Hell, they don't get you. People holler at you, that's all."

"Did they ever catch you?"

"Sure, three times. So what? Nobody put me in jail."

"Were you scared?"

"The first time."

"Did they tell your pa?"

"So what if they told him?" Rosalie said sharply.

Clara saw some kids coming and wanted to cross the street, but Rosalie wouldn't. The kids—three boys and a gawky, scrawny girl—let them get past, then they began whooping and throwing stones at them. Clara and Rosalie started to run. "Dirty bastards!" Rosalie yelled over her shoulder. The kids behind them yelled too, laughing. A stone hit Clara's back but didn't really hurt, it just made her angry. She and Rosalie ran wildly down an alley, across another dirt lane, and through someone's junk heap. A battered old kettle struck her leg, knocked down from higher up on the pile, and she cried out with pain.

Then they were in a backyard, behind a fence. They stared at each other, panting. Their eyes were big.

"Where are they? Ain't they comin?"

"I don't hear them—"

They waited. Clara whispered, "I'd like to have a knife like my pa does, to kill them. I'd kill them."

"I would too."

After a while Rosalie looked over the fence. "We might could run out the front way—I don't see nobody back here—"

They caught their breaths and ran, Rosalie first. Down a nice brick walk and out onto the street. Clara kept waiting for someone to yell out the window at them.

"Look at the grass they got here," Rosalie said.

It was like a rug on the ground, green and fine.

"Jesus Christ," Rosalie said. They walked along the street, bumping into each other. They had never seen such nice white houses. "The people that live here got money. They're rich," she said.

"We better get out of here," said Clara.

"Yeah ..."

"We better go back. . . ."

Clara was staring at a house some distance from the street. It was a bright clean white like the house in that schoolbook, with trees in the front yard. There were two stained-glass windows in the entryway. For some reason Clara started to cry.

"What the hell?" said Rosalie. "You sick?"

Clara's face felt as if it were breaking up into pieces. The stained-glass windows were blue and dark green with small splotches of yellow. "I could break that window if I wanted to," Clara said bitterly.

"What, them windows?"

"I could break it."

"Well, you ain't goin to!"

Rosalie pulled her along. She acted nervous. "We better be goin back, I'm hungry. Ain't you hungry?"

"Or I could take that," Clara said. She was pointing at a flag that hung down from the front porch. The porch had been screened off with dark, green-gray shades.

"Yeah, sure."

"I could take that easy as anything," Clara said. She rubbed her eyes with her hands, as if to make the red-and-white-striped flag smaller, to get it into clear focus so it wouldn't mean anything. "I ain't afraid—"

"You are too."

"Like hell I am."

"You're so smart, go on and take it!"

Clara stepped on the grass. Her thudding heart urged her on, and the next thing she knew she was running and was up on the porch steps, then she was tugging the stick out of its slot. It was a thin little pole that weighed hardly anything. Rosalie stood back on the sidewalk, gawking.

"Hey—Clara! Clara!"

But Clara did not listen. She tugged at the stick until it came loose. Then she ran back to Rosalie with her prize, and both girls ran down the street as fast as they could. They began to giggle hysterically. Laughter began deep inside them, rushing up to the surface like bubbles in the soda pop that forgotten man had given them.

7

A month later, about six o'clock in the evening, Nancy was sitting in the doorway, smoking, her legs outstretched in front of her. Both her arms rested comfortably on her stomach, which was beginning now to get big. Clara was scraping food from the supper dishes into a pail. She sang part of a song she heard out in the field:

> Whispering hope of his coming . . .
> Whispering hope . . .

She had a thin, tuneless, earnest voice. Everyone in the camps sang, even the men. Clara's father did not sing, though. People sang about someone coming to them, someone saving them, about crossing the bar into another world, or about Texas and California, which were like other worlds anyway. Clara asked Rosalie about Texas, was it so special, and Rosalie said she couldn't remember anything. But Rosalie always laughed at everything; she didn't take anything seriously. She was like her father and that whole family. Clara liked to laugh at things too but she was like her father and knew when to stop laughing. In a group of men Carleton would be the first to smile and the first to stop, because he was smartest. Then he would sit back on his heels or turn his face slightly away and wait until the rest of the men finished laughing.

"Clara, get me a beer," Nancy said.

Clara got a bottle of beer out of the cupboard. When Nancy turned to take it from her Clara saw that her face was creased with tiny wrinkles. She was always frowning these days. Clara waited while Nancy opened the bottle and stopped to pick up the bottle cap. Those little caps could cut somebody's feet; Clara went around picking them up in the cabin and around the cabin, outside, where Nancy and Carleton let them roll.

"Is Rosie better now?" Clara said.

"No, she ain't better, and you ain't goin to go an' find out," Nancy said.

Clara hadn't been able to see Rosalie for four days. Rosalie didn't go out to work in the morning, and when Clara got back on the bus with her family they wouldn't let her go down to see Rosalie. Rosalie's father, Bert, was out working today and Clara had noticed how cheerful and nervous he was—he mixed with work crews from other camps and was always in the center of the loudest group, where people were laughing and talking and maybe passing bottles around. This was against the law. You weren't supposed to mix with the people from a certain camp because they always caused trouble, there were lots of fights, but Bert did whatever he wanted to. He liked everyone.

"Somebody said there was a doctor out," Clara said.

Nancy did not bother to turn. "What's it to you?" She sat with her shoulders slumped inside a soiled shirt of Carleton's. Her hair was stiff with oil and dust from the fields; everything she said or did was slowed down. Clara, who remembered how happy Nancy had been a while ago and how, at night, she used to laugh and whisper from the mattress where she and Carleton lay, felt sorry for her— she had never been jealous of Nancy's happiness, because she thought that anyone's happiness would turn out to be her own someday. Now, Nancy's slurred words and irritated face frightened Clara because there was no reason for them. She could not understand what was wrong.

Rodwell and some other kids ran past the shanty, yelling. Nancy did not bother to look at them. "He better watch out, that big kid's gonna beat him up," Clara said. The kids were gone. They ran between two of the shanties, pounding against them with their fists as they passed, as if they wanted to break the shanties down. Roosevelt was out somewhere, Clara didn't know where. Their father was out talking the way he was every day after supper. When Clara was through with the dishes she'd go out to find him, squatting on the ground with some other men, and when she came up to them she would hear important, serious words that made her proud: "prices," "Roosevelt," "Russia." She did not know what these words meant but liked to hear them because they seemed to make Carleton happy, and when he came back home later in the evening he would often talk softly to Nancy about their plans for next year. He would tell Nancy and Clara and whoever else wanted to listen that the country was going to change everything, that there would be a new way to live, and that when they went through a town the next time he was going to buy a newspaper to read up on it. Nancy was not much interested, but Clara always asked him about it. She thought that "Russia" was a lovely word, with its soft, hissing sound; it might be a special kind of material for a dress, something expensive, or a creamy, rich, expensive food.

It began to rain outside again, a warm, misty drizzle. "Christ sake," Nancy said sourly. "More mud tomorrow."

Clara couldn't see much out the window, because it faced the back of another shanty, so she went over to Nancy and looked out; she had to be careful because Nancy didn't like anyone standing behind her. A few people across the way were standing in their doorway too. They were a funny family no one liked because they couldn't talk right. Clara and Rosalie didn't like the girl, who was their age, because she talked funny and had thick black hair with nasty things in it. Nancy told Clara that if she came home with lice she could sleep under the shanty. She could sleep out in the outhouse, Nancy said. So Clara and Rosalie and all the other kids pretended to be afraid of the kids in that family, circling around them and teasing. The people in that shanty threw their garbage out in the walk, too, and that was against the rules.

"Lookit them pigs over there," Nancy said. "They ought to be run out of this here camp; this is for white people."

"Are they niggers?"

"There's a lot more niggers than just ones with black skin, for Christ sake," Nancy said, shifting as if she were uncomfortable. "Where's your father? We're s'post to go down the road, what the hell is he doin with it rainin out?" Her voice went on listlessly, with a kind of dogged anger. It was as if she had to stir herself up when she began to forget about being angry. She scratched her shoulder. Clara watched how the worn green material of the shirt was gathered up and then released by Nancy's fingernails. It was hard to believe that Nancy was going to have a baby: Nancy was not much different from Clara.

"I'm gonna see Rosie," Clara said.

"Like hell you are."

"How come I can't?"

"Ask your father," Nancy said. "What about them dishes, anyway?"

Clara splashed cold water from the pan onto the dishes. Each day when they came back on the bus she went out to get water from the faucets, then kept this water around until the next day. She washed the plates by putting them in a big pan and pouring water on them and swishing her fingers around. Then she took the plates out and put them facedown on the table to dry, so the flies couldn't get at them. There was old, faded oilcloth tacked on the little table, and Clara liked the smell of it. She liked to clean the oilcloth and the dishes because they were things she could get clean while other things were always dirty—there was no use in scrubbing the walls or the floor because the dirt was sunk deep into them, and if she tried to clear away the junk around the cabin it would just come back again.

"I'm goin out now," Clara said.

"It's rainin."

"Everybody else is out."

"So the hell with Rodwell and Roosevelt," Nancy said, drawling. "If they want to get worse colds, let them."

Roosevelt was bad: he ran out anytime he wanted, and he never got over being sick. He was sick all the time now and wouldn't lie still. He wanted to come along to the fields with everyone else, then when he got there he wanted to play with the little kids and not work; if Carleton slapped him he would mind the way an animal minds, not wanting to but doing it out of terror. "Roosevelt's poison, that kid, an' Rodwell ain't much better," Nancy said. "I told him I wasn't goin to bring up no baby of mine around them. I told him that."

Clara's face got warm.

"I could leave here anytime I fuckin want," Nancy said. She drank from the bottle, noisily. "He don't give a damn, that's his trouble. Always talkin about some goddamn half-ass job with buildin a road or somethin—when was he ever on a road crew, huh? There's all kinds of bastards lined up for that work, and chop down son-of-a-bitch trees, any kind of crap you can think of. *Buy me! Buy me!* Sonsabitches saying women are whores, well all of 'em are fuckin whores. And this here, crawlin in the mud, this is so shitty nobody wants to except niggers. You tell him that, huh? Tell him Nancy said so."

Clara was trying to understand this, that flew past her head like a swarm of riled yellow jackets. "Pa said we were goin to leave real soon," Clara said apologetically. She felt older than Nancy, sometimes. It made her tired. It would come upon her suddenly, a sense of expansion, something dizzy, too much for her to bear; like in those dreams where you are running, running, running—but where? Or, awake, like your eyes are rubbed raw, you see things other people don't see, or don't wish to see.

"Shit, I heard that before."

"Pa says—"

"Pa says, Pa says! A lot of crap Pa says and he ain't gonna fool me with it anymore." Nancy finished the bottle and tossed it out onto the ground with a flourish wanting it to break. It made a noise but didn't break.

After that, Clara would not remember anything clearly.

Except: the woman from the cabin next door running up. She was holding a newspaper over her head to keep off the rain and her face looked twisted and rubbery with excitement. "They're right here now—they just come in! They been trying to burn a cross, and the rain keeps putting it out."

"Oh, Jesus." Nancy got to her feet stumbling and scared.

"It's the Klan. Like people said. They're here."

"Jesus help us, I heard of them torching a whole camp—"

The woman stood barefoot in the mud, toes curling. She was shivering with excitement and her face had gone crafty. "They ain't gonna do that. They can't. There's men from the camp gonna protect him. The camp owners, they ain't gonna let the place get burnt down. This cross, it's taller'n a man, it's ten feet, it's soaked in gasoline and that burns but it don't burn for long, then—"

"Is Carleton down there?"

"He's there."

"Oh, Jesus." Nancy moaned with fear. "Can't somebody call the sheriff?"

"It's all the Klan. All of 'em. Out of Tom's River, like people been saying. Half the sheriff's deputies, people say."

Clara came up behind Nancy, shoving fingers into her mouth.

"Who's comin? What's wrong? Where's Pa?"

She saw the women exchanging a quick, secret look. They were frightened yet suddenly both laughed, the way a dog barks out of nervousness. Clara said, scared, "Where's Pa?"

"None of your business, Clara. This ain't business for a young girl, you get back inside."

Nancy tried to push Clara back but Clara squirmed free of her hands. There was a brief struggle then Nancy gave up, cursing.

"Go to hell, then. Like you're goin to go, miss. *I* ain't your pulin old ma."

Nancy and the woman hurried away in the rain. The newspaper flapped out of the woman's hand. Clara jumped down and ran after them. A cross? A burning cross? A torch? Something had been going to happen that night, people were saying. Everybody knew, but nobody would tell Clara. Now older kids were running in the mud, kids she knew and was a little afraid of, but she ran after them not minding the rain or the mud. "Where's it? What is it?"—Clara asked but nobody bothered to hear her.

Clara saw men in the rain, in front of Rosalie's house.

Maybe it was a sickness? Some bad sickness like they'd had in one of the camps: *meningitis.* It was just sounds to her she'd memorized: *bacterial meningitis.* And there was chicken pox they'd been inoculated against, a nurse-looking woman giving you shots in the upper arm from a needle. Nancy hadn't wanted to be inoculated, Nancy near-to fainted like a big baby, but Clara thought the hurt hadn't been so bad. And clothes and things from the camp had been burnt in a big fire, and everybody stood around watching. And it had been fun, kind of. Except it wasn't like that now. What they'd tried to burn was two wooden planks nailed together to make a cross like a cross on a church. Maybe why Nancy said *Oh Jesus.*

There was Carleton, you could see him he was so tall. With some of the other pickers. But they were standing at the edge of some louder men, angry men you could see weren't from the camp. It was like Hallowe'en—some of the men were wearing white sacks over their heads, with holes for eyes. White robes that, when they walked fast, kicked open to show their pant legs. Something to do with the cross? Like priests? Except they were carrying shotguns and rifles and were angry-looking, and yelling. Clara shrank from men yelling, it wasn't like women and kids yelling. At such times you are made to know *Something bad will happen now.*

The men in the white hoods were dragging Rosalie's father Bert out of his cabin. The man was pleading, crying. Hanging on to the doorframe so one of the men with a shotgun rammed the butt against Bert's fingers and Bert screamed with pain and let go. All this while Clara was whimpering, "Pa! Pa . . ." She could see Carleton at the side grimacing, clenching his fists, but he couldn't do a thing, couldn't push free to help his friend. Clara saw the gang of white-hooded men how they'd taken over, so many of them, there was nothing you could do except stand aside, and watch.

Clara tried to push through men's legs but people just pushed her back. Somebody leaned down to shake her—"Little girl, get the hell back home." There was a surge in the crowd and Clara slipped or was pushed and fell into the mud bawling, "Pa! Pa! Rosie!" A man's booted foot came down on her hand, but the mud was soft, it didn't smash her fingers.

They were beating Rosalie's father. Clara couldn't see but she could hear him pleading with his assailants, and she could hear the whacks of the blows. Up at the cabin there was Rosalie's mother in the doorway, she'd been screaming and screaming and in the rain her clothes were soaked through, and her face and hair were streaming wet. "His property! His property! You got no right!"— over and over she was screaming this, till one of the white-hooded men slapped her, hard.

Some of the men in white hoods, they'd pushed them back now

so you could see their wet glistening heads. They were like any other men you'd see in Jersey, Clara thought. Like her own pa, not that different. It was surprising to her, and confusing. Clara was calling, "Pa—" and there came Nancy to grab her by the arm and yank her free of the crowd. "You, Clara! Oh what did I tell you!" Nancy's face was white and twisted-looking like a rag. She made Clara run with her out of the crowd, panting and stumbling, and told Clara not to look back, though the men's shouts were heightened, and something seemed to be happening. Clara whimpered, "Where's Pa—" but Nancy paid no heed. Nancy had slung her arm tight around Clara's thin shoulders. So Nancy didn't hate her! Clara was thinking she would forgive Nancy speaking so cruel of Pearl. *Pulin old ma* Nancy had said but maybe she hadn't meant it.

Farther back into the camp, near where the Walpoles' cabin was, people stood in front of their cabins in the rain, worried-looking but just watching. Somebody asked Nancy what was happening, had they got the man they'd come for, was it that man that his daughter was having a baby, and Nancy shook her head wordlessly and pulled Clara on. And now Clara knew: Rosalie was having a baby. A baby! It was a stunning fact and yet it didn't stay with her, there wasn't time. Like rain falling, running down her face and arms. Like the men's shouts. You were so scared hearing them, when the shouts stopped you wanted to forget right away.

There wasn't going to be any cross burnt. The camp wasn't going to be torched. They'd got who they came for.

"Roosevelt! Get in here. Your pa's coming in a minute."

Nancy gave a swipe at Roosevelt who was squatting in the mud. Clara's brother's head had been shaved, for lice, and that gave him a retard look; he was twitchy and nervous all the time, and now so scared when Nancy went to grab him he flinched like a dog fearful of being kicked, which pissed Nancy so she cuffed him, and hauled him into the cabin. "You damn kids! Goddamn you kids! —Where's Rodwell?" Nobody knew where Rodwell was.

Inside, Roosevelt hunched himself in a corner, bawling. Nancy was saying in a voice trying to be calm, "Now we're just goin to shut this door. We're goin to shut this door." She shut it, and dragged a chair in front of it but was too nervous to know what to do, to secure the door from being shoved open. Clara tried to help her but they were both too nervous. Out the window you couldn't see much that was happening. Clara's teeth were chattering bad and she had to pee. Nancy said, "Goddamn, Roosevelt, I'm gonna warm your ass if you keep bawling. Drivin me crazy." The boy crawled into the next-door room and lay on the mattress he shared with his brother, like he wanted to burrow into it and hide. Nancy said loudly, "Look, they ain't comin here. That's the Klan you saw. Klansmen. They punish people need to be punished. They don't hurt innocent people. See, it's to protect us. Like against niggers, and bad people. We ain't done a thing wrong in this house. No daddy ever touched his daughter in this house. You kids, your pa is a good man, a Christian."

Clara thought of her father, and why he was different from Rosalie's father. And how the Klansmen would know.

She was seeing Rosalie's father when they tore his fingers from the doorframe. His face, when they grabbed at him. She was hearing him pleading. A spurt of blood at his mouth, she believed she had seen.

"No gun went off," Nancy said. "I never heard no gun."

Clara asked, when her teeth weren't chattering so bad, if maybe they'd shoot Carleton, if they mixed him up with somebody else; and Nancy said vehemently no they would not, *no.* Clara persisted, what if they shoot Pa, what if they beat him bad like they were beating Rosalie's father, and Nancy said *No!* "Nobody's goin to shoot Carleton Walpole."

But Clara had to wonder, did any of those men in the white hoods even know her father's name.

The cabin was darkening. They huddled in the dark. Whatever was happening, it was passing them by. Clara crawled over to crouch beside Roosevelt, where he was huddled on the mattress, and would fall asleep. Drew her bare legs up to her chest and hugged them tight and in the morning she would see mud marks everywhere, not just hers but prints made by the others, too. She would see, and she would know. *Whatever it was, it passed us by.*

—

Waking later to hear Carleton's low voice in the other room. Saying, "We couldn't do nothin. One of them hit me with his gun and—I couldn't do nothin for him. They about broke his face in with their gun butts. They dragged him out to this pickup they had waiting. Some of them was sheriff's deputies, not wearing their uniforms but you could tell. Where they took him, I don't know." Clara had not heard her father speak in such a way, almost quiet, and wondering; Nancy was asking questions, but Carleton talked slow and solemn like a man trying to explain something to himself he knew he could not, but had to try. Clara snuck to the doorway to see her father hunched over in a chair like an old tired man. His hair was wet, in strands on his face, and you could see the bald patches, and parts of his scalp showing through. Clara was shocked to see how beaten-looking Carleton's face was, blood and sweaty dirt like a mask. Nancy kept saying, "He ain't killed. They wouldn't do that. I just don't believe they would do that."

Carleton laughed harshly. In that low flat dead voice saying, "He'd wish he was killed, then. When they're done with him."

"Look here, Carleton: they're Christian men. They swear by the cross. My folks in Alabama, some of them are Klansmen. They only punish people who need punishing."

Carleton laughed again. It was a sound like ashes being shaken in a woodstove.

In a softer voice Nancy said for him to come to the sink so she could wash where he'd been cut, it looked dirty. This shirt was ruined, nothing to do but throw it away. Carleton muttered to leave him alone but Nancy persisted and finally he heaved himself to his feet like it was a heavy task, and he was swaying so Nancy had to help him and there was Clara crouching unseen in the doorway telling herself *My daddy is safe. My daddy.*

8

Island Grove, Florida. It was a hot afternoon in late summer, Clara was alone minding Nancy's baby. Thinking how, goddamn, if it'd been some other time, and a thousand miles to the north, she'd be with her friend Rosalie. Even picking oranges together, warding off flies, she'd like better than this.

A knock at the door! Kind of hesitant, soft. Nobody knocked, ever. Just called your name or barged right in.

In this Island Grove they were living in an actual building long and low and flat-roofed. Fifteen units in each building and concrete floors that could be hosed down; each unit had two rooms and two windows, one in front and one in back, and the buildings were sided in beige asphalt that was rough like sandpaper, and there were roofs that leaked only in heavy rain. At the far end of the camp the outhouses had concrete floors, too. Clara had never seen anything like it.

Except there was a harsh chemical smell here. Like lye Carleton said, made him cough and wheeze. Clara had gotten used to the smells of the other camps, that were mostly garbage and outhouse smells; but this was worse, not a natural smell but one to burn your nostrils and mouth and make your eyes water. When they'd first moved in they'd been amazed at the way the garbage and trash were hauled off to be burned in a big dump pile at the edge of the camp, and at how women could wash laundry for free in a big roofed place like a barn; there were showers, and sometimes hot water. And soap you squirted onto yourself out of a big jar. Even Carleton was impressed, there was an actual doctor and a nurse from the county who came to examine the workers, it was "mandated" that everybody be examined including blood tests but some refused, or just didn't show up; including Carleton who said he didn't want any damn doctor poking at him and taking his blood and next thing you know they're telling you you have blood-cancer or TB and have to be quarantined; but for sure Carleton wanted his kids examined, and of his kids Clara especially. *Pa, why?* Clara asked, and Carleton said *Because I say so.* In fact, Clara had liked being examined. Strangers touching her, caring about her. It made her feel happy. The nice youngish doctor said, " 'Clara Walpole'—your teeth! Don't you ever brush your teeth?" He was shaking his head, but smiling. Out of a big box of toothbrushes Clara was given one, with a red handle; she was proud of having it but didn't use it much, the bristles either tickled her sensitive gums, or made them bleed.

And there was a grocery store they could go to with special tickets so you didn't need actual money. And, with the strong smell, there weren't so many insects, though always a few palmetto bugs for as Carleton said, This is the fuckin Sunshine State. The burning smell stayed with them, though, even out in the orange groves amid the sweet pungent smell of oranges.

That day, Nancy wasn't picking but sorting oranges in the big sorting shed at the edge of the camp, and Carleton had gotten lucky with a county crew doing emergency roadwork on some highway. They'd been living here for five weeks now and Clara had decorated some of the walls, cut pictures out of magazines and flower shapes out of oilcloth and tacked them up to make the place pretty. You could always find something to make a place prettier than it was, like covering up places where people'd squashed bugs on the walls.

When Clara heard the knocking she was nervous thinking it was maybe these older guys, seventeen, eighteen, who'd been hanging around and bothering her, who knew that Carleton was away. She wasn't sure she wanted to see them, Nancy warned her what guys were after, still she put the baby down in his crib and glanced at herself in Nancy's mirror, propped up on the windowsill.

"Y'all come in"—Clara saw it wasn't the boys, and it was nobody she knew: two ladies outside, standing awkwardly on planks that had been placed in the muddy walks.

"Hello!" The ladies' voices were bright and hopeful and you could see they were nervous. Town ladies, wearing hats and boxy shapeless knit suits—the one an ugly bone-color, the other a puke-pale green—that must have been expensive because there was no other reason to wear such clothes. Their faces were soft and powdered and their mouths had been reddened with lipstick that gave them a frantic look in these surroundings where no women or girls wore makeup during the day, and only on rare occasions at night. One of the ladies wore tortoiseshell glasses like a teacher, so Clara looked at her.

"I'm Mrs. Foster," she said, "and my friend here is Mrs. Wylie, we're from the First Methodist Church over in Florence. We came out for a little visit—"

"Y'all want to come inside?" Clara said again, because she knew this was the polite thing to ask; but the ladies seemed nervous of stepping up the cinder blocks and into the building, like there might be something inside they would not wish to see. "Nobody's home right now but me and this baby I'm minding."

The lady who'd called herself Mrs. Foster was saying how they'd been made welcome here by the orange grove owner who was a Christian and a good citizen and how they'd seen Clara's flag hanging out—"Brought us here right away." Clara had mostly forgotten about the flag, it was just one of her decorations, hanging out the window on a two-foot pole. Nancy liked it fine and Carleton said it "added class" (maybe Pa was joking, twisting his mouth in that way of his) to their quarters. This flag was so small, and now so faded and limp, it wasn't much like flags Clara saw sometimes at the tops of tall buildings or flagpoles; those were usually whipping in the wind with a proud look. Clara's flag was just a rectangular piece of red-and-white-striped cloth hanging down. Still you could see it was an American flag. And seeing it through the church ladies' eyes, Clara was proud it was there.

"Yes, it shows such a . . . an interest—"

"Brought us here right away," Mrs. Foster said in an earnest, happy voice. "There is nothing so important as—loving your country."

Clara was glowing with pleasure. "I'm real glad you like it," she said, hoping the ladies would take the burden of talk from her. Smiling so hard! It was like that strange excited feeling she'd had pushed up against the man in the car driving her and Rosalie into town in New Jersey—that she had to hook onto the other person, she had to make him like her, had to make these smiling ladies like her, and fast. But she couldn't think of much to say to them, who were looking at her with that mixed look you get from mother-types—like they can see things to improve in you. Clara felt a stab of shame, her hair was likely snarled, and her clothes were likely not too clean. And she was barefoot.

The ladies were clean of course. And they wore stockings and dress-up shoes. And white gloves.

Gloves! Clara smiled happily to think that she had been singled out by ladies wearing white gloves. She hoped everybody in the units was watching her, who was home. For these were women who lived in real houses and went to church and had all the money they wished to spend, and nobody ever yelled at them, or cuffed them.

Such a cordial voice inquiring of Clara, "What is your name, dear?"

Clara saw some kids gathering to watch a short distance away. Goddamn if those brats ruined this.

"My name is Clara Walpole." Like at school, Clara spoke clearly.

"And where did you say your family is, dear?"

"Oh, they're—out. My stepma is down at the sorting shed, and my pa is—away somewhere." Clara began to speak more rapidly, out of a fear of running out of words. "Like I said, I'm minding the baby. Roosevelt is picking oranges I guess, and Rodwell is—" Clara pointed toward the kids hanging out across the way, one of whom was her brother, and when the women shaded their eyes to look around, the kids waved with exaggerated enthusiasm and made animal noises. So mortified! Clara shook her fist. "Damn you, shut up!" It occurred to her immediately that she shouldn't have yelled, she surely shouldn't have shaken her fist—she saw how the ladies exchanged startled glances. "They don't mean nothin," she said weakly.

Next door the old man wandered out and, Jesus!—Clara saw his pants were unbuttoned, she hoped to hell he wouldn't piss right in front of them but the ladies were trying not to look. The one with the tortoiseshell glasses adjusted them, and peered at Clara with her hopeful smile, and said maybe yes they could step inside, just for a minute.

So Clara held the screen door open for Mrs. Foster and Mrs. Wylie, who brushed past her seeming to be holding their breaths, into the "unit," and Clara saw with dismay how messy the kitchen was, dishes soaking in the sink, damp towels and clothes hanging on the backs of chairs, Nancy's flypaper twist hanging down from the light fixture above the table covered in flies and moths. Some of these were dead, and some were still living. "We only just moved in," Clara said, as if the flypaper twist wasn't their fault. She was noting a discrepancy between the ladies' pink-lipstick mouths that were smiling, and their eyes that looked frightened and quivery. "Here is Esther Jean," Clara said proudly, picking up the baby, such a hot little bundle in her arms she had to smile, "ain't she cute?"

"She isn't—is?—no, she isn't—"

"—isn't her baby, Catherine. Really!"

The ladies were murmuring together. Clara laughed at what they were saying. "She's my stepma's. I ain't married—I don't have any baby." The ladies appeared embarrassed.

"Dear, the purpose of our little visit is to inquire whether . . . anyone in your family would like to accept an invitation to visit our church." Mrs. Foster spoke in a rush of words, twining her white-gloved fingers around one another. "We of the First Methodist Church of Florence wish to extend to you a warm welcome from the Reverend Bargman and we hope—we hope that you will accept."

An invitation. Clara smiled at the word, it had a sound she liked. "Oh, I'm real interested in church!" she said. "I just never been, much."

"Your family isn't aligned with any particular church, then? But you are Christian, yes?"

"Oh, yes. Christian. But not—not particular about it."

Clara shook her head solemnly. *All eyes* she'd gone in that moment, as certain of her girlfriends teased her when guys hung around her and tugged at her hair sometimes; Clara wasn't conscious of behaving any differently, only just her gaze seemed to soften and melt and she lifted her face like a flower to whoever was talking to her. It always seemed to have some effect, as now the ladies smiled at her startled and pleased.

"We are having a prayer meeting tonight, in fact," Mrs. Foster said quickly. "At seven. A lovely child like yourself, you would be so very welcome. And of course your—stepmother, you said? And your father, and—anyone else. All of you are welcome."

They all smiled at one another, as if a difficult hurdle had been overcome. The ladies examined the walls decorated with pictures of snowcapped mountains and southern plantation houses and careful cutouts of yellow oilcloth in the shapes of flowers; Clara was wishing she'd taped up a picture of Jesus Christ, like some people did, because the ladies would be happy to see it and like her better.

Clara walked with Mrs. Foster and Mrs. Wylie back to their car, that was parked at the front of the camp. She was deeply ashamed of the units they were passing, where laundry was hanging out, and all kinds of junk lay in the lane; little kids everywhere, fat little dark-skinned boys with no pants, and their peckers bobbing. *Just like animals* Clara knew the ladies were thinking. Clara kept up a bright stream of chatter in the way of Nancy when she'd been drinking and trying to deflect Carleton out of a bad mood.

Almost they'd made it to the ladies' car, where a beefy boy of about twenty was sitting behind the wheel listening to a loud radio, when some kids from the camp came running by, splashing mud and shouting what sounded like *cocksucker! fucker!* and laughing like hyenas. Mrs. Foster gave a little shriek, and Mrs. Wylie clutched at her purse as if fearful it would be snatched from her. Clara saw to her mortification that that damn asshole Rodwell was running with the gang, they'd done it to embarrass her.

"Never mind them," Clara said hotly. "They're just animals."

At the ladies' car it was decided that Clara should wait at this spot after supper, and she would be picked up and driven to the church. The boy behind the wheel, who'd had to turn the radio down at Mrs. Foster's murmured request, was staring at Clara without as much as a smile.

They drove off. Clara waved goodbye. "Don't forget me!" she called after.

———

There wasn't any supper that night except what Clara put together for herself. Luckily Nancy came back to get Esther Jean, to take her to a friend's place (where they'd be drinking real late, Clara knew) so Clara could wash her hair in the sink, and comb it out to dry, and put her favorite little blue barrettes in it. She wore a blue dress, too; a castoff somebody had given her. And flat black shoes called "ballerina" shoes and were only a little scuffed. "I'm going to church tonight in town. A special invitation." She spoke to herself in a friendly way like somebody bearing good news.

By six-thirty Clara was out on the road waiting. Seeing cars she knew didn't belong to Mrs. Foster, she scrambled through a ditch to hide behind some bushes. At about five minutes to seven the stocky boy arrived, in a swirl of dust. He stared at her. "You all that's coming?"

Clara said apologetically she guessed so. Her father and stepmother couldn't come.

"O.K., Blondie. Jump in."

He was smoking a cigar as he drove and it smelled bad. Clara tried to make herself like it, as if it were the sign of church, of a new world. She kept glancing at him nervously and when he looked at her she smiled. He said nothing. Clara thought he drove sort of fast.

"Is it hard to drive a car?" she said.

He shifted the cigar around in his mouth and took a while to answer. "Depends on how smart you are."

"How old do you need to be?"

"You ain't old enough."

He said no more. Clara was staring out at the houses they passed, at people who had nothing else to do but sit on their front porches and watch traffic go by. She felt something ache in her that was mixed up with the heavy sweet smell of lilacs from the big bushes by everyone's front porch.

At the church—not as big as Clara had hoped, but clean and white—the boy said to Clara, "When you get sick of that crap in there, come out. I'm gonna be over there." He pointed down the street to a gas station.

Mrs. Foster was waiting inside for her. She held a book pressed up against her chest, and when Clara came in she seemed almost ready to embrace her. "Ah, yes, yes," she said, smiling sadly, "so wonderful that you could—such an opportunity for you—"

Clara looked around, smiling in her confusion. The church reminded her of a schoolhouse. There were maybe eight people there, sitting in pews right up at the front.

Mrs. Foster kept talking about the "opportunity" Clara had. She walked with her up the aisle, whispering and nodding sadly. Mrs. Wylie was sitting by herself in one of the pews, her head bowed, whispering to herself. Clara noticed that the other people—three men and four women and a crippled boy with a crutch propped up near him—were also whispering to themselves. The men's voices occasionally turned into murmurs.

Mrs. Foster had her sit on the side. She felt cold and shaky. At the front of the church was a raised platform, and on that was a podium for the minister. Off to one side was an organ. She waited, glancing over now and then at the praying people, who seemed very serious and unaware of anything except their prayers. After a while there was a bustle in the back and Clara saw an enormously fat woman in a dark silk dress come in. She smiled at Mrs. Foster, who was back at the door waiting for people to come in, and her eyes were fast and bouncy like a girl's. Clara saw that her dress was stuck to her legs and looked funny. Then another man came in, tall and thin and stoop-shouldered. He whispered to Mrs. Foster and they both looked over toward Clara. She began to smile at them, but they did not quite see her—not exactly her. Then the man came over to her and put out his hand for her to shake. Clara saw that there was a dull red rash on it, as if he'd been scratching himself there hard.

"My dear, I am Reverend Bargman. Mrs. Foster has told me about you. Let me say we are all so happy you came tonight."

Clara smiled. He was a tall, earnest, gawky man, with a smile that cut the lower part of his face in two. "You may be entering the threshold of a new life. A new life," he whispered. Clara nodded eagerly. He went on for a minute or two, using the words "threshold" and "opportunity." Then he excused himself, stood for a while near the wall with his hands behind him, staring at the floor, and finally shook his head as if to wake himself. He strode to the front of the church, scratching the back of his hand.

He began:

"My dear brothers and sisters in Christ, let us give thanks for our being here this evening—for our church, our wonderful new building— And let us begin by singing hymn number 114. All together—let us rise and sing all together—"

They moved slowly. He seemed to be pulling and nudging them with his hands and little prodding movements of his body; everyone stood. Clara stood. She had found a hymnbook on the pew beside her and leafed through it. They had already begun singing, without any music behind them, before she found the hymn in the book. They made a thin, discordant mixture of voices that kept trying to waver apart. Clara stared hard at the music in the book. She had never seen music before. And the words were big words. She felt perspiration break out on her and she wondered if everyone was waiting for her to sing her part— Just ahead of her the fat woman sang, raising and lowering her head with a deliberate meekness. She was a warm, energetic partridge of a woman, with damp spots on her dress that looked like wings folded back.

Clara had thought the song was ending but it began again. The back of her neck was damp. She raised the book closer to her face and tried to read the words. Then she noticed that the minister was crying! He sang words that Clara could not even make out and these words were so sad that he was crying. He shook his head sadly. Clara waited tensely, wondering what there could be in words to make a person cry. She only cried when something real came along. But she never did find out what the words meant. After the song ended a few people cleared their throats, as if self-conscious at the silence. The minister closed his hymnbook and everyone else did the same. They sat.

"I see," he said, with a special little smile, "that I have not worked hard enough this week. I have not worked hard enough."

There was an intake of a breath or two. Clara did not understand. "Only this child is new to us," the minister said, looking kindly at her. "I have not worked hard enough this week. I have not brought people to our worship of Christ."

Mrs. Foster sighed.

"No, I have not worked hard enough. Just this child . . . And it is through the efforts of Mrs. Foster and Mrs. Wylie that . . . No, I have not worked hard enough." He did not wipe his eyes or even his nose, Clara saw. He let the tears run down as if he were proud of them, and when he smiled she could see tears glistening around his mouth. He bowed his head and clasped his hands before him, out before him as if he were going to help pull someone up there with him, and prayed aloud. Clara stared at the top of his head. It was thick with dark hair in some places but thin in others; she wanted to laugh at it. Everything made her so nervous that she wanted to laugh. He prayed in a loud, demanding voice that got more and more angry as it went on, about Christ and blood and redemption and little children and sin and the world and money and city life and the federal government and the Sunday collection and Pontius Pilate . . . and his voice was angry and hard as any man's, not about to cry at all, and he began to pace tightly around on the little platform as his voice rose higher in a sudden upward swerve, as if something had caught hold of it and jerked it right up toward heaven. "God is watching! God is listening! You people in sin, how can you think God isn't with you all the time? Right now, tomorrow, yesterday, next year—always—God is always with you—"

Just when his voice was hardest, though, it collapsed down into a sob. He could not get his breath for a moment. Clara pressed her hand against her mouth to keep from smiling. In the center section women were crying freely, their heads bowed; the men stared down at the minister's shoes. Only the crippled boy was looking around the way Clara was. Their eyes met and he seemed not to see her; he had lines on his forehead and around his mouth like a man getting old.

Someone had once told Clara that God was watching her, or maybe Christ, someone was with her all the time and watching her. She hadn't bothered with it because it didn't make sense. It might or might not have been true, like many complicated things, but since it didn't make sense she forgot about it. But tonight when the minister said the same thing, it struck Clara that if God was watching anyone, it was not the people here. He was probably watching other people who were more interesting. Clara knew that God would never bother with her and she thought this was a good idea.

The minister was clearing his throat and Clara cleared her throat involuntarily, in sympathy with him. She felt the way she felt when her father or Nancy was acting silly, wanting to help but a little impatient. Then something extraordinary happened: The fat lady with the damp dress lumbered out of the pew and headed for the platform. Clara wondered if she was going to hit the minister or do something violent—maybe she was his wife. She could see the woman's thick, pale, doughlike arms, the flesh swinging free just beneath the sleeves, and her legs in brown stockings round and thick as tree limbs, working her up to the front. There she knelt, heavily, and buried her face in her hands. She was sobbing too and the minister bent over her and let his eyes streak across the pews as if drawing everyone else up to him. A pouchy-eyed spider he was, drawing the buzzing flies to him. "To Jesus! To Jesus!" he whispered loudly.

A man in a bulky drab-yellow suit coat and brown trousers gave a little sob—"Amen! Jesus!" He pushed clumsily—desperately—over knees and legs to get out into the aisle. He was panting and his face was oily-slick with happiness. "Amen! Oh Jesus, have mercy!" Clara had to pinch herself not to laugh aloud, was everybody in this place *crazy?* This man hurried to Reverend Bargman, too, and knelt so hard you could feel the vibrations. There came an older man, with a face like something rotted, and there was a nice-looking lady who might've been Mrs. Wylie's sister, they looked so much alike. And a chunky teenaged girl with bad skin, leaking tears behind her hands. It was so strange! What did it mean! Clara was scared something would draw her forward, too; like a magnet; she could feel invisible things in the air, like waves; like the beating of birds' wings; or maybe they were spirits, nudging and bumping against her. Why was everybody so happy, and why was everybody sobbing? Why would you sob if you weren't hurt—except out of a fear of being hurt in the future? Was it to stop God from wanting to hurt you? To show how weak you are? Clara was smiling so hard her cheeks felt like bursting. If she could fix her gaze on God she'd have gone *all eyes* and make Him like her but—where was God? Where was Jesus?

Crock of shit Carleton said of religion. Clara hoped if there was a God, He wouldn't blame her for her pa's opinions.

But here was her chance, Clara saw. Her opportunity. She slipped onto her knees onto the hard floor. She hid her face in her hands like God seemed to want, and made herself weak and placating praying for Rosalie. Clara had no prayer for herself, she would take care of herself, but Rosalie needed her help, maybe. After her father was taken away the rest of the family disappeared overnight and the rumor was they'd been given bus tickets back to Texas. Clara prayed *Jesus let Rosalie into Heaven. Jesus let Rosalie's baby that died into Heaven. And Rosalie's pa. Jesus have mercy.*

That was enough. Either it would work, or it would not.

Clara was out in the aisle. On her feet, and in the aisle. She wasn't going to be drawn to Reverend Bargman though she could see he was waiting for her, his pouchy eyes greedy upon her. He'd seen her praying, on her knees. He'd seen, and he was waiting. But Clara just laughed at him, ugly old spider, turned and ran out of the church. She was so happy! She could feel her hair flapping between her shoulder blades. *I'm not a sinner like these people. Whatever they have done, I'm not one of them.*

Outside, she discovered the damn old hymnbook in her hand, she tossed it down on the top step where they'd be sure to find it.

9

First they went to a little restaurant near some railroad tracks. There were several trucks parked outside, and inside were men who shouted and laughed in one another's faces. Their fists and elbows struck the tables accidentally and made them wobble. Clara, who had never been in a restaurant before, said right out to the young waitress: "I'm hungry, I want some hamburgers. I want a Coke."

The boy was older than Clara had thought. He had a blotched, heavy face with eyes sunk back into his skull. He kept joking and interrupting himself and laughing nervously; he played with his car keys for a while. In his shirt pocket were five cigars wrapped in cellophane. Clara smiled at him and showed her teeth and kept pushing her hair back out of her eyes. With the table between them and other people around, what did she care? "You got out of there faster'n I did," he said. His name was LeRoy. He was Mrs. Foster's only son and he was going to join the Navy and get out of Florence forever, as soon as he had some operation he had to have before they'd let him in. "My old bastard of a father that's dead now, he had me carry anvils and junk all around the barn. That's what done it," he said sourly, smiling and twisting the cap on the ketchup bottle. He got ketchup on his fingers and wiped them underneath the table.

A song began on the jukebox. It was a country song with a twangy, forlorn, sleepy voice. Clara tried to imagine what that man would look like and she knew he wouldn't look like LeRoy. But LeRoy hummed along with the music, grinning and squinting at her and turning the cap on the ketchup bottle nervously. He seemed so excited he couldn't sit still.

"Don't you want nothin to eat?" Clara said.

"I'm just gonna sit and watch you."

He shook his car keys once more and dropped them in his shirt pocket. He laughed and snickered at something he thought of, then put his elbow down on the table and his chin in his palm and watched her. Clara ate her hamburger fast, licking her lips and then licking her fingers. She drank the Coke so fast it hurt her throat. This made LeRoy laugh. "You're such a cute little girl," he said. "I bet you know that."

He wanted to drive out to the country, but Clara said she knew a place she wanted to go—it was a tavern she'd heard about. People from the camp went there. She wondered if she had made a mistake, going with him, when he did not quite turn into the tavern drive but idled out on the road, saying something vaguely about a better place a few miles on. He hadn't looked at her. "Like hell," Clara said. So he turned into the drive. Clara got her door open fast and was outside before he had even turned off the ignition. He jumped out and ran around the car, his feet making heavy crunching noises in the gravel. He started breezy little sentences that went nowhere, like "If my ma— What a night— That's the way things are—" He opened the screen door for her and Clara went inside as if she'd never seen him before. "My sweet Jesus," the boy said, wiping his forehead.

Clara felt a little dizzy with excitement. The man behind the bar, who looked like LeRoy, said: "How old are you, sweetheart?"

"How old do you need to be?" she said.

The man and LeRoy both roared, this made them so happy. Clara took the bottle of beer someone handed her and sipped at it, looking around. Her eyes darted from face to face, not as if she were looking for someone she knew but as if she supposed there was someone here who might know her. Her hair was hot and heavy about her head. One time in the evening LeRoy took a bunch of it in his hand and Clara jerked away like a cat.

"O.K., no scratchin, no bitin!" LeRoy laughed. He put out his hands to defend himself. Now that he had been drinking a while, his laughter was wheezing.

People kept coming in. Clara noticed a man with blond hair at one of the back tables; her heart gave a lurch, she thought it might be her father. But when he turned she saw it wasn't, thank God. He was maybe twenty, maybe twenty-five, she didn't know. She forgot him and then saw him again and felt the same tripping sensation around her heart. He sat leaning back precariously in his chair, legs crossed at the knee, listening to what his friends were saying but not saying much himself. Reminded Clara of a hawk: just waiting.

Nancy liked to play cards, solitaire. Slapping the sticky cards down. You were supposed to value the king the highest but Clara had an eye for the jack. Jack of spades was her favorite.

The blond man had a look of the jack of spades, Clara thought. She smiled, biting her lower lip. One of the blond man's friends had nudged him, he'd turned to look in her direction, but not smiling as you'd expect; eyes narrowing as if he didn't much care for what he saw, a scrawny-armed blond girl in a cast-off cotton dress staring at him like she knew him, had some claim on him. LeRoy slid his heavy arm around her shoulders in clumsy possessiveness. "Honey, know what you are? A pretty li'l cat." LeRoy stroked her disheveled hair and Clara shoved at him with the beer bottle she was holding, struck him on the chest. Observers, men who'd been watching the two, laughed.

"Get your hands off, you. I ain't no cat to be petted."

By this time the blond man had turned back to his friends. Something rushed into Clara's head, hot and pulsing, desperate. LeRoy was sullen for a while then began jabbering and laughing at his own damn-dumb jokes, and Clara just stood and walked away. Pressing the sweating bottle against her cheek. Somebody collided with her and Clara seemed hardly to feel the impact. Her eyes were fixed on the blond man, dilated. A wild shrill sensation rose in her, a sense that she was in danger of losing her balance, falling; as at the church she might have suddenly run up to the front bawling like the others, and gave her heart to Jesus, and to the Reverend Bargman. But she'd stayed where she was. She'd knelt on the floor at her pew and prayed for Rosalie, and that was it. That wildness that's dangerous, but you have to trust it. She was feeling it now, suffused through her body; could have done something crazed with her hands, her nails, even her teeth. She was approaching the blond-haired man. The man reminding her of the jack of spades. From where she now stood, about ten feet from him, it seemed to her that the God of whom the minister had spoken was present, in this place. He was this hot pressure that hung over her, this force lowering Himself into her body. That God was still hungry, the hamburgers hadn't done Him any good, and He made her think of all those nights she'd lain and listened to Carleton and Nancy—not hating them, not hating Nancy, but just listening and listening to know how it would be with her someday, since when it happened to her she wouldn't be able to know any more than Nancy knew.

There was one woman at the table and three men. Clara looked at her once and then forgot her. The blond man's head seemed to become vivid in the dim light, just as she watched. Waves of heat seemed to tremble about it, the hair pale like her father's, but the man's shoulders stronger than his, younger and straighter, a different person—he was a different person. Clara's lips were dry. She stared at that man and stood lost in a trance, a little drunk, sweaty and tired, her eyes aching from all the smoke. She might have stood there all night if he hadn't turned around. He did not smile. After a moment he got to his feet.

"You looking for someone, little girl?"

He came right up to her and bent to look in her face. Clara stared at him. He was a little different than she had imagined—his eyebrows were strange, hard and straight so that they almost ran across his forehead in a single line. His chin was square. Clara wanted to cry out in terror that she had wanted someone else—someone else! But she said nothing. Her eyes felt glassy.

"You here with anyone?" he said. He looked around. "What are you doing here alone?"

Clara brushed her hair back out of her eyes. She could not think of anything to say.

"I'll drive you back to where you're going," the man said.

"I don't want to go anywhere."

"I'll drive you there."

He took hold of her arm and pulled her along. Clara hurried to keep up with him. They stepped out into a cloud of moths and mosquitoes. The man said, "Are you from around here?"

"From Texas," Clara said.

"What are you doing here, then?"

He looked at her in the blast of light from the neon sign. At his car he opened the door for her and pushed her inside, the way children are pushed here and there, as if it were easier to just push them than to explain what they should do. He got in beside her. He said, "You're not from Texas or anywhere near. You don't talk like it." He backed the car around. "Now, which way do you want to go?"

"Out that way," Clara said, pointing down the road.

"Nobody lives out there."

He paused, not looking at her. Then he drove out onto the road and turned back toward town. He had not looked at her since they'd left the tavern. "You're not thumbing your way through here, are you? Because you better be careful doing that."

"I can do anything I want to," Clara said.

Before he came to the town he turned into a drive. The house there was a big, three-story building with a wide veranda; lights were on in some rooms and off in others. "I'm in and out of this place myself," he said. "Tomorrow I'm leaving." He turned off the ignition. Clara waited. Something hot and swollen was inside her head so that she could not think right. "You're on your way to Miami, probably, but I'm not," he said.

"Ain't goin to Miami," Clara said.

He turned off the headlights and turned to her. Clara smelled whiskey around him; it reminded her of Carleton. He took hold of her and would have hurt her shoulder if she hadn't twisted free. She was breathing hard and her head ached. But the dizziness inside her made her want to press forward against him, hide herself against him and fall into sleep. It wanted to stop her seeing anything and thinking anything. The man reached over and opened the door on her side and pushed her out, and slid out with her. Standing out in the driveway, where everything was dark and quiet, he put his arms around her and kissed her and then let her go, his breath nervous. "My place is around back," he said, pulling her along. Clara stumbled on boards propped up around the corner, against the house. The man opened a door in the dark and they went in together. There was another door right inside.

The room must have been an addition on the back of the house; it was made of boards that were just boards, rough and unfinished, and the floor was the same way. A cool draft came up through cracks in the floor even though the night was warm. There was a bed and a stand with a basin on it that had a rusty bottom; there was just a little water in it. On the floor there was a hot plate with just one burner.

The man shut the door and nudged her over toward the bed. He was as tall as Carleton. He took off his shirt and his chest was covered with dark blond hair. Clara stared at his chest as if hypnotized. She felt the cool air rising between the floorboards.

"How old are you?" he said. "Seventeen or eighteen or what?"

Clara shook her head.

"Or thirteen?"

He screwed his mouth up into a look that meant he was judging her. She had seen people from town, or farmers who owned land, looking at her and her family that way. They looked at everyone that way who lived in the places she lived and did the work she did. It did not occur to Clara that they might have looked at her another way. She felt sleepy, and so she lowered her head and moved toward this man. She closed her eyes against his hot, damp skin. When his mouth pressed against her throat she drew in her breath sharply, thinking that she would not have to do anything at all; she would just press herself against him. But she must have stumbled backward because she knocked the basin over. The man kicked it against the wall, laughing. He pulled her over to the bed and they fell down together. The bed had been made up, just sheets and a pillow but still someone had made it. It felt cold. The ceiling and the wall wavered over Clara, seen through her hair or through his hair and then blotted out by his face. He was lying on top of her just as Clara had imagined someone lying on her, years before she had ever seen this man. And she held her arms right around his neck just as she had imagined she would.

She caught sight of his face in the shadow and saw that it was sleepy like her own, slow and hungry. Something ached in her to see him like that. She clutched against him wildly. "Do it to me, don't stop," she said. "Don't stop."

But he did stop. He fell back beside her. She heard him breathing and in that moment her body just waited, suspended and frozen in a daze of sweat and disbelief. He said, "How the hell old are you?"

"I don't know—eighteen."

"No, you're just a child."

That word was one that had nothing to do with her—she exhaled her waiting breath in a sound of contempt. "I'm not a—child," she said angrily. "I'm not a child, I never was."

He swung his legs around and sat on the edge of the bed. "Christ," he muttered. Clara watched him. Far away there was the sound of a car horn fading. Clara felt how alone they were and how dark it was outside, how easy it would be for them to be lost from each other. A pool of darkness seemed to open at her feet, chilled by the night, and this man could fade away into it and be lost.

"I love you," Clara said bitterly. "I never was any child."

He looked around back at her. There were little lines around his eyes, as if he was used to squinting too often. She could see fine light stubble on his chin, she wanted to touch it, to move her hand over it. But she did not dare. His skin was damp, his hair damp. Looking at him, she seemed to be seeing more than he wanted her to; he made a face and turned away.

"No, please, I love you. I want you," Clara said. She spoke violently. A pulse in the man's neck jumped and she could have slashed at it with her teeth. Her body ached for him and he was keeping himself from her, it wasn't right, everyone always said how any man could be ready for a woman anytime. "I want you, I want somethin!" Clara said. "I want somethin!"

"Look, where are you from?"

"I don't know what I want but I want it! I don't know what it is," she sobbed.

"I sure as hell don't know either."

After a moment he got up. He went out. Clara heard him in the corridor, heard a door open. She lay still, panting, her jaw gone rigid with anger. She could not remember how he had looked now that he was gone. When she thought of men, of love, she had always thought of an impersonal heavy force, a man that was no particular man but just a pressure, coming against her and letting her fall asleep within it and taking care of her—arms that were just arms to take care of her, a body that was heavier and stronger than hers but would not hurt her—and she would pause no matter what she was doing, dreamy and entranced, a kind of sleep easing over her brain until she had to jerk herself out of it and wake up— Now she felt that languorous sleep move over her, weighing down her eyelids, and the man who had just been with her was no more real than the ghostly men who had come and slipped away when she bent to pick beans or strained up to pick oranges, either way tempting that flood of warm dizziness into her brain that marked the point at which she stopped being Clara and became someone else with no name.

She could ease into that darkness and become a girl without any name: someone who wanted, wanted, who reached out in the dark for someone to embrace her in turn.

The man came back. He was carrying a bucket of water. He closed the door behind him with his foot and went to the hot plate and set the bucket down. He plugged the hot plate in. Clara watched him in silence, wanting to laugh because it was all so strange, so nervous. He squatted by the hot plate and watched the water, his bare shoulders twitching as if uneasy with her staring. But he himself was not uneasy.

He said to her, "Take off your dress."

"What?"

"You're dirty, take it off."

Clara's face went hot. "I'm not dirty!"

"Take it off."

"I'm not dirty—I'm—"

He had blue eyes, a cold blue-green. They were not like her own eyes. His eyebrows made one shadowy ridge over his face. He was squatting a few feet from the bed, one hand lazily on his knee. "I'm dirty too. Everyone's dirty. You want to take that off or should I do it for you?" he said.

Clara sat up. She had kicked off her shoes. "You take it off," she said spitefully. He did not move at once. Then he grinned at her, a grin that flashed on and off, and got up. She let her head droop forward as he reached under her hair to undo the buttons at the top of her dress. He unbuttoned them and Clara stood so that he could pull the dress off. She snatched it from him and threw it down onto the floor. "What are you going to wear out of here except that?" he said, and picked it up. She was standing in a short cotton slip on which she had sewed pink ribbons. She tore one of the ribbons off before he could stop her. "You said I was dirty!" she cried. "I hate you!"

"You are dirty. Look at this." He rubbed her wrist and tiny rolls of dirt appeared. Clara stared. His fingers made red marks on her skin. "Your hair too," he said. "You should wash your hair."

"My hair's nice!"

"It nice but it's dirty. You're from that fruit pickers' place, aren't you?"

"People always say my hair's nice," Clara sobbed. She looked up at him as if waiting for him to say something different, something that would show he had only been joking. "Other people think I'm pretty—"

He parted her hair with his fingers and bent near. He thinks I have lice, Clara thought. She felt sick. "Son of a bitch, you son of a bitch," she whispered. "I'll get my father to kill you—he'll kill you—"

He laughed. "Why would anyone want to kill me?"

She tried to push away but he caught her. He pulled off her slip and made her stand still so that he could wash her. Clara shut her eyes tight. She felt the angry pressure of tears behind her eyes, but another pressure, a sweet feeling, that did not let her cry. She thought that no one had washed her for years. Her mother had washed her years ago but she almost couldn't remember that. Maybe she couldn't remember it at all. Now this man rubbed soap between his hands and washed her, and she shut her eyes tight with the feel of his warm, slow, gentle hands. She knew that the ache in her loins for him would never go away but that she would carry it with her all her life.

He washed her and dried her with a thin white towel. It wasn't big enough and got wet right away, so he finished drying her with his shirt. Clara stood with her hair fallen down one side of her head. She felt the man's breath against her face, against her shoulders. When she opened her eyes he was handing her clothes to her.

"You're going back home," he said.

She nodded meekly and took her things.

"I don't want them to hurt you back there." Clara turned slightly, shyly, as he spoke. "Do they knock you around much back there?"

"You mean my pa? No."

He helped her button up the dress. Clara stood obediently. "I'm tired," she said. "I don't feel right." He said nothing. When he was finished, Clara turned sharply. "I lost my purse," she said.

"What?"

"I lost my purse—"

"What purse?"

She looked around. She saw nothing.

"I don't remember any purse," he said.

They went outside and he drove back to the camp. It was late; Clara could smell that it was late. She wondered if Carleton was back. The dull, sullen ache in her body for this man did not go away but grew heavier at the thought of what might happen to her if Carleton was home.

She opened the door. Insects were swirling around his headlights.

"You want money to buy another purse?" he said.

"No."

"I thought that's maybe what you wanted."

Clara had never thought of that. She felt hot and ashamed. After a moment the man said slowly, "Look, if you want to see me before I leave—come early tomorrow. But you better stay away."

She nodded and ran down the lane.

Her brain was pounding with terror. She had never done anything like this, had never gone so far. She felt driven by the same God that had possessed the minister, making his voice shrill and furious at once, making his legs jerk him about on that platform. God had torn out of that man's mouth sobs and groans of desperation; Clara understood what he must have felt.

She ran along the big low building until she came to their place. Then she stopped. The door was open and the lights were on. "Is she out there?" her father's voice said. Clara paused, outside the circle of light, then came forward. Carleton was sitting inside, on the end of his cot. Clara saw Nancy's face. Roosevelt and Rodwell were hiding behind her. Carleton got to his feet and came to the doorway. He walked so carefully that she knew he was drunk.

"Somebody seen you where you shouldn't of been," he said. His face was ugly. Clara did not move. She saw his arm draw back even before he knew what he was going to do.

"Bitch just like your mother!" he said.

He began to beat her. Inside, Nancy shrieked for help. Clara tried to break away but could not because he was holding her. Lights came on. Someone yelled out. Carleton was swearing at her, words she had heard all her life but had never understood, and now she understood them all—they were to show hate, to show that someone wanted to kill you. Then Carleton let her go. He stumbled backward and she saw that two men were holding on to him. "They want to get up an' leave, they don't stay home, they run off—the bitches—just like their mother," Carleton shouted. "They don't stay home but run off! Bitches don't love nobody— Clara don't give a damn, my Clara—" He began to sob. Someone shook his shoulders to quiet him down.

"You let that girl alone tonight, you hear?" a man said.

"She run off an'— Dirty filthy bitch like all of them—"

"Walpole, are you goin to let her alone?"

They got him inside and on the cot. He fell asleep almost at once, as soon as his head was down. Clara rubbed her face and saw that it was bleeding. She looked at Nancy just once and then quit looking. She knew that Nancy had been in the tavern somewhere, that Nancy was the one who'd seen her, but she did not care. The blood that ran into her mouth was the only real thing: she could taste that. Roosevelt and Rodwell, her brothers, were nothing to her. Let them look. Let them snicker. Nancy was nothing. Her father, snoring damply on the bed, his face flushed and his shirt unbuttoned to show his sunken chest and his soft, spreading stomach, was real to her now but not for long.

The neighbors went back to bed. Nancy turned off the light. They lay in the dark and listened to Carleton snore, and then everyone went to sleep except Clara. She lay still and thought. It was as if a great cooling breeze had been blowing toward her for years and now it had overtaken her and was going to carry her with it. That was all.

10

Carleton woke up. Someone was shouting in his face.

"What's wrong with you? Get up!"

He opened his eyes to see a strange woman shouting down at him. She had a round leathery face with exaggerated eyes that could have been anyone's—a man's or a woman's.

"How long are you goin to lay there? Goddamn you! Your darling little daughter is run off and we got to get to work—it's goin on six, what the hell's wrong with you?"

He pushed Nancy away and sat up. His eyes darted around the room.

"We got to get out there before the bus leaves," Nancy said viciously. "I fed the kids while you laid there snorin—what's wrong with you these days? Can't take a little drinkin no more? It ain't like you worked those two days—what a big joke! Get all the way out there an' the man tells you poor bastards it's all off—"

Carleton got to his feet. He was wearing his clothes from yesterday; his shoes were still on. Inside his stomach a hard knot was forming. He stood with his shoulders hunched and his head bowed, listening and not listening to Nancy, paying close attention to the knot in his stomach. It was familiar but might get out of hand yet. He was getting ready to think about Clara.

"You all right?" Nancy said.

She put one arm around him. He did not move. "You look kinda sick," she said. Carleton pushed her gently away. He did not want to move fast for fear he would get something into motion he could not stop. "Yeah—like I said about Clara—she ran off," Nancy said. She had a whining, defensive voice. "You shouldn't of hit her like that, she ain't a bad kid. You know it. I don't blame her for runnin off, I run off myself, I wasn't goin to take none of that crap from nobody—"

Carleton bent over the basin and splashed cold water onto his face. It was strange, but he could feel the water running down the outside of his skin as if it were far away from him, while he himself contemplated it from somewhere deep inside.

"We better get out there. It's goin to be hot today," Nancy said. His silence made her nervous; she was speaking almost quietly now. "Honey, are you all right?"

The ball in his stomach threatened him for an instant but he fought it down. He didn't want to throw up and have that taste in his mouth. The water on his face made his skin itch and he watched his hand come up to rub it. He watched his fingers scratch at his skin, then he forgot about scratching and stood with one hand up to his face in a pose of abstract thinking. His brain was just now waking up. It told him harshly that he had a lot of thinking to do—he had to get things sorted out. For weeks, months, years he had been letting things accumulate. If he did not get them straight and understand them he would never be able to get free of them and begin a new life.

"Is the baby all right?" he said.

"Sure." Nancy sounded touched by this.

"How much money do you have?"

"What?"

"How much money?"

"You mean—right now?"

"I gave you three dollars Friday."

"I—I had to buy food—"

"Here. Take this." He reached deep in his pocket and took out a soiled ball of material that might have been silk. He unwrapped it and gave her a few dollars from it; he did not notice how she was staring at him. She might have been waiting for him to hit her, so white and strained was her face. "That should help, then you'll make somethin today. Twelve or fifteen today, you an' the kids."

"Where are you goin?"

He put the rest of the money back in his pocket. At the mirror he crouched so that he could see his face. The knot in his stomach grew tighter: that did not seem to be his face staring helplessly back out at him. "Christ," he said. He rubbed his eyes, his mouth. Everything was stale from his drunken sleep. An image came to him of Clara cringing back from his hands—but he shook it away. He knew that he would have a lot to shake out of his mind before he could stop thinking.

"Honey, are you goin after her? Carleton?"

He left the room and stepped into the bright, innocent sunlight, making a face. He might have been walking past a stranger who was pleading with him, pulling at his arm. Nancy said, frightened, "Where the hell will you look? Carleton? I mean—where are you goin? She'll be back! You don't want to make no trouble with people from town—"

Carleton tucked his shirt into his trousers, raising his aching shoulders as high as he could. His two boys were waiting patiently outside. They looked at him. He glanced at them as he might have glanced at two strange boys, one with a lowered, pinkish head and the other with a careful blank face that was poised upon a body about to break into a run at any second. They both had Carleton's look—a long, narrow, thin face—and he had the idea that they would never get much bigger than they were. "You mind Nancy," he said to them.

She followed him along the lane, tugging at his arm. "Look, she'll be back. Clara likes you real well—she'll be back—she only took a few things, an' no money—"

She followed him out to the road. Carleton pushed her back, still without looking at her. He walked in a precarious falling motion forward, as if he were listening to something ahead of him. Nancy began to cry. She cried loudly. As he walked toward town he heard her swearing at him, shrieks of words that flew right by his head and did not hurt him. "I'll kill that baby! That goddamn dirty baby!" she screamed.

He listened to her screaming, then he stopped hearing her. He seemed to pass beyond her screaming and beyond her life with no more effort than he might have walked past a crazy woman on the road.

When he reached town he was soaked with sweat. A dusty clock in a gas station said four-thirty but he knew from the sun that it was around six. The town had not yet gotten out of bed, only a few places were open. He walked along the road until there were some dirt paths and he walked on them, up the incline to the railroad tracks and then down on the other side. There were lots of weeds growing by the tracks and many junked and rusting cars and parts. On the other side of the tracks he saw a restaurant that was open. He went inside and asked about Clara. A few truck drivers were sitting at the counter. They watched him closely, as if there were something in his voice that he himself did not know about. "I did see a girl like that last night," the waitress said. She had high-piled brown hair and a very young face; as she spoke to Carleton the freckles around her nose seemed to get darker, showing how young she was. She was almost as young as Clara. Carleton waited, listening to her with his shoulders back and straight even though they ached. He did not seem surprised that the first person he should ask would have seen Clara. The girl talked earnestly, about that other, lost girl she'd seen, about her long blond hair and blue dress and even a yellow purse—she was excited to think she could remember so much and looked up at Carleton as if awaiting praise for so much information. "Who was she with? Who was he?" Carleton asked, cutting her off. The girl gave a name Carleton had never heard before, but he knew he would not forget it. "Where does he live?" he said patiently, again cutting her off. She told him. It was necessary for her to come out from behind the counter, pretending to be a little frightened, glancing at the truck drivers as she spoke to Carleton. She went to the door and even outside with him, pointing down the street.

He walked off, not hurrying. He did not even want to hurry; it wasn't to maintain his pride that he walked slowly. It was just that he knew he had to go a certain distance before he allowed that hard ball in his stomach to take over.

The house was a nice little house on a side street. In the front yard were beds of flowers that confused him—he had not expected flowers. But when the door opened and a middle-aged woman stared up at him, her face drawn and pale and her hair untidy, he was not surprised. "Is your son home?" he said politely. She clutched a robe of some kind around her. It smelled like mothballs. He could sense her thinking of something to say and then forgetting it because she was so upset. He waited while she went to get her son. Standing on the porch, inside the veranda that was so nicely shaded with big round leaves, he did not even bother to glance in the house, through the door she'd left ajar. He had no interest in anything but groping his way to Clara through a number of people, and those people could interest him only faintly. He might have felt excitement at meeting the boy, but he seemed to know that this was too fast, too easy; it would take more time than this.

The woman was gone quite a while. It might have been ten minutes. Then Carleton began to hear footsteps. They were on a stairway, heavy and reluctant. Someone was whispering, then there was silence. A young man emerged out of the dimness of the house and blinked at Carleton. "You know anything about my daughter?" Carleton said. The boy wore baggy yellow pajamas. At first he stammered and swallowed, he knew nothing. Then Carleton asked him again. He made a hissing sound that was a laugh, raised his eyebrows, scratched his head. "There was someone, I guess," he said slowly. "She was with this guy who comes here once in a while—he don't live here—mixed up with whiskey or somethin—that's what somebody said—I—"

"Where's he stayin?"

"He goes to this one place when he comes in town," the boy said. He had the waitress's sincere look. He stared right into Carleton's eyes as if the two of them were friends involved in a mutual problem. "Yeah. Yes. Over on the other side of town, a big dirty house where the woman has ten kids—she rents rooms—there's one like her in every town—"

Carleton made a gesture that he hadn't meant to be threatening, but the boy stammered and was silent. "Thanks," Carleton said.

When he got to the house he could feel sweat running off him. On the big veranda with its peeling paint and broken boards he talked to a youthful woman with a ruined, blemished face. She kept staring off over his shoulder as if every word he said pained her. "We need money here," she said, whining, "we don't have nothin to do with anybody who—"

"Where did he go?"

"He had that room two other times he was in town," she said. "He never made no trouble, I liked him. His business was his own business."

"Where did he go?"

She fumbled with the neck of her dress. Her lower lip protruded in thought, then relaxed. "You can look in his room," she said. "I ain't fixed it up yet. I heard him drive out last night, real late—I was in bed—"

Behind her a man was shouting something. The woman stared over Carleton's shoulder as if the voice were coming from a great distance. Then she turned sharply and yelled back through the screen door: "You shut your mouth an' keep it shut!" When she turned back to Carleton her face was already composed and she was moving. They went down the rickety steps and around to the back of the house. In the soft morning light of this land everything was softened by moisture, even the rotting wood of the house. There was a pile of lumber around the corner, some of it propped up against the house as if children had been playing with it. Carleton and the woman walked in the driveway, which was rutted and wet. Two cars were parked in it, at angles. One of the cars looked as if it had been there for quite a while. Carleton thought he could get it going, maybe, if it was his own car. The only trouble would be getting it out of that mud.

She showed him the room. A flood of sunlight fell onto the bare floor and partly onto the bed. Carleton looked around. The very bareness of the room satisfied him. He knew it was still too soon to find her. "Where does he go after he leaves here?" he said.

"Why, he drives to Savannah. I think. To Savannah maybe," she said pleasantly, as if offering Carleton a gift. "I don't know why I know that...."

"What does he look like?" Carleton said. His eyes moved slowly around the room. He saw a film of dirt on the window. The room was so empty he might get lost in it, somehow fall in its secret silence and be unable to get out. He kept looking around as the woman described that man, again pleasantly, like the young man and the waitress leaning a little toward him as if about to offer him some of their energy as well as their truthfulness. When she stopped, he felt his mind jerk like a muscle. He jumped forward and began tearing the bedclothes off.

"Here," the woman said nervously, "you don't want to get hot this early in the day—"

When he was outside again he felt better. At first the woman did not want to sell him that car because the kids played in it, and because the man who owned it might be coming back someday; her forehead creased with honesty. Carleton had the eerie, unreal feeling that this morning everyone was sympathetic with him as they had never been before in his life; it might have been that they believed his life was over. But he took out his money and counted it patiently. "Well, maybe you got a hand with cars," the woman said, looking at his money. "It'll maybe start an' maybe won't." Carleton said nothing. She laughed breathlessly and went with him over to the car, tiptoeing and hopping in the mud. "The keys are inside there," she said. Carleton got the creaking door open and slid inside. The broken fake-leather seat was hot as acid from the sun. "This'll do just fine, I thank you."

It took Carleton a while to get the motor started. A small crowd had gathered by the time he backed the sputtering car out of the rutted driveway. A mile away was a gas station, he turned the shuddering car into it where a bald-headed boy was standing staring at him with an amazed smile as if he'd been waiting for him, Carleton Walpole. The boy stared at the car as if trying to place it. He moved slowly with the hose, filling Carleton's gas tank. Carleton asked, "Which way to Savannah?" and the boy said some words in a quick mumble Carleton didn't catch, and went to fetch him a road map. Carleton opened the damn map that was so large he could hardly see it and his heart lurched at the challenge it was: an infinity of lines of differing, coded colors and small-print names of towns, cities, counties, rivers. Carleton laughed, an angry laugh. All he needed now was his eyes going bad: old-man eyes.

"This'll do just fine. I thank you."

———

There was a river he was crossing on a high bridge with an open wire floor through which you could see the water below and the bridge was vibrating and humming like an electric chair as the current was thrown: his eyes took in a name that was Indian-sounding ending in *-oochi* but he had no idea what it meant. Many times he'd crossed the Mississippi River but he didn't believe this was the Mississippi for it wasn't so wide, and he was in another part of the country—wasn't he? Sunlight flashing on the water below like flame.

Didn't believe in God, it was all a crock of shit, yet God might be laughing at him now. *Seek and ye shall find.* He was seeking her, but he had not found her. Yet. Because the sun had shifted in the sky and was assaulting his aching eyes from another, new angle.

Even the Mississippi River had looked shallow in places. That was deceptive. You have to know that there are undertows, swift currents in some places, like slithering snakes; in others, the water appears muddy and no-account. Carleton, Sr., cautioned his sons to preserve their strength as men for things that were *of account*. He had been a blacksmith and a farmer and had not gone to school beyond a few grades but he had eyes in the back of his head, nobody could put a thing over on him. Carleton laughed aloud—"That old man ain't dead." Suddenly he knew. And knew, too, that the farm had not been sold: that was just to fool him, and to punish him. Because he'd gone so far from Breathitt County. And he'd never repaid that debt.

His pa had said much in life is *no-account*, and a whole lot of that is a *crock of shit*. It passes without leaving any impression like clouds in the sky. What is *of account*—getting born, dying, buying property, getting married and having children and honoring your father and mother and defending the honor of your family—are all that matters.

Everything else was no-account. Carleton's life was adding up to *no-account*.

Stopped at a filling station paying in dollar bills, nickels and dimes. A penny that slipped through his shaky fingers, he bent to pick it up but the gas station attendant, a lanky kid, was quicker.

Which was the route to Savannah?

Savannah what? Florida, or Georgia?

Carleton thought it was Florida, maybe. Or, if it was Georgia, maybe the other was on the way.

You trusted to the sun, as a picker. In the field you can gauge the time by the sun in the sky. Even if it's overcast, you feel it.

He was back in the car and driving. "Now what?"—God was laughing at him. He'd maybe taken a wrong turn. He had not known there was more than one Savannah. So a map could not help, one hundred percent. But if one was on the way to the other, then it might. Hours passed. It was night, and another day, and again morning and he had not slept; or, if he'd slept, it was in his car with his mouth agape like an old man, snoring so hard he woke himself in a panic. And then he was driving into the sun: saw a clock in a barber shop window: eight-twenty. But which eight-twenty, day or evening? And which day, and which month?

Wasn't sure if he was still in Florida. Maybe he'd crossed the state line without knowing. YOU ARE LEAVING FLORIDA THE SUNSHINE STATE COME BACK SOON!

This was confused with God commanding him as God had commanded him once. *All the corners of the world shall ye seek and one day ye shall find.*

Except his skin, he'd be judged. His skin was white. Yet the Klansmen had been scornful of him. A white man and an American like them except they'd kicked him in the groin as you'd kick a dog, and one of them had struck his face with a rifle butt when he'd lain writhing in pain. Now he favored his left leg. He was not an old man but sometimes walked like an old man. What they'd done to Bert, he had not seen. Like you'd castrate a hog it was said.

There was a sign—CUMBERLAND ISLAND 19 MILES. Cumberland! But he guessed it wasn't what he wished. He kept driving.

Stopped in a place called Brunswick. At least he was headed

north on route 17, and he was headed for Savannah, Georgia. His head was pounding so, almost he couldn't get out of the car. Outside, the air was steamy, worse than in the car. Hugging close to his body in a kind of halo. Inside the diner that was also a tavern, a few flies buzzed lazily. No one at the counter and no one behind it. Carleton sat on a stool and waited. Folded his battered scabby hands and waited. *Seek. Ye shall find.* There were festive sounds from the kitchen, laughter, a hammer pounding. After a while Carleton went to peer through the doorway and saw that the kitchen was cluttered and messy but there was a floor fan going and at a table sat a fat, shirtless man wielding a hammer. A nerve in Carleton's eye twitched when the fat man struck the table with the hammer— "Gotcha, fucker!" A girl in a soiled waitress's uniform was leaning against a stove, giggling. Her cheeks bounced with hilarity. The fat man struck again at the table and she giggled louder. Carleton saw that for all his fat, the man had a deft aim: he'd mashed maybe a dozen flies on the table.

Still, Carleton was served. Had a cold bottle of Coca-Cola to soothe his nerves, tried to eat a ham-and-cheese sandwich on rye, but the ball of tiny snakes in his guts was acting up. He decided to take the sandwich along to eat in his car. No knowing when he would eat again. He smiled to think—"A sandwich can outlive who tried to eat it."

———

WELCOME TO SAVANNAH his eye discerned without comprehending at first. So tired . . . Saw a clock in a billboard sign: two-thirty. But maybe it was a painted clock and not real. He could not have said which of the blond-haired girls he was seeking: the one named Pearl, or the one named Clara.

Had to wonder: Does God keep a promise?

He parked his car, had to piss so bad. Behind a boarded-up warehouse. A long shaky steamy-hot stream of piss like poison. When he was finished he swayed on his feet. Flies moved in.

Bitch just like your mother.

Why he said those things he did not know. In fact it wasn't Carleton who said them but some drunk with his mouth. He would ask to be forgiven, he hadn't meant to hit her. (Maybe he hadn't hit her.

His own girl. It wasn't like Carleton to hit a woman let alone a girl his own daughter who adored him.) He was walking somewhere looking for his car he'd parked by a— He would remember when he saw it.

"Clara." That was her name.

He was walking, and he was favoring his left leg. That bad knee. His skull pounded. Hammer-hitting: whack-whack! A nerve twitched in his eye. He understood that God was mocking him more directly, openly. Yet he had his dignity, you didn't look up to acknowledge it. Always he would have his white skin, that was a fact.

Time was slowing down for him. Never before in his life had time slowed down so you could feel it, like melting tar. This meant that the rest of his life would stretch out before him like that long hot highway to this city whose name he'd already forgotten. He did not think that he could bear it, unless it had already happened and was finished.

Came to a church. A church! Remembering that the girl had been taken to a church. He'd begun to lose her, then. And he had not even known at the time.

This church was made of dark red stone, and it was a big old church nothing like the small tidy white shingle board with the cross at the top where he and the little blond girl who'd hardly come to his shoulder had been married. His eye took in *Gethsemane* vague as a word glimpsed through water. He was stumbling inside, into the relative cool of the stony interior.

A strange place. Like a mausoleum. A high ceiling like no church ceiling he had ever seen. He squinted up at it, and could not see where it ended. In the half-light, rising from the stony floor, figures stood motionless observing him. He believed he heard a soft murmur. *There he is.* Seeing then that the figures were statues. Tall, garishly costumed statues, more than life-sized. They were wearing long robes, but their heads were bare. Their hands held no visible weapons. One of them was Jesus Christ contorted on his cross like a worm on the hook, spikes through his bare white feet graceful as a woman's feet. Carleton stared, and shuddered. The sweat on his body was turning clammy. Like a man losing his vision he groped his way along the pews, intending to approach the altar. For you were drawn toward the altar in this church. But the altar was far away, floating in white. White drapery, tall white candles. White flowers in vases. Above the altar was a stained-glass window. He had to sit suddenly, his left knee pounded with pain. Turning then to look behind and seeing how the statues were spaced through the church so that each section of pews might be observed. So that the church was never empty. If you half-shut your eyes, the statues seemed to move. There were low excited murmurs *There! there he is.* In this shadowy place like a mausoleum something seemed to draw everything upward, toward the altar and the stained-glass window that was a perfect egg shape. In the sides of the stone walls were other stained-glass windows, smaller and narrower. They were like eyes. Unblinking eyes. Carleton was the only figure in the church not moving, because he was being observed. In the windows the eye-aching colors—vivid reds, blues, yellows, greens—glowed and faded, sinking back into themselves then pulsing up again as if behind them a heart was beating. Everywhere there were vertical lines and juttings, arches high up the walls, that vibrated as if about to come to life. The shadowy ceiling might not even be a ceiling but the entrance to some other world. Ghostly and quivering the close, stale air was filled with invisible shapes like birds' wings. Spirits. Carleton was shivering, he did not believe in the spirits of the dead returning. He did not! Shut his eyes to ignore them seeing a melting-tar highway stretching off to the horizon, sun-baked. Sunshine State and God laughing at him and crushing him under His foot that was a fuckin cloven hoof.

"Fucker."

It was a groan, coming from his gut. The ball of spite-snakes rousing themselves. He was looking for her—his daughter—that one daughter—the only person he had ever loved—he wanted to understand this, and he wanted these witnesses to understand. They were judging him, and he wanted them to know he was a Walpole, and the name Walpole signified a certain kind of man, a man who honored his family even to the grave.

But he felt these facts sliding away. Memories he should have sorted out years ago so that when the time came he could put them all together. *Of account* these were. He could not die because that would mean all these things would be lost—who else was there except Carleton Walpole to bring them together? Everything—everyone—was joined in him. Like Jesus on his cross, these things came together in you, piercing and spiking you in place. Only in Carleton Walpole. He was the center of it, without him everything would melt away into nothing. Already he was losing their names, that were familiar to him as his own. And he had a new baby now back at the camp, he had to live for her. And Clara who'd run away with a man he had never seen. *Pa no. Pa don't hit me. Pa!* He held back his hand, he had not struck her. It was the others he wanted to hit, the others he wanted to murder.

Struggling to pull off his shoe, goddamn he was angry: threw the shoe at the nearest of the stained-glass windows but it struck the wall, and fell harmlessly to the floor. Carleton heaved himself to his feet. Grabbed whatever it was—a heavy iron stand for a candle—reared it up and swung with it, striking one of the long-robed statues, a female it appeared to be in a long blue and white robe, and a halo around her waxy face, Carleton laughed at the expression in the face as he swung and struck and battered and crumbled the thing and it fell in pieces at his feet. Turning then, panting and partially blinded, bits of grit in his eyes, he swung the iron stand in wild arcs striking the pews, denting the hardwood pews but not otherwise injuring them, he stumbled in the aisle uncertain which direction to take as at a crook in the road where there's no fuckin sign you can't make a decision, yet finally you do, he was laughing stumbling toward the door, he had one shoe on and one shoe off and his knee was numb, the pain had abated, as in his gut the tiny snakes were taken unaware, and could not stop him now. At the front of the church he swung and toppled in single strokes two fountain-looking things, milk glass on pedestals that held water, and the shattered glass went flying, and the water went flying. And a voice called out—"Stop! Stop!" and Carleton turned to see someone hurrying toward him, and ducking, wordless, remembering to breathe through his nose, Carleton swung the thing in his hand and caught the man on the side of the head, the man went down like a shot duck, hit the stone floor with a soft moaning sound, and Carleton dropped the iron thing beside him, and stumbled away. Both his hands were throbbing with sensation but it was a good sensation. Outside then in the sunshine, stumbling along the pavement one shoe on, one shoe off. Witnesses would think he was a drunk well fuck them let them think what they fuckin want. He saw faces regarding him with astonishment. White faces like his own yet regarding him with astonishment. In a sudden rage he tore a whiplike thing from a car, a metal strip it was, he'd use it like a whip, he was striking at people's faces who came too close, warning *Get away! Get away I'll kill you!* and it seemed to him not even himself any longer who was doing this, it was the whip-thing in his hand that was alive, and there came a youngish thick-bodied man in a policeman's uniform, bulldog face yet astonished behind curved dark glasses— *Mister lay down your weapon, I am warning you mister lay down your weapon*—and in his hand was a pistol cocked and aimed at Carleton's heart and Carleton felt the trigger jerk as he rushed his enemy wielding the whip, swinging it until something exploded into his chest and his vision went out, and his brain went out. And that was all.

II.

LOWRY

1

"Kid, you don't cry much, do you."

It wasn't a question. It called for no answer. Lowry had no questions to ask of Clara, or of anyone. He was a man who knew the answers to questions, not one who depended upon others to supply them.

He likes that Clara thought. *A girl who doesn't cry.*

Those long dreamy hours driving with Lowry, sitting beside him in the front seat of his shiny-dark new-looking sedan, drinking Colas they stopped to buy—Clara was the one to run into the store, clutching coins Lowry gave her—and sometimes he let her have a few swallows from a bottle of beer, driving those hours Clara had no thought of any destination. Just to be in motion: to escape. Watching the sun shift in the sky behind the scrub pines beside the highway Clara thought nervously, fiercely *Nobody's going to get me now. He isn't going to, ever again.* Observing the nameless road before them that the man named Lowry overtook always at the same speed, trying to imagine it running back beneath them and into the days preceding: the distance and time her father would have to conquer if he were to get her, claim her. Lay his hands on her. And she saw Carleton Walpole blundering, failing. For he could not overtake the younger man whose face in profile was the sharp-etched face of the jack of spades on a playing card. And so she smiled. She laughed.

See? I don't need you, goddamn you. No more.

Dozing off and waking to his upraised hand, his actual fist, seeing the scabby knuckles before his hand struck . . .

"He made my face bleed," she'd told Lowry in a thin, outraged child's voice. Her anger was for that sensation of being helpless, a sight to be pitied by others. "He never hit me like that before. He hit my brothers but not me, I could taste the blood and some people were watching, and—" She would shudder, raising her knees to catch her heels on the car seat, hug her knees tight against her chest as a boy might do, staring through the bug-splattered windshield at the road that had no name for her, as the places through which Lowry drove had no names and were fleeting, inconsequential. Sometimes she would turn to peer over her shoulder, to see the highway moving back steadily behind them, misty in the morning light; and something about the way it disappeared so swiftly frightened her. Lowry said, "You're afraid your old man will find you. But you're afraid worse he won't."

Lowry laughed, and Clara felt her face burn.

"Goddamn it ain't that way. No."

But Lowry just laughed, and reached out to squeeze her knee.

Like you'd squeeze a dog, the nape of its neck. Out of fondness that was superior, condescending.

Sometimes, Clara told him *Go to hell*. Muttered so maybe he heard and maybe he did not hear and she climbed over the back of the seat clumsy and indignant and stretched out in back to sleep. That weird sensation of lying flat in the back of a car as the car is moving, you feel the vibrations, a shivery feeling between the legs sometimes, and thoughts coming like long slow flat shapes and in her sleep she heard a child sobbing and her heart was filled with contempt for such weakness. *You don't cry much, do you.* Waking then she was confused not knowing where she was, maybe on one of the buses, then she realized the moving vehicle was small, contained: only just Clara lying on the backseat amid Lowry's things, and shimmering green outside the window flowing past like water, and there, the back of Lowry's head, the blond hairs that were different shades in the sunshine, some so pale they appeared silvery, others darker, almost brown, and he wore his hair long, straggling to his collar, and almost Clara could not recall his face, staring fascinated at the back of his head feeling calm now thinking *There he is. He hadn't ever gone away.*

———

Stopped at places along the road. Small restaurants, taverns. Lowry, entering such places, seemed always to be recognized: if not his actual face and name, his Lowry-self. The way he smiled, knowing that people would smile back at him; knowing they were grateful to see his smile, and not something else. He said, in the way of a man speaking to himself, to reason out a thought to which Clara Walpole was a witness only by chance: "You're a certain size, people look at you a certain way. Say I'm on crutches. Say I'm in a wheelchair. These same fuckers looking at me, think they would respect me like they do? Or if I was a woman."

Clara said, sly and mean, "If you were a woman, there'd be some bastard drives a car just like yours and the same color hair as yours to knock you on your ass every time. Wipe that look off your face."

Lowry laughed. He liked it when Clara spoke to him in a certain brash way long as she didn't cross over into something else. Like a dog that's been trained to rush barking to the very edge of his master's property, but not to take a step over. Or he'd regret it.

In the places they stopped, Clara ran to use the rest room and fixed herself up. So happy! Sometimes she thought *Just to pee. Just to wash my face. Just to run water, it don't need to be hot.* She slapped her cheeks that looked pallid, sallow, to get some color into them, like she'd seen Nancy do. Wetted her eyes to make them clear. Smiled at herself in the mirror in that way she had not needing to show too much of her teeth, and thinking that she looked all right, she had a hopeful-seeming face, nobody would wish to hurt that face.

Smiling because there was Lowry out there waiting for her.

(And what if Lowry was gone and left her? She knew, this might be. Any place they stopped it might be. And so walking out there she had to appear hopeful and happy like a girl who'd never had such a mean thought.)

Lowry might tease when she returned breathless to slide into a booth across from him, "Kid, I was worried where you'd gone: thought you'd fallen in." Or, to make her smile and blush with pleasure, all the more if a waitress was there looking on, "Kid, you look like a million bucks. That's my girl."

She wasn't, though.

She wasn't Lowry's girl. Not the way Carleton would think, or Nancy. Or anybody who saw them together, maybe.

If Lowry was in one of his moods, it was like Clara did not exist. Or she was some kind of thing tied to his ankle, or a duffel bag slung over his shoulder, a weight, a burden but not too much of a burden; for Lowry wasn't the kind of man who endures much of a burden.

"What's he, some kind of ex-soldier? Marine? Good-looking guy."

Women asked such questions of Clara when Lowry was out of earshot. Cutting their eyes at her thinking *What's so special about you, he chose you? What about me?*

Waitresses, bar girls, shifting their shoulders just-so, in Lowry's presence. Must be an instinct like a cat arcing its back to be petted, a female displaying her breasts for a man's drifting eye.

Clara stroked her small hard breasts in secret. Pinching the nipples to make them grow.

"Naw," she'd say, keeping a straight mouth, "he's just out of Leavenworth, y'all know what that is?"

The looks on their faces! If, say, Lowry was playing pinball or dropping coins in a cigarette machine, hearing Clara giggle he'd glance around to see the woman startled and fearful-looking backing away quick.

Lowry liked it that Clara struck up conversations with people they met, he said it wasn't healthy for a girl her age, a growing girl like her, to talk with only him. "Sooner we get you where you're going the better, kid."

Clara heard this clearly. Clara heard the statement beneath *Sooner I can get rid of you the better.* But she pretended not to hear, just laughed. There was a high breathy laugh you heard on the radio, a feminine way of laughing. And twining her hair strangers said was the prettiest hair around her fingers in a way she'd seen Nancy do, in the days when Nancy had been younger, prettier; and Carleton Walpole had liked to look at her.

Clara had heard the two of them in the night lots of times, on their mattress in a corner of whatever room in whatever tar-paper shanty or cabin or unit, Nancy whimpering and moaning and Carleton panting, grunting hard, and groaning too like somebody was raking his back he could not bear it, yet had to bear it. *Going at it* was the expression Rosalie had used. *Going at it like dogs in heat* Rosalie had said of such behavior spitting in disgust.

Clara said to Lowry she'd known a girl once up in Jersey, had a baby that was born dead and guess who the daddy was?

Lowry, lighting a Camel and shaking the match out, tossing the match onto the floor, looked at her with a mean-playful smile saying, "Her own daddy. Right?"

Clara felt her face burn. Goddamn: she'd meant to shock Lowry and she never could.

"Are babies like that always born dead? That's some kind of curse?"

Lowry shrugged. He had a way of dismissing Clara's willfully naive questions the way you'd dismiss the prattling of a baby.

"If you believe in curses, kid, that'd be one of them."

———

Did she believe in curses, no she did not. For some folks maybe but not for her. She figured that God had more important things to care about than Clara Walpole.

———

"Where're we going, Lowry? You got to tell me."

"Where's who going? You, or me?"

Clara hesitated. She knew this was a tricky question.

"Both. I guess."

"Naw, kid. I told you, you got to make your mind up what to do." Lowry paused in his eating, and wiped his mouth on a napkin in a way that maddened Clara, made her want to tear the napkin from his fingers. "Happens that I'm going to where I'm going day after tomorrow, sweetheart." He paused after saying this.

Clara stared at her plate. Oh, she'd been so hungry!—and so happy eating this gristly hamburger with ketchup and mustard both, and greasy french fries, sugary coleslaw. Even the stale bun was delicious. Now she wanted to push her plate away like Carleton used to do with the heel of his hand, signaling he'd had enough and had not liked what he'd had.

" 'Day after tomorrow.' What's that mean . . ."

Clara felt her lips go into a pout. She'd have gone *all eyes* leaning over the sticky tabletop but Lowry just returned to his eating.

A damn pig, he was. Men were. Hear them eating, chewing; hear them guzzling beer; hear them belching. Enough to make you sick.

It was true, sometimes Clara ate a lot, herself. Nancy used to tease her, try to shame her. Sometimes Clara was ravenous with hunger, ate and ate till her belly swelled tight against the elastic band of her underwear; not that she ate as much as Lowry, but she ate as long, and sometimes longer. And she drank from his beer, if nobody was watching to scold saying she was underage. Sometimes in a sad mood, or her head aching from the day's drive, Clara chewed food without tasting it and felt it settle into her stomach like a hard little knot and even Lowry's beer left a bad taste in her mouth; this was one of those times when she felt like laying her head down on her arms, and crying.

Lowry signaled the waitress: another beer. Might've been sitting in the damn booth alone for all the notice he gave Clara.

"Fucker."

Clara mumbled biting her lip. Lowry could hear, or choose not to hear.

One thing Clara knew, they were headed north. Wished she had a map to see where they were, where they'd come from and speculate where they were going. She had only a vague sense of geography from some faded old map hanging down a blackboard at some school in a place now forgotten but she knew that Carolina and Virginia were still *south* but Pennsylvania was getting to be *north*. She wondered if they would pass through Kentucky, or if they were going some different way, and would not. She'd told Lowry about Kentucky and he had seemed more interested than he usually was in her talk. Actually asking her questions like where her father's people were from? and her mother's?—but Clara was vague. Asking had her relatives worked the mines?—and Clara asked what kind of mines? She didn't know. What she knew was Pearl's stories of being courted by Carleton Walpole, her wedding when she was only just fifteen ("Maybe Ma wasn't old enough to be served beer in some damn old tavern but she was old enough to be married") and the wonderful snapshots Pearl had had, that Nancy had denied she'd tossed away. Clara's eyes filled with tears of indignation thinking of that bitch Nancy taking Pearl's place and showing poor Pearl no respect.

Lowry had asked why Clara's mother had died, and Clara had to say she didn't know. "Pa told us it was her time. That's all he'd say over and over. 'It was your ma's time.'"

Now Clara said, shoving her plate from her, "I'm gonna pay you back for all this, soon as I can. I don't take no charity."

Lowry smiled at her, picking his teeth with a toothpick.

"Sure."

"I am! Goddamn you, I'll get a job and pay it back."

"You will, will you? Where?"

"Anywhere I can."

"So what's your skill, sweetheart? Name one."

"Name one? Name a dozen: I can pick fuckin green beans, I can pick fuckin tomatoes, I can pick fuckin strawberries, I can pick fuckin lettuce—"

Lowry laughed, relenting. "All right, kid. Any other skill?"

"I can take care of a baby. I can clean house. I can cook, sort of. I could be a waitress, I bet. I could . . ." Clara paused, thinking a sly dirty thought: *I could lay down on my back and spread my legs. Be a whore.*

This word Clara had not uttered aloud, for fear of getting her face slapped by someone. But she'd heard it plenty of times. Had no idea how it was spelled but it was pronounced *ho'* and always with an intonation of contempt.

Lowry saw her cat eyes going flat and calculating and must've known exactly what she was thinking.

"Best thing for you's to get married soon as you can. A girl with hair your color, and trusting as you are . . ." Lowry made a gesture signaling there's no help for such a one.

"Married! Shit, I ain't gonna get married, ever." Clara spoke vehemently, bravely. "You just end up having babies. Whoever you married don't give a damn for you once you get pregnant. *He's* tom-catting around, and never home."

Clara made herself laugh scornfully. She felt a stab of love for Lowry, a sensation of desperate helplessness like drowning. At the base of her spine was a cold numb place into which all her blood ran leaving her sickened, faint. She loved this man for his handsome face and his strong arms and the way he'd protected her, saving her from harm; but she was coming to hate him for the way he didn't give a damn for her really, she was just some stray mutt he'd found along the roadside and pitied, and would get rid of as soon as he could. He meant to do the decent thing by her, she guessed. And she hated him for that, too. She hated him for how, in any public place, his eyes could move about alert and restless and affable and his mouth shape itself into a smile, that easy smile of a man who knows he's attractive to women, and to men, too; and forgetting her who stared at him so avidly it was like a flame in the air between them, of which he took no notice. She hated knowing that Lowry could toss a few coins on the table of this booth for the waitress and stroll outside to his car whistling and if Clara didn't trot after him, damn if he wouldn't drive away without her. And no looking back.

Clara asked, pouting, "What kind of a job d'you have, where you're going?" It wasn't for the first time, and she guessed he would not answer.

Lowry just shrugged. That look in his face like he's getting bored.

"Why couldn't I be with you, Lowry? I could cook for you some. I could clean house for you. What women do . . ." Clara spoke clumsily, her tongue too big for her mouth.

"Clara, you're just a child."

"Fuck! I am not a child."

"I can't be dragging you around with me. You're underage."

"Don't you like me?"

"Oh, Christ—"

"Don't you think I'm—pretty?"

"No."

"Hell you don't! You do."

But Clara was shaken, uncertain. Lowry was looking like a man who could walk out on her any minute.

"There's lots of pretty girls. Damn good-looking women. A man can have his fair share, and more. That's not it."

Then what is? Clara wondered. She wondered why, if Lowry felt like this about her now, he'd ever looked at her the way he had back in that tavern, after she'd left LeRoy. Maybe he'd thought she was older than she was, maybe he hadn't looked at her close. And now he'd looked too close. She trembled with rage, suddenly.

"You better listen to me, mister!"

"Yeah? Says who?"

"I can love a man like any grown woman. I can do things for a man like any woman. I can! You got to let me prove it."

Lowry smiled at her, amused. But he was looking at her with interest, as if seeing her for the first time.

Clara said, "I don't want no damn old picker's life. No more, it ain't gonna kill *me*. I want more things than just babies, I'll show you."

"I bet you will."

"I will! Even if I can't name it yet, I want it."

"Going to steal it?"

"If nobody gives me what I want, I'll steal it. I want somethin—I'm gonna get it."

"Calm down, kid. You're talking kind of loud."

Clara's heart was pounding furiously and out of her rage came something like joy. She knew now, from the way in which Lowry was watching her, with a certain wariness, as you'd watch a coiled snake, that she would discover what she wanted; and she would get it.

"First I got to learn how—how things are." Her words were plaintive suddenly, her voice was almost apologetic.

Without a word Lowry slid out of the booth, tossing a handful of coins onto the table. He was halfway out the restaurant door before Clara caught up with him flush-faced and craven, yet without his having seen she'd pocketed one of the silver quarters he'd left behind in his improvident generosity.

I can steal. I will. If you make me.

—

After that, things changed between them.

He was more respectful, Clara thought. But he didn't touch her as he had, the way you'd touch a child, or animal. He did seem wary of her. More frequently he spoke of *getting to where he was going*.

Each night they'd slept in the car. Clara fell into a doze while Lowry was driving, sometimes she crawled dazed with exhaustion into the backseat and slept, waking to discover the car stilled, in darkness like the darkness at the bottom of a deep pond, and only after some minutes of disorientation would Clara realize that Lowry was asleep in the front seat, his breath wetly audible. Clara would listen to him breathe, scarcely breathing herself. So many years of sleeping in the same room with her family, now she was sleeping almost-alone, and almost-lonely; for Lowry kept himself from her, at nighttime. She had believed that he would love her in that way she'd been warned men and boys would wish to love her, yet he had not, and would not. *Don't touch me like that, Clara. You're underage.* He'd spoken sharply, he meant it.

All he'd given to her of himself was his name: Lowry. And she could not be certain of that.

Clara lay huddled in the backseat listening to the sound of nocturnal insects outside. So loud! She thought of her pa who was somewhere behind her. She would not have minded being hit by him, she'd known she had deserved it, but his words shouted at her had hurt. *Bitch just like your mother!*

That was wrong, to speak so of Pearl. To speak so of the dead, who can't speak for themselves.

Clara smiled to think that Carleton would never catch up with Lowry. He was too old, Lowry was younger. Lowry slept in the front seat of his car with no fear of being discovered and attacked. Carleton had killed a man once, but he'd almost been killed himself. If it came to a fight, Lowry would beat Carleton down with his fists.

Clara drifted back into sleep thinking *He will never find me. I am nobody's daughter now.* Jamming fingers into her mouth as she'd done as a little girl, for consolation.

———

Next morning they were driving north into New York State.

Hill country, but as the sky lightened Clara saw that the hills close beside the country highway fell back in waves to mountains, and that the boundary between the mountains and the mountainous clouds in the sky was feathery and unclear. Like between waking and sleep, you couldn't know for certain. Clara drew her knees up to her chest and hugged herself like a little girl. The mountains were so beautiful!

"Lowry, I bet you're from around here."

Lowry glanced at her, surprised. His jaws were glittering with blond stubble. "How'd you know that?"

Clara just smiled mysteriously.

Somehow, she'd known.

Lowry was taking pride in this landscape, you could see. Descending one of the long broad hills, the blacktop road and the land spread out so vast Clara thought you could get lost in it, so much for the eye to see, and sunlight in patches, and cloud-shapes of shadow swift-moving across the fields. There were cornfields, and wheat fields, and what was maybe rye fields, rippling-green like water, and there were small farms, houses, barns, outbuildings amid acreage neatly plotted as a map; and the rest was trees, some of them of a kind Clara had not seen before, white-barked, growing in clusters. Straight as she could Clara sat staring. Her new home: Lowry was bringing her to her new home.

"I love you."

It was the merest whisper. Wind rushing through their rolled-down windows, Lowry couldn't be expected to hear.

In a loud voice she asked, were they going to stop somewhere around here?—and Lowry said, "Maybe."

An hour later they were descending into a town: TINTERN POPU-LATION 1650, Lowry said it was an old river town, the name of the river was the Eden River and the time of Tintern as a "living" town had been a hundred years ago, when his folks had first arrived. Clara stared at brick streets between tall gaunt steep-gabled brick and stone houses that looked like elderly toothless men. Here was a town that looked like a city, what Clara would have believed to be a city, but the neighborhood was old and run-down and there were children playing in the streets—white-skinned, but noisy and frantic like kids in the farmworkers' camps. You didn't think that people could be poor in a city, only in the country. This was a surprise.

The funny old brick street narrowed as it began to ascend to a high, humpbacked bridge so narrow vehicles could pass over it but one at a time. Clara's heart began to thump.

"Jesus! I'm scared we're gonna fall in. . . ."

Lowry just laughed at her and continued across the bridge that made a nervous whirring noise beneath the tires of his car, not slackening and not increasing his speed. Clara tasted panic: you could see the water through the grid of the bridge's floor! If she'd been driving, she would have maybe fainted, the damn car would crash through the railing—

Lowry pointed out buildings along the river, most of them shut-down and boarded-up. Railroad yards, granaries. A tomato-canning factory that was still in operation part of the year. "The Depression hit Tintern pretty hard. Lots of people I knew left, but not me." Yet he spoke regretfully as if he'd wanted to leave, and somehow hadn't been able. Clara listened closely to these rare words of Lowry's, for he'd never answered questions she put to him about himself, in all those hours of intimacy in the car; as if now, seeing this town, that was run-down and jumbled but somehow beautiful he was shaken in some way, and moved to speak.

On the north side of the river, as Lowry spoke of it, there was a Main Street; there was a River Street, and there was a Bridge Street; there was a railroad depot where trains only stopped a few times a week now; along the downtown streets were three- and four-story buildings, made mostly of dark brick, with false fronts Clara was curious to see: from the front the building looked sort of impres-sive, but from the side and back it was some old run-down thing. Clara's eye lit onto taverns, a restaurant, a movie house, clothes stores and a shoe store and a Woolworth's Five & Dime. She hoped they would be living downtown: she hoped they would be living somewhere above a ground floor.

"This road continues all the way to Port Oriskany, on Lake Erie," Lowry said. "North of town, the road leads to Lake Ontario." As if Clara knew, or, staring so hard at what lay before her, gave a damn for these places. Erie? Ontario?

Lowry pulled his car to a stop. Clara was practically leaning out the window, staring so hard. They were at the edge of the down-town on the crest of a hill; here you could see some of Main Street, and you could look back to that scary bridge and buildings on the other side of the river. Lowry was saying in a voice that sounded different, somber and almost-scolding, "Clara, there's a place for you in Tintern, I made some calls. But you need to keep quiet about yourself and don't make any trouble. Like if somebody asks where are your folks, you say politely, 'I don't live with my folks right now. I've been on my own since sixteen.' Whatever hell age you are, sweetheart, say you're sixteen."

Clara laughed, biting her lip. "Goddamn, I am sixteen."

"Anyway, say it. If the wrong people catch on to you, you'll be charged with 'runaway.' You'll be placed in some juvenile facility. They'll try to contact your family back in—wherever. Or put you in an orphanage. That's the law."

"Well, I'm not goin back. I'll kill myself first."

"That kind of talk, you keep to yourself. That's the first thing that'd get you taken into custody, talk like that."

Clara tried to make her face serious. " 'I don't live with my folks right now. Been on my own since sixteen.' " Goddamn, she kept wanting to laugh she was so nervous, or excited.

Lowry said, "I've made some calls like I said. There's maybe a job for you if you can make change. Learn to use a cash register."

" 'Make change'—?"

"Like, changing a dollar bill. Five-dollar bill."

"Sure! Sure I can do that."

Clara had done this for Pearl lots of times. Even before Pearl got dreamy and dopey. Nancy, too. Buying things in a store, they hadn't wanted to figure out the coins, themselves. And knowing what kind of change you were going to get back, so you wouldn't be cheated.

Eagerly Clara said, "It's easy: you think of a dollar as being one hundred pennies. Then you—" but Lowry cut her off.

He turned the key in the ignition, to start the car motor again. Going to take her somewhere now, she guessed. He had never spoken to her like this before and Clara was fearful of him now and fearful he was saying goodbye to her. "Lowry, I could—do things for you. Like women do. I could—"

"No. I told you, Clara. I don't stay in one place long. And nobody comes with me. I don't marry any of them, either. Erase me from your head because you're just not the one, kid. Not just you're too young which you are, but what I want is a—voice. A way a woman talks to me, says things to me I don't know and am astonished to hear and I'll know her as soon as I hear her. Or maybe I never will hear her, and that's all right, too. Because my father was poison to women, and damned if I will be, too. And some things, the worst things, run in your blood."

Clara nodded numbly. Not wanting to think this could be so.

Saying desperately, like a pleading dog if such could speak, "Lowry, why'd you ever bother with me?"

Lowry, driving his car, pulled to a traffic light and didn't answer at once. Didn't look at her, either.

"It wasn't 'bother,' Clara. Don't think that."

"You helped me. Saved me. You—"

"Maybe I always wanted a little sister. Maybe that's it."

2

"I have a job. I'm on my own now."

Astonishing to Clara who had expected to be working out in the fields, or scrubbing some rich ladies' toilets, she had a job in the Woolworth's Five & Dime right on Main Street. Somehow, Lowry had arranged for her to be interviewed by the fattish middle-aged manager Mr. Mulch, and she'd been hired right off. A store! In town! Clara couldn't believe her good luck. She smiled to think how Rosalie would envy her. Clara Walpole, a salesclerk in a *store*.

It was like the world had been broken into pieces and tossed into the air and come down again in a nicer arrangement. Yet an arrangement Clara could not believe had anything to do with her— what she deserved, what she'd earned. Sharing a long counter with another girl, who'd quit school in ninth grade a few years back and was passing time till her fiancé could afford to marry her; selling sewing supplies—scissors, threads of all colors, ready-made ruffled curtains, cloth of all colors and prints. On a slow day, if the manager wasn't around, you could drift over to visit Joanie at the candy counter who'd give away broken-off bits of peanut brittle, ribbon candy, stale old bonbons and marshmallows about to be removed from the display case and tossed into the garbage. And there was the magazine and pocket book rack, where you could leaf through *Silver Screen, True Romance, Collier's* and *Life*. There were paperback novels Clara stole away for overnight reading—*Lamb in His Bosom, So Big, Honey in the Horn*. Lowry was impressed, Clara spoke of such books. She meant to demonstrate to him how mature she was, and independent.

Goddamn, though: she wished she'd learned to read better. It took her an hour sometimes to read a dozen pages, pushing her finger beneath the words and mouthing them like a first grader.

Being a salesgirl at the five-and-dime was glamorous-seeming, and Clara was proud of her position, but it was harder work than you'd have guessed. Waiting on customers was the easy part. Also you had to unpack merchandise at the back of the store and carry it to the front; you had to repack old merchandise, back into grimy old cartons. You had to help sweep up. You had to help wash the big fly-specked windows. The five-and-dime was in a block-long row of brick buildings infested with roaches and rodents, and under Mr. Mulch's disgusted direction you had to deal with these: nasty-smelling poisons set out for the roaches, and traps with wicked steel springs for the mice and rats. The tricky thing was, the rats could devour the mice's cheese bait and if the trap sprung it didn't hurt them one damn bit.

Clara had to laugh, she'd used to think a store in town was so special. Now she knew better, but it was a kind of secret you kept so people outside the store didn't know. So funny! Joanie made them all laugh complaining of rodents breaking into her candy display case in the night, that was supposed to be rodent-proof, eating just parts of some candies and leaving the rest, and tracking goddamn turds she had to brush off by hand. Mr. Mulch's byword was *What the customer don't know don't hurt 'em.*

Lowry asked Clara how she liked her job at Woolworth's, and Clara said she'd never had a job she loved so much. And Lowry seemed pleased, and maybe proud of her.

"Mulch says you're learning fast. 'Sharpest-eyed girl in the store.'"

—

So happy! Lowry had found a furnished room for Clara, with its own tiny bathroom, and had paid her first three months' rent. This he'd done without telling her, exactly—that was Lowry's way. The room was on Mohigan Street around the corner from Main, above a hardware store. Through her rear window Clara could see, slantwise, that high old nightmare bridge and a slice of the Eden River. For a long time she sat dreamy-eyed in her windows gazing out. She imagined herself telling Rosalie *I live by myself now. On a second floor.*

Mostly, she'd ceased thinking of the past. She did not wish to think of Carleton, Pearl, her brothers. Her sister Sharleen she had not seen in years and would never see again. She did not wish to think of her spindly limbed child-self she'd rapidly outgrown.

From the five-and-dime discards Clara acquired old melted lipsticks, broken packages of face powder, bent tweezers. Eyebrow pencils. Plucking and arching her eyebrows in the style of Joan Crawford, or Katharine Hepburn, or Bette Davis whose movies she saw for ten cents, in the movie house on Main Street. Clara loved best those movies where a man and a woman met, and fell in love; and the man went away; and the woman missed him, and waited for him; and the man returned. Emerging into the evening air, Clara wiped at her eyes.

So happy! This was her new life, and there was a man she was waiting for. There was a man her hopes could fasten upon, always.

Yet: sad sometimes. Lonely sometimes. As she'd never been sad and lonely in her old, lost life she had believed she despised.

For now, suddenly, there were two times in Clara's life, and disproportionate times they were. When Lowry was in Tintern, and would take time to see her; and when Lowry was away.

He'd warned her not to speak of him to anyone, and so she had not. Seeming to know that if she boasted of him, or complained of him, he would disappear from her life as abruptly as he'd appeared; and she would be left alone in Tintern, under the eye of Mr. Mulch.

Lowry was beginning to take notice of her, Clara thought. For she was older now, living alone and spending so much time in her own thoughts. Tilting her head like Katharine Hepburn, fixing her eyes upon a man's face like Claudette Colbert. And her hair, she'd begun to trim and curl with bobby pins, parted neatly on the left side of her head in the way of Joan Fontaine, whose hair was ashy-blond like Clara's. Lowry took her driving in his car, along the river; rarely did he take her to a restaurant or tavern in Tintern, only elsewhere. He was ashamed of her, she guessed. She understood, and did not blame him.

As a dime-store girl, Clara was able to buy things at a reduced price. Sweaters, blouses, skirts, sometimes even dresses. In those towns in the Eden Valley to which Lowry drove her she appeared older than fifteen in her gaudy, tight-fitting clothes and high-heeled shoes. Lowry, in public, seemed always in a hurry and walking with his face slightly averted, as if he were both with her, yet not with her. Sometimes he was in good spirits, playful; at other times he behaved like an older and remote relative of hers, a cousin or uncle entrusted with her for the evening. If Clara dared to take his hand, and stroke his fingers, as she'd seen women do in movies, Lowry stiffened but didn't always draw away at once.

Sometimes, as if unconsciously, his fingers closed about hers.

"My little girl's getting growed up. Happens fast, sometimes."

Clara smiled, in that way she'd perfected of not showing any more teeth than she needed to show. Her heart was suffused with happiness. *My little girl.*

One Saturday night Lowry drove her to Lake Shaheen, which must have been about twenty miles to the north. The Anchor Inn was on the lake and overlooked a boatyard. Clara had never been inside so nice a place: it excited her that Lowry seemed to be known here. The main room, with a timber ceiling, was crowded and romantically dim-lit, and people were dancing. Some of the women were young, nearly as young as Clara. "I want to dance. Oh, let's dance!" Clara begged.

But Lowry left her in a booth by herself, drinking a Cola and eating pretzels. He'd told her he had friends to see, to catch up on, and Clara had smiled and said that was all right; she was happy sitting by herself in such a nice place, and listening to music. Her eyes followed the dancers, eagerly. Just watching, she was learning: it was like the movies. It was like ringing up sales at the five-and-dime, you learned by doing. In fact she'd learned to smoke, from Lowry. She'd needed something to do with her hands.

For when Lowry drifted away from her, talking with women he hadn't troubled to introduce to her, Clara needed something to do with her hands.

At the Anchor Inn that night, Clara waited. Thinking *I can wait. I've been waiting fifteen years. I'm happy.*

Lowry returned, she saw a smear of lipstick on the side of his face. He might have checked his reflection in a mirror and missed that smear. "Sorry, sweetheart. Something came up."

In the car driving back to Tintern, Clara spoke quietly of a man who'd befriended her. Took her to the movies. In fact he was the hardware store owner, and Clara believed he was a married man, but she didn't tell Lowry this. "He said, any new dress I wanted, in any shop in Tintern, he'd buy for me. If I wanted it."

"What's that mean?"

"I don't know. What it means."

"You want to get pregnant?"

"Get *pregnant?*" Clara was incensed, insulted. "All we do, mister, we go to the movies! That's all."

"How many times did your mother get pregnant?"

"None of your damn business. Damn you!"

Clara was smoking, trying not to cough. A flame of pure hatred pulsed over her, for this man beside her.

"You don't care about me. You never did. I'm just some old mangy kicked dog you found along the highway."

"Is that so."

"Somebody would marry me. People say I'm pretty."

Lowry, driving, leaning his elbow out the window, said nothing.

"Then I wouldn't be a bother to you."

"Clara, you aren't a bother to me."

Clara was thinking: if she could read better—if she could write— if she didn't have to struggle so with words, things would come easier for her. There were times when an idea brushed her mind, but she couldn't seize it. Like a butterfly fluttering out of her reach.

Lowry said, in the way of a man reasoning something out for himself that surprised him, "You were just a kid then. Not that long ago, but you've changed. I don't believe I had ever done one damn thing in my life I was proud of or cared even to contemplate, but I was glad that I could help you. And I didn't take advantage of you, either."

"That woman back there, at the tavern," Clara said carefully, "is she—"

"None of your business. That's what she is."

At Mohigan Street, Clara waited for Lowry to say goodnight to her but instead he asked could he come upstairs, see what her place was like? "Sure!" Clara said. "I'll make coffee for you."

"*You*, coffee?"

"I can do all sorts of things, mister. You'd be surprised."

Upstairs she unlocked the door eagerly. She'd hoped for this: Lowry coming to see her. The small furnished room held a bed, a card table she'd draped with a floral print cloth from the dime store, a few chairs. Waterfall and sunset scenes she'd framed in dime-store frames and hung on the walls, like real pictures. "This is new. I got it at the store, marked down." A small lamp of dimpled milk glass and a shade decorated with pink satin bows. Lowry smiled, and switched it on.

Uninvited, Lowry sat on the edge of Clara's bed. There was no bedspread yet, she was saving for something nice. But the bed was neatly made, and she knew he was seeing that, taking note. A dark blue blanket primly drawn over the single pillow. On the floor at Lowry's feet was a small oval rug of some fuzzy material, also dark blue. Lowry looked at it for a second too long.

"For when I'm barefoot and it's cold," Clara said.

Clara fumbled to make coffee. She'd learned at the five-and-dime, where instant coffee was sold. Lowry glanced through some of the magazines Clara had brought home. She was embarrassed, damn old dumb movie magazines, a *True Romance* her friend Sonya had given her. "Clara, why don't you go back to school? What grade were you, when you dropped out?"

Clara said quickly, "I'm too old."

"If you want a life different from your parents' lives, you need to be educated, at least some. I could help you."

"I said I'm too old."

Clara bit her lips to keep from crying. That flame of hatred for him came over her, she felt weak, dazed as if he'd struck her.

She was fumbling, preparing coffee. Her double-burner hot plate, in a corner of the room. Here too was a small enamel sink with a rusty faucet. Above the sink, a calendar with a photo of a baby in a bonnet playing with two kittens. Clara began to chatter nervously telling Lowry about working at the store; and about her girlfriends she liked so much, and trusted—Joanie, Sonya, Caroline. She'd told Lowry about them before and he'd never seemed interested as if Clara's life apart from him was of no significance. How many times she had tormented herself over the months with Lowry's words *What I want is a voice. A woman, a voice.* Her own voice was thin, nasal, persistent as a head cold. "Caroline, she's engaged, too. She's only eighteen. Her fiancé works on that big farm up the valley."

"The Revere farm?"

Lowry's voice was alert, edgy.

" 'Revere.' I guess so. D'you know who it is?"

Lowry didn't reply at once. Then he said, "The same family owns the gypsum land, too. The mines." He paused again, like a man who isn't certain what he means to say, listening to his own words. "They were neighbors of ours. The Reveres."

"That's where you live now? Up the valley?"

"No."

Lowry's answer was short, curt. Clara knew she must not ask more. She poured coffee for Lowry, carefully into one of her good, clean cups; the hot steaming coffee smelled good to her, but was too strong for her to drink at this time of night. Lowry said, shrugging, "They bought out my father. He hadn't any choice but to sell. What's called the Depression now, nobody knew what the hell was happening then. It was like the earth opening up and swallowing some people but not others, their neighbors. Though I know it was more than that, I know there was human blame. Fuckers!"

Clara nodded vaguely. The Depression: Carleton had spoken of it sometimes, resentfully. The Depression kept farmers' prices low, so pickers were paid low. The Depression shut down factories, businesses, so there were too many pickers for the jobs, the jobs went to the cheapest labor. The Depression made Clara think of a sky of ugly thunderhead clouds, bruise-colored.

"My folks wanted to own things, lots of land. More than they could farm. So they lost it all. I'm not like them, I don't give a shit for owning things. Just my car." Lowry spoke with an air of bemusement. He sipped Clara's coffee not seeming to mind how hot it was.

"I want to own lots of things!" Clara said. "I love these things here, my rugs and pictures. The bed I don't own but the sheets and things. My own sheets . . . I have my own toothbrush. I'm going to get a certain bedspread at the store, it's kind of gold-colored, with embroidered flowers. Then, a goldfish."

Lowry laughed. "What the hell you want with a goldfish?"

Clara felt a little hurt. "I like them. At the store, it's nice to watch them. . . . I feel sorry for them, see, in the damn old tank they live in."

"Goldfish." Lowry shook his head, smiling. "What do they cost, thirty cents?"

Clara felt her face burn, but it was a pleasant sensation. She loved being teased. Nobody except Lowry teased her now, not in a long time.

"Well," Clara said, biting her lip to keep from smiling in an angry, hard way, "that woman you were with tonight—"

"Christ! You're really jealous, aren't you?"

"No! 'Cause you're with me here, and not with her. So goddamn her to hell."

"I'll see her some other time. We keep in touch."

"But right now, you're here with me."

Clara spoke with childlike obstinacy. She wanted to throw her cup of coffee into Lowry's face.

She was too restless to sit down. If she couldn't sit close beside Lowry on her bed, which he wouldn't like, she couldn't sit anywhere for long. Felt like a cat, cooped up in this small space, a cat in heat, Nancy had said the poor things really suffered, wailing and moaning if you kept them cooped up at such a time. Clara leaned against the sink seeing through the small oval mirror she'd hung on the wall Lowry behind her, lifting the coffee cup to his mouth and drinking, bemused, not even looking at her.

"Where'd you go with her? In your car?"

"Who wants to know?"

"You fucked her, did you? That's what you did?"

Lowry shrugged. Now he was looking at her, but not taking her seriously.

Like none of it matters. Fucking.

None of it matters much.

"Does she do that with other men?"

"How do I know? Possibly."

"Does she like it, too? Do women like it?"

"Sure, why else would they do it?"

Clara turned to face him, smirking. She was beating her thighs with her fists lightly, half-consciously.

" 'Cause men want them to do it, I think. So they do it. 'Cause they love the men, they want the men to love them. I think."

Lowry shrugged. His expression was casual, indifferent. An edginess in his eyes, that were fixed on Clara as if he thought her childish, someone to be humored.

"My ma used to tell me it would hurt real bad," Clara said earnestly. "But that was just to scare me, I think. Now I'm bigger, I'm different. Anyway I wouldn't care, if—"

"Clara, drop it. I told you."

"—if I loved who it was. The man."

"You don't know what the hell you're talking about, actually. You're just a kid, what—fifteen?"

Clara fumbled for a hairbrush, and began brushing her hair. Like a movie scene, this was: Bette Davis brushing her hair in quick angry strokes. Eyes glaring like a cat's.

"You don't like me. You feel fuckin sorry for me. My new dress, you didn't even notice."

"Sure I did. It's a very pretty dress."

"It isn't! It's a cheap stupid dress. It's what I can afford. And if some guy wants to buy me a dress, you tell me no. Fuck *you*."

Lowry laughed. Watching her now, more alertly.

"Damn dress is all wrinkled and wet now, I been sweatin." Clara pulled at the collar as if she wanted to rip it off. Rip the dress off herself. "I'm gonna take it off. *I can't stand it.*" Fumbling at the buttons Clara removed the dress, yanked it over her head and let it drop onto a chair. Standing now in her slip that was a soft amber color, a fabric smooth like silk, or almost, she'd purchased at the dime store at half-price. Clara was panting, tears in her eyes. She saw how Lowry stared at her, not smiling now. "Someday you might want to love me, and I'll tell you to go to hell. I'll say—'You're the wrong age. You're too old.' I'll be married then and I'll drive past your car in my car and honk my horn at you, to get out of my way."

"You do that, honey. I deserve it."

"I will! Goddamn I will."

Lowry said, in a softer voice, "Hey. I didn't mean to laugh at goldfish. If you're lonely, get a goldfish. I'll buy you as many as you want."

Clara said, wiping at her nose, "You have to buy the bowl, too. And seaweed to put in it, and fish food."

"In Woolworth's?"

"Sure! Real nice ones. Not just only gold, but black and pink and white, stripes-like. Different sizes."

Clara dared to touch Lowry's leg with her bare foot; she'd kicked off her shoes, that were hurting her feet. She smiled in her slow sly way she'd practiced in the mirror. "I washed my hair in this special stuff, just for tonight. For you. I know I look pretty sometimes, if I don't talk loud or rough. I see it in people's faces." Lowry swiped at Clara's bare foot as if he wanted to capture it but she was too quick for him. She came to sit beside him on the bed, arched her back, eager and trembling she leaned forward to kiss him. It was a movie kiss, magnified: slow and sweet and concentrated. Because she knew he would not kiss her back, it had to be her act solely. Sliding her arms around his neck as she'd never done before, and letting him feel her breasts against his arm. Pressed her cheek against his. Lowry's warm skin, the smell of his hair, his coffee-tinged breath. "You're gonna come next week, Lowry? Please?"

"Maybe."

"I'll be so lonely, if you don't."

Clara felt his hands, hesitant, on her back, on her bare skin. His thumb nudging the strap of her slip. Beneath the silky fabric she was wearing only underpants. Like a warm ripe peach her flesh felt to her, and she was in dread that he, the man, would be revulsed by it, and by her.

"If I come next week, are you going to bitch again?"

"No." Clara spoke sleepily.

"If we go out somewhere, and I leave you for a few minutes—are you going to bitch?"

"No, Lowry."

"You're gonna remember I'm your friend?"

"Yes, Lowry."

"And nobody else?—any other bastard, you won't let touch you?"

"Yes, Lowry."

"Then maybe I'll see you next week. Maybe."

After he left Clara replayed this conversation, staring at her reflection in the mirror. Close up, her face looked feverish, wounded. She was exhausted as if she'd been arguing with Lowry for hours. Her body ached, between her legs and her nipples, a dull throbbing ache that would stay with her in her sleep, she knew. She shut her eyes to recall kissing Lowry. She had done it: she'd kissed him, full on the mouth. That could never be undone. That could never be forgotten between them. She remembered the way he'd detached himself from her, when Clara was leaning against him, on the bed; his fingers careful not to hurt her, but firm, the way you'd grip an obstinate child, to bend her to your will. And, at the door, when Clara had stood on tiptoes to kiss him again, Lowry had laughed, flush-faced, and kissed her on the forehead.

She loved him, goddamn she would die for him. Goddamn him he didn't wish to know it. But she'd felt how hard he was, through his trousers. That, Lowry couldn't undo, either.

"But someday I'll get back at him," Clara said aloud.

3

Wedding! Clara was shivering with excitement.

She was in her friend Sonya's house. An old ramshackle farmhouse on the outskirts of Tintern. Always Clara liked visiting her girlfriends in their houses allowing them to think it was natural for Clara Walpole, to have friends who lived in their own houses; it was natural for Clara Walpole to have friends, girls of about her age who seemed to like her. Sonya, a big girl, was standing before a narrow vertical mirror brushing her hair, and Clara could see herself in the mirror beyond Sonya's head and shoulders. She'd told Sonya about Lowry, finally. These months, Clara hadn't been able to resist.

"What if he comes while I'm gone, and doesn't wait? What if I don't get back in time?"

"Hell with him. You got better things to do than wait around for him."

Sonya was a wide-shouldered, wide-hipped girl with bristling dark hair and a smooth, oily, olive-dark skin; her fleshy shoulders and arms exuded strength, confidence. She was brushing her hair impatiently. When she moved aside, Clara's glimmering-blond hair glowed out of the mirror. Clara stood in her good high-heeled shoes nearly as tall as Sonya, staring at her reflection and breathing lightly through parted lips. They were going to their friend Caroline's wedding, and they were both dressed up. There was an odor of something sharp and oversweet in the air, like lilac—their perfume, Sonya's, which they'd shared—and their bright clothing gave the attic room a look of frantic, festive disorder.

"Any guy you wait around for, he's gonna take you for granted."

Sonya spoke with that emphatic yet vague air of a woman watching herself in a mirror. She was a good-looking girl though her skin was coarse and her eyebrows heavy; she had a way with men, you had to admire Sonya Leznick. Clara watched her friend nervously, not wanting to be judged. Yet knowing that Sonya was right, for of course Sonya was right. Lowry had said he might drop by that day, but it hadn't been a promise, had it?—not really. *Look, kid. If I can.* She'd wakened with the conviction that, yes Lowry would be dropping by to see her that evening. After Caroline's wedding. In the mirror, despite the distortion of the cheap glass, the look of Clara's face made her blood tingle.

She was damned good-looking, she knew. With her face made up, and her hair curled and brushed. Long as she didn't get nervous, and stammering like a dope.

"I left a note on the door, if he comes early. Told him where he could find me ..."

Sonya approached the mirror and turned her head from side to side, critically. She was only eighteen but the pouting, dissatisfied slant of her brows and mouth made her appear perhaps a decade older. When Sonya smiled it was like a nudge in the ribs, a ribald surprise, so you wanted to make Sonya smile. Especially, men did.

"Caroline's real lucky, ain't she?"

"Yes." Clara spoke dreamily. It was of the wedding they were thinking, not the marriage to come. Neither would have wanted to marry Caroline's fiancé Dave Stickney. *But maybe they have to. Have to get married.* Clara wondered if, if Lowry made her pregnant, he would marry her.

It was more than two years now. Since she'd first seen him, in that tavern in Ocala, Florida. He let her kiss him sometimes, and run her hands over him. Like it was a game, the man himself wasn't exactly playing.

"You look nice, Sonya. Your hair like that."

"Shit. It ain't what I wanted."

"No, it's nice. Let me—" Clara took the hairbrush from her friend, and gave Sonya's thick, manelike hair several deft swipes. She wanted to hide her face in Sonya's hair sometimes, or maybe just to lift it to her face, to smell. Reminded her of, what? who?— maybe Nancy. The way Nancy had slung her arm around Clara's shoulders that time, running with her in the mud.

"And like this, Sonya, see? So the bangs don't hang down straight."

Sonya smirked cross-eyed at her reflection. Still, she liked it that Clara primped her. A feeling passed between the girls, that they could trust each other. A man, a boy—you couldn't trust them. Sonya was always saying she couldn't trust her bitchy sisters, either.

An automobile horn sounded out front. The girls descended the stairs from the attic, which were so steep they had to make their way sideways in their high heels. Clara was conscious of her smooth silken legs and the way her dress, a bright electric blue, clung to her body. She dreaded Lowry laughing at this dress, that had a kind of cobwebby netting over the bodice, and a rhinestone pin the size of a silver dollar. She knew he'd laugh at her white gloves.

White gloves! Clara had to laugh, herself. She was giddy with happiness. Infatuated with everything about herself and about this day, a wedding on a balmy Saturday in May. Sonya pushed Clara along to the front door of the house which was a door the Leznick family rarely used except for visitors, themselves rare. "Hey, how do I look?" Sonya asked, rolling her eyes. "Really."

Clara told her she looked beautiful. Really.

———

Beautiful, wasn't it beautiful! Isn't the bride beautiful!

Like Clara's head was trapped inside a bell. Ringing, ringing the same words *beautiful beautiful* which she heard uttered in her own voice, too. After the ceremony in the little gray shingle-board church, and after the bride and groom had driven away in their crepe-paper-festooned car.

Clara decided, no I can't. Can't stay for the reception.

In the church she'd had to grind the heels of her hands into her eyes. Christ, why was she crying! Not her but Caroline was getting married, four months pregnant the rumor was. Not her but another.

Blurred faces. "Clara, hello!"—"It's Clara, isn't it? Hello, dear."—"Clara? Where are you going?"

These people, mostly women, she knew from the store. They were customers, they recognized her face and her pale blond hair. They recognized her aloneness. *That Clara, in the five-and-ten. Doesn't that girl have any people?* Even as the minister spoke in a warm smothering voice of God, Jesus Christ, love, even as the organist pumped away at the organ, Clara was hearing *White trash. That one is white trash.* They were kind to her in that way you might be kind to a dog with three legs.

Oh, she hated them. Even Sonya sometimes, she hated. Because they were kind to her, they pitied her. In these pews, in which families crowded. In this place where it all became clear who was alone, and who was not. She did hate them. She hated their eyes on her. Like Lowry. Sons of bitches she did not need them, any of them. She needed only Lowry.

Sonya said, surprised, hurt, "Clara! You can't leave yet. Hey—"

"I can walk. I don't need a ride."

"But, Clara—"

Oh, why didn't they let her go! It was enough that Caroline tossed her bridal bouquet in Clara's direction, and another girl had leapt for it, quick as a long-beaked heron snatching a fish out of shallow water. It was enough that Caroline had hugged Clara so tight the girls' faces nearly collided. "You'll be next, Clara. I have a feeling."

The reception was being held in the minister's house next door. The minister's wife, mannish and bossy, stood on the front porch and waved people inside. "You, where are you going? You in the blue dress!" she yelled.

In a few minutes Clara was free. She hurried along the road, walking in the middle so her shoes wouldn't get dirty. They were already flecked a little with mud. Around her, sunlight shone with that peculiar wet intensity it has in spring, and if she were to lift her eyes from the road she would see the range of mountains to the north glimmering and dazzling in the light—the boundary to another, savage, unpopulated world. The Eden River had carved for them this deep, long valley out of the foothills, and to the south and east hills rolled for miles, endlessly. Clara had always had the strange idea, in this part of the country, that the very sweep of the land did not let people stay small and allow them to hide, but somehow magnified them. Here one's eye was naturally driven to the horizon, to the farthest distance, run up against that uncertain boundary where the misty sky and the damp mountains ran together like the blending of heaven and earth in one of Clara's cheap little prints.

She heard an automobile coming up behind her. She supposed she had to stand aside, to let it pass. So she made a waving gesture and turned to the side of the road, walking cautiously, both arms outstretched as if to help her keep her balance. The road was muddiest at the side. In the car was a man with dark hair that had turned partly gray. He had a severe, critical look that made Clara want to turn away in shame.

"Would you like a ride?" he said.

Clara smiled feebly. "I don't mind walking, I'm used to it," she said.

His car slowed to a stop. She did not know whether he was afraid to splash her with mud or if he was really stopping. She saw that he had a large, heavy head, that his eyes were framed with tiny creases that gave his face a depth she had never noticed in anyone else.

Then the car struck her eye: it was new, big. It must have been expensive. She narrowed her eyes at the sight of it and wondered who this man was.

"I couldn't stay for the reception either," he said. "I'll drive you back to town."

She did not answer at once. His voice was an ordinary voice, but behind it something was pushing, prodding. "Get in," he said. Clara felt the warm sunlight on her face and the image of herself she had been reserving for Lowry released itself: she felt strong and her body coursed with strength. She smiled at the man and said, "All right."

When she went around the front of the car she reached out with her white glove to almost touch the hood, in a half-magical gesture. She opened the door herself and stepped up into the car. It smelled rich and dark and cool inside. The man wore a dark gray suit and a necktie with tiny silver stripes in it. Clara thought at once that no woman had picked that out for him. He had picked it out for himself.

"Are you a friend of Davey's?" she said shyly.

"Yes."

He drove on. Clara looked around and saw that the countryside was changed a little by the windows of this car: the cider mill and the empty fields and the houses set back from the road looked clearer, sharper. Clara thought that sunshine revealed everything cruelly—the drab little town had looked better in winter, hidden by dirt-streaked slivers of melting snow.

"You can let me out anywhere," Clara said. She saw that Lowry's car was not parked out front. But she could not control her excitement. In the future lay everything—everything. Lowry in the doorway of her room, Lowry in her arms, his face, his voice, his calm stubborn will that was a wall she kept hurtling herself against—"Thanks very much," she said, polite as any child. She was about to get out, but her excitement prompted her to talk. She chatted the way she'd chatted for other men: "It was nice that you stopped because now my new shoes didn't get all muddy. . . . Wasn't it a nice day today? I'm glad Caroline and Davey are married and happy and everything. . . . Thanks very much for the ride."

"Do you live in town here? Where?"

She glanced at him, still smiling. "Upstairs there," she said, pointing. It somehow pleased her that the man bent a little to look.

"Your whole family lives there?"

Clara hesitated. "I live alone," she said, looking down. Then she said shyly, "I work at the five-and-ten there and got the whole day off today, so did Sonya, just for the wedding. And somebody's coming to visit me today, a friend of mine. . . . It's all so nice, the day is so nice. It smells nice when the sun comes out. . . ."

She laughed in embarrassment at her own joy.

When she ran upstairs she saw there on her door the note she'd left: "Dear Lowry, I am at a wedding and will be back soon please wait for me Love Clara." Sonya had helped her write it. She had hoped Lowry might come and discover it and be pleased to think that she had written it all herself, that she had learned so much from his teaching.

She waited in her room.

Hours passed, the afternoon passed. She thought of her friends out at the reception. But she had things to do: sewing, mending. There were two stuffed dolls on her bed now, made of old scraps. Clara did not take off her dress and shoes but stayed the way she was, ceremonial and uncomfortable, waiting for him. She sang to herself, breaking off now and then as her heart tripped violently over some small obscure sound that was never explained and never led to anything else. Her bed had a pink bedspread on it now. On her dressing table were bottles and tubes and glittering, gleaming things she was proud of. Sonya's boyfriend had driven her and Sonya to a larger town about twenty miles away where they went to a store that had clothing just for women and children—nothing else—and Clara bought a sweater there; it was folded neatly in one of the bureau drawers and she had the drawer pulled out so that she could look at it.

Her card table was now covered with a scalloped cloth. On it lay Clara's white gloves and her pale blue purse, waiting. They continued to lie there in that alert, expectant way even after Clara herself had given up.

4

It was as if Clara were living in two worlds and two times: the one
bounded by her room and her job and the drugstore and the now-
familiar limits of Tintern, and the other spread out aimlessly across
the country, dragged back and forth with Lowry in an invisible, insatiable striving. She did not understand him, but she sensed something familiar about the hardness with which he lived. It was her
father's hardness brought into sharper focus.

"But what the hell do you care about him?" Sonya and Ginny
complained. Her friends kept up long monotonous arguments
against him, annoyed by the clammy infatuation Clara did not try
to hide. Over at Ginny's house, playing with the baby, Clara would
have the sudden catastrophic vision of this baby as her own and
Lowry as its father, but a father who never stayed in one place and
who wouldn't know his own baby—no father at all. She felt icy with
apprehension, as if she were inching out too far on something precarious. It was not that she was afraid of losing control of herself or
of her knowledge of how things were; like everyone she knew, there
was no speculation in her about what was real and what wasn't. It
was only the secondary, underlying conviction that she was being
betrayed so coarsely by her wishes that frightened her. She hated
this backlashing tendency in herself that cut away at the simplicity
of her life. "My mother worked all her life and had kids," she told
people. "Anything better than that is all right with me." But she did
not quite believe this herself.

She loved Ginny's children and her love spread out to include
Ginny herself and her husband Bob, a man of about twenty-two
who was temporarily out of work. He had pumped gas at a gas station but the station had burned down. Ginny was one of those
women who expressed themselves in bursts of generosity, with
food or affection or anger; she had a round high-colored face that
put Clara in mind of country girls she'd seen walking on back roads
all her life. Her husband was thin and gave the impression of lung-
ing when he walked or reached for things. His silence and the passivity with which he watched his own children gave no indication of

his impatience. "Gonna get a car from a guy," he'd brag to Clara, and grabbed her by the back of the neck to make it more emphatic. When he kissed her she thought in a panic that Lowry would find out. She pushed him away. "What the hell are you doing?" she said, making a face as if she had tasted something bad. They all must have liked her because she could take nothing seriously—Ginny's husband and other men who bothered her, married or unmarried—as if, in having committed herself to a hopeless infatuation, she was therefore kinder and more forgiving with them.

The less she saw of Lowry, the more she thought of him. When he did come, his face and voice were less real than what she imagined. She felt as if she had loved and married him and endured an entire lifetime, while Lowry himself was still young and indifferent. "I already have a boyfriend," she explained to men who did not believe her, but she did not think to extend this perfunctory defense to the man who had driven her back to town from the wedding—and it happened that he showed up again in a few days, in the five-and-ten. It would never have occurred to her to turn away from him, because she understood that this man was not like anyone else she knew. He did not want the same thing from her.

"How long have you been here, living alone?" he said. She told him, toying with a shining pair of scissors on the counter. Before this kind of man—one who "owned" things—she was shy and a little stubborn; she sensed that what gave her power with simpler men would have no effect on him. "Do you really live alone?"

"I'm of age," Clara said. She flicked her hair back out of her eyes and met the man's steady, gray, impenetrable stare. "I take care of myself."

"Do you go to church?"

She lifted one shoulder in a gesture of indifference and then stopped before the gesture was completed—it was better to say nothing bad about religion because it might do her harm one of these days. "Well, my folks never went to church."

"That's too bad." His hands rested on the edge of the counter and were perfectly still. Clara noticed things like hands: her own were always doing something, Lowry's fingers were always tapping impatiently, Sonya was always fooling with her hair. "At your age you need guidance. You need a religious foundation for your life."

"Yes, sir," Clara said.

Two tiny lines appeared between her eyebrows. She said, feeling a little embarrassed, "But I can take care of myself." This came out more aggressively than she had wanted, so she softened the effect of her words by brushing her heavy hair off one shoulder and letting it fall loose on her back. "Where I come from," she said softly, "you learn to take care of yourself when you're a little kid."

He leaned forward as if he could not quite hear her. "Where do you come from?"

She bit her lip. She almost smiled. "Oh, from anywhere. From all over." It was not flirtation, though it had the style of flirtation; she stared at him seriously to make him understand this. "We didn't have no particular home, we traveled on the season."

His silence indicated that he knew what she meant. Then he said, in a harsh, paternal tone, "People should have done more for you than they have. Society has failed you."

"Society—"

"There are probably hundreds of girls like you—" He reddened slightly. "Have you gone to school?"

"Oh, there was some woman in asking about me, from the school board here or something, I don't know. She asked me did I go to the doctor this year or to the dentist, things like that. Somebody said they could take me out of here and put me in some home or reformatory or something—but they can't because I'm of age. Can they do that?"

"I don't know."

She felt a little disappointed at this answer. "Well, look, I don't want no home with other girls, I want everything I have right now the way it is and I want to be free and the hell with charity. My folks never took no charity, nothing. My pa—"

"I don't know the county board," he said quickly.

"Yes, well, that's all right. I was just saying." Clara lowered her gaze. The man inhaled deeply. Clara was conscious of other people in the store either watching them or very carefully not watching them, but they were not forced into any kind of unity because of this. They stood alone, awkward and a little resentful, as if each had somehow failed the other.

Clara said, "Did you want to buy something?"

"My wife wanted some thread," he told her, and already his eye was running along the rows of thread. "Gold thread—"

Clara looked through the spools of yellow thread. It was smooth, smooth, packed down to an incredibly satiny smoothness; it was delightful to touch. "What about this one?" she said dubiously. He nodded and she saw the dark yellow transformed to "gold." "Is this all, mister?"

"Yes."

He made no move to leave but leaned on the counter, rubbing his hands against the lower part of his face. She saw that he wore a wedding band. What kind of a man would wear a ring? she thought at once. His hands were like any man's except for the ring, and the edges of his white shirt by his wrists and the dark sleeves of his suit coat. He was wearing a suit and tie in Tintern on a Wednesday. Clara believed she had seen him somewhere before having come to Tintern, or perhaps a picture of him: why did she think that? He summoned up in her blood a vague trembling response, inarticulate. She did not resent the way he looked but she resented a little the way he made everything around him look cheap and inadequate. Lowry, beside this man, would not stand straight enough; Clara would want to be poking him to make him stand straight. This man's shoulders and back were straight and firm, and nothing could tease him into looking any other way. She had no idea how old he was.

"My name is Curt Revere," he said.

"My name is Clara."

"Clara what?"

She rubbed the damp palm of her hand along the spools of thread, turning them slowly. "Oh, just Clara," she said. One of the spools jerked out of place and rolled down to the edge of the counter. It would have fallen to the floor but the man caught it.

"Did you run away from home?" he said.

"There wasn't any home, how could I run away from it," Clara said sullenly.

He waited for her to continue. She stared at the spool of thread he was holding. "What the hell business is it of yours!" she said suddenly. Her face felt as if it had cracked. She began to cry. He fitted the spool back into place, taking some time. Clara wept bitterly without bothering to turn aside or hide her face. She was used to crying. "You leave off askin me those things," she said in a child's voice, and as she looked up at him the memory flashed through her mind of where she'd heard his name before: Lowry had mentioned it and that man had mentioned it. Caroline's husband worked for him. The corners of her eyes ached as she tried to get him into focus. There was something wrong, something terrible about him, she was on the brink of a precipice, her whole life could be ruined: he had money, power, a name. The very air about him seemed to tremble. He had a name that people knew.

"Well," he said gently, "if you don't have any last name then you don't have any. Maybe you lost it somewhere."

He tried to smile but was not too good at it. After a moment he moved uncomfortably, a little abruptly. Clara felt paralyzed by her recollection of who he was, as if he were an enemy she had been hiding from all her life. She tried to remember where she had seen him before, or what she had seen that he reminded her of. . . .

"I could suggest that they stop bothering you, the people from the county board," he said. Clara, hearing this, drew her hands together in a meek, prayerful gesture. "You are obviously able to take care of yourself, no matter what your age—"

"I'm over sixteen."

"Yes." He paused. Clara waited stiffly for him to continue. "In my car the other day you said something about—about— You said you were happy. You seem to be happy. You're obviously able to take care of yourself—"

"I'm happy," Clara said rigidly. "I can take care of myself."

"You said you like the weather. . . . You were happy." He smiled a little. His smile was the kind directed to dogs and babies; it did not anticipate any response. Now he noticed the thread in his fingers and said, "How much is this?"

"Five cents."

He took out a coin and handed it to her. "You want a bag or

something?" Clara said. He said no, he'd put it in his pocket. As soon as it dropped in something touched Clara, some near-recognition. She felt different at once. "Your wife is sewing something made out of gold," she said, with one of these mysterious spurts of daring she was to have several times in her life. She smiled. "Somebody told me you lived on a big farm," she said, talkative now that he was ready to leave, "they said how nice it was—lots of hills and trees and horses— Nobody has big farms around here, but if they do they're land-poor; you're different. I don't know why," she said, moving along the counter in the direction of the door, urging him along by running her hand on the edge of the counter with a playful meticulous precision. "I don't know much about it because my folks never had a farm or any place that you could settle down on, but anyway the ones that did lost them—the banks took them or something. I don't understand any of that. But you, you didn't lose yours, I'm glad for that." She reached the end of the counter and leaned a little forward; for the first time she was conscious of her bare arms and the pale gold hairs on them. In the sunlight she would be sleek and golden. She looked at her arms and then slowly up at Revere.

Revere stared at her. He seemed not to have heard any of her words, but only the musing, singsong tone of her voice. Clara came around from inside the counter and walked with him to the door, as if she were seeing him out of a place that belonged to her. Outside, his car was parked by the walk. Two children were in it. One of the back doors was swinging idly open and a boy of about eight sat with his legs out; another boy was struggling with him, trying to slide his arm around his neck. They argued in low, hissing voices, as if they had been forbidden to make any noise. Clara said, "Do you have any other children besides them?" "Another boy, two," Revere said. She shaded her eyes. She and Revere stood in the doorway. Clara had the door open, holding it there with her body. She was wearing a pale yellow dress whose skirt now fluttered about her knees in the wind. "That's real nice," she said. But she said it sadly. Revere said nothing and she did not look at him. Silence fell upon them as it had in the store, but she felt somehow linked to him by it—they were both looking out of this silence at his children, who were fighting with each other and had not noticed them.

When she went back inside, Mr. Mulch was waiting for her. He sat most of the day in the back room, drinking, and came out into the alley to watch the Negro boys unload things from trucks that stopped a few times a month. He wore a white shirt and a tie and showed by his dress that he was different from other Tintern people; he had a malleable reddened face. "How much did he spend?" he said. Clara smelled about him the odor of the store itself—something sour and unused. "Five cents," Clara said, smirking. "Five cents," he repeated. He almost smiled. "That goddamn cheap bastard. That dirty son of a bitch of a cheap bastard. Five cents." "Maybe he never came in to buy anything," Clara said. He seemed to catch her words as if they were a trifling little blow directed at him, and he jerked back his head in a gesture of mock surprise and mock humor. "Then what did he come in here for?" he said.

5

"I'm thinking of how quiet it is."

"That isn't anything to think about."

"I can hear it, all this quiet. I think about it a lot."

They were standing on a bridge, looking down at the river. It was July now and the river had begun to sink. Clara leaned against the rust-flecked railing and stretched out her arms as if appealing to something—the river disappointed her with its slow-moving water, its film of sleek opaque filth. Its banks were far apart but the river itself had dwindled to a low, flat channel in the center of rocks that looked made of some white, startling substance that would flake off at the touch, like chalk.

"It's real quiet here," Clara said. "It's like this all over but you don't hear it."

Lowry kicked some pebbles off the bridge. Not much of a splash: the pebbles just disappeared into the water. Clara waited for him to speak. But it was like waiting for that splash—the more you listened for it, the less you heard.

On both sides of the river the banks lifted to a twisted jumble of trees and bushes. These banks eased in to obscure the river's path, twisting and writhing out of sight. "Rivers go like this," Lowry explained, making a line in the dust with a stick. "First they go straight like this; they run fast. Then they get slow and go like a snake. They pick up dirt and junk on the corners then and slow down. So they meander more. They meander bigger and fatter until this happens." And he surprised her by running a straight line through the very center of the curves, jabbing the stick in the dust hard to show the first river back again—the straight line.

"Is that the truth, honest?" Clara said lazily.

Lowry tossed the stick over the side of the bridge. It seemed to fall slowly and hit the surface of the water without a sound. They watched it float under the bridge and away.

"This river is dirty," Clara said. "By the other side, there, it's awful dirty. People let all kinds of junk drain into it, sewer junk, Sonya told me. That makes me sick."

The heat seemed to flatten out against them. Clara shook her hair out of her eyes. This silence of Lowry's was just like the silence she always listened to and so it did not surprise her. She pressed her fingers against her eyes and made the sunlight do tricks for her; she'd done that on the buses and trucks they had taken, years ago. If a person wanted something bad enough, Clara thought, he should get it. If he wished for something hard enough, he should get it. She took away her hands and the placid river returned, unchanged. She looked up at Lowry, who was leaning back against the railing; he smiled. His hair had bleached even lighter in the summer sun. His face was tanned and his eyes were a mild thoughtful blue; he looked as if he had two parts to him, the outside part and the inside part that wanted to get out. She supposed that when he was anywhere his eyes showed he was thinking of another place, and when he was with anyone he would be thinking of someone else. His trouble was never to be where he wanted to be.

"You don't have much to say, do you?" she said.

"Might be I don't."

"What did you do with yourself since you came out here last?"

"Oh, one thing or another."

"You're awful secret."

"You're awful nosy, little girl," he said. His smile showed that he was using only the top part of himself with her. Clara would have liked to seize him and stare into his eyes, deep into his eyes, to locate the kernel at the very center that was Lowry—why was he such a mystery? Or was he an ordinary man, the way all men would be if they were free and weren't held down? She could half close her eyes and imagine herself moving toward him invisibly, trying to embrace him in an invisible embrace, and Lowry dancing forever out of her grasp.

"Do me a favor?" Clara said.

"What?"

"Look at me serious. Say my name serious."

He was lighting a cigarette. He stopped sucking at it and said, "O.K. Clara."

"Is that serious as you can get?"

"Clara. Clara," he said, the end of his breath making the word droop suddenly into a seriousness that was dismal. It struck Clara that her name, which was the sound for her in people's minds, had nothing to do with her at all and was really a stupid name.

"I wish I was someone else. I mean, had another name," Clara said. "Like Marguerite."

"Why that?"

"I heard that name . . . somewhere."

Each time Lowry came to visit she had to worry about his leaving too soon. It was a tugging thing, the way he would get restless and be ready to leave even before he had thought of it. Clara always thought of it, dreading it, and ideas came to her of ways to put off that time as long as possible. She might have been in a contest only with herself. "Let's go walk down there," she said. He was agreeable. His car was parked off the bridge and up on the side of the road, a new car. They passed it without comment and climbed down the embankment. A few feet from the bottom, Clara jumped. A shock went through her when she landed flat on her feet. It did not hurt: the shock was that she had so solid, so responsive a body and that the earth had pressed back so hard against it, yielding up nothing. Lowry came slipping and sliding down, holding the burning cigarette in his hand as if he were a city person awkward in this business but not giving in to it.

They headed for the riverbank. In July there were many kinds of insects, so Clara stepped carefully through the weeds. "It's real pretty here," she said shyly. "Nicer than up on the bridge." She looked over to where they had been standing and could not imagine herself and Lowry up there together. "Don't you like how peaceful the river is, Lowry?"

"It's nice."

As if to ruin its peacefulness, he picked up a flat stone and threw it sideways. The stone skipped three, four times, then sank.

"Did you do that when you were a little boy?"

"Sure."

She smiled to think of it, even though she could not quite believe he had ever been a little boy. She picked up a flat stone and tried to throw it as he did, slanting her wrist sideways, but it sank with a gulping splash. "Girls can't do that," Lowry said. He walked on and she followed him. Down by the riverbank there was a path fishermen used. They followed it along and walked away from the bridge. Clara heard, past the noises of the insects, the silence that covered this whole countryside. She felt as if she were walking through it and disturbing it.

"Don't you ever get lonely, Lowry?"

"Nope."

"Do you do a lot of thinking?"

"Nope."

She laughed and slid her arm through his. "Can't you say anything but nope?"

"I don't think much," Lowry said seriously, "but there are pieces of things in my mind. Broken pieces. They buzz around like wasps and bother me."

Clara glanced up at him as if he'd admitted something too intimate.

"But I don't worry."

"I don't either," said Clara.

He laughed and she pressed herself against him. "Look," she said, "can I ask you something?"

"What?"

"How come you're here with me right now?"

He shrugged his shoulders.

Clara ran from him. She jumped down into the creek bed, where it was dry. "Look at this, Lowry," she said. It was part of an old barbed-wire fence, lying frigid and coated over with bleached grass. Lowry's look said clearly, So what? Clara said, "You would wonder how things get where they are. This thing here—think where it used to be. Over there's a bicycle tire somebody owned. Wouldn't you like to know how things end up where they do?"

"Maybe."

"They get in the water, then drift down here. . . . I'm so happy," Clara said exuberantly, hugging herself, "but I don't know why. I love everything the way it is. I love how things look." She actually felt her eyes sting with tears. Up on the bank Lowry sat down heavily and smoked his cigarette. He wore the faded brown trousers he had been wearing all summer and a tan shirt with rolled-up sleeves; he brought his knees up to lean on them and his ankles collapsed themselves in the grass, so that the outside of his feet were pressed flat against the ground. He looked as if he would never get up again and never care to. "You don't listen to me!" Clara said angrily. "Goddamn you anyway!"

His gaze was mildly blue. She saw his teeth flash in a brief smile.

"You think I'm just something you picked up on the road, and when you can't find some bitch to lay around with you come around here and visit!— Oh, Christ," Clara said, heaving a large stone out into the water. She laughed and her shoulders rose in a long lazy shrug. "What do you think about when you're with them, then?"

"Clara, I don't think about anything."

"When you're with them?"

"Sometimes I don't remember who they are."

She liked that, but she did not let on. Instead she picked up another stone and threw it out into the water. It sank at once. "But I'm happy anyway," she said. "That's because I'm stupid. If I was smart I wouldn't be happy when everything is so rotten."

"What's rotten?" he said at once.

"Oh, nothing, nothing," she said, waving to dismiss him. She flicked her long hair out of her eyes. It fell far down her back and she'd washed it the day before, somehow expecting him to come, so she knew it must shine in the sunlight. She knew she was pretty and now she wanted to be beautiful. "When things get better I will be beautiful," she promised herself. If Lowry would stand still long enough and she could climb up into his arms and sleep there forever, the two of them entwined and not needing to look anywhere else, then she could relax: then she would grow up, she would become beautiful. She was standing now on a large flat rock near the water, which flowed in a fairly rapid stream in the center of the riverbed. She leaned over to see herself. There was a trembling vague image, not hers. She felt as if love were a condition she would move into the way you moved into a new house or crossed the boundary into a new country. And not just this one-sided love, either; she had enough of that right now. But the kind of love held out to her in the comic books and romance magazines she was able now to read for herself, which she and Sonya traded back and forth wistfully: love that would transform her and change her forever. It had nothing to do with the way other girls got pregnant and fat as cheap balloons—that wasn't the kind of love she meant. The only real love could be between her and Lowry. You couldn't imagine any real love between Sonya, for instance, and her boyfriend who was married. They never felt about each other the way she and Lowry would. . . .

"I remember you that night way back in Florida," Clara said. "I think about that a lot. Who were you with then?"

Lowry shrugged.

She had thought of it to get her mind rid of that memory of Lowry and everything that came with it: going back to his room with him. If she got her mind stuck on that she would be miserable to him, and maybe he was casting his mind around for some excuse to get away from her earlier—here it was about six o'clock and they would have to get some supper. Clara had told him she would make it herself. A tiny churning sensation began in her stomach and subsided at once, at the thought of the food she had bought that might still be there the next morning. She said, "I'm going to walk in here.

It's cool." The stream of water was deep on her side. She could look right through to its stony bottom.

"You're going to wade in that?"

She kicked off her shoes. Her feet were tough from going barefoot so much in the summer. Clara stepped into the water and was surprised at how warm it was on top. "I like to wade," she said. "I used to do it when I was a kid." It was the kind of remark other girls probably said; Clara did not really think of herself as lying. The edginess in her voice must have made Lowry conscious of this, because when she glanced around he was looking at her. "What about you, did you play in cricks when you were a kid?"

"I grew up too fast," Lowry said.

She moved slowly through the water, staring down at her pale feet. Her legs were wet up past the knee. She pulled the skirt of her dress up higher. At first her legs were cool where they were wet, then the sun got to them and made them burn. She had to keep flicking her hair out of her eyes when she turned back to speak to Lowry. "I grew up fast, too. I'm just as old as you are if you look at it right."

He made a snorting sound.

"Damn you, don't laugh at me," she said. She bent to pull something out of the water—a barrel stave encrusted with scum and tiny snail-like things. She dropped it at once.

"Lowry," Clara said, "did you love your family?"

"I don't know. No."

"Why not?"

"I don't know."

Clara lifted one foot out of the water, gingerly. "I loved my family. I couldn't help it."

"Well, I was born able to help such things," he said. He shifted around, straightening out one leg. She thought there was something uneasy in his voice but she did not want to be so conscious, so meticulous with him. She walked farther out, gathering her skirt up around her thighs. Lowry flicked his cigarette out from him and it landed on the dry riverbed. "I never could see what it was—things between other people," he said seriously. "I mean invisible things. Ties that held them together no matter what, like getting flung up on the beach and dragged out again and flung up again, always to-gether. —Don't walk any farther out, you want to fall in? I'm not coming in after you."

"I'm all right."

"I'd like to have everything I owned in one bag and take it with me. I don't want things to tie me down. If I owned lots of things—like my father did—then they'd get in the way and I wouldn't see clearly. Once you own things you have to be afraid of them. Of los-ing them."

"I wouldn't mind that," Clara said sullenly.

He did not seem to have heard her. "If I have to kill myself for something, I want to know what it is, at least. I don't want it handed to me. I don't want it to turn into a houseful of furniture or acres of land you have to worry about farming—the hell with all that."

Clara glanced back at him. He was just far enough away so that she could not see whether those tiny wrinkles had appeared again around his mouth. "You're getting beyond me," she said, afraid to hear anything more that he had to say.

He was silent for a moment. Then he said, in a different voice, "Clara, are you about done messing around in there?"

She looked up at the sky, feeling her hair fall down long and heavy on her back. In Lowry's voice there was something she had heard once before but now, in her wonder, could not quite recall. She closed her eyes and felt the sun hot against her face.

"Come on out from there," Lowry said.

"Go to hell. You're bossing me around."

"Come on, Clara."

"Now you called me Clara. How'd you know that was my name?"

"You're going to walk where the water's going fast, and fall in."

"I am not."

"Well, I'm not going to carry you out, ma'am."

"Nobody asked you to."

"We should be getting back. . . ."

"I'm in no hurry."

"It might be I am."

"You aren't, either," Clara said, letting one shoulder rise and fall lazily. But she stepped out of the water and onto the dried rocks, which had a curious texture now beneath her cold feet, like cloth. She spread her toes on the whitened rocks as if they were fingers grasping at something. Then she saw, between her toes, a dark filmy soft thing like a worm. "Jesus!" Clara said, kicking. She jumped backward and landed on the other foot and kicked again violently. "Get it off, Lowry!" she screamed. "Lowry—help— a bloodsucker—"

She ran at him blindly and he caught her. Everything was speeded up, even Lowry's laugh, and he was still laughing when he picked the thing off. With a snapping motion of his wrist he flicked it away. Clara knew that her face was drained white and that her muscles had let go, as if that bloodsucker had really sucked away all her blood. She lay back, sobbing, and when her eyes came into focus she saw that Lowry was not smiling any longer.

He bent down by her. "You oughtn't to have done that," he said, not smiling, and Clara stared bluntly into his face as if he were a stranger stopping out of nowhere. He kissed her, and while she tried to get her breath back from that he moved on top of her, and she remembered in a panic that he had done this before, yes, years ago, and it all came back to her like a slap in the face, something to wake her up. "Lowry—" she said in a voice all amazement, entirely removed from whatever was giving him such energy and half-trying to push him away—but everything that might have shot into clarity was ruined by his damp searching mouth and his hand thrust under her, getting her ready in a way she only now realized she had to be gotten ready. In amazement the blue sky stared back down at her, wide and impersonal, deep with the unacknowledged gazes of girls like Clara who have nowhere else to look, the earth having betrayed them; the blue shuddered with a panic that was not fear but just panic, the reaction of the body and not the mind. Her mind was awake and skipping about everywhere, onto Lowry and past him and even onto the Lowry of a minute before who had surprised her so, trying to figure out just what had happened in his mind to make him turn into this Lowry—filling out the gestures of her imagination without having to ask what they might have been. It would never have seemed to Clara that love could be such a surprise, so strange, that she could just lie limp and have it done to her and never be clear enough to anticipate any more even when she had tried to figure out what they would all be years in advance— then her amazement turned into pain and she cried out angrily against the side of his face.

She felt him pushing in her, inside her, with all the strength he had kept back from her for years. She pulled at his shirt and then at his flesh under the shirt, as if trying to distract him as well as herself from what he was doing. Lowry's hot ragged breath came against her face and she caught a glimpse of his eyes, not fixed upon her and not ready yet to see anything, and for the first time the kernel behind those eyes gave a hint of itself. She groaned and tightened her arms around his neck, hard, and Lowry kissed her with his hot open mouth and she gasped and sucked in his breath, squirming with this new agony and waiting for it to end, thinking it couldn't last much longer with a kind of baffled and staring astonishment— until Lowry, who was always so calm and slow and seemed to calculate out how many steps would be necessary to take him from one spot to another, groveled on her with his face twisted like a rag in a parody of agony, and could not control what he did to her. She felt as if her body were being driven into the ground, hammered into it. She felt as if it were being dislodged from her brain and she would never get the two together again. Then everything broke and she felt his muscles go rigid, locking himself to her and waiting, suspended between breaths that must have made his throat ache. A soft, surprised sound escaped him that was nothing Lowry would ever have made, and Clara let her head fall back onto his arm without even knowing she had been holding it up and waiting for him to stop.

He lay on top of her and his chest heaved. Now that the day was clear again she touched his hand, smoothed his hair off his forehead. Between her legs her flesh was alive with a pain that was so sharp and burning she could not quite believe in it. She felt as if he had gone after her with a knife. She felt as if she had been opened up and hammered at with a cruelty that made no sense because she could not see what it meant. That logic was secret in Lowry's body. In her imagination—lying sleepless in her bed at night, or dreaming behind the store counter—she had known everything Lowry felt and had felt it along with him, because that was part of her happiness; but when it had really happened it was all a surprise. He had made love to her and it was all over and she knew nothing about it, no more than this pain that kept her veins throbbing.

"Jesus, Lowry," Clara sobbed, "I must be bleeding—" He brought his damp face around and his lips brushed hers, but she pushed him away. She tried to sit up. The pain had shattered now into smaller pains that shot up toward her stomach. Lowry wiped his face with both hands and, still breathing hard, lay down beside her. He was like a man who has fallen from a great height. Clara lay back. Tears were running down both sides of her face, into her mouth. Whether the sky was in focus or not she could not tell. Lowry lay beside her, on his back. Her body burned where he had been. She thought that she would never get over it and that he would never be able to do this to her again. So she lay very still with her pain, as if what she felt had more power over either of them than any other feeling she had showed.

Finally Lowry said, "Now you're not a kid, sweetheart."

She wept bitterly. "I never needed to grow up," she said. "I never needed to be gone after with a knife."

"I'm sorry."

"What the hell made you do it?"

He laughed a little. He seemed to be asking her permission to laugh, by the sound of it. "I thought you loved me," he said.

Clara sat up and smoothed her hair back from her face. She took hold of it and twisted it up and back, away from her neck. The perspiration on the back of her neck made her shiver. She looked down at Lowry, who was lying now with his arms behind his head. He smiled at her, then his smile broadened. Clara's face remained rigid. "If I said I loved you, could be I didn't know what I was talking about," she said.

"Could be you don't yet."

She bent her head back again suddenly to look at the sky, but did not see it. In spite of the pain she felt a sensation of joy, something unexpected she didn't want Lowry to see yet. "So, after two years," she said. "You wouldn't ever do it when I was ready, or when

I wanted you to or thought I wanted you to. That would have been too easy."

"I didn't want to do it, honey."

"If you find yourself not wanting to do it again, let me know," she said. There was a twist to her mouth she'd copied from Sonya. "I can get something else to do that day."

He smiled at her toughness. "It doesn't mean anything, honey."

"I know that."

"I'm serious. It doesn't mean anything except what it is."

"I knew you would go on to say something like that."

She tried to get up but froze. A sigh escaped her that was a sound of regret for everything, but not serious regret. The only thing that was serious was the pain and she knew now that it would not last long.

Lowry put his arms around her waist. From behind, he embraced her and pressed his forehead against her back; she could feel him there, and she turned a little as if she were listening to his thought with her body. "You are such a bastard," she said. "Do you know that?" His fingers locked together. He lay still. Clara looked down at her bare feet and blinked when she remembered how it had all happened—and there was the spot between her toes, pink from where the blood had been but now smeared around, a tiny dot of blood that was all that was left from the bloodsucker.

Lowry said, "I'm not going to marry you. You know that."

"All right."

"I can't think of you that way. Don't you think of me that way either."

"All right."

"I'm ten, eleven years older than you, sweetheart. . . ." His words sounded sad. Clara glanced down at his fingers, which were making wrinkles in the cloth of her dress; but it was probably ruined anyhow. Her eyes ran along down her thighs to her legs and feet and back up again. She smiled slightly. She would have drawn in a great exultant breath, except Lowry's embrace kept her back. "How do you feel?" Lowry said.

"You must have made me bleed."

"Does it hurt bad?"

"No, it's all right."

"No, really, does it hurt?"

He straightened up and turned her head to him. He kissed her and Clara made a slight gesture of impatience, mock disgust, then he held her head in his hands and kissed her again. She felt his tongue against her lips and smiled while she kissed him. She said, drawing away, "You never kissed me like that before. You're going to love me if you don't watch out."

"That might be," Lowry said.

It was late when they drove back to Tintern, between ten and eleven. Clara's hair was tangled and her face drawn with exhaustion; she lay with her head against Lowry's shoulder. She thought he was holding the steering wheel in a strange way, with a precise, almost drunken attention he had never showed before. Lowry said, when they were parked outside her place, "Are you going to go in or what? You want to say goodbye?"

"No," said Clara.

"Or would you like to take a few days off and come with me?"

"Yes, Lowry," she said. It surprised her to see where they were, even though a moment before she had watched them drive up and stop. The stores on the main street were darkened; only the drugstore was open. Someone sat in the doorway on a folding chair, and another figure was behind him. "Where would we go?" Clara said.

"Thought I'd take a drive to the ocean."

"The what?"

"The ocean. You'd like it too."

"All that way? Drive all that way?"

"I can do it."

"Without sleeping?"

"We could maybe sleep first."

"Yes," she said gently. She tried to open the door but could not pull the handle down hard enough. On her second try she succeeded. Lowry slid over behind her and put his arms around her, his hands over her breasts, and buried his face in her hair. Then he pushed her out and followed her upstairs.

When Clara woke off and on that night she felt no surprise at all that Lowry was with her. It might have been that in her sleep she had been with him so much, that now the real Lowry was nothing to alarm her. Being so close to him was like swimming: they were like swimmers, their arms and legs in any easy position, blending together, breathing close together. Her toes groped against his. She thought, It's all decided now. I am a different person to him now. When he made love to her the next morning she began just at the point she had left off the night before, and she had already learned to feel past the pain to the kernel in her he was stirring that was like the kernel in himself he loved so well, that inspired him to such joy. She said, "I love you, I love you," in a kind of delirium, her ears roaring with the flow of her own blood and fit to drown out the silence that had been with her all her life.

At dawn they drove off in his car to the ocean some hundreds of miles away. She brushed her hair with her blue plastic hairbrush, languid and pleased as any married woman, letting her hair fall down onto the back of the seat. She hummed along with the songs on his radio. On the front of the dime store, for the manager she had left a note: "Have been called home, emergency. Will be back Thursday latest. Clara." It was with the little dictionary that Lowry had given her one time that she had looked up, by herself, the word "emergency." This had pleased him. Everything about her pleased him now. She lay back, comfortable in the sun, and thought that now it would be decided between them—what they were to each other, how they had to stay together—and she had only to wait for Lowry to explain it to her.

6

"You sure as hell don't want to get pregnant, Clara."

It was Lowry's somber mode: calling her *Clara*. She'd grown to like best those times Lowry called her *sweetheart, honey*. Even *kid*.

There were to be three sun-drenched days in what Lowry called a resort town, that had formerly been a fishing village on the Atlantic Ocean; these days would remain in Clara's memory for the remainder of her life. Then she found herself back in Tintern— Tintern, that had once seemed so exciting to her!—on the Eden

River, alone; her brain dazzled by what had happened to her, and what had not happened.

Lowry was always at the center of her thoughts. Like the sun, you needn't even glance up to see it, let alone feel it. You could even forget it, in a way. So Clara concentrated upon what surrounded her—working at Woolworth's, going out in the evening with whoever was around, gazing dreamily out her second-floor windows, sleeping alone and touching herself gently, in love, as her lover had touched her, though not always gently. *Clara. Beautiful Clara.*

Sometimes Lowry's voice was so clear, she woke from a dream of overwhelming happiness. *Clara: I don't want to hurt you.*

She wasn't sure what that meant. An apology ahead of time.

A warning?

———

" 'Beautiful Clara.' " It was so: she'd changed. Customers in the store regarded her closely, and smiled. Even the women lingered, friendlier than she remembered. And on the street. In that way that people smile at a good-looking girl or woman, with no thought for why, what logic.

Now it seemed to Clara that Tintern had grown mysteriously less beautiful. Stricken with the hot-humid air of August, that made you sweat inside your clothes though you'd just had a bath, and had talcum-powdered your body with care. Clara walked on Main Street, and on River Street, and on Bridge Street, and sometimes on the gaunt old nightmare bridge, gripping the railing when vehicles passed, and the structure shuddered. In her old life—she'd come to think of her life before Lowry had made love to her as old, bypassed—she'd have been scared as hell, but now the sensation thrilled her. As if Lowry were close beside her. She knew herself radiant and buoyed by happiness. If men or boys approached her, she laughed and told them that she was engaged, her fiancé was out of town.

That word: *fiancé.* Speaking it, with a smile.

Drifting into a dream open-eyed. Her mind was a thousand miles away, in that seaside town on the Atlantic Ocean.

Atlantic seaboard Pearl had murmured solemnly.

"Then it's decided. He has decided." So Clara had thought on the first day, and on the second day of lying in the sun with him and observing other people live out their lives—parents, children— who were staying at the shore as she and Lowry were doing, though probably for longer. "It must be all decided, he doesn't even need to think about it." Lowry would lie for a while on his stomach, and if she leaned over to gaze at his face she saw how vulnerable it was, his skin that was a man's skin, coarse, pitlike scars at his hairline from some accident long ago, or fight. At the beach, Lowry soon became restless. He read, or tried to read: paperback books, newspapers, magazines. Sometimes turning the pages so swiftly, Clara supposed he wasn't really reading. If she leaned against his arm, and began to read aloud, haltingly, as a child might, Lowry laughed and caressed the nape of her neck, "Go on, good. Don't stop." But Clara invari- ably stumbled over a word, and shoved the book from her.

At other times, after making love, Clara sat beneath Lowry's gaze and brushed her hair that fell now to nearly her hips, staring out at the ocean. That slow dreamy time Clara wanted to last forever but knew would not. Lowry became gigantic to her: a presence more than the sun, that could cut the sun off from her. He'd grown to fill her mind most of the day, and at night he was a presence she slept curled against and would have clung to if he'd allowed it. "He must not be thinking of it, even," she told herself, waiting to ask him what plans he had and whether he was keeping in mind that note she'd left for the dime-store manager about Thursday. Would that day come, and Clara would be back in the damned store? She could not believe it.

Yet a part of her mind must have accepted it, because she felt no great surprise, only a faint, wan disappointment, when she was back in Tintern on Thursday, just as Lowry had said.

The days at the shore were a flashing, blurred interruption of the summer, and all that Clara retained of it, to hold in her hand, were two snapshots: Lowry and Clara snuggling together like teen- aged lovers in an automatic photo stand, smiling into the camera's blank eye. Clara had been sunburnt, her hair windblown and tan- gled, and Lowry hadn't shaved for a day or more, grinning with mean-looking wires pushing from his jaws. The edges of both photographs were clouded. One of the snapshots was for Clara, and one was for Lowry, but Clara discovered both snapshots among her things.

And she had also this tanned sensuous body, and certain memories, and Lowry's promise of returning again in two Sundays—it was the earliest he could make it, and he kissed her goodbye with genuine regret—and a vague suspicion that her awkwardness about *taking care of herself* in the way that Lowry wanted might have consequences.

Still, Clara had no way of knowing yet.

And even if her period came late, that might not mean anything. For her period sometimes came late, and sometimes early. Clara was so stricken with self-consciousness, she could not bear to speak of such things to another person, let alone a man. When Lowry had said, "You sure as hell don't want to get pregnant, Clara," she'd heard the word clearly, but turned aside, blushing. She knew: Lowry did what a man did, sometimes: slid things onto himself, thin-rubber ugly things that she, Clara, did not acknowledge, could not bring herself to acknowledge except in repugnance, afterward. *Pregnant* was not so uneasy a word, or an idea; you heard *pregnant* often, though not as often as *going to have a baby*, which was somehow easier to utter. Clara had a vague idea—hadn't Rosalie said so?— poor Rosalie, who'd gotten pregnant, so young!—that you couldn't get pregnant so fast. Or maybe it was Sonya who said so. Based upon her sister who'd tried so damn hard to get pregnant, and it had taken years. Sonya's attitude caught on with Clara, who could imagine her lumbering sardonic friend sneering at other people's advice. (Sonya was involved with a married man, a gypsum mine worker twelve years older than she was.) Trouble was, Sonya seemed always angry these days, and Clara avoided her afraid she might hear something she didn't want to hear. The serenity of Clara's face might annoy Sonya, for with Sonya love made things jagged and troublesome and brought out blemishes on her face. Clara had softened. If her face looked empty it was because her mind was occupied, sorting out and arranging memories. In four days there had been less of them than she would have thought, because moments blended into one another and were almost the same moment. But she had certain images to love: Lowry doing this, Lowry looking at her in such a way. One day a man had said something over his shoulder to Clara, and Lowry had grabbed him and pulled him around, and the man had jerked away and told Lowry to let him alone, and Lowry had waited a second and then gone after him again, pushing him along with one hand and showing by the stiffness of his bare back that he was furious. When he came back to Clara she had been ashamed, not because he had been so angry on her account but because he had been angry just for something to do. That was one of her memories. And all the times when she had said aloud to him, "I love you," the words tortured out of her by a force that was like a devil squirming inside her, lashing out in his frenzy. Sunlight in at the window—they stayed in a boardinghouse that was clean but a little noisy—and certain water marks on the ceiling, and the eating stands and taverns, one after another, and Lowry squeezing her shoulders or swimming in loose circles around her: she had these things to think about.

As the days passed she began to think more and more of Lowry's baby. Her mind broke through to the surface of the day, shattered by the sunlight, and she was positive that she was pregnant—she knew it must be. But she waited. She fell into the habit of dreaming about Lowry and the baby together, as if the two of them were somehow one, and what had begun as a thought that frightened her turned into a daydream she looked forward to. If she had a baby it would be his and it would be something only he had given her, something he had left her with. After the first several times he had never again said to her, "Are you taking care of yourself, Clara?" because it embarrassed her. Sometimes they would fall asleep and he must have known she was doing nothing, but forgetfulness came down upon them like the lazy heat of the beach and told them that all was well. Clara thought that all was well forever and that the future would stretch out before them the way the ocean and the beach did, stretching out of sight but always the same, monotonous and predictable. She supposed it would be that way with Lowry once he settled down. She supposed that in his mind everything had been decided—that he was going to keep her with him from now on—but, back in Tintern a while later, she had had to give up that idea and start working on this new one.

On the surface of her mind was this worry, was she going to have a baby? Or could it be that her body was thrown off by Lowry? It was only on the surface of her mind, however. What she really felt came out when she said to Sonya one day, "It would be nice to have a baby," and then stopped to think what she had said. Sonya made a contemptuous noise that was like something ugly kicked out before you, for a joke. This did not bother Clara. She felt like a plant of some kind, like a flower on a stalk that only looked slender but was really tough, tough as steel, like the flowers in fields that could be blown down flat by the wind but yet rose again slowly, coming back to life. Her first thought was, "Lowry will be mad at me for not taking care of myself "; then she thought, "It's his more than mine because he's older," and remembered the many times he had been gentle with her, drawing her close with a casual gesture that meant more to her than anything else. They came together at moments like that. On the beach his dreaminess had been a dreaminess that drifted out for miles, while hers was a dreaminess of motion content to remain still for a lifetime; but still they had come together at certain moments.

Ginny's children, especially the baby, drew out Clara's love. On Sunday she went to a charity picnic with them, just to have something to do while waiting for Lowry to come (he had said not before eight), and she kept asking to hold the baby even when Ginny said she didn't mind carrying it herself. Ginny was pregnant again. Her husband Bob had not found work yet and he and Ginny were living with her mother.

They walked slowly about together, a little group. Clara thought that everyone at the picnic looked different, special. The old women wore hats, round black straw hats with bunches of artificial flowers, usually violets. Many of the men wore suits, though they looked awkward and hot in them. Ginny wore a filmy long-sleeved dress that was already stained with the baby's milk, an accident they had in the car, but her face was freshened by the music and the excitement of the picnic and she did not seem to mind the way Bob walked a few steps ahead of them. Clara returned looks she got with a slow, dreamy smile, not surprised that people should think her worth staring at but rewarding them for it. She saw Sonya and her boyfriend standing at the Volunteer Firemen's Beer Tent, the biggest tent of all, but she did not go over to say hello. Ginny nudged Clara and said, "Don't they have a nerve?" but Clara just shrugged her shoulders. She was in a warm, pleasant daze, trying to balance the secret she was now certain of about herself with the color and noise of the picnic, dazed by what she knew that no one else, not even Ginny, could know.

They stopped at the bingo tent and the two girls played a few games, while the baby whined and tugged at Clara's skirt and the boy tried to swallow the dried-up corn kernels they pushed around on the dirty old bingo cards. A fat lady, the wife of the man who owned the drugstore, stood by them and chattered at the baby. She wore an apron with special pockets sewn in it to hold change. "Too bad you don't have better luck, you two," she said to Clara and Ginny. On the last game Clara had no luck either, and sat toying with the kernels of corn and staring down at the card with a small fixed smile, her mind already fallen beyond the noisy tent of bingo players and the shaking of the numbered balls and the recorded music to those days by the ocean with Lowry. But those days seemed already far away. . . . Then someone yelled "Bingo!" and, as always, she wasn't ready just yet to hear it. Ginny said, "Crap," and pushed her card away. Clara swung herself around on the bench and let her legs fall hard. She thought, "Six or seven months and I won't be able to do that." This thought, which came out of nowhere to her, was more real than all the memories she had been reliving.

They found Bob at the beer tent, which was naturally where he would be, and stood around talking with people. There was just a slight wind and it picked up dust—the land was dry in August—and Clara sometimes reached down to keep her skirt by her knees. She wore yellow high-heeled shoes and no stockings, which was a mistake because a blister had begun on one heel, and a pale blue dress that reminded her of Lowry's eyes, though her own were about the same color. That morning, and every morning since Thursday, she had washed her face with cream in a blue jar she bought at the drugstore (it cost fifty-nine cents) and stood dream-ily massaging her skin in small circles, looking beyond her own eyes in the mirror. After she finished with the cream she washed it off her face carefully and then leaned close to the mirror and plucked at her eyebrows, until they were shaped in thin rising lines and made her look a way she had never looked before—delicate and surprised. She had always had the look of a girl standing flat-footed, but now she looked like someone else—it might have been the girl in that dime photograph she was imitating. Herself, but a better self. Whenever men glanced at her and their eyes slowed, Clara turned her head a little to loosen her hair just to give them some-thing more to look at; being with Lowry had done that for her. She thought that all men were like Lowry in some way, or trying to be like him. At the beer tent Bob joked around and jostled her and then, when Ginny had drifted a short distance away, talking to someone else, he had taken hold of her upper arm and squeezed it. Clara looked at him as if she did not know who he was, doing such a thing. She had listened for months to Ginny's weeping over him, and she knew that Ginny was right, but now this hard, sullen young man confronted her with a look of trouble that was all his own and she could not really identify him. It crossed her mind that he too could have done what Lowry did to her, and the baby she might be going to have could be his baby, that it could be any man's at all—and the idea was astonishing. Except for Lowry, everyone was common.

She got away from him and caught up with Ginny, and was hold-ing Ginny's baby and wondering at its out-of-focus eyes when some-one approached her. It was Revere. She smiled at him and made the baby's hand wave at him, as if it were natural he should just step up out of a noisy crowd at the Tintern firemen's picnic. Clara chat-tered about the baby: "His name is Jefferson and this is his mother here, Ginny, and that's his father down there—where they're all laughing and carrying on. Isn't it a nice picnic?" Revere stood with one hand in his pocket, awkwardly.

"Clara, give him back. You go have fun," Ginny said. She sounded maternal and bossy, like her own mother, but it was really meant to be critical so that Revere could catch it: after all, he was here alone and he was married and hadn't he just fired Caroline's husband for drinking too much? She took the baby from Clara's arms and left Clara just standing there, facing Revere.

"You seem to like children," he said.

"I love babies especially," she said. She thought of Lowry and of any baby that Lowry might father—it would be half hers and might look like him around the eyes, and she would let him name it—and a sensation of faintness rose suddenly in her. She and Revere began to walk together. She felt this dizziness, this uncertainty that was not at all unpleasant, and wondered if she should tell this man about it. He seemed to have nothing to say and so she went on, chattily, "I'd like to have seven or eight children, lots of kids, and a big house and everything. Nobody is happy in a house without a baby, right? —I was just over visiting by the ocean, all that ways. I went with some friends and was swimming and out on the beach."

She turned to him with a dazed, dazzling smile, as if she were still a little blinded by the sun. But he did not smile with her. He looked uneasy. "A friend of mine is coming to visit me tonight," Clara went on. In her excitement she wanted to tug at Revere's arm to make him understand how important this was. "I have lots of things to do and have to get back home—I just came to the picnic with a friend—"

"Would you like to talk about them?—your friends?"

She thought this was a strange question. She glanced at Revere and was a little slowed down by his eyes, which were fixed on her in a way she remembered Lowry's had been. The faintness swelled out inside her. She wanted to turn and get back to Ginny, where it was safe, even if Ginny was angry, and get rid of the time somehow until eight o'clock when Lowry would come. She said, "My girlfriend Ginny—" but was cut off by some boys running past.

They strolled through the picnic grounds and stopped at the edge of the parking lot. The "parking lot" was just a field where cars could park for the picnic. From here the music sounded thin and sleazy. Revere said, "I think I'd like to talk to you. I don't ask anything from you." Clara smiled nervously. She kept listening to that music and thought how far away it was, so quickly, and here she hadn't been with this man for five minutes.

"Yes," Clara said, "but my girlfriend— I'm supposed to have supper with her folks."

"I can get you something to eat."

"Something to eat?" Clara said blankly. "But my friend is coming at eight."

"Is it a boyfriend?"

She said cautiously, "Just a friend," and turned to him as if to get them on their way back to the picnic. But her gaze swung around past his chest and did not dare reach up to his face. She was conscious of his standing there, of his watching her. She was conscious of his name. His name floated about him like perfume around a beautiful woman, touching people before he even came near, defining and fixing him in a way he himself could never know about. Lowry himself had known this man's name. . . .

They stepped through the weeds and went over to his car, which Clara recognized at once. She must have looked at it more closely than she knew. She said, "Someone told me your name is Revere," and he laughed and said, "I told you that myself." But she did not mean him.

"You look a little different than you did before," he said.

"Yes, I know it."

She got in his car. The seat was hot and burned the backs of her knees. "Maybe," she said weakly, "we could not drive far but just a little ways? Just a short drive?"

He drove out to the road, over the bumpy field. Some kids were playing around the parked cars. A boy with a toy cane stood on the roof of a car and waved his cane at them, calling something. Clara closed her face against them.

"What did you want to talk about?" Clara said.

He seemed a little embarrassed. She wondered if there wasn't something resentful about him, about the way the corners of his mouth drooped in profile as if he were puzzled himself over what he was doing. "I should be back to have supper with them," Clara said, relaxing a little so that she could enjoy the drive, "they're real good friends to me. I don't have any family or anyone and they invite me over a lot. . . . I'm friends with a girl named Sonya too. But you probably don't know her. . . ."

He might have been waiting for her to get through with this kind of talk. Clara shrugged her shoulders in miniature at his silence, not for him to see. She thought of Lowry probably on his way driving to her, and of how they would make love that evening. She thought of the ways she might use to explain to Lowry what was wrong with her—unless it was just a mistake. She would have liked to talk to Revere about Lowry but did not know how to begin. Anyway, you should not confide in adults, especially men; it was better never to say anything secret to anyone.

They drove up the highway and kept going, not fast. Clara looked out the window and enjoyed it, though she'd had quite a bit of driving with Lowry the week before. Moving around and getting somewhere so long as you were more or less already on your way back always struck her as nice; it was nothing like riding on the crop seasons. She said, "I loved the ocean. I loved driving there and seeing everything. You can see more of the mountains on your way out. . . . Do you travel around much?"

"Mostly to Chicago."

"Chicago?" Clara said. "In this car?"

"By train."

"Oh," she said, pleased. She liked that expression, "by train." Anyone else would have said "on the train." She imagined him speeding through the countryside in those straight, relentless lines railroad tracks made, cutting through backcountry and eating up distance like nothing. She looked over at him as if he had performed a magic feat. "Mr. Revere, what was it you wanted to say?"

He brought the car to a stop as if he were far enough now from what had bothered him back there. They were at the top of a hill and could look down to some scrubby land where there was a narrow angular lake—"Mirror Lake"—dotted with trees and the stumps of trees on its north side. Young people swam here and had picnics, but today there were only a few couples; everyone was at the charity picnic. Clara could hear someone's car radio blaring, all the way up the hill. The memory of those days with Lowry came back to her like a stab in her breast. Clara felt how far she was from them already, just the way Mr. Revere must feel far from those young people who were swimming and carrying on around Mirror Lake.

Revere rubbed his face. He might have been, like Clara, trying to wake up out of a dream. "There are some things I can't understand," he said slowly. His words were a little harsh. Clara noticed that they cut at the air more than the words of other people did; there was something impatient about them. "I don't think I can explain them. But—when I was your age I stayed with an uncle of mine who lived on a ranch in Dakota. I spent the summer there. He drove my cousins and me into town and it was hardly a town at all—much smaller than Tintern—just a muddy street with some stores. Back from the road there was a shack and a big family lived there. Nine children. There was a girl my age. She had long hair that was almost white and dressed just in rags and she was—like you. . . . She was Swedish."

"I ain't Swedish," Clara said suspiciously. "I'm American."

"She was happy," Revere said.

Clara wondered at that. She did not understand what this man was talking about. What he was saying had something to do with another girl, someone who was grown up now and old, lost, forgotten, someone Clara had never even seen. "That was nice," Clara said uncertainly. "I mean—her being happy."

"My first wife was from a family in the valley here," Revere said. "She was my own age. Then she died and I married Marguerite—"

"Yes," Clara said, "somebody said that was your wife's name."

He took no notice that someone had been talking about him. He said, "We have three boys but she's never really been well since before the first one was born. She's a fine person . . . her father was a fine man. It's all in her, behind her . . . her family. . . . But her heart is heavy."

"Why?"

He looked off to one side, as if Clara had asked a foolish question. "Most people are that way, Clara," he said.

Clara did not know what to say. Should she make a joke, or smile, or what? What made her uneasy was the knowledge that she would not be able to tell anyone about this conversation, especially not Lowry. She said, gropingly, "Your boys are real nice, anyway the two I saw— There ain't something wrong with the youngest one, is there?"

"No."

"But—then—"

"There's nothing wrong."

"Is your wife sick bad?"

"I don't know."

"Does the doctor come out a lot?"

"Yes."

Clara thought about that. "It's nice he can come out a lot," she said. "A doctor looked at me once. He gave me some shots in the arm that stung a little. . . . My pa, though, was real scared. Grown-up men get scared sometimes too. But he wasn't scared of anything else," she said quickly. Revere was still looking out the window. Outside, some blackbirds were fighting over something on the ground. "Tell me," Clara said suddenly, "are there books in your house?"

"Some."

"Are they—up on the walls?"

"On shelves? Yes."

"Oh," Clara said, pleased, "that's nice."

Revere smiled at her. "Do you like to read, Clara?"

"Yes! But I have trouble, sometimes." She paused, twining her hair around her finger. "I'm kind of slow, I guess. I have to say the word to myself when I read, and it takes so long, it makes me tired. If I have kids, I want for them to read. I would give them lots of books so they could read all the time." Clara thought of Lowry skimming his paperback books and magazines at the shore, and giving her the dictionary; of course, Lowry would want his children to be educated. *If you want a life. Different from your parents.* "If I'd gone to school and learned things right, I'd be—I'd be different than I am now."

"But Clara, why do you want to be different?"

She felt her cheeks coloring. She laughed. This man was saying he liked her the way she was. "I guess I don't want to be different."

Revere gazed at her solemnly. If Curt Revere was a playing card, Clara thought, he was one of the kings. Heavy-jawed, inclined to brooding. Not fast and sexy-treacherous like the jacks. You were supposed to think that the king of spades was stronger than the jack of spades, but that wasn't so. Having so much, knowing so much wore out your soul, for you knew that you could lose it.

"Ginny and her folks are gonna be . . . wondering. Where I am."

But Revere didn't seem to hear. With his first and second fingers he was squeezing his lips, thinking. She could feel the resentment in the air about him, and something else, too—that steady brooding weight of his stare that meant that Clara had been selected out of the visible landscape—and maybe the invisible landscape, too—just for him. He saw in her face a face that Clara herself could not see, and she felt a moment's confused power, brief as a flash of heat lightning. And Lowry was on the road returning to her, and in a few hours they would be together again: it wouldn't even be dark yet.

In Clara's purse were loose snapshots. Two were of her and Lowry taken at the shore, another was of Clara alone, taken more recently in an automatic photo booth in the drugstore. She was tempted to show Revere all three, but she took out only the one of herself. "This is me, I had it taken last week. My girlfriend and me . . ." She faltered, not knowing what she meant to say. Revere took the snapshot and examined it. The way he frowned made Clara uneasy, she hadn't meant anything special by offering the picture. In it, Clara had wetted her lips and was posed *all eyes* and her hair sliding into her face like a *Screen Romance* starlet and her shoulders raised to accentuate her breasts in a snug cotton-knit sweater—Clara and her girlfriend had laughed themselves silly with their poses, almost wetting their pants. And now: Here was Curt Revere taking it seriously. He said, "This doesn't look like you exactly, Clara. But I would know you anywhere. Clara." She put out her hand for the picture, but he was still looking at it. "It's very strange," he said. "I don't ask anything of you. . . ." Clara held her breath for some reason thinking he would mutilate the snapshot. Instead, he placed it in his shirt pocket.

"I didn't mean. . . ." Clara began weakly.

"Can't I have it, Clara?"

He wasn't begging exactly. A wounded sound in his voice, you don't expect to hear in a man like Curt Revere.

"Oh, sure! Sure."

Revere said slowly, not looking at her, "My first, young wife died. In childbirth. It wasn't supposed to happen, she had the 'very best prenatal care.'. . . The baby died, too. So long ago, she was young enough to be—she could have been—my daughter now. It's very strange for me to think that."

Clara nodded, embarrassed. When older people talked of their age, how could you respond? It was so shameful, somehow.

She wanted to put out her hand. Wanted to touch this man's face that was so heavy with thinking. It frightened her to think that somewhere—when she shut her eyes, she imagined the place precisely: the pickers' camp in Florida where she'd last seen him—her father Carleton Walpole might be brooding over her. Swigging his cider jug in that way he'd perfected where he spilled only a few drops . . .

"You have a lovely smile, Clara."

Smile? Had she been smiling?

Inanely Clara said, "I guess . . . I don't see myself."

"Is your mother alive, Clara?"

"Oh, yes."

"Where is she, dear?"

"This place in Florida, I guess. Where they had a little farm." Clara paused, confused. "I mean, orange grove. Outside Savannah."

"Savannah?" Revere frowned, considering. "And what about your father, Clara?"

"My father? I don't know," Clara said, laughing edgily, "what about him? I ran away to leave him."

"Why?"

"Why'd anybody run away? He was hitting me."

"Did he hurt you, Clara?"

"Naw." For suddenly an idea opened at the back of her mind: she hadn't run away from her family because Pa was hitting her but because it had been time. Like stealing the flag, it had been time for that. Like falling onto her knees in that church and praying her heart out for Rosalie, the first and last time. That was why she was sitting here in Revere's car this afternoon on an August Sunday years later. Defensively she said, "My pa had some bad luck. He got cheated lots of times. He used to get drunk and hit us kids and I had a chance to leave and . . ."

"You sound regretful, Clara. Did you love your parents?"

"Sure."

"Even your father, who hit you?"

"Sure."

"But why?"

Clara shrugged. This close questioning was getting to her.

"Why did you love your father if he hit you?" Revere persisted.

"He was my father. I said."

"But—is that enough?"

"He was my father." Clara spoke sullenly now. She was beginning to understand this man's power: he pretended to be gentle with you, even humble; it was his way of making you think he was no different from you. But of course he was different. There was some picking, precise look in his eyes, a tension in his face, that reminded her of Lowry when Lowry wasn't his teasing self but somebody older and more serious who scared her.

"You don't stop loving somebody just 'cause they hit you," Clara said contemptuously, as if the thought was childish, silly. As if you'd have to be goddamned weak to give in to such.

Revere thought this over. Clara half-closed her eyes and tried to think of her father but her mind shrank from the memory; it was a memory that came unbidden at night, and not in daylight. Instead she smiled thinking of her and Rosalie tramping along the street, two pickers' kids in town, and there was that house, that flag. Oh, that flag! Clara smiled remembering running up boldly to snatch it and could see herself, as if all the action had been done by another person. Then in the next instant everything fell away, years vanished, and she was sitting here with this strange man. What had her father to do with it, then? But she could not explain this to Revere.

"Are you going to be married soon?" he said.

She looked at him. "How come you say that?"

"Are you?"

"I don't know. I guess not."

"But you might?"

She laughed shyly. "I don't think so."

"Is there somebody in mind?"

"Mister, can we go back now? Please?"

He looked at her the way he had looked at the photograph. "All right," he said. "We can go back."

———

She sat up straight, with the docile alertness of a child who may have done something wrong. The land back into Tintern moved unhurriedly to them, and Clara measured with her eyes the distance they had yet to go. And Lowry was on the way to her and would be with her in a few hours. She felt slow and peaceful, as if warmed by the sun. Revere was even more of a stranger to this town than she was herself, she thought. She stood between him and the ugly little clump of buildings and the clearings that were only halfway cleared and the dusty lanes with weeds growing in their centers; he might have owned some of it or all of it but he was more a stranger than she was.

When he let her out he looked tired. She thought he must be almost forty; it was the first clear thought she had had about him. "Take care of yourself," he said, echoing Lowry's words. Clara was a little shocked at that echo. She shook her head yes, smiled yes, with her hand on the doorknob just waiting for its freedom, waiting for his sad, heavy gaze to release her. Why his resentment, why that bullying set of his mouth? Clara wanted to tell him that she was free and belonged to no one at all. And if she ever did, it would be to another man. But she did not know what he wanted. She had never met anyone like him, she did not know how to talk to him. All she felt when she left was a sense of relief at being away from the pressure of his gaze.

When she climbed the stairs to her room she felt that relief ebb out of her. Revere's look stayed with her, the look her father should have given years ago if he'd known how—but of course he hadn't—and that would have kept her home, kept her from running. From Lowry too. And from this new, stunning knowledge—she let her hand fall against her stomach. Yes, it was true. Was it true? How could she know for certain? She stood at the top of the stairs breathing heavily.

She opened the door, half-expecting Lowry to be inside, but the room was empty. The air was very hot. A few flies buzzed about when she entered, annoyed at being disturbed, then they quieted down. Clara sat on her bed and stared at the opposite wall for a few minutes, thinking of nothing. Then Revere's face returned to her, and then the knowledge about her life she'd had in the car: what had brought her all this way to Lowry and to what she believed she might be carrying inside her had just been an accident. Was that it? Life was a sequence of accidents and nothing more?

She lay on her bed and lit a cigarette and waited. Trying to think what she was going to tell him, which words to use. "I'm afraid I got some trouble, Lowry," or "There's something wrong you need to know," or "I feel bad about . . ." It might have been the ease with which she mouthed this that made her know she would never get to say it, that things did not go that easily.

When Lowry finally came it was late. Clara had taken off her dress but still lay on top of her bed, waiting. In the darkness she could see objects without bothering to figure them out; she knew where everything was. She lay with her feet curled up under her, half-sitting, propped up by a pillow, with an ashtray tilted on the bed. She was just lighting her sixth cigarette when she heard the unmistakable sound of Lowry's car outside; she hadn't known that she had known what his car sounded like.

He knocked and came inside. Clara had stood. "No, don't turn on the light," he said. He closed the door and she could hear him breathing hard.

"What's wrong?"

He seized her and pulled her over against him. "I can't stay, I'm in a hurry. I did something," he said. Though his voice was rushed, he was not frightened. "I'm on my way through. I can't stay. Are you all right, Clara?"

"What's wrong?"

"For Christ's sake don't cry—stop that," he said. He embraced her and lifted her off the floor. There was something reckless and joyful about him that terrified her. "Little Clara, it's all right, I'm not hurt or anything—just in a hurry— How the hell are you, kid? How's everything here? I missed you—"

He pushed her back toward the bed and sat her down. "Look, I can't stay. Maybe I could write you a letter or something—O.K.? O.K., sweetheart?"

"Did you do something?"

"Christ, yes, it's about time," he said. "I was fed up with this two-bit business, this two-bit goddamn junk I've been doing. Next time you see me I'll be different. I'm sick to death of myself the way I am—what the hell am I?" He sat down heavily beside her. His released joy made his body heavy. "I'm going to Mexico, sweetheart."

"I'll go with you—"

"What? You stay here. You grow up. Do you need some money?"

"Why are you going away?" Clara said wildly. "What's wrong? Did you kill somebody?"

"I've never been down to Mexico, that's why I'm going there. I'm going to do lots of things— Look, do you need some money? How the hell are you?" He took her jaw in his hand and looked at her, this new, loud, strange Lowry. She could feel his anxious breath on her face and was paralyzed. No words came to her. "You're a sweet little girl but look, look, I never fooled you, did I? I never lied to you. I told you all along how it was. O.K.? Are you O.K.?"

He lay back with her on the bed and held her in his arms. But she had already retreated from him, grown small. She felt small, and her body was numb and dead in his arms, something foreign to both of them. Lowry kissed her and kept on talking in that low, explosive way, his energy threatening to damage her with the very innocence of its joy, and she could not understand it. She had shrunken far inside her body and could not control its trembling and could not understand what was happening. Lowry said, getting up, "Clara, I've got to get going. I'm in a big rush. If somebody comes looking for me, tell them to go to hell—right? I'm only taking what's my own. If he follows me I'll smash his head in. Tell him that. Here, Clara, I'll try to see you sometime again—remember me, all right? Here's something for you. Remember me—I took good care of you, didn't I?"

Then he was gone. Clara lay still. When she finally turned on the light she saw money on the table, bills scattered carelessly as if the wind of Lowry's passing had blown them there by accident. It was some time before she could make herself get up to put them away. She moved slowly, woodenly. She wondered how she would live out the rest of her life.

7

The day Clara took her life into control was an ordinary day. She did not know up until the last moment exactly how she would bring all those accidents into control, like a driver swerving aside to let a rabbit live or tearing into it and not even bothering to glance back: he might do one or the other and not know a moment before what it would be.

She was sixteen now, and by the time the baby was born she would be seventeen. Every morning after Lowry had left she woke up to the clear, unmistakable knowledge of what had happened to her and what it meant. The dreaminess of the past two weeks had vanished. She stared long and hard at things. It might have been that she didn't trust them—that she wanted to make sure they stayed still, kept their shapes, identities. She thought about the baby obsessively and of Lowry who would be kept alive in this way even when—in Mexico, or anywhere—he really did die. Lowry would remain alive through his baby and its eyes might resemble his, its mouth or way of speaking—and it would answer her when she called it, a baby boy maybe who would come running breathless and laughing when she called him, to her.

To people in Tintern she must have looked very like their own girls, the kind who'd grown up too quickly and were anxious to grow up even more. She knew people were talking about her. When Lowry came to Tintern they talked and now that he failed to come to Tintern they talked even more. She felt their eyes, following her.

She cried, and cursed herself for her weakness! It was those dry, exhausted hours when she had no more tears or curses left that hurt her most. Lowry had been cruel to her, a selfish bastard—she knew. Yet, so long as Lowry himself did not know, she supposed he was innocent of harming her. And he did love her, in his way. She would always believe this.

One afternoon when Clara was out walking by herself along a back lane a mile or so from her room, thinking these thoughts, murmuring and laughing softly to herself, she saw: Revere's automobile, parked. And in that instant she understood what she was going to do and what she'd been planning to do for nearly four weeks.

It had been that long: four weeks. She thought it could have been four years. Clara had never paid much attention to the workings of her body, but after that trip with Lowry her attention had turned inward so violently and resentfully that she would never be able to think of her body any other way. Lowry had changed her. But she was healthy despite this. The trouble was that her body's health had nothing to do with her personally, with Clara; its workings and demands were not hers. She sometimes dreamed that Lowry was making love to her and her mind did not want this at all—it was disgusted and angry. She would press both hands against her stomach when she was alone, or even sometimes in the store, and think of how her body had continued in its way while her mind had tried hard to go in another; but in the end there was no choice. Time kept on passing, she kept on growing into it, drifting into it. There was no choice.

When she had nothing else to do she went out walking by herself. In Tintern there were always people walking, kids or old people or anyone at all, maybe attended by dogs that ran barking and sniffing everywhere. Some of the old men carried heavy branches to use as canes, some of the kids carried branches that were supposed to be weapons. Clara walked back on the dusty lanes that led past closed-up storage barns and frame houses and fields that had never been cleared. She avoided walking by the creek because so many people hung around there, and she never went past the Tintern "hotel," where mill hands rented rooms or just hung out. One day she saw Revere's car parked up on the shoulder of the road; back a distance was a new building, a small office that had something to do with the lumberyard. It looked as if it had been built out of new raw lumber just the other day. The lumberyard itself was large and not very busy. The sawmill, some distance away and facing another road, was noisy and crowded with men; Clara was afraid of it.

This was the very end of August. The air was motionless. Clara was used to perspiration on her forehead, her neck, her body, but she did not like it because it made her feel dirty. Lowry disliked dirt. So she wiped her forehead with the backs of her hands and stood at the side of the road and waited. If she stared straight ahead, she could see the tall ungainly buildings of Tintern, one of them the building she'd lived in now for over two years. Seen from the back, they looked hollowed-out and strange; women had clothes hanging up to dry, drooping from line to line, on the back porches. Two girls came from the turnoff of Main Street, riding bicycles, heading down toward her. They were about twelve or thirteen and lived somewhere on the other side of the town, in those neat identical white frame houses bought by men who had managed to save money for twenty years or so in the sawmill or at the gypsum plant, doing steady work, therefore different from Clara and her people. She felt this difference now more and more often. When she had been with Lowry—no matter where his imagination had been— she had never noticed such things. She must have lived in a daze. But now she did notice, now her eyes had taken on the characteristic of narrowing shrewdly when she met someone, as if sizing up an enemy. The girls were laughing shrilly together and as they approached Clara they fell silent. Clara stared at their sweaty, smeared faces, their little mouths and eyes shaped for secret wonder and laughter about this strange blond girl Clara, whom everyone knew and talked about, who didn't have any family, who lived by herself in that dump—!

The first girl pedaled faster and shot by Clara, saying nothing, then the other was by too. Once they were past, they giggled again. Clara watched them ride away—the second one had a boy's bike, old and battered—and wondered what they had been saying about her. She did not feel any bitterness. She did not feel anything toward them at all. She watched them ride down the lane and wondered why she had never had a bicycle, why she hadn't trained her legs to go up and down like that in tight controlled circles, so that the muscles of the calf showed, even on those skinny girls. They wore blue jeans that were baggy and faded, they stood up on the pedals in a breathless rigidity that waited to see where it would be taken to, the girls calm and unalarmed by bumps and rocks in the lane. They zigzagged back and forth, calling out to each other, their words flattened now by the distance. The soft pale dust of the lane was marked by their tire prints, a vague blurred confusion of lines that no one but Clara could understand. Clara looked after them and felt how old she was, how far she had come while never having ridden down back lanes like this with a friend, on bicycles, before supper.... Then she heard some men talking and looked over to the office, where Revere and two other men stood. Revere was backing off from them.

He must have seen her because he backed away, still talking, and then turned and headed to her. She was serious when he approached her. She watched him come and saw how his eyes emerged out of the distance, fixed upon her. She had not quite remembered them. He said hello, but she hesitated, unwilling to say anything across that space of dirt, when here she had been standing and waiting for him so obviously—anyone could tell that.

"Is anything wrong?" Revere said. He brought a sweet, fresh smell of new lumber with him on his clothes. But it began to fade at once in the afternoon heat. "Did you want to—see me?"

Clara almost shivered, but she had felt it coming and controlled it. She must have been looking at him with a small, fixed, strange smile. Revere wore no suit coat today and no tie, and the sleeves of his shirt were rolled up. But he still did not look like a man from this country. Just as Clara, dressed up, looked like every other girl for miles, so Revere looked like no one else even when dressed like them.

"I was out walking and saw your car," Clara said flatly. She kept staring at him as if to force him into saying something, doing something. Revere was slowly folding up a slip of yellow paper, then he seemed to forget about it and held it between his fingers absently. "It's hot, it's awful hot. I feel all heavy and sick with this summer," Clara said. Her voice had gone breathless, amorous in a tired way, and her eyelids drooped as she spoke, not knowing at all what she was going to say. But she did not think she had to say much of anything. She was so aware of him standing there that her throat kept wanting to close up, to swallow in terror; his movements too were stiff. They might have gone through this before, many times. Clara did indeed feel that she had said something of this nature to him before, and that he had looked at her as he was looking now. Clara glanced down at herself, as if to guide Revere's eyes, at her bare tanned arms and bare tanned legs, at her black ballerina slippers that had cost $2.98 new and were already run over and smudged and looked like hell. Everything she had, Clara thought, looked like hell sooner or later. She said, tossing her hair back out of her eyes, "Do you own this place here—this lumberyard?"

"Not all of it," he said. He tried to smile.

She still had not smiled and so she felt ahead of him. "You own lots of things in town, though," she said flatly.

"In Tintern? Yes, something. It isn't important."

"How do you get to own things?"

"What?"

"How do you get that way?—How would a baby end up like that? A baby that was just born and had nothing?"

"You look a little tired, Clara," he said. He came to her. Clara watched his hand approaching and thought, This can't be happening. He touched her arm. It was the first time he had touched her but it too seemed familiar. "Is something wrong? Have you been ill?"

"I must be ugly in all this heat," she said, turning away. She felt real revulsion. She brought one hand up to hide her face from him and he stepped around to look at her, the way a child or dog will press after someone who has retreated. He looked so strange, so uneasy and nervous, that she was afraid she would do something crazy just to end what they were going through.

"No, you're not ugly," he said.

"I'm tired—"

"You're not ugly."

He said it sadly. She did not want to meet his eyes. Her heart had begun to pound heavily. Revere pressed his hand against her forehead, just for an instant, a light, casual gesture that was meant to calm her but instead made them both nervous. Clara thought,

Somebody is watching from the lumberyard. She thought, The whole town is watching. But when she swung her eyes around, as if trying for freedom, she saw no one at all. Nothing.

"I can drive you back," he said.

He waited for her to acquiesce. It took a moment or two. Then he pushed her gently toward the car. This was the way Lowry had pushed her—not a real push, but just a nudge, something to get her started and guide her a little, but really just an excuse for touching her. "You work too hard in that store. You shouldn't have to work at all," Revere said.

"Yes," Clara said, thinking of how she had worked all her life and had never known any better, while other people owned the farms she and her family had worked on, and still other people owned the trucks that drove up to buy the vegetables and fruit, and others owned banks and sawmills and lumberyards and factories and grocery stores in town that sold the things she and her family had picked, and the children of all these people were free to ride bicycles up and down quiet dusty lanes throughout their whole childhoods, never growing old.

She got into the car and let her head droop down toward her chest, just for an instant. It was all she allowed herself. In the next moment she would know, she thought: it depended on which way he turned the car. If he drove back into town (the car was headed in that direction) she would have to start thinking about getting out of this place, but if he turned around and went the other way, she had a chance. Revere started the car and drove it a little jerkily up onto the lane, then backed up into the lumberyard driveway so he could turn the car around.

She knew they were talking to each other, even though they had nothing to say out loud. All she had were questions, questions. She was fearful of being injured, broken, dirtied beyond anything Lowry could ever fix up. But she had trained herself to think, "That bastard," whenever Lowry's name came to mind, and the blood pulsing from her anger for him gave her courage. In a few minutes they had overtaken and passed the girls on the bicycles. The girls were standing and resting, their legs on either side of the old bikes, and Clara let her eyes brush past them with something like a for-lorn, wistful affection—but they were just brats anyway, girls with fathers and mothers and families who dawdled around the dime store handling things and who stared a little too often at Clara and Sonya. In the instant Revere drove by them Clara wanted to catch their eyes and toss out to them a look of contempt, but when she turned, her look changed into one of confusion, of clumsy affec-tion, as if she would have liked somehow to be nothing more than a third girl with them, on another bike, and not in this car heading out toward the country and whatever was going to happen to her out there.

He was saying, "I didn't know if you'd want to see me again. I don't want to get you in any trouble."

"Yes," Clara said.

"I mean with people in town."

"Yes."

"I stopped by the picnic to see you. But you belonged with those young people you were with."

Clara said nothing.

"It's strange," Revere said. His voice was not warm. "I didn't think I would see you again."

Clara looked out the window. The hot sun, facing them, gave her a vague reflection in the side window so that she could see herself. She rolled down the window and the wind poured in, whipping her hair back. She closed her eyes. After a moment Revere said, "There's a house I own out here. I bought some land and a house came with it. . . ." Clara opened her eyes and waited for the house to come into sight. She expected it to materialize out of nowhere. "I own this land here," Revere said. "There are two hundred acres to this. But the land's no good."

"No good," Clara echoed, not quite questioning him. She won-dered why anyone would buy farmland he couldn't farm on, but she was too nervous, too oddly tired, to ask.

When they reached the house her face and body were damp with sweat that had turned cold. She did not bother wiping her forehead. Revere, helping her out of the car, touched her with a hand that was cold with perspiration too. She wondered what he was thinking or if he was thinking at all. They were some distance from the road, parked in the overgrown driveway. The farmhouse was probably a hundred years old. Clara saw feverishly that its roof was rotted in one part and that some of its windows were broken. Tall thistled grass grew everywhere. There were sharp weeds that brushed against her legs but she was too nervous to avoid them. Revere was indicating something, very seriously, and she turned and saw a few old barns, washed by the rain to no color at all. They went on toward the house. Clara was watching her feet. She did not want to stumble on the back steps, which looked wobbly. She thought that if she stumbled she would fall apart, everything would crack into pieces. Revere helped her up. Since he had first touched her back on that lane she had grown weak, as if she did indeed need help getting in and out of cars and walking up three or four steps. Revere pushed the door open and it moved away from his hand, opening by itself. Clara swallowed hard. In her body everything was pounding with heat and fear and heaviness.

Just inside the house she turned to him miserably, sobbing. He took her hands and tried to comfort her. She felt his pity, his own uneasiness, and that hard strength behind him that she had to count on now. She was giving herself over to him and it would be done the way Lowry would do something, thinking it through, calculating on it, and then going ahead. All her life she would be able to say: Today she changed the way her life was going and it was no accident. No accident.

"I'm afraid—I don't want—" she began. But Revere pressed her face against him, hiding her face. He was trembling. Clara shut her eyes tight and thought that she would never go through this again, not anything like this. She would never be this terrified again.

"No, don't be afraid. Clara. Don't be afraid," he said.

Her teeth had begun to chatter. She thought of Lowry, that bastard Lowry, and of how he was making her do this, making her heart swell and pound furiously in her chest like something about to go wild. It was of Lowry she thought when Revere made love to her. They were in what must have been a parlor, surrounded by drifting bunches of dust and the corpses of insects and odd pieces of furniture hunched beneath soiled sheets. The ceiling was covered with cobwebs that swayed a little though there was no breeze at all.

8

By the time the first cooling thunderstorms came in late September, that house had been fixed up—the roof mended, the steps and porch strengthened, the inside painted and even papered with a special wallpaper Clara herself had picked out of a big book, pale pink with tiny rosebuds. When she was alone in the morning she would sit out on the porch as if waiting for someone to come, or she would stare off across the land that had come with this house, untended and belonging to no one really, since Curt Revere did not bother to put anything into it. She would try to think what she was doing and how this had come about: she tried to imagine the old people who had lived out their lives here, a couple who had built everything and worked the land and who had died and lost it so that Clara could sit on their porch and stare out with a stillness that she must have sucked in with the air of the old house, the intimate breaths of that old couple.

Revere had said of them: "They were eighty or more, both of them—the man died first. Their children were scattered and nobody wanted the old farm."

Clara thought that she had never heard anything so sad.

Sometimes she went walking out in the fields, carrying herself as if she were a vessel entrusted with something sacred or dangerous, something that must not be jostled. As often as she thought of the baby—which was nearly always—she thought of Lowry, and even when Revere was with her she could gaze past his face and into Lowry's face, wondering what he was doing at that moment and if he ever thought of her, knowing that the energy she needed to keep hating him was more than he deserved. These long months were a kind of dream for her. Looking back, afterward, she was never able to remember how she had passed all that time. If Revere had allowed her to ask Sonya out, or if Caroline and Ginny had been able to come (their people forbade them), she would not have needed to drift about so in this sleepy confusion, waiting for the baby to be born. She was waiting for pain too. She could remember enough of what her mother had gone through to expect the same thing. The long, groggy months of pregnancy kept her heavy and warm, slow, a little dizzy with the awareness of what her body was going to accomplish and of the extraordinary luck she had had: where had Revere come from? He stayed with her for hours and held her in his arms, soothing her, telling her how much he loved her and how he had known this at once, the first time he saw her, telling her of all the things he was going to do for her and the baby; and out of all this Clara stared back at the way she had come and tried to figure out what was happening, but it always eluded her. She was like a flower reaching up toward the sun: it was good luck that the sun happened to be there, that was all. Like a flower she basked in the warmth of Revere's attention, never quite certain in those first few months how long it was going to last. When Revere stayed with her in the old house or when they walked slowly about the fields, talking, she believed she could hear past them the vast silence that had always followed her about, a gentle roaring that was like the roaring of the ocean when she'd been lying with Lowry out in the hot sun or like the monotonous rattling noise of the engines that had carried her and her family around for years....

He bought her a car, a little yellow coupe, and gave her driving lessons. They practiced on the lonely dirt roads where no other cars ever appeared, once in a while a hay wagon or a tractor, that was all, or some kids on bicycles. Clara loved those lessons and sat very straight behind the wheel, throwing her hair back out of her eyes with an excitement that was nearly hysterical—she could have been thinking of the complex system of roads that led from there to Mexico, a system she might be able to figure out. A map told you one astonishing thing: no matter where you were, there was a way to get somewhere else, lines led there, crossing and recrossing, you just had to figure it out.

But when Revere didn't come she only drove the car around in the driveway and in front of the house. She couldn't go into town, where people would stare angrily at her—she figured it would take them a while to get used to her and Revere, so she would give them that time—and Revere would not allow her to drive over to Sonya's, and it was too far to go to another town; anyway, she did not want to leave. If she couldn't go to Mexico she might as well stay home. She had a home now that was all hers and no one could kick her out. She had someone to take care of her and she wouldn't ever have to worry about being slapped around or him coming in drunk—as far as she knew he didn't even drink, which was strange. She explored the old house so thoroughly that she accepted it as hers and no one else's, as if she had been living there all her life. For weeks she seemed to be sleepwalking through an immense warm dream that had the dampness of October in this part of the country but none of the clarity of afternoons when the sun finally broke through, and the passivity with which she had had to accept Lowry's baby inside her kept her passive about other things as well. Revere brought her anything she wanted: sewing machine, cloth, odd pieces of furniture. It was her home.

The birth of Lowry's child was coming upon her the way death had come upon the house's first tenants, a warm sullen breeze blowing toward her from some vague point in the future. Whatever Revere brought her or decided to do to the house, she accepted as if it had always been planned, as if he were just filling in an outline. When they walked out in the fields or along the old lanes, Clara pulling at weed flowers or sucking grass, Revere sometimes lifted his shoulders in a strange forceful way he had, as if arguing with himself, and Clara had only to close her eyes to see not Revere but any man, a man, the idea of man itself come to take care of her as she had supposed someone must, somehow. She did not think enough about the peculiarity of her situation to come to the conclusion that she was the kind of girl someone else would always protect. This would have surprised her. But Revere might have been a promise someone had made—that someone was Lowry—when he had taken her away to save her from the old life back on the road, in another world now, and it would never have occurred to her to thank him for it.

He liked to frame her face in his hands and stare at her. He talked about her eyes and her skin; Clara hated this but put up with it, then it came to be something she expected Revere to do. If they were outside, she would smile up at the sky and let her mind loose from this place, wandering everywhere, and at the end return suddenly to this man who was staring at her—and she would be startled by the love she saw in his face. How could this stranger love her? Were all strangers so weak, no matter how strong they looked? But then, Lowry had been a stranger too, and so had her father, and everyone else. The only person not a stranger to her was Lowry's baby, the only thing she really owned. But each time she looked at Revere she saw more of him, until her shyness began to fade and she wondered if maybe she wouldn't end up loving this man after all, not the way she had loved Lowry but in another way. She knew that his mind did not flit around everywhere when he was with her; she knew he was looking at her and not through her at someone else.

"You're smart, Clara. You catch on quickly," he said, teaching her to back up the car. She had had no compliments in her life, and her face burned with pleasure when Revere said this. She took his hand and pressed it against her cheek. All this drew him to her, fascinated him, and it was only to be in later years that she would do it just for the effect. At this time in her life everything was new and spontaneous. She was hypnotized always by the wonder of her being here at all: how had it happened? Had she really done it herself, made the decision herself?

Out of the lonely, dark winter days in the house she had this idea: to make of Lowry's child a person to whom everything would make sense, who would control not just isolated moments in his life but his entire life, and who would not just control his own life but other lives as well.

They acted out two roles, not quite consciously: Revere was the guilty one, because he believed he had made her pregnant, and Clara was the victimized one, made softer and gentler by being victimized. She told him of her fears about having the baby, about the pain her mother had had each time, about the last baby that had killed her—this memory mixed up with a card game some men were having while, in another cabin, Clara's mother was bleeding to death. When she cried she was amazed at the sorrow she felt. She must have loved her mother in spite of everything, in spite of really having no mother for many years—so she wept until her head pounded, wishing she could call her mother back from the grave and give her all these gifts Revere had given her; why hadn't her mother had anything? Revere soothed her, rocked her in his arms. The fact of her pregnancy meant that she was his and, like any stubborn, lucky strong man used to getting his own way, he loved what was his own. He talked of "making up for everything" and Clara listened, her eyes still glistening with tears, accepting his apologetic caresses at the same time she might be thinking about Lowry, if he might write someday and what if someone at the post office, just to be mean, got hold of the letter and ripped it up? At some point Revere's sorrow for having "hurt" her made her feel guilty and she said, "But I love it already. I can't wait to have it. I love babies," and by saying this everything would be returned to her, even the joy of having been in love with Lowry, though it had lasted only those few days. "But I'm not going to no hospital or anything to have it," she said. "I want to have it right at home here."

"We'll see about it," Revere said.

"No, I want to stay here. I'm not going away."

"We'll see."

She was fierce with love for her home. From her old room she had brought things along for her bedroom, which was the first "bedroom" she had ever even seen, let alone lived in. She had a bed and a bureau of good polished wood, and a mirror rising from it that was like no mirror she'd seen before, and a closet just for her clothes, though she hadn't many, and a chair with a pillow on it, and a table alongside the bed on which Revere put his wristwatch when he stayed with her. On the wall opposite the bed was a print of a sunset, all spreading oranges and reds like pain flicked carelessly into water, with trees starkly silhouetted in black—Revere never said anything about the picture, which Clara had picked out herself. If she sat and stared at it long enough, strange, sad thoughts came to her and she would begin to cry, for no reason. Never in her life had she bothered to look at a real sunset; she heard sometimes on the radio a twangy-voiced man singing about a world "beyond the sunset" that also inspired her to tears, but still she did not bother to look at real sunsets. Paintings and music were meant to turn things into other things, Clara thought, so that the sunsets in pictures could make you cry while the real thing had no meaning at all. How could it? Even the picture of a house in winter, banked by clumps of evergreens, on the cover of a box of candy Revere had given her, meant more to her than the frequent picture she had of her own home, seen from the lane or the road. She could be moved by such things but not by reality, which was something that just lay stretched about her, indifferent and without meaning.

And just outside her bedroom was a corridor that led first to the kitchen—a big old drafty room with a pump at the sink, which Revere was going to fix up and which had already been painted a bright yellow—and then the parlor with its high gloomy windows that could hardly be stirred to life by the sun shining through them, then to another room that was left empty. There were heaters in three of the rooms. The house had an attic, but no one had bothered to fix it up; there were old boxes of junk—clothing dampened and mildewed, and Christmas ornaments of a wispy silvery type, many of them broken, and ugly furniture. Clara had been through everything many times. She felt closest to the old people when she looked through the Christmas ornaments, fingering the bulbs and the prickly lengths of trim that left silver flakes on her hands, thinking how unfair it was to those people that the things they had loved so ended up with Clara, a stranger. Then she put everything back carefully, as if she expected the owners to return and make their claim. Left alone in the attic, in sunny air or air heavy with gloom, she tried to think whether Revere was coming that evening or not. Sometimes she could not remember what he had promised.

One day someone drove down the lane in a rusty station wagon and Clara ran out onto the porch. It was November now and cold, but she stood waiting for the man to come up to her, her face set for a surprise, for something pleasant. But the man was about sixty, cranky and nervous. He said, "If somebody lives here now there's got to be a mailbox out front. Why ain't there a mailbox?"

Clara looked out toward the road as if checking to see if one might be there. Then she said, "There's nobody going to write me a letter."

"You need a mailbox regardless. Are you gonna get one?"

"I don't need none."

"What's your name?"

"Clara."

"Clara what?"

"Just Clara. I don't have any last name," she said sullenly. She stared down at the man's feet. Of course he knew who she was and that Revere owned all of this, but he kept at her with his eyes and his angry voice until she said, turning away as if she were a married woman with other things to do: "Oh, go to hell!"

Through the parlor window she watched him turn the station wagon around and drive back out, fierce and in a hurry. She thought with a kind of slow nervous power that maybe Revere could take that man's job away from him if she bothered to complain. But when Revere came out that day she said nothing. It was too shameful—she remembered the way that old man had looked at her, as if she were dirt, and how it was like everyone would look at her if they got the chance.

After a while she began to think about Revere's wife, who fed him meals on those days when he didn't eat with Clara, and the same sensation of power she had felt about the mailman rose up in her. What if . . . ?

She sometimes said, "What does your wife say when you're not home for supper? Does she get mad?"

Revere could signal her to be quiet without ever saying a word himself, but at times she chose not to understand his gestures. She would lean against him and let her head droop against his shoulder as if overcome with thought or worry, and he would always answer her. "This has nothing to do with her," he would say finally. Clara did not like this answer but she did not believe it, either. She would smile into Revere's face as if she knew better. He sometimes said, a little coldly, "You shouldn't worry about her. She's a very strong person."

"What do you mean, strong?"

"Strong. Like her family."

He never wanted to say much about his wife but Clara drew it out of him gradually, over the months. She did this with an actual picking gesture, touching his arm or shoulder and drawing something away from him, bits of lint or minute hairs she would hold between her fingers for a second and then discard with a deliberation that had nothing to do with thought. He must have been fascinated by her, by her words or her face, something, because she noticed how he would always answer her questions in the end. He seemed always to see another Clara, not Clara herself. "She isn't like you, Clara," Revere said once. "She isn't a happy woman." And Clara had stared at him, wondering if he thought *she* was happy—then she decided that of course he did, what did he know about her hours of being alone and thinking of Lowry, always Lowry, and her fear of what might happen in childbirth? He couldn't guess any of this. She was a girl who had been walking one day in the middle of a muddy road, dressed up, proud, excited, waiting for a man but not the man who had driven up behind her and stopped to give her a ride. Or she was the girl at the firemen's picnic, dressed up again but too excited and too reckless to know anything about how she should look, or about how people should look at her. Or she was the girl who ran out to meet Revere on the porch of this house, or out onto the hard frozen grass, shivering so that he would scold her as he embraced her, and so far as he knew her life had begun that day on the muddy road after someone else's wedding and had its reality only when he was able to get free and drive over to see her. So it was no wonder he thought she was happy; and she knew she would have to stay happy if she wanted a last name for Lowry's baby.

"But why isn't your wife happy?" Clara said, pretending surprise.

"I don't know. She isn't well."

"How bad is she sick?"

"She isn't sick. But she isn't well."

Clara would pretend to be baffled at this, as if such complexity lay beyond her. She was learning to play games with him to take the place of the passion she had felt for Lowry—you had to do something and say something to a man, and what was there to talk about that made any sense? Everything that was serious about life had to be kept back because Revere could not know about it. He could never know. Even if someone in Tintern hinted to him about Lowry, about another man involved with Clara, he wouldn't believe it. He did certainly think he had discovered her and that he had almost seen her born, that he was almost her father in a way. "She isn't like you," he would tell her. "You're very beautiful, you don't worry about anything. . . . You're just a child."

"I'm not a child," Clara said.

"You enjoy everything in life. You don't worry," he said.

That winter he began to bring a cousin of his over to visit her, a thin, lanky man who had not yet married, who was in his thirties. His name was Judd. While Revere sat with his feet out before him on the heater, firm and confident, Judd was restless and made Clara want to run to him and calm him down. He had a bony, earnest face that might have been handsome if something hadn't gone wrong, some angle pushed out of shape by his prominent cheekbones.

She listened to the two men talk about horses and the weather and their families and business contracts; evidently Revere had forced one of his competitors out of business. Clara sat listening, not quite knowing what they were talking about but sensing that Revere wanted her to stay on the periphery of his life, except when he crossed over to her of his own accord. She did not mind. Life out in the country had infected her with its silence; she imitated the cat Revere had brought her from home, a long-haired gray cat with a shabby, gentle, lazy face. The men talked, Revere more than Judd, about people Clara would never know, some of them living far away, others already dead. "Yes, sir, he is asking for trouble. He is asking for someone to sit on him," Revere would say, but smiling. Judd would make a flicking motion with his fingers, as if dismissing this person. A minute later Clara found out they were talking about the governor of the state. It made her smile in alarm, to think she could listen to a conversation that tossed that man's name about so casually; she felt a strange surge of power, as if Revere's quiet, bemused strength might someday turn into her own. But all she did was pet her cat, who lay sleeping at her feet and paid no attention to them at all.

They taught her to play card games. Revere always won; he was an apologetic winner. Clara made mistakes because she could never remember the rules. She thought card games were silly but they belonged to the world of men, so there must be some point to them.

Staring at a hand of cards newly dealt to her, trying to make sense of the numbers and suits, Clara understood that her brain could go so far and no further. She was limited, like a dog tugging at a chain. Somehow the two men could work these cards, toss down combinations right in the middle of talking, but Clara had to work hard every second. Perspiration came out on her forehead, tiny beads of sweat because she was ashamed of being stupid. She did not want to lay down her hand for them to see because it would be like opening her brain to the daylight and revealing how limited she was.

From Revere and Judd she got a picture, gradually, of a vague web of people, the generations mixed together and men present in their talks simultaneously with their grandfathers, and Revere and Judd as children; it was like a great river of people moving slowly along, bound together by faces that looked alike and by a single name. How wonderful to be born into this name and to belong to such a world. . . . Clara thought of Lowry's child among them, even if she herself could never quite make it. She thought of this child pushing its way through, appearing before the legs of aged people and pushing them aside, impatiently, with somewhere to go. Her child would be strong, Clara thought, like Lowry. It would be like Lowry. It would push its way through like Lowry did and yet it would be happy, while Lowry had never been happy, because it would be born with everything Lowry had been seeking. It would have a last name and a world and want nothing. . . .

They alluded now and then to relatives, in an oblique, glancing way that was difficult for Clara to follow. She gathered that the most wealthy of the Reveres lived in the city, in Hamilton. She gathered that there was some kind of quarrel between the city and the country Reveres, but that it would be straightened out. Revere's father had been a great fat man who'd died at the age of forty, knocked off a horse that ran under a low-hanging branch; he had been drunk at the time. Clara could not reconcile this with Revere himself. That story about his father was almost a joke, but nothing about Revere himself was a joke. And they mentioned a cousin of theirs, an older woman who traveled everywhere and never came home. She lived in Europe. Revere screwed up his face to show disgust for her. Judd defended her, saying, "People can't help what they believe. She says she just can't believe in God." "She'll believe in hell, though, fast enough," Revere said coldly. Clara sat leaning a little forward, her eyes lowered. She was learning. In those love magazines she used to read there were many stories of girls screaming at married men who had promised to marry them but never did marry them, and the point of the stories was that you got nothing by screaming but might get something by shutting up. Clara was learning that that was so.

During the long days when he was traveling or could not leave home, she talked to the cat and carried it around in her arms until it struggled free, or she worked at the sewing machine or tried to cook. She wandered through the rooms and looked out the windows at the snowy fields where white lay upon white out to the very horizon of the mountains. She cried out in silence for Lowry to come back to her, but nothing happened, no one came except Revere and once in a while his cousin Judd. She learned how to be still. Her hands would fall innocently upon her stomach and rest there, and she could not remember what she had done with her hands before. Kneeling on the sofa and staring out into the heavy winter sky, she thought: "I will not think about him. I will think about nothing all day long. Nothing. Nothing." The cat was so lazy it made Clara sleepy, so she slept during the day and felt that it was good for her. Then she and the cat sat in the kitchen together, she gave the cat warm milk, and talked to it off and on.

Because she was alone so much, she looked in the mirror often, as if to seek out her reflection as company. She liked to look at herself. She wondered if this was the face Revere saw, or did he see someone else? Her face was fine-boned, her eyes were slanting, like pale blue glass, eyelashes thick and innocently pale, almost white; she had a sleepy, lazy smile that could come out of nowhere even if she never felt like smiling again in her life. She held the cat up to the mirror and tried to interest it in its reflection; it did not respond. "Mighty strange, not to see yourself in a mirror," Clara said aloud, feeling sorry for the cat. What if people couldn't see themselves? It would be like living in a vast desert. The cat's name was Rosalie. When Revere and Judd sat in the parlor talking, she held the cat on her lap, her own expression shaped and suspended like the cat's, sleek and sleepy at once, so that Revere could stare at her with that look she was beginning now to control; she thought, "He fell in love with me the way another man falls into a swamp," and was able to think of herself as this swamp, something Revere could sink into and lose himself in. And if Lowry ever saw her again, she thought, he too would sink and drown; she would get him.

That bastard Lowry, she thought, clear-eyed and awake when Revere dozed off beside her, his heavy arm around her to keep her still and close to him. Sometimes she lay sleepless until dawn, when the night turned into day abruptly and awkwardly as light shot over the ridge of mountains—and where all that time went she could not say. She could watch Revere's face define itself into the face she now knew and was beginning to love: the lined, stern forehead, the eyes that did not seem to relax even when closed. Clara's long hair would be twisted with sleeplessness.

She thought of Rosalie, the first Rosalie, and how that girl had had a mistake happen to her and had not known where to run with it, on whose lap to dump it. Clara had known what to do before she had even known she would have to do it.

She thought of her mother—all those babies gouging themselves out of her, covered with blood, slippery and damp as fish, with no more sense than fish and no value to anyone. And how her mother had died!—she knew more about that night than she had ever let herself think about.

And she thought of her sisters, and of her brothers—lost somewhere—and of her father, who would probably be on the road right now, as always, drinking and fighting and going on, getting recruited on one crew after another, and that was going to be all. Had she betrayed them by running out? What did she owe them or anybody?

Her hands fell onto her stomach and she thought fiercely that she would betray anybody for this baby; she would even kill if she had to. She would do anything. She would kill Lowry himself if she had to.

In the morning she drank a cold glass of water to help keep her nausea down and felt the bright new coldness fall inside her as if there were nothing to stop it. And she would stand in her bare feet, shivering on the rough kitchen floor, and look out the window past the rust- and snow-flecked screen that was still left on it from last summer, to the barns that were stark black against the snow and past them to the decrepit orchard and as far as she could see to the horizon, to the sky, and hear silence easing down to her.

One day Revere drove her down through the valley and across the river and into the city of Hamilton, which she had heard about but had never seen. It was a port at the branch of two great rivers. Clara saw its smoke rising fatly up into the winter air for miles as they approached the city, driving on smart paved highways and passing cars that were often as good as Revere's. Back from the highway were the occasional shanties with their tar-paper or tin roofs, abandoned or filled with some hint of forlorn life, and along the highway were pieces of thrown-away junk, iron scraps, rusted mufflers that just fell off cars, sometimes even automobiles, and the frequent unsurprising signs for Royal Crown Cola or hotels in Hamilton with rates for the family or Lucky Strike cigarettes, everything sad and misty in the gray air. That soot on the edge of the signs, Revere told her, was blown out from the city they were coming to.

They crossed the Eden River on a high gleaming bridge. It was the same river Clara had waded in while Lowry watched, so long ago, and she thought grimly that it was really a different river this far out of Tintern and at this time of the year. It wasn't the same river at all. The bridge was high and new and Clara's stomach cringed to think of how high they were. She stared down at the water far below, winding tightly between two bright banks of ice covered with soft powdery snow; she was afraid she might be sick. She wondered if this trip might be a trick and if Revere might be going to abandon her somewhere, six months pregnant as she was.

They kept on driving for some time. The sun tried to shine through the gray, misty air, and finally they were driving in traffic and Clara looked out narrow-eyed at girls her age waiting to cross streets, their arms loaded with books. They wore bright wool socks that went up to their knees, and plaid wool skirts, and coats that hung carelessly open as they stood about with a vague purposeful air of having somewhere to go but feeling no hurry about it. It was about noon. There were many trucks on the road. Everything brightened and Revere turned off onto a winding street that led down toward the river. He said, "This is upriver from Hamilton." Clara tried to think what that meant; was it something special? Upriver, they maybe didn't get polluted water.

The homes here were set far back from the street, on hills that faced the river. Great immense homes with rows of windows that caught the sun and flashed it out indifferently, bounded by spiked iron fences and gates or high brick walls. The houses gave no sign of life. Clara stared out at them. Revere slowed his car in front of one of the hills. "Look at that," he said. It was nearly hidden from the street, high behind clumps of evergreens, a dark gray stone house with columns. "Does someone you know live here?" Clara said. "One of my uncles," said Revere. Clara's jaw muscles involuntarily tightened as if she were biting down hard on something, unable to stop, and she could feel the baby hard and tight inside her, demanding this already—the house and the columns and its heavy brutal look. She said, teasing, "Are you going to take me up to visit?" but he was already driving past. He didn't like to joke about things like that. "I thought you were going to take me in," she said. She did not call this man by any name. She certainly did not call him Curt nor did she even think of him by that name; she did not think of him by any name at all. If she had needed to call out for him to come to her she would have said, "Mr. Revere!" like everyone else.

"Someday, who can tell?" he said, trying to match her own tone.

He drove on for a while until they passed over into an area where the homes were closer together, all on a level, and Revere's surprise was a visit to a doctor—Clara had been against doctors all along. She had thought his silence meant he agreed with her. So she sat in the car for a while, trembling with anger while he talked to her. Then she gave up, close to tears. "All right, goddamn it," she said, and allowed him to get her inside the waiting room so that she could sit with him, without a wedding ring, in this room filled with women and their husbands who stared at her as if she were on display. "I hope it's born dead, just to get back at him," she thought, imagining Revere's sorrow and her own righteous hatred of him for what he had caused. She clasped her hands together, turned away from Revere to refuse his murmured conversation, and stared fixedly at the feet around the room—boots and rubbers and women's boots tipped with fur and unhooked farmers' boots (these were Revere's) that were leaving a small puddle on the floor. Good. It showed they were from the country, making a mess, and her without a wedding ring (and she would not hide her hands), while a skinny scarecrow woman with hair like straw looked up from her magazine at Clara, and a man with a round pumpkin face watched her too. There was a glassed-off partition behind which a nurse sat, answering a telephone, and in this glass Clara could see a vague reflection of herself. When they had come in, Revere stooped to talk through the hole in the glass; he had said, "Clara Revere," as if this were really her name, as natural as anything, and he didn't expect anyone to be surprised, not even Clara. She had wanted to interrupt and say, "Clara Walpole," but had no nerve. So she sat now and waited, and when that strange name was called—Clara Revere— she got up and refused to look at Revere as the nurse led her out.

When she came out again she must have looked awful, because Revere got right up and came to her. He took her hands. Clara was certain everyone thought he was her father and of course they had noticed she had no wedding ring—every woman had seen that in the first instant—so her face flushed with the shame of this situation he had gotten her into, just as it had flushed with shame before the doctor. The doctor called Revere inside to talk to him and Clara put on her coat and sat sullenly in it, thinking of nothing. Her feet were out loose on the floor, ankles turned out the way Lowry had sat that day on the riverbank, as if he had abandoned walking forever and would have been content to sit there doing nothing the rest of his life.

Revere came back out in a few minutes, his boots flopping, and Clara stared at them as if they were objects she could not quite place. Out in the car she cried with that hopeless, inflectionless passivity that cost her the least effort, while Revere talked to her, saying everything that was sensible and reasonable and that Clara would agree with in time but not right now. She was struck and weakened by his love for her, which was crazy, out of focus. "And I'm not going to a hospital. I'm not," she said. "Nobody I ever knew went to a hospital and they were all right...." After a minute or two she sensed that she should carry on no longer, that he might lose patience, so she wiped her eyes dry and was quiet.

"I wanted to get you something," Revere said apologetically. This was downtown, where the traffic fascinated and frightened Clara and the buildings were taller than any she had seen. On the sidewalks women walked past quickly in high-heeled shoes, as if they were used to wearing them on an ordinary weekday. They passed a big dirty-gray building with a statue out front: a horse rearing up toward the sky, a military man on his back, both of them tarnished a hard dead gray-green. It looked like something fished up from the bottom of the ocean. Revere parked the car and put a coin in the meter; Clara tried not to look too hard at the little flag that jumped back inside it. She had never seen that before. The air was frosty and impure here but no one seemed to notice. "Along this way," Revere said, not touching her. She walked along slowly, staring. Her lips were parted. Revere brought her to a small shop with only a few yards' coverage on the street; it was a jewelry store with a sign bearing a long foreign name Clara could not read.

There were no other customers in the store, which was narrow and deep, consisting of one long counter that led to the back. Clara stared about at the gleaming clockfaces and silver plates and tea sets, placed out in the open so that anyone could steal them, and down past the flawless clean glass to the jewels on dark velvet. She felt dazed by what she saw.

"Maybe you'd like something here," Revere said.

An old man waited on them. He was servile and smiling; he wore glasses. Clara stared down at the man's fingers as he brought out rings for her to look at—this could not really be happening, she thought. He indicated she should try a ring on. She slid it on her finger and saw how her hand was changed by it. "What's that, an emerald?" Revere said. The man said yes. Revere took Clara's hand and stared critically at the ring. "Well," he said, releasing her, "pick out any one you want. It's for you."

"But I don't know—what kind they are," Clara said. She stood flat-footed and awkward. She had a terror of picking something too expensive, or something Revere thought was ugly.

"Take your time. Pick out something pretty," Revere said. He stood a little apart from her. He was not uneasy, not quite, but Clara saw that there was something guarded in the way he spoke. She picked up a ring with a purple stone and tried it on.

"I like this one," she said at once.

"That's an amethyst," said Revere. Clara wondered what this meant.

"I guess I like it," Clara said shyly.

"Look at the others."

The old man pulled out another tray. Clara's heart beat in confusion and alarm at everything she had to see, touch, think about. Her instinct was to take the first thing and have done with all this awkwardness, all this pain. But in Revere's world, evidently, you stared hard at everything before you made your choice. The stones sparkled at her and their settings were intricate and beautiful, gifts from another world she had no right to and that she was stealing from those who really deserved them—not girls like herself but women who were really married, who were not choked with shame in a doctor's office. She was stealing from them and from Revere's wife, who should be here in Clara's place. Her fingers went blindly to another purple ring with a gold setting, placed high and cut into a dazzling intricate shape with many facets, and she turned it over and saw the price tag—just the number 550 in dark ink—and this did not register at once. When it registered she put the ring back. There was an ugly roaring in her ears. She would be able to wear on one finger something worth more money than her father had ever had at once, something worth more than anything her mother had owned, ever, and it was all coming about with no one showing any surprise except herself—the old man behind the counter wasn't surprised, maybe he was even bored, and Revere looked as if he did this every day. This was how life was.

In the end Revere wanted her to take that one. It was a little large for her finger but she said it was all right, she didn't want to bother anyone. All the way back home she stared at her hand, looking off at the colorless countryside and back at her finger, at the rich deep purple stone, her mind so overcome by it that she did not think of it as something she had stolen—from Revere's wife or her own people or anyone. It was hers. Clara brought the ring up and touched her face with it, then raised it to her eye so that she could see the sharp tiny reflection of the moving countryside in it, shadows and blurred forms that were like the passing of time in a world you could never get hold of.

"I thank you for this," she said to Revere.

The baby was born in May, a few weeks overdue by her reckoning, but that was lucky: it was just on time, according to Revere. And what she went through turned out to be no great surprise—it was not as bad as the times she had suffered along with her mother, having to watch helplessly. Revere drove her in to Hamilton, to a hospital, because this was what he had wanted and in all things that did not really go against her wishes she would give in to him; and the son she had, hers and Lowry's, was delivered over to Revere forever.

9

As soon as she became a mother with a baby to care for, time went quickly for Clara. She learned to live by the baby's rhythms, sleeping when he slept and wakening when he woke, fascinated by his face and the tiny eyes she imagined were like Lowry's eyes, coming so slowly into focus and one day looking right at her. Revere named the baby Steven, and Clara said that was a fine-sounding name, but her own name for him was Swan; she liked to whisper "Swan, Swan" to him, and sometimes when she fed him her hand would come slowly to a stop and she would sit leaning forward, frozen, staring at this creature who had come out of her body and had now taken on life of his own, putting on weight as if he knew what he was doing—and there he was, looking at her. "You smart little baby, darling little Swan," Clara would sing to him, hurrying around barefoot when it was warm enough at last, taking in the air of spring with a joy she had not felt since Lowry had left her. She made up tuneless tireless songs about him:

> He's going by train and by airplane
> All around the world. . . .

Revere was a little shy with the baby. "Why do you call him Swan?" he said. Clara shrugged her shoulders. With the baby born, she had work to do now—she did not bother fixing herself up for Revere but sat wearily or with a pretense of weariness, her long bare legs outspread and her hair tied back from her face carelessly, interested only in the baby. When Revere held him, Clara could hardly tear her eyes from the baby's face to look at Revere and to listen to his words. "I like the name, I picked it out myself. It's my baby," Clara said stubbornly. But she knew enough to soften anything she said, so she leaned forward to touch Revere's hand. She said, "I love him and I want lots of babies all like him."

She could tell that Revere didn't know how to hold a baby or how to feed him, it was just a nuisance to have him around, but she kept quiet about how she felt. She could outwait anyone, outlast anyone.

She would never have known what people thought of her from just the things Judd said if she kept asking him, except one day in July, when she thought Swan was sick, she drove into Tintern by herself. She had the baby bundled in a blanket, lying on the front seat beside her, and as she drove she kept leaning over to touch his face; she was sure he had a fever. "Don't fall asleep, that scares me," she said. "Swan, you wake up." She heard her voice climbing to hysteria. So she stopped the car and picked up the baby and pressed her face against his; then it struck her that this was crazy and that she should have called Revere on the telephone, hunting him up wherever he was, instead of taking the baby out into the heat. "You're not going to die. What's wrong, why don't you wake up like you used to?" The baby looked drugged. Clara began to cry, then she stopped crying and put the baby down and drove on, and when she got to Tintern the dusty little town opened up before her eyes like a nightmare picture someone had made up just for a joke. She thought how dirty it was, how ugly and common.

When she ran into the drugstore, barefoot, a few people at the counter looked at her. They were sipping Cokes. "Mr. Mack?" Clara said. A fan was turning slowly above the counter, making noise. "Where is Mr. Mack?" Clara said. "My baby's out in the car sick. I need help for him." Her voice accused those people who stared at her as if they were complete strangers and hadn't lived in the same town with her for two years. The woman behind the counter, Mr. Mack's niece, looked at Clara for maybe ten seconds and said, "He's takin a nap an' don't want nobody botherin him."

"My baby's sick," Clara said. She went past them and kept going. "Mr. Mack?" she called. At the doorway to the back she hesitated, her toes curling. There was a beige curtain pulled shut across the doorway. She did not push it aside, but said, "Mr. Mack? This is Clara here— Can you come out?"

He was not an old man but he had always looked old, and in the while she had been away from Tintern he had grown to look even older. No more than forty-five, but with a reddened face that was pale underneath its flush, and hair thinning meekly back from his forehead: he brushed the curtain aside and looked at her. She saw how his eyes narrowed, remembering her.

Clara's words came out too fast, tumbling over one another. "My baby's sick, out in the car. He's got a fever or something—he don't wake up right."

"Take him to a doctor."

"What doctor?"

He looked behind her, as if making out the face of a doctor somewhere in the distance. "In the city. Don't your man take you to a doctor in the city?"

"I need some pills or something," Clara said. She was trying not to cry. "He's real hot. You want to come out and see him? He's in the car—"

"How much money do you have?"

"I don't know—I—I forgot it," Clara said. They faced each other silently and Clara thought in panic that she should have brought the baby inside, not left it out there, or was she afraid to pick it up? At the counter people were watching. And there was some noise outside that meant her little yellow car had attracted attention already; but she did not turn around. Finally Mr. Mack said, in a voice that let her know what he thought of her:

"All right. Just a minute."

Clara hurried back out, past a big mannish woman with great

shoulders she had seen once or twice before—a farm woman—and those two girls of maybe thirteen who had ridden past her that day on their bicycles. She did not look at them. After she had passed and was out the screen door, she heard someone laugh. "Bastards," she thought. "Sons of bitches, I'll get them." But this took only a second and already she was lifting the baby out. His eyes were closed, milky-pale, and she bent her face against his to see if he was breathing—but she could not tell—and her heart stopped beating for a moment as she wondered if she was standing here with a dead baby, out in the sun with people drifting over to look. There were some little kids across the way; they called something out to her.

Mr. Mack took his time coming out. His face was furrowed like an old man's. "Remember, I ain't no doctor," he said. "Let's see him."

"He's hot, ain't he?"

"Take him out of the sun," the druggist said. His face showed disgust. Clara wished he would look at her, acknowledge her. They stepped back against the building. Mr. Mack touched the baby's forehead with the back of his hand, as if he were afraid of catching something from him.

"Look, I'll get money," Clara said wildly. "You know I can pay for it; just take care of him. It ain't none of that baby's fault—"

"He's got a fever."

"Is that bad? How bad is that?"

Mr. Mack shrugged his shoulders.

"What if he dies?" Clara said.

"He won't die."

"But what if—"

"Then he dies."

Clara stared at him. "Look, you give me some pills or something. You better give them to me."

"I'm not a doctor, I don't prescribe."

"Please, mister. Give me some pills or something—"

"All right, just a minute."

He went back inside. Everything was silent. Clara did not look around to check out this silence. The baby's eyelids fluttered as if he were struggling to get awake. He choked a little. "What's wrong?" she said. "You wake up, now. Why don't you cry or something?"

Mr. Mack returned and handed her a bottle. "You can rub this on him," he said. He wiped his hand on his thighs, uneasily, indifferently. Clara stared at the bottle's label: Rubbing Alcohol. "Give him some of these, too. Can you read?" he said. He handed her a little bottle of children's aspirin.

"I can read," Clara said.

"All right. There you are," he said, glad to get rid of her. He was about to turn away but Clara stopped him.

"How much do I owe you?"

"Nothing."

"Why nothing?"

"Forget it."

He turned away. Clara forgot the sick baby and said, "My money's good enough for you!" Mr. Mack did not acknowledge this. He let the screen door slam after him. Clara wanted to run to the door and yell something out, something to make them all sorry. . . . But she put the baby in the car and tried to get quiet. He was fighting at the air now, kicking. She took that for a good sign. "What the hell do we care for these people," she muttered. She wiped the baby's mouth on her skirt. She opened the blanket and unbuttoned the baby's shirt, and using her skirt again she dabbed some of the alcohol on his chest for a minute or so. Then she wondered if maybe this was a joke, that Mr. Mack had played a trick on her. . . . But she guessed it must be right: it said Rubbing Alcohol. She had never heard of it before; she thought alcohol was something you drank.

Across the street the kids were saying something. "Gonna give us a ride, Clara?" one of them yelled. He was big and had a familiar face: one of Caroline's brothers.

"What the hell are you asking?" Clara cried.

She climbed in the car and closed the door behind her, awkward in her haste, suddenly panicked by the children there and the other faces attracted by the commotion—someone was coming out the drugstore door to watch. She felt how they were all together and how she was alone. "I'll tell him and he'll kill you," she muttered.

She was thinking of Lowry; Lowry had maybe killed someone already and he could do it again. She tried to start the car but the engine must have been flooded. It was very hot. One of the boys yelled again and Clara did not look around, remembering how she and other kids had yelled at people, making fun.

A pickup truck turned the corner and approached slowly, driving down the middle of the street. Clara sat with her head bowed over the steering wheel and saw through a mass of hair one of the local farmers driving the truck. Some farm boys were in the back, their legs dangling over the edge. She felt heat push in on all sides of her and tried to start the car again.

"You havin trouble, you want a push?"

The driver stopped right by her, leaning out his open window to look into hers. He had a broad, thick, tanned face, and hair everywhere on his body that you could see—Clara's face went hard just to see him. "Little Clara, huh?" he said. "You want a push somewhere in your new car?"

"Go to hell," Clara said.

The boys in the back thumped against the roof and shrieked with laughter about something. Clara saw the farmer's face break into a happy grin and she did not bother to listen to his words, but cut through them viciously: "Go to hell, you fat old bastard, you fat-assed son of a bitch of an ape! You monkey's ass!" They were silent for a moment just out of surprise. Clara fumbled with the ignition and this time got it started.

"Whose car is that?" someone yelled. There was a rising, buoyant joy in everyone but Clara; she could sense it. "Whose baby is that? Whose baby?"

Clara got the car going and it leapt ahead, away from the truck. She saw heat glimmering over the road like figures dancing to distract her. In a minute she would be out of this and safe. Nothing like this would ever happen again. Those bastards, she thought, her mouth like a slit outraged by pain, and as she turned the car into the center of the street to get out of town she felt and heard something crash against the roof. A clod of mud burst there and fragments flew to all sides. Her first instinct was to press down on the gas pedal, but something made her look back—she could not help herself. Caroline's brother was running after her with something else to throw, and while she looked right at him he slammed another heavy clod of mud against the back window. People laughed. The boys on the pickup truck had jumped down. Caroline's brother ran at her, yelling "Shoo—shoo! Scat!" as if he were chasing chickens out of the yard.

Clara sat frozen, the engine idling, her body twisted so that she could see them all—these boys and those young men, running after her car, drawn by something feverish and hunted in her face. "Shoo! Get on home—you stink! Clara stinks!" the boy yelled, pounding his fists on the side of the car.

She must have had a moment in which to think, to choose, but at once she opened the door and got out of the car. She ran right at the boy, running into him. He was about twelve years old and as tall as she was. She surprised him so, butting him like that, that he fell backward and his mouth jerked open. "You little fucking bastard!" Clara screamed. She kept on screaming and pushed into him, digging at his face with her nails. The other boys stood around, amazed, and Clara kept striking at Caroline's brother with her furious blows, and when the boy recovered enough sense to fight back she was ready for him and met the blow with one of her own, pounding the soft inside of his arm with her fist. "I'll teach you! I'll kill you!" Clara screamed. Something kept her going—rising in her like madness, pushing her forward and running her into the boy so that he never got his balance, but only yelled at her in desperation. She had the feverish vision of his face streaked with tiny bands of blood, then she lunged at him again and caught hold of his hair with both hands and swung him around. She kicked him as hard as she could between the legs and let him fall groveling in the street. "There! I told you!" she cried. She turned to taunt them all, her hair loose and wild about her face, and all their faces were just one blurred face to her—then she was back at the car and pressing down on the pedal. They let her go.

If Revere ever found out about that he said nothing to her and she certainly said nothing to him. Sitting on the floor with the baby, playing with him, Clara could forget her humiliation in his face and the clumsy motions of his hands, fascinated by how everything was diminished in Lowry's baby that had been so hard, so strong in Lowry himself. If she had been insulted because of the baby it was nothing—she could go through it again and again, what did she care? "What the hell do we care?" she murmured to him.

She sang:

> He's going by train and by airplane
> All around the world....

She imitated the baby's patience, the cat's long sleepy patience, the turning of the days into nights and the relentless trancelike motion of the seasons, feeling herself sinking down to a depth that was not quite unconscious but where all feelings, emotions of love and hate, blended together in a single energy. She remembered her father's anger that had never been directed toward anything that made sense and Lowry's insatiable yearning, a hunger that could take him all over the world and never give him rest; these impulses belonged to men and had nothing to do with her. She could not understand them. The most she did was ask Revere about his house sometimes, innocently: "Is it drafty like this house? Is there a special room for a baby?"

She got the impression of something vast and unexplored, a big stone house with elms around it, the house a century old and in better condition than new houses—everything must be perfect there. Judd had told her the barns had the name REVERE painted on them in big black letters; Clara had been struck by that. She closed her eyes and tried to imagine what that might be like, to see your name written out like that. It was hard for her to put together the man who sat in the kitchen of this old farmhouse, watching Clara and the baby playing together, and the man who had barns with his name on them: how could he be the same person? How could a single man be so expanded? Or how could it be that a name on a barn, something so big, could be diminished into this man who was tall and strong but weakened by his love for her?

She asked Revere: Did the boys have anywhere special to play around that house? Were they getting big? Did the house have a porch where you could sit out in the summer at night? Did the house have lightning rods? Was there a nice garden? Was there a fireplace? Was the kitchen nice and clean, or was it big and drafty like hers?

That winter passed by and in the spring she began to dream about Lowry again. She had the idea he might be coming back. There were hours when she wandered around outside with the baby, staring off toward the road and waiting for someone to appear without knowing what she wanted. If she understood what she was waiting for, she rejected it angrily; there really was no room in her life for Lowry now. She would give up nothing of it for him. But she kept looking and waiting and there were times at night when she rose dizzy with sleep and tried to get her head clear, wondering at the power of her body and at the deep vast depths of herself where there were no names or faces or memories but only desires that had no patience with the slow motion of daily life.

In the summer after Clara's eighteenth birthday, Sonya died and Clara went to her funeral. Revere was gone away to Chicago and so Judd was good enough to come and watch Swan, and Clara drove by herself to the little country church ten miles from Tintern where Sonya was going to be buried. She had forgotten Sonya for some time and the news of the girl's death was at first something oblique and impersonal, like a newspaper item. Then it began to eat into Clara and she thought of the many times they had been together—already years ago, in what had been left of their childhoods; but even then they had not been children.

Everyone was silent in church. Clara saw Sonya's mother and a few kids who were Sonya's brothers and sisters, and some relatives, old women she had never met before, sitting up in the second pew wearing black and looking sick and heavy. There were not many people in church. Clara recognized some of the faces and sensed that these people could look at her today without any special hatred, believing that she was like Sonya and therefore destined to be punished for everything sooner or later, like Sonya. And it did happen, Clara thought, that you were punished sooner or later. It happened whether you did anything wrong or not. So she sat in a black cotton dress with a wide-brimmed black hat on her head, pulled down a little over her forehead to hide her bangs, and watched the coffin as the minister talked over it, wheedling and prodding them into thinking about a strange invisible world of God that was somehow simultaneous with this world but never found in it, until she wanted to cry out to the man that he should shut up—what did all that have to do with Sonya? "There are some bastards that don't do nothing but talk, talk all their lives," she thought.

No matter what he might say, trying to turn facts into something that sounded better, Sonya was dead and that was that. The top of the coffin was closed. Sonya had been her best friend in those days before Revere came and changed her life, they'd slept in the same bed and talked all night long, but now Clara sat healthy and erect in the pew and Sonya lay dead while everyone stared gloomily up at the coffin as if a little put out that they had to be here on this beautiful day. Clara could see the side of Sonya's mother's face—a pale hawkish profile that showed no grief. Everything eroded downward in that face and whatever happened that was ugly just etched the lines in deeper, convincing her she had been right all along. But then, Sonya's mother was supposed to be a little crazy; she wouldn't know what to feel. How did you know what to feel? Sonya had been strangled by the man she'd been living with for nearly a year, and now the man was in jail waiting to be killed himself and his wife was going around making trouble everywhere, drunk half the time—so how did you know what to feel? Sonya just hadn't gotten out in time, that was all.

The ceremony came to an end. Clara heard the minister's words stop a moment after they had actually stopped; she had been so wearied by them. Everyone stirred and the church felt hot again. Sonya's oldest brother and some other young men went awkwardly up front and picked up the coffin. Clara flinched when they lifted it into the air, feeling the sudden heavy weight of Sonya's body on their shoulders—but they picked it up with no effort and walked out into the sunlight and around back, their young faces grim and faintly sullen in this company of women; they were out of their own world. Everyone else filed along behind with that pretense of hurry that disguises a confused reluctance. The outdoors made everything different—a little unreal. Clara smelled sun-drenched, sunburnt corn and wheat, and her eyes moved involuntarily to the sky where the future lay eased out forever, without boundaries. There, anything could happen: you need only be alive. The pulsing of her veins and the slight trembling of her body made her feel light, while Sonya in that coffin must be heavy, gravitating already down toward the dry earth. It was not fair, Clara thought, but she was alive and Sonya was dead. Something gleamed and caught her eye: the amethyst ring Revere had bought her.

The grave was ready. Clara caught up with everyone and then stopped still; there was nowhere farther to go. She stared from face to face at those people on the other side of the open grave, and felt tears at last coming into her eyes. She could not quite believe that Sonya was in that box. She had not seen Sonya for many months, for a year. What had she to do with Sonya? Everything was unreal, faintly incredible—the soft warm air and the hard black coffin, the songs of birds and insects invisible all about them and the minister's droning voice, the hole there dug right out of the earth that was so peaceful on all sides, with its ancient tilting gravestones and weeds and forgotten, forlorn flowerpots with dried-out plants in them like tiny skeletons. . . . In the middle of all this, while the minister went on with something he had to get said, Clara thought quite clearly and desperately of Lowry. She could not live out her life and die and never see him again. She could not die and be buried, like Sonya, with strangers standing around who did not give a damn, or who believed God's will was being done, sin punished, while Lowry was somewhere else—or maybe dead himself, buried by people who also did not give a damn and who could not have known who he was. Something wanted to claw its way out of her, made wild by this thought. She covered her face and wept.

Then it was over. People turned to leave, relieved, their eyes skidding away, breaking up into little clumps—family, mainly. Those people who hated one another and fought every evening in their homes banded together comfortably out of loyalty, or habit, or spite; Clara was the only person who was really alone. The minister would have walked with her, to prove something or other, and to make Clara think seriously of her own future—as if anyone was ever going to strangle her! But she walked fast to avoid him. She said nothing to anyone, not even to Sonya's mother. She had nothing to do with these people. She had nothing to do with Sonya either, now that Sonya was dead.

She drove quickly away, not even glancing back to see the cloud of dust she made and to wonder what they thought of her—frowning, disapproving eyes, waiting for her to get punished the way Sonya had. As she drove she cried silently, feeling the tears run hot down her face. She was thinking of Lowry. Her heart churned inside her at the memory of him. She pictured him, she tried to remember how he talked; her head jerked a little as if in silent conversation with him. Outside, the land flowed by without her noticing it. She did not know which direction she had taken. Whatever road it was, it wasn't the right road; it was some dusty country road that led nowhere. She drove for quite a while, faster and faster, with the tears now burning her eyes and her mouth set sullenly against the pressure that would make her turn the car around and drive back home.

About an hour later she approached a town: FAIRFAX POP. 2500. She had never seen Fairfax before. It looked like Tintern except it was on a hill, jumbled and awkward. She let the car slow down to drift through the town, and she noticed a gas station. It was an old, small building painted green some time ago. There were just two gas pumps, giant ugly things, and the drive was all dirt, bleached pale by the sun. Clara turned into the station.

She sat breathing hard, her heart still pounding. An attendant came out of the little building, hurrying toward her with his head bowed, or with his body shaped in the pretense of hurry. Behind him she caught sight of another man standing in the doorway. Something rushed in her, a sensation of drowning, choking; but the man was a stranger. His height and his slouched shoulders had made her think of Lowry and she hated herself for that. . . . The attendant hurried around to her and she said sullenly, not caring what he thought of her reddened eyes or windblown hair, "Give me some gas, some expensive gas." She picked up her purse as if to indicate she had money, then let it fall back on the seat. The attendant was a skinny man in his forties with a dull, freckled face. Clara got out of the car. She let the door swing open. Her heart was still pounding, everything seemed about to tilt around her, and yet she did not know why—it could not still be on account of Sonya, who was gone forever now, and why should it be because of Lowry? She hated him. She did not give a damn about him.

The sun was hot and bright about her. She walked around the car as if testing her legs. She looked at her bare arms, at her wrists and hands, at the ring that gleamed so darkly in this rich light, and only after a moment did it occur to her that she was doing all this for the man inside the building. She looked over at him. He was just lowering a soft drink bottle from his mouth. She saw him wipe at his mouth with his sleeve, and a smile began to itch at her mouth. He stepped down onto the packed dirt and tapped to check his cigarettes in his pocket, some little ceremonious gesture that meant he was conscious of her, and Clara let her head fall back as if to dry her eyes in the sun or to show off her face. He walked right up to her car and put one foot out against the fender, as if appraising it; then he looked sideways at Clara.

"Somebody's been drivin fast," he said.

Clara brushed her hair back from her face with both hands. She felt cunning and lazy; what had been wild inside her a few minutes before was now waiting quietly. She said, "You work here or something?"

"Hell, no."

He finished the bottle of lime pop and turned to toss it back against the building. It struck the side and left a white streak. "What are you doin?" the other man said, up front by the car hood. The man just laughed. Clara smiled and saw him watching her and as he watched she let her lips move slowly back to show her teeth, the way a cat would smile if it could smile. He had dark, damp hair and he wore a pullover shirt with something faded on its front, and blue jeans old and faded with grease; Clara saw that his face was young and impatient. He took hold of the radio antenna of her car and bent it toward him slightly, then let it go. He looked at her. Clara kept on smiling. He wiped his forehead, then his mouth, and his fingers closed into a loose fist while he watched her.

"You ain't from around here, that's for sure. Where're you from?"

"Driving through," Clara said.

"Where're you goin?"

She lifted one shoulder vaguely and then let it fall. "Somethin happened, maybe?" he said. "You been cryin?"

Clara turned away and said to the gas attendant, "How much is it?" He told her and she reached inside the open window to get her purse, one leg raised from the ground to balance herself, and then she took the dollar bill out and handed it to the man; the other man, the one who had been talking to her, had come up close so that she could see a small white scar almost lost in his eyebrow. She said to him, "If you live outside town and want a ride home, I can drive you."

She said this so dreamily, staring right at him, that he had no time to let his gaze drop somewhere so that he could think— instead, he said at once, "Fine with me," and nodded once or twice. Clara ran around the car and got in and he was already beside her, his long legs awkward, smelling of perspiration, glancing sideways at her with the same kind of taut calculated smile she herself had.

She drove down through the town and out from it, out into the country again. "You like living here?" she said to him.

"I'm goin in the Army next month," he said.

"What if they go in with all them people fighting?" Clara said. She knew only what she overheard from Revere and Judd: fighting in Europe. The young man made a sound that expressed contempt for the war and for her question. "You maybe could get killed," she said.

She glanced over at him and saw that he was maybe twenty-two, twenty-three, and that if he was going to die shortly he would need her now. He was watching her as she drove. His face was damp again, though he'd just wiped it and his shirt was soaked through; on his hard muscular upper arms the sweat looked oil-slick. "I thought you were somebody else, the first sight I had of you," she said. She spoke softly and coaxingly. He said, stirring as if he were uncomfortable, "Sorry I ain't that man." "There's no need," Clara said. "Yes, I am real sorry," he said. She stopped the car and they sat for a moment, not looking at each other, then they got out of the car and seemed almost to be testing the ground with their feet. He came around to her side, dragging one hand across the hot hood of the car. Right next to the road was a thick woods that was posted.

Clara said, "You think they're going to get the state troopers out if anybody walks in there?" He took her arm and helped her across the ditch. He lifted the barbed wire for her to go under, holding it up as high as he could. Clara ran through and into the woods with her hair loose behind her, feeling something pushed up to suffocate her, almost, in her chest and throat. It kept pushing at her, goading her into a wild feverish smile she turned toward the woods but not toward the man.

He caught up with her and took hold of her as if he had been waiting for this for hours. Clara heard his breath come brokenly. They lay down and he was ready for her so fast that it seemed this must just be another dream, Lowry's face obscured from her while she gripped him around the neck, tensing herself, the cords in her throat getting taut and anxious. "Come deep. Deeper," Clara said. Then she stopped thinking and abandoned herself to this man, sinking down to that great dark ocean bed where there were no faces or names but only shadowy bodies you reached out to in order to calm yourself; nothing came before and nothing came afterward. She shut her eyes tight and had no need to think of Lowry, who was with her in this stranger's body, and at the end she moved her teeth hard against the bone of his jaw to keep from crying out. Afterward he didn't roll off her but stayed where he was, holding her down as if she were a prize he had won by force, and he kissed her to make up for what they had not done before. His chest was heaving, his body drenched with sweat. Clara brushed his wet hair back off his forehead and framed his face with her hands while she kissed him. She felt as if she were drowning in the heat of his body, in the heat of everything wet and drugged that she could not control or get clear in her mind, and that she loved whoever had come to her like that, she was lost in love and would never get out of it.

When she got back to the house it was early evening. Revere's cousin Judd was playing with the baby in the front yard. Clara saw that he had a weak, vulnerable face and that something in the urgency of his look meant that he had been worried about her. She got out of the car and looked down at her wrinkled dusty dress and her dirty bare feet, and for no reason at all she set the black hat on her head and came over to meet them. She picked the baby up and kissed him, closing her eyes with gratitude. The very earth before her feet seemed to her solid and transformed; the baby's happiness was her own happiness; her body had not been like this since those days with Lowry. Seeing Judd's look she said, "I got lost somewhere," and pressed her face against the baby so that she would not have to look at Judd.

10

"Honey where are you? Swan?"

Clara was working in the side garden and it occurred to her that the boy had been gone for a while. She let the hoe fall. "Swan? Where are you?"

Revere said she fussed over the boy too much and she knew it, but it was partly just loneliness; anyway, she liked to talk, and if Swan wasn't with her she couldn't talk without thinking herself a little crazy, like a few women in the vicinity she could name. She looked around the garden and out toward the orchard, letting her eyes move easily from thing to thing, all her possessions. She had been living here for four years now; she was twenty-one. If she thought of the time behind her, she felt no regret, no doubts at all. All those years when Revere came to visit her and occasionally stay the night were kept here in the look of the land he had gifted her with, the slightly shabby farm with its tilted and moss-specked barns, the wild grass that to Clara was so beautiful, the wildflowers and weeds and bushes sprung out of other bushes like magic—all this was hers.

She tilted her head back to let her hair fall loose. Her hair was warm and thick, too thick for August. Sometimes she wore it pulled back and up, in a great clumsy knot that fell loose all the time and made her feel childish; most of the time she let it fall wild. It was bleached by the summer sun, like her boy's, almost white, a pale gleaming moon-colored blond that seemed to be kin to the burnished tips of certain weeds and the way the sun could slant its light off the tin roof of the old barns. Clara said, "Swan?" without bothering to raise her voice and went through the garden toward the back of the house. It was a large garden for just a woman to handle, though Revere and Swan could help her. But it was her garden and it bothered her to have someone else working in it. A year ago, before his marriage, Revere's cousin Judd had put in some large-petaled roses for Clara, and in a way she had minded even that—though she had not let on. Now, since his marriage, Judd never came to see her. His wife would not allow it. So it was Clara's garden and no one else's, and when her eyes moved from plant to plant, pausing at each dusty familiar flower and occasional insects she'd flick off with an angry snap of her fingers, a feeling of accomplishment rose up in her. The garden was as much of the world as she wanted because it was all that she could handle, being just Clara, and it was beautiful. She did not want anything else.

Her mother had never had a garden, Clara thought. If her mother were still alive she'd maybe like to sit on the back porch and look at this garden, and be pleased at what her daughter had done.

To Clara it was all transformed by the sunlight that bathed the land every day, changing those old rotting barrels out back and the dilapidated chicken coop and everything her eye might come across into things of beauty. Even the most dwarfed of the pear trees could be beautiful: she only had to look at it with that fierceness of satisfaction that had now become part of her. And if Swan should run back there with the dog, jumping and playing in the grass, she would stand transfixed, as if she were at the threshold of a magic world.

Clara came through the backyard. Revere had bought a few chairs for it from a store in the city—tubed metal, painted bright red (the color Clara had thought she wanted) and glaring like splotches of paint dashed right on the land itself. She paused to look through the back screen door, thinking he might be in the kitchen somewhere. "Swan?" she said. On either side of the back stoop were great lilac bushes banked up close, not in bloom now but heavy with leaves. Over the house elms seemed to be leaning, like people watching Clara, and she thought of how quiet everything would be except for Swan's dog and how the world had moved back from her—the worry and bother of which old person was sick now in Tintern or what Ginny would do with that boy of hers whose teeth had to be pulled, all of them—all rotted—and who would win the war over in Europe, so far away from her on this land and impressing itself upon her only through the few signs she saw nailed on trees and in town: JOIN NAVY, RED CROSS, WORK AT GARY, WORK AT DETROIT, WORK AT WILLOW RUN, GIVE BLOOD. "Give Blood" made Clara think hard; it was the only sign that got to her. She went into town as much as she wanted now, no one bothered her—most of the men were gone and quite a few of the families, following their men down out of the mountains to work in the defense factories, disappearing. Many old people were left and the mail now was everything to them; they were jealous over one another's letters. The world had suddenly opened up the horizons falling back far beyond the ridge of mountains that had seemed at one time to be the limit of their world. And so nobody cared about Clara now; after four years, she was almost as good as Revere's wife, and so they did not bother her.

"Give Blood," those signs said. Clara sucked at her lip to think of what that meant, why it was nailed up everywhere. Men were dying, drained of their blood; did it sink into sandy soil, or into dust, or into mud, across the ocean where Revere would never have to go?—when you owned what he did you went nowhere, you stayed home and managed things, even Judd did not have to go, but that was for a different reason: nerves. But the husbands and sons and brothers of people in town, Caroline's husband and Ginny's husband (though Ginny's husband had already left her) and anyone you could name, many of them were not just gone now but dead or reported missing, which was the same thing. Clara could not keep this in her mind and there was the remote, haunting idea that she should keep it in mind and think of it all the time, that someone needed to be thinking of it—it was so strange, this sudden opening up of the world. But she put it all out of her life and thought instead of Swan, who was a child and therefore safe. When she went to town and someone cornered her, some woman, she listened with her eyes lowered as she heard about some young man or boy who was "all right," didn't she think so, because everyone knew they were treated well in the prison camps? She thought instead of Swan.

Out here, north of Tintern and south of the Eden River, in the slow gentle slope of the valley that encompassed so much land, history had no power for her. It was hardly real except if you listened once too often to one of those old women. Clara kept up her house and sewed for herself and the boy and worked outside and made supper for Revere and took care of him when he came to her, telling him what he wanted to hear and letting him love her and say to her what he always said, as if he were kept young by saying these things, pressing his face against her body and losing himself in it. Out here time might pass, but it was just weathertime or daytime, seasons blending into one another or days turning into night, nothing that got you anywhere: she was older than before, maybe, but she looked better than she had ever looked in her life. Time had nothing to do with her.

The dog was barking. It rushed around the corner at her eagerly as if it had something to tell her, a dog of no particular type Revere had bought her one day. Clara ran around the house and saw first a car parked out by the road and thought *That's strange,* and then she saw a man at the end of the drive, just where it branched off to go to the barns and back along one of the old pastures. Swan was standing by this man. He was facing him and the man was bending a little to talk to him, his hands on his thighs. Clara approached them and the dog came up behind her and overtook her, barking. Once or twice she had been bothered by strangers and one winter morning she had even discovered footprints out in the snow, under her windows. . . .

The man was Lowry.

As soon as she saw that, she stopped. She stopped, panting, her hand against her chest as if she were stricken with pain. They looked at each other across the patch of scrubby grass, and the boy turned to look at her too. When she got her senses back she walked to Lowry, slowly, and he came to meet her. Clara said in a voice that was too faint, "What the hell do you want?"

Lowry looked the same. Or maybe not: something was different.

He wore a blue shirt and dark trousers and shoes smudged with dust from the walk down the lane. His face was the same face, with its thick firm jaw and that expression that played for innocence, as if he'd been gone a week at the most and why did she look at him like that?

"Mommy—" Swan said.

She wondered, staring at the boy, if Lowry knew. But how could he not know? She let Swan push against her, he was frightened; in another minute he would hide behind her legs. "It's just a visitor," she said, a little sharply. She wanted him to be brave in front of Lowry. "You go over and play with the dog."

The air between her and Lowry must have been choked with heat. He kept looking at her, smiling. No one should be able to smile that way, Clara thought. But she could do nothing in return, not make her face ugly or hard against him. She felt rigid, as if a small ticking mechanism inside had suddenly failed.

"Well, what do you want? What do you want?" she said.

"I came to see you, that's all." He held out his hands, not to suggest an embrace but just to show that he was carrying nothing, had no surprises.

"You—you dirty bastard," Clara said. She looked over to where Swan was playing, pretending to play, then her eyes shot back to Lowry. "Why did you come here? You want to ruin everything for me? Didn't they tell you about me?"

"Sure."

"You asked then in town?"

"I asked them in town."

"Well?" Clara said shrilly, "what do you want, then? He isn't here now, it's lucky. You want to see him?"

"Why should I want to see him?" He leaned toward her and laughed. She heard the familiar laugh but saw something flash from inside his hair, something flat against his skull; this frightened her. It might have been a scar around which hair wouldn't grow. "I just came to see you. I thought you might want to see me."

"I don't know why in hell you thought that," Clara said, trying to make her words hard enough to keep down her trembling. She turned away from him suddenly to stare out at the fields that ran to the road—thick with dandelion fuzz that was white and fragile as she felt. Out there his car was parked. "Why did you leave your car out there?"

"I don't know."

But she thought it was strange. He had come back to the house on foot. "How did you find me?" she said.

"They told me. But they didn't think I should come."

"Well—what do you think? What do you want?" she said. She stared at him and felt in this instant that she was too young to go through such things, that this moment was terrible for her because she knew what he wanted and what she would say to him, as if everything had been rehearsed in her dreams for years without her knowing about it.

"Honey, I came back for you," he said. He took her hand. He slid his hand up to her wrist and jerked her a little as if waking her. "He's a real cute little kid," he said, nodding over toward Swan. "I knew he was your kid right away—he looks like you. I knew I was at the right place then."

"But—what do you want?" Clara said.

"Do you love him, this Revere?"

Clara wanted to say something but could not. Her lips parted but Lowry's eyes had too much power over her, they wanted too much. She felt that she would fall helplessly from him if he released her wrist.

"I said, do you love him?"

"I don't need to love anybody."

Lowry laughed. His face was not as tan as one might think, this late in August. "Aren't you going to invite me in? Have supper or something—what time is it?"

"Suppertime almost, but I don't have anything fixed—I—"

"Don't you want me to stay?"

She looked around to where Swan was kneeling with one arm around the dog's neck. They might have been whispering together or crying together. The impulse to tell Lowry that this child was his was so strong in Clara that for a moment she could not speak at all. Then she said, "You can come in. I'll feed you. He isn't coming over tonight."

"That would be real kind of you."

"You're probably hungry."

"I'm hungry."

"You look tired—you've been driving a long time."

"That's right."

At the door her foot slipped and Lowry had to catch her. "Swan, come on in," she called. The boy was waiting on the path, his clever, silent face turned toward them. Then Clara said, confused, "No, never mind. You don't need to—it's hot inside." She started to cry. It had something to do with her foot slipping on her own doorstep—mixing her up, frightening her. Lowry laughed and put his hands on her waist and pushed her up into the house.

"This is nice," he said, "but Revere could do better for you."

"I know that."

"Don't you mind, then?"

"I don't want anything else. I told him to stop buying me things a long time ago."

He walked through the kitchen and looked into the parlor. There Clara's plants were everywhere, on the windowsills and on tables—broad, flat leaves, ferns, tiny budlike leaves, violets you might almost miss if you didn't look closely enough. She saw Lowry looking at them. "You have a house all your own now," he said.

Clara followed him into the parlor where it was cool. She was still crying, angrily. Lowry turned and said, "I see you got grown up."

"Yes."

"When did that happen?"

"After you left."

"Not before?"

"No."

"They said you've been with him a long time. Four years, maybe? That's a right long time, it's like being married."

"Yes," Clara said.

"You like him all right?"

"Yes."

"What's this here?" And he reached up to take hold of the small gold heart she wore on a chain around her neck. "So he gives you nice things. This is expensive, right?"

"I don't know."

"What about his other wife?"

"He's only got one wife."

"What about his other sons?"

"I don't know."

"They don't mind you?"

"I suppose they hate me—so what?"

"Doesn't it bother you?"

"Why should it?"

"Being out here like this—for him to come visit when he wants."

"You used to do that too," Clara said, pulling away. He let go of the heart. "I suppose you forgot all that."

"I didn't forget anything," Lowry said. "That's why I'm here."

Then the trembling started in her, a rigid violent trembling that began far down on her spine and passed up her back to her shoulders and arms, a feeling she had never known she could have. All those years with Revere were being swept out into sight and considered and were maybe going to be swept out the back door, as if with a broom Clara herself was whisking about impatiently.

"Let me get you a beer," Clara said.

"Are you cold?"

"For Christ's sake, no," she said, looking away. "It's summer out." She felt the shivering start again and made herself rigid. Lowry sat down and she went to the refrigerator and got two bottles out. At the window she saw Swan by one of the barns, alone and lonely, a child without other children, with a mother who was now about to desert him and betray him, just as she must have always known she would. And the worst betrayal of all would be her giving him this father who had come down the lane without even driving up, apologizing for nothing and already bossing them around. She saw Lowry through the doorway, his legs outspread and his hands fallen idly across his flat stomach.

She sat on the arm of his chair. Drinking together like this made them quiet, quieted something in her. Lowry said, "I went to Mexico and got married."

"You what?"

"Got married."

Clara tried to keep her voice steady. "Where is your wife, then?"

"I don't know."

"Well—that's nice."

"We got rid of each other before the war. She was trying to teach down there, just for something to do. She was from Dallas. I guess," he said, closing his eyes and pressing the bottle against them, "I guess we were in love, then something happened. She kept at me, she kept worrying. She was afraid I went after other women."

"What was she like?"

"I don't know. What are people like? I don't know what anyone is like," he said. "She had dark hair."

"Oh."

"This was all a while ago. She divorced me."

"Divorced?"

The word was so strange, so legal, it made her think of police and courthouses and judges. She stared at Lowry as if she might be able to see the change this divorce had made in him.

"Are you all right now—are you happy?" she said.

Lowry laughed. She saw the lines at the corners of his mouth and wondered for a dazed instant who this strange man was.

"That depends on you, honey."

"But what do you want from me? You son of a bitch," she said, bitterly. "I'm a mother now, I have a kid. I'm going to be married too."

"That's nice."

"I am, he's going to marry me."

"When is this going to take place?"

"Well, in a few years. Sometime."

"When?"

"When his wife dies."

Lowry grinned without there being anything funny. "So you're waiting around here while she dies, huh? They said in town she was sick but she'd been sick for ten years. You want to wait another ten years?"

"I like it here."

"Stuck out here by yourself?"

"I'm not by myself, goddamn it. I've got Swan. I've got Revere too," she added. "There was nothing else I ever wanted in my life but a place to live, a nice place I could fix up. I have a dog too and some cats. And all my plants—and my curtains there that I sewed—"

"It's nice, Clara."

"Sure it's nice," she said. She drank from the bottle. "You're not going to take this away from me."

"You could just leave it, yourself."

"What about Swan?"

"He comes too."

"Where do you think you're going, then? You're so goddamn smart. You always had plans, you always knew where you were going," Clara said. She bit at the neck of the bottle, hard. Lowry was watching her as if he felt sorry for her, suddenly, after all these years, and as if the emotion were a little surprising to him. "You came and went, you drove up and you drove away, I couldn't think of anything but you and so you went away and that was that— The hell with me. You never thought about anybody but yourself."

"Don't be mad, honey."

"You're a selfish bastard, isn't that true? You go off and leave me and come back, what is it, four years later? And I'm supposed to love you, I'm supposed to go with you—to the beach again maybe for three days. Then you'll give me and the kid a ride back and kick us out—"

Lowry sat back in the chair. He looked tired.

"I didn't think about you like that, honey," he said. "I mean—the way I thought about the woman I married."

"You don't need to tell me."

"I wanted something else, honey. I couldn't talk to you."

"But you could to that woman down there, huh?"

"Yes."

"Is that why you left her? If you like her so much go on back and find her," Clara said furiously.

"I don't want her."

"Why the hell do you want me?"

"I'm tired of talking."

"What? What does that mean?"

"I'm tired of talking, of thinking the way she did. I'm tired of thinking."

Clara raised the bottle to her mouth again, trying to rid herself of that trembling she hated so. She felt that her body was moving off from her, going its own way and paying no attention to what she wanted.

"I joined the Army, honey," he said. "I came back to the States and enlisted just in time."

"You what?"

"I've been over in Europe, you know where that is? I want some-body who doesn't know where that is," he said. He was not smiling. He caressed Clara's arm and she did not move it away; she watched his hand moving on her skin. There were tufted blond hairs on the backs of his fingers and she thought that she remembered them, yes, she remembered every one of them. His fingernails were thick and milky, ridged just a little with dirt. Lowry was staring at her. "You've changed quite a bit, Clara. You really are a woman now."

Clara looked away.

"I know why he loves you. I don't blame him. But he's already married and he has a family—he won't be able to do anything for you. You know that. You could never fit in with those people, you're nothing at all like them. He won't marry you."

"Shut up about that."

"Clara, you know I'm telling the truth."

"He loves me. And anyway this is none of your—"

"But sitting around here waiting for someone to die—a woman you don't even know—"

"I don't know her but I hate her," Clara said viciously.

Lowry was amused at this. "How can you hate her if you don't know her?"

"He'll marry me after she dies," Clara said.

"You'd really like to be his wife?"

"I would."

"I don't believe that."

"Go to hell then! What's wrong with you? You want everything handed over to you—even a son like that, a kid given to you.

Right?" She drew her breath in sharply, watching him. She felt as if she were on the brink of something terrible.

"If he's your kid. . . ." Lowry said. But his answer was just vague enough to lessen the tension between them. "He's a quiet boy."

"He's strong and growing fast. He's smart too."

"I could see it was your boy right away. . . ."

"Lowry, why did you come back?"

"I was meaning to come for a long time. I sent you a letter, didn't I?"

"What letter?"

"A letter from Mexico."

"I never got it."

"Sure you did."

"I never did."

"Didn't that bastard give it to you. . . ?"

"No." Clara rubbed her hands against her eyes. "What was in it, news about your wife? A wedding invitation?" Then she stared at him. "Or did you really write a letter, really? I don't know whether to believe you or not. . . . You were married and everything. . . ."

"Honey, don't be so jealous. You're still jealous after all this time."

"I'm not jealous. I really don't give a damn."

"I thought I wanted a different kind of woman, that's all. You and she are nothing like each other—honey, a man wouldn't bother looking at her if you were around. But I thought I wanted something that it turned out I didn't."

"Now you want somebody stupid, somebody who can't talk or bother you," Clara said. "Somebody to make love to and forget about, right? And you know you'll always be welcome when you come back, so what the hell? *She* threw you out right away."

"No."

"What the hell kind of a marriage was it?"

"Clara, don't be so angry."

"I'm not angry."

"Drink your beer, finish it up."

"I don't want it, I feel like puking."

Her being like that, being vulgar, was just enough to make him laugh a little. She could not trust herself to look at him too steadily. It was like staring at a light, at something blinding; in a few seconds the center could fade away and she might see nothing.

"So I left her and went back to the States and enlisted. I went to England for a while, then over to France. Someday I'll tell you about what happened."

"You were over there all that time?"

"For two years."

"You really were in the Army?"

"Sure."

"And I didn't know it. . . . What if you were killed?"

Lowry laughed bitterly. "There were a few of us who got killed."

"But Lowry, you couldn't die. What if— You—"

She ran out of words. It was so close to her, this knowledge of Lowry and Lowry's death, a possibility Lowry himself maybe could not see. He took her bottle from her and set it down and pulled her into his lap. "Would you have worried about me, honey?"

"Yes, Lowry."

"You didn't get that letter?"

"No. Never."

"Did you miss me?"

"Yes."

"Did you wish I was here?"

"Yes."

"What about Revere, then?"

"He loved me, he took care of me—"

"Do you love him? Did you?"

"I don't know—"

"Was it hard for you, having the kid like that? Without being married?"

"No. I didn't think about that."

"You didn't care?"

"No."

"You wanted the kid, huh?"

"Sure I wanted him."

Lowry smoothed her hair back. He looked at her as if she were really some distance away. After a moment he said, "He isn't my kid, is he?"

Clara's lips parted in shock. "No."

"Does he look like Revere?"

"Mostly he looks like me."

"I used to know Revere," he said. "I didn't tell you this but my family was like yours—except my father did farmwork. He went from farm to farm, always getting kicked out. Finally he took off and left us, and my mother took the kids back to her mother. I was fourteen then. Once my father worked for Revere. . . . I didn't tell you that."

"But I thought—"

"We're like each other, you and me, except I went places and tried to find out some things and even got shot for my trouble, while you camped down and got everything you wanted. Those are real nice plants, honey," he said. He kissed her. "I can't tell you how much I like them. I like this house. If I hadn't been told whose house it was—"

"Lowry, I thought—I thought your family—"

"Just white trash, honey."

"But you had a nice car, and had money to spend—"

"I was helping somebody run whiskey. My family was all gone by that time."

"Run whiskey? Was that it?" And she could not keep the flat surprised sound of disappointment out of her voice.

"I pulled out and tried to get something going in Mexico, I had a few thousand dollars I'd taken from this bastard I worked for, and I wanted to start something—some business—but nothing turned out. I didn't know enough. I met her then—"

"Your wife."

"She was sort of bumming around but she was a teacher too, she had a job she could point to. Her family kept sending people after her, trying to get her back home—she was staying with me then— and she maybe married me to get back at them, to make them shut up. She told me I was fooling myself with my life, running around and never getting anywhere— She was right, but what the hell."

"No, she wasn't right—"

"What the hell."

"Did you say somebody shot you?"

"Nothing much, just in the leg here."

Clara touched his thigh. "Is it all right?"

"It's all right now."

"Did it hurt awful?"

"I don't know."

"Lowry, for God's sake—"

"What?"

"You were in the war and everything, you got shot—I never knew about it—"

"Lots of people get shot. They're getting shot right now. Or bombed to pieces, that's even better. I don't want to talk about it."

"Were you in a hospital?"

She saw his mouth jerk as if he had to taste something ugly, so she let that pass. He was quiet. She was not angry. She said, "Were you surprised about me?"

"No. Maybe."

"What did you think?"

"I didn't think you'd still be around here. Or I thought you'd be married."

"This is the same as being married."

"Not quite."

"I have a kid."

"Revere doesn't live with you, honey. How often does he come over?"

"When he can."

"These days he's a busy man. How much money do you think he's making off the war, him and his people?"

"I don't know anything about it. He never says."

"They say he's making money off it. Why not? All the trash from around here and all the hillbilly backwashes in the country that didn't get shipped over to die are working their heads off in the factories, making lots of money. Or so they think. Your friend has investments in things like that."

"He never says—"

"Why should he? When he comes to you he forgets about it. But I knew you first, I brought you here. For two years I've been thinking about you. I didn't even think about her—my wife—I thought right past her to you."

"Did you?"

"I thought about you all the time. I thought that if I got back here and they let me out—"

"What?"

"If I got back I'd come right here and get you and we'd go somewhere. Even if you were already married I was going to come back and marry you."

"Marry me?"

"Now I'm going to do this: I'm going up to Canada, to British Columbia. They're giving away land there, practically. Thousands of acres. I have a little money and we're going to get clear of everything except the outdoors, we'll have a farm, I can learn how to work on one again—"

"Lowry, you're crazy—"

"Why am I crazy?"

"I don't know, it's just—I—"

"Why are you afraid?"

Clara pushed away from him and got to her feet. Her teeth had begun to chatter; she felt that the very air about her had turned brittle. "I don't want to hear it," Clara said. She closed her eyes and shook her head slowly. "Don't say anything to me. I'm afraid what I might do. How can I change . . . ? Once there was a man that looked like you, in a gas station—"

"And?"

"He made me think about you all over again."

Lowry got up. "Honey, everything is beautiful here. This old house is beautiful. Out the window there—those trees—it's all beautiful. We'll have a place just like this in Canada, by ourselves."

"Lowry, no."

"You don't know what you have here, how beautiful it is. You don't understand what it is," he said. "Over there I thought about you all the time, Clara. You were at the center of what I was trying to think about. I remembered how it was by the ocean, and down by the river that day—how nice you were to me— Nobody was ever as nice to me as you were, Clara. I know that now."

Clara went out into the kitchen and stood at the screen door. She heard Lowry following behind her. Her fingernails picked nervously at the screen, at tiny rust specks or dirt embedded there. Outside, Swan was digging a hole by the fence that cut off the orchard from an old pasture. "Swan?" she called. "What are you doing?"

He looked around. "This here," he said, his small clear voice a surprise to her. He lifted the spade. After a moment, staring at her and at Lowry behind her, he turned away self-consciously.

"Suppose that was your kid, what then?" Clara said.

"It wouldn't matter, I would want him with us even if he wasn't," Lowry said. And that answer, that should have sounded so good to her, somehow didn't; she had wanted something else. "I'm thirty-two," he said. "I had my thirtieth birthday over there and I never thought I'd get that old. Now I'm back here and I could maybe forget about all that, if I could begin everything over."

Clara stared at him. She did not understand.

"You're worried he's going to come?" Lowry said.

"No."

"What are you worried about?"

She pushed past him. "I've got to fix supper," she said.

"Forget about supper."

"You've got to eat, and Swan—"

"Forget about it. Come back here with me."

"Lowry, I can't."

"Come on."

She stared miserably at the floor. Everything was draining out of her, all her strength, all the hatred that had kept Lowry close to her for so long. It struck her that she had fed on this hatred and that it had kept her going, given her life. Now that he was here and standing before her, she could not remember why she had hated him.

"You bastard," she whispered. "Coming back here like this— You—"

"Let me make you quiet," Lowry said.

She looked up at his smile, which was exactly like the smile she remembered.

———

"That boy is still outside playing," Lowry said. From the bed he was leaning to look out the window. Clara, lying still, watched the long smooth curve of his back. "Any other kid would come bothering you, but he doesn't. How does he know that much?"

"Smart, like his father."

"Why is he so quiet?"

"He isn't quiet. He was afraid of you."

"He shouldn't have been afraid of me."

"A strange man coming up the lane, walking up the lane like that. . . . I was afraid of you myself."

"Are you afraid now?"

She wanted to say angrily that she would always be afraid of him, that there was nothing she could do to keep herself from him and that this was terrible, this power he had over her. But she lay still. Her hair was tangled around her damply; she felt soiled, bruised.

"I'm sorry if . . . I upset you," Lowry said gently.

He pressed himself against her again, hiding his face against her, and she felt how soft even a man's flesh can be, lying so delicate on top of his bones; and if it had all been blown apart, shot apart, what then? If the bullets that had shot about Lowry in the dark, over there in Europe, across the world in Europe, had hit him instead and stopped dead in his body, what then? He would not have come back to make love to her. Lowry's body, which was all of him that she could see and touch, would be rotted over there in a ditch in a place she would not even know by name, could not even imagine because she would not have the power to do so . . . and what then? She caressed his back and her hand came away wet with sweat. That was all she had to go by. She felt how weak they both were, she and Lowry, how the terrible power he had in his body and in his hard muscular legs passed over into this weakness that was not at all like the weakness before sleep but was something heavy and close to death, like lying on the bottom of an ocean of sweat, their bodies still trembling from all the violence they had suffered. She felt as if a wound had been viciously opened up in her, secret in her body, and that all her strength had drained away through it and left her helpless again.

"What is Revere going to say when I tell him what we're going to do?"

"He's got a wife."

"But he loves me," Clara whispered. "He wants to marry me."

"The hell with him."

"He loves me."

"I don't give a damn about another man's love."

"He loves Swan too. . . ."

"Well, I don't give a damn about that either."

"What if you get tired and leave me again?"

"That won't happen."

"How do you know?"

"I know."

They fell back into silence. Clara listened to his breath, felt his breath against her. She said dreamily, "But you . . . Lowry, with you everything is just what comes into your head. It comes out of somewhere like in a dream and you want it and then you get it, then that's over. . . . People or places to go to or things to do. The world is just spread out as far as you can see or feel it. I could fall out of that world, get pushed over the edge or something. Then what?"

"Clara, don't talk crazy like that."

"And the kid too. He might get forgotten. You're in such a rush. . . ."

"No."

"I'm not just a kid now, Lowry. I'm afraid what you'll do to me this time."

"I always took care of you, sweetheart."

"Oh, Christ—"

"You just wanted more from me than I wanted to give."

Clara sat up. She did not want to look at him. It was as if they were criminals together, weak and suspicious together, not happy with each other the way she'd been with that man from the gas station—who had made her feel Lowry inside her without having to really be Lowry. The air was warm and sultry. This bedroom, which Clara had always loved, now seemed to her someone else's room. It was not just Lowry who did not belong in it, but Clara herself.

She let him embrace her again. Her mind stumbled backward to other embraces of his, and back all the way to that night in Florida years ago, when he had taken a washcloth and cleaned her up to suit him, to make her good enough for him. Or was she wrong about that, was she judging him wrong . . . ? She remembered that Lowry and she remembered herself, as if she had been outside her body all along and watching. He was the same man and she wanted him just as violently; making love with him cost her everything, every agonized straining to give life to that kernel of love he would always keep inside her. She would never be free of him. But she knew what she was going to say just the same.

"No. I guess I'm not going with you," she said.

"What?"

"I'm not going."

He touched his forehead with his fingertips—a strange gesture. He was stunned. Clara closed her eyes to get rid of that sight. She felt sick.

"You're not coming with me?" he said.

Clara got out of bed and put her housecoat on. It was made of pink cotton, rather wrinkled and not too clean. She went to the window and stared out. Lowry had not moved. After a while she looked over her shoulder at him, narrowing her eyes against anything she might see that she would not want to see. Lowry was tapping at his teeth with his fingers, watching her.

"You changed your mind?" he said.

"I never really thought any other way."

She let her head droop. Her hair moved about her face languidly, lazily. She knew she must have the look of a woman in a picture who had everything decided for her, who had never had to think, whose long complicated life had been simplified by some artist when he chose one instant out of it to paint: after that, the hell with her.

"You want to spend your life waiting here for another woman to die?"

"If I have to."

"Does your kid know about that?"

"I don't know what he knows. He's just a baby."

"Maybe he knows more than you think."

"Maybe."

"And what about Revere, what if somebody told him I was with you?"

"Are you going to tell him?"

"Suppose I did?"

"If you want to, go ahead."

"Suppose I told him about before, too. Four years ago."

"Go on and tell him."

"Don't you care if I do?"

Clara looked down. "You won't tell him, Lowry."

"Why not?"

"Because you won't tell him. You won't do that."

They were both silent. She raised her eyes to his, narrowed.

"Why won't I?" he said.

"Because you know I love you. Why would you want to hurt me?"

"If you love me, why the hell—"

"I'm not like I was!" she said. "I'm different now—I'm a mother, I'm grown up— I had all this time to think about things—"

"Clara—"

"There's all these things you think about that I can't understand," she said. She spoke softly and quietly, trying to keep her voice still. "You always go past me. That was why you wanted another woman, and you'd want one again—"

"If that's it—"

"No, that's not it. I'd go with you anyway. I'd take that chance if it were a few years ago—what the hell would I care? But it's different now."

"Clara, you could do so much for me if you would."

"I can't do anything for you."

He was breathing hard. "It wasn't just being shot that hurt me, it was other things," he said. The way his mouth twisted showed how he hated to say this. "I had some trouble for a while. I was in a hospital over here, in Washington. They had to keep me quiet—try to keep me quiet—"

"My God," Clara whispered.

"I don't want to go back to it, I mean I don't want to think about it," Lowry said harshly. "Up in Canada we could start over again, and the kid too, a kid is so young he doesn't know anything—and we could have other kids—"

"Lowry—"

"I can't understand things. Life," he said. He shut his eyes tight, as if to get rid of something flying around him, at him. "I don't mean around here. Here, everything is quiet. Your garden here. . . . It stays in one place. But over there— Nothing stays still long enough for you to understand it. How do you know what you're doing, what's happening? I can't live that way."

"Lowry, please."

"I can't live that way. It would kill me."

"Lowry, I just can't go with you."

He waited a moment. "All right," he said.

She went out in the kitchen to wait for him. Swan must have caught sight of her because he came up on the porch. A slender, shy boy, with his father's face and Clara's hair, standing out on the porch and looking in as if he were on the precipice of time, not really born yet. He waited shyly out there. Clara looked at him as if he were a stranger. There was only this child between herself and Lowry: without him she would throw some things together and the two of them would run out to his car and drive off, and that would be that. Whatever happened—Canada or no Canada, more babies or not—she would not have given a damn.

But the boy was out there, watching. She said, "Swan, come inside, I'm going to fix up supper."

He hesitated.

"That man's leaving," Clara said.

The boy came inside. He remembered to shut the screen door without letting it slam. His eyes moved carefully, almost shrewdly around the kitchen, as if looking for things out of place. Clara touched his head and let her hand fall a little heavily onto his shoulder. He flinched a little but said nothing. They waited for

Lowry to come out. "Did you dig some nice holes?" Clara said. "Did Butch help you?"

He shook his head, no.

Lowry came out. "I'm going to fix up some supper, you stay for it," she said.

"I'm not hungry."

"Everybody's hungry," Clara said. She did not mean her voice to be so harsh and hopeless. Lowry and Swan looked at each other, both of them strangely shy. In Lowry there was something stunned and withheld, in Swan there was the kind of timidity Clara hated in all children, especially boys. "For Christ's sake, people have to eat," she said. "You want something or not?"

"I said no."

She and Swan followed him out onto the back porch. "You got a few more hours before it gets dark," Clara said. "Do you expect to drive far, or . . ." They kept up this kind of talk in front of the boy, Clara feeling herself pushed forward further and further toward that precipice, so that she wanted to scream at Lowry to get out of here before it was too late and everything was ruined. If he said just the right thing, if he looked at her in just the right way—

But he did not know this. If he had known, he might have changed her life; but he was exhausted, he had given up, something had drained out of him and left his face ashen. Instead, he took hold of Swan's chin and bent down to look into his face.

"You ever killed any snakes or things, kid?"

Swan tried to jerk away.

"Let go of him!" Clara cried.

"I just want to ask him: you ever killed anything?"

Swan shook his head no desperately.

"You're lying. I can see in your face you killed something already and you're going to kill lots of things." Lowry's own face twisted into something ugly that might have been there all along, through the years, without him or Clara knowing of it. Clara saw how his mouth changed, how his grayish teeth were bared. "I can see it right there—all the things you're going to kill and step on and walk over."

And he released Swan. He straightened up, stepped back. The

boy ran to Clara, too terrified to cry, and she stood without bending to embrace him and watched Lowry walk away. He walked out along the side path to the lane and out along that, taking his time. The last she saw of him wasn't even him, but the dust that rose behind his car as it moved out of sight.

"You forget about him, you hear?" Clara cried. "Don't you think about him again—he's going and he won't be back! You're going to get things that he could never give you, you're going to get a last name, a real name, and a whole world to live in—not just a patch of a world— You hear me? You hear me?"

She had to be careful or she would go crazy, Clara thought. She had to be careful. The boy's face, drawn and strangely old, seemed to her suddenly the one thing she had to hate, the only thing that had lost her Lowry.

III.

SWAN

1

The man said to be Swan's father had shoulders that stooped a little, as if to minimize their obvious strength. His hair was gray, a mixture of many shades. All his life Swan had been seeing this man, but today, when he looked at him, his vision seemed to blotch, as if trying to protect him from some mysterious injury. He was a child, seven. His vision would pound and tiny nervelike veins around his eyes pulsed a warning to him, but a warning of what? He was seven now and getting big and had no patience with babyish fears; he himself could measure how fast he had grown this year by the limb of the apple tree he had never been able to reach before.

That morning they had been driven to the man's house many miles from their own, in the man's car that was heavy and solid as a piece of farm machinery. Though the man's house was said to be a farmhouse it looked like no farmhouse Swan had ever seen before. It was made of dark weatherworn stone with long narrow windows, more windows than Swan could count, and shutters painted green. There were three brick chimneys. Behind the farmhouse was a barn, painted dark red, larger than any barn Swan had ever seen; what was even more startling, the barn was positioned at the top of a small hill, and it had sides that enclosed the barnyard. There was a copper weathercock on the highest peak of the barn and on its front was painted in big black letters REVERE FARM. There were two tall silos in good repair beside this barn, and there were several other outbuildings: Revere pointed out the stable, the cow barn, the chicken coop. He had a pleased, embarrassed way about him, and glanced often at Swan who was staring through the windshield of the car, squeezed in beside Clara.

Clara leaned down to Swan, gripping his thin shoulders and bringing her head level with his. She was excited, gleeful as a child. "Oh Swan, look! Did you ever see anything so—" But Clara's voice faltered. *So big* she might have meant. But she had no adequate words. Swan felt the poverty of his mother's language, and knew it to be his own.

The driveway from the road was long, perhaps a quarter-mile. It was lined with tall evergreens so evenly spaced you understood that they had been planted deliberately. At REVERE FARM, little was left to chance.

Swan wanted to shut his eyes. He knew this was meant for him, that was why Clara was gripping his shoulders so tightly.

As they were walking into the house, Clara murmured in Swan's ear, "Don't be afraid of him, Swan. He loves you. What the hell is wrong with you?" She poked him, pinched him. Swan bit his lip to keep from crying. Inside, he was taken into the parlor as Revere called it, a room that smelled of furniture polish and something dark and moldy. Revere was breathing hard, and his face had a warm copperish glow; he sat heavily in a chair with a high back and a thick cushion, and drew Swan to him. *Loves you. Loves you.* Swan held his breath against the man's smell. "Steven. This will be your home." Revere's voice was husky, as if he were on the verge of crying. A grown man, an old man! Swan balked, and would have wrenched away if Clara's deft fingers hadn't caught him.

Clara said to Revere, as if Swan were not present, or were some sort of animal to whom language had no meaning, "See what it is for him—your son!—to be afraid? Of his own father, afraid? And in his father's house for the first time at age seven."

Revere said nothing. Perhaps, staring at Swan, he wasn't listening.

Clara had never been in this house before but she looked boldly around, with her calm, narrowly interested gaze, at the furniture that was so heavy and polished and nothing at all like the things in their old house, and she was not afraid. In the very air of this great stone house there was an odor that could never have belonged to their own house—an odor of weight and darkness and time, of things oiled and cared for. At one end of the room there was a great fireplace, big enough for Swan to stand in if he wanted, and above it a mantel with silver candlestick holders on either side. He knew what silver was, more or less. His mother had some silver things. And she had a golden ring and a golden necklace too, gleaming, delicately glittering things that lay so gently against her tanned skin that you might worry about their getting lost or being thrown aside when she was in a hurry. Once she had lost a little heart Revere had given her, and Swan had hunted for it and found it in the weeds by the back door.

But they were in this house now. Clara swallowed, and stared, her eyes slightly narrowed as if she were looking into a blinding light. When she spoke it was impulsively, nervously. "Those chair legs—why are they twisted like that?"

Revere said, bemused, "That's the way they are."

"It's—like an antique? That's what it is?"

"Yes, it's French, I think."

Swan waited expecting Clara to say it was strange, she didn't like it, but instead Clara looked elsewhere. "That man in the picture— he's somebody you know?"

"It's a painting of my father."

"Your father!"

Clara approached the portrait, cautiously. She stood with her hands clasped before her, staring, frowning, while Swan and Revere watched. Out of a vague brown-hued background the man said to be Curt Revere's father gazed down at her, imperturbed. A chill white light illuminated his face, that put Swan in mind of a sharp, clever dog's face. Clara glanced back at Revere, comparing the faces. "He has your eyes. But not so nice as yours." Half-teasing, she said, "Will you look like him when you get that age?"

"Clara, I'm older now than my father was when he died."

Revere made a sound that might have been an embarrassed laugh, yet it might have been reproachful as well. Clara didn't catch this. She frowned as if trying to solve a riddle: what exactly had Revere said? Swan saw her give up, and turn back to them, smiling. She was conscious of her new, expensive dress and her long silky legs. When she sat down she drew her skirt carefully over her knees.

"Ah, well," she said, "people live, and people die. It keeps on."

She stretched out her legs. She would make herself lazy and comfortable as a cat, even here, even today, while Revere sat stiffly, as if listening for something from upstairs or outside that he was afraid he might hear. He wore a dark suit. He smelled of something harsh—maybe tobacco—while Clara smelled of the perfume in the amber jar Swan had always loved. He would sneak into her room and hold the jar up to the light to look through it. Through that glass the backyard became mysterious and fluid with a grainy, fragrant light. The ugly old pear tree, dying on one side, became serene and frozen in the glare of that special light—even if there were those pouches of cloudy cocoons filled with worms high up on the tree, it did not matter. Swan could look at them without disgust through that bottle.

"Steven," Revere said, "what is your last name going to be now?"

Swan looked up at him. This man's natural expression was muscularly pleasant; his smiles faded easily into one another. He had big squarish white teeth that seemed to smile too. He was a man who belonged outside, not in this parlor. He had already tried to take Swan hunting with him, out behind Clara's house, and his strides through the grass had drawn him away from Swan, who hurried along nervously and could not look away from the grass for fear he would trip over something and the gun he had would go off. It was out of the high grass the pheasants and quail flew, and their flight terrified Swan so that he had burst into tears. He remembered that.

"Tell him," Clara said, nudging him with her foot. "What's your name going to be? Don't be so shy, kid."

"I don't know," he said.

That was bad, a mistake. He sensed their impatience. "Don't you know?" Revere said. He smiled. "It's Revere. You know that. Say it now—Steven Revere."

There was Clark, and Jonathan, and Robert, and now Steven: all brothers.

"Steven Revere," Swan said softly.

He wished he had another name to blot out this one, to take its place, but he had nothing. His mother always said with a laugh that she had no last name—it was a secret—or better yet, she had forgotten it—she had been kicked out by her father, she said.

"Steven Revere. Steve," the man said slowly. He peered into the child's eyes as if trying to locate himself there. Swan stared up shyly—he had the feeling for a moment that he could love this man if only he wouldn't take him out hunting and make him handle guns and kill things. Why was there always so much confusion and danger with men?

He edged over toward Clara but she was talking to Revere about other things. They talked about people who were coming, about the house, about Revere's sister. Swan, who spoke so little when he was with anyone besides Clara, tried to force the dizzying flood of words and impressions into coherent thoughts—this was all he could do. The only power he had was the power to watch and to listen. His mother could pick things up and toss them out in the garbage; she could slap him, spank him, hug and kiss him; she could yell out the window at some kids crossing through their property; she could sit smoking in the darkened kitchen, smiling at nothing. She was an adult who had power, and because Swan was a child, he had no power. This man here, this kindly man with the strong hands and the urgent, perplexed look—he too had power, the power suggested by this large house and the barns and land behind it, the enormous sweep of cultivated land that belonged to him while so many people owned nothing at all. He could walk confidently across his land and know that he owned it because he was a man, an adult, he possessed the mysterious power of strength that no child possessed, even those boys at school who pushed Swan around. But even those children had no real strength; adults owned them. Everyone was frightened by someone else, Swan thought.

"Well, what do you think?" Revere said, smoothing down Swan's hair. "You're not worried about the boys, are you? They're good kids. You'll all get along."

"They'd better be nice to him," Clara said.

"They won't bother him," Revere said. "They're good kids."

"I know what kids are like. . . ."

"Don't worry him, Clara. You know better than that. Steven," Revere said, leaning to him, "you know your mother will take care of you. There's nothing to be worried about. It's just that now we're going to live together in one house. We've been waiting a long time for this. And you'll have three brothers to play with—you won't be alone anymore."

"He never was alone," Clara said.

Swan knew these "brothers." His terror of them was based on the fact that they had never spoken to him but only looked at him, unsmiling. They were big—ten, twelve, and fifteen—and had their father's heavy squarish shoulders, the dark hair, and the dark quiet blue eyes. They seemed to be waiting for him to speak, to do something. The times Revere had brought them to meet Swan, Revere had done all the talking and even Clara had been silent. Revere had talked about them hunting together, fishing, playing with the horses. He had talked about doing chores together. He had talked about school. . . . But the boys had said nothing except what was dragged out of them by Revere and those words had no meaning.

"Look, everything will be fine. You know that," Revere said to Clara.

She shrugged her shoulders but she smiled. She had taken out a cigarette and now she leaned forward so that Revere could light it; Swan, forgotten for the moment, watched in fascination the burning match and the tiny flickering glow at the end of the cigarette, as if he had never seen these things before. He wanted to pay attention to every small thing in order to keep time going slowly, because something important was going to happen that day and he was afraid of it.

"It isn't good for boys to be . . . without a mother," Revere was saying.

Swan had always watched people closely when they were around his mother. He saw how they caught from her a certain catlike easiness, no matter what anger they had brought with them. Even this big Revere, with his squarish jaw and his wide, lined, intelligent forehead, was squinting at her now as if something misty and dazzling had passed between him and Clara. Swan looked quickly at his mother as if to see what it was that Revere saw in her; but he did not see it, not exactly. His mother smiled at him, a special smile, for him. It told him, right in front of this man whose big hands could have hurt them both, that they were here at last, here they were, what good luck!

"I know what you need around here," Clara said. "Some windows open and some airing-out. Some of this old stuff cleaned, right? What's that thing you're sitting on, honey? I can see the dust in it, eating right down. Doesn't your sister care about the place?"

"She isn't well," Revere said clumsily. Swan saw how the man's gaze faltered; Clara must have been frowning. "It's only been a month since the funeral, after all. She just hasn't gotten over it yet—they were like sisters."

Swan looked at the man's shoes: black stiff-looking shoes without any mud on them, not even a faint rim of dried mud around the very bottom.

"They were a lot alike," Clara said softly. "People said so. Your sister is older than—than your wife, though." The child stood between them, listening. He took everything too seriously and had not learned to laugh; he knew that, didn't his mother tell him so every day? But he had the idea that he must watch and listen carefully. He must learn. Living was a game with rules he had to learn for himself by watching these adults as carefully as possible. There had been one other adult in his life—not the schoolteacher, who didn't count, but one other man, almost lost in his memory, a strange blond man who had touched him and who had vanished. . . . Once in a while he found himself thinking about that man, trying to remember what that man had said to him. But it was fuzzy and lost. He had been too young. Now the memory of that other man, awakened by Revere's attention, swept down upon him like one of the big chicken hawks everyone hated, with its dusty flapping wings and its scrawny legs, and Swan could almost smell the fetid odor of that breath. ("Never say a word about him," Clara had told him, just once. She did not have to tell Swan things twice.)

"Look—Esther was like a sister to her too, not just to me," Revere was saying. Swan knew that their attention had moved completely away from him; he was relieved. "Out in the country like this, and not ever getting married—she liked Marguerite better than she liked me, really. She never caused any trouble. She never came between us. But she has nowhere to go now, she's too proud to ask anyone. The house is just as much hers as mine—"

Clara made a disgusted sound.

"Our father left it to us both."

"Who keeps it going? Who has the money?" Clara said breathlessly.

"She has money of her own, that's not it. I don't care about that. Anyway, she doesn't want to live in Hamilton, she doesn't like it there and I don't blame her. She doesn't like my uncle. My sister and I have never really been close, but . . ."

"How she must hate me!" Clara said.

"She doesn't hate you, Clara."

"She never told you?"

"No one ever said anything, all these years."

"They were afraid of you, that's the only reason. But they hated me anyway and they'll always hate me. Are they really coming today?"

"Yes."

"Every one of them? Really? The women too—Judd's wife too?" Clara said greedily.

"They do what I ask them to."

Swan sensed something brittle and dangerous in the air about them. A faint warning began in his stomach, as it did when he was inching out on ice, but his mother must have felt nothing, for she went on teasingly, "Your wife didn't do what you asked."

Revere shook his head. "That's finished."

"If she'd done what you wanted," Clara said, "you and I would be married now. Not like this, with the kid seven years old and us going to be married finally—what a laugh! But no, no, you can't budge a woman like her. From a good family with a good German name, is she going to give a divorce to a man to make him happy? Never! She's going to sit tight with her nails dug in you to keep you as long as possible."

Clara made a vague spitting gesture; then, to soften the movement, she frowned and picked a piece of tobacco off her tongue. "So your kid here has to be taught his last name, and he's afraid of you. Your own boy afraid of you. Are you proud?"

"No, I'm not proud."

"Men are always proud, they think more of that than anything. But not women," Clara said. She crossed her legs. The blue silk dress was drawn tight about her thighs in tiny veinlike wrinkles.

She had lean, smooth legs; because she was wearing stockings today the curve of her calves was not shiny as usual. "Women have no pride. They do what men want them to do, like me, and to hell with it. If some bastards turn their nose up at me, let them. I never asked for any of them to like me."

"After today everything will be all right," Revere said. "The past is over. Marguerite is dead. I can't think anything bad of her now."

"I don't think bad of her either," Clara said quickly. She had the look Swan sometimes saw on her face when she was about to throw something down in disgust. "I don't think bad of the dead. She was a good woman to give you three sons—I don't think bad of anybody dead. I never knew her. And when I'm dead myself I won't give a damn if they're still talking about me."

"After today it will be different," Revere said.

Clara smiled a smile that could mean anything: that he was right, that he was wrong.

Today was a holiday; his mother was going to be married. Swan knew all about it. She had told him the night before that nothing really would be changed and he shouldn't worry; she was doing this for him. "We're going to live in a nice big house, not like this, and there's even a woman to help in the kitchen—think of that! And Revere, he likes you so. He loves you. We're all going to live together starting tomorrow. How will you like that?"

Swan said, "I'll like it," but he meant that he would like it if she did. It was clear his mother liked the idea. She liked everything. If something in the house made her angry she would break it or throw it out, if the dog bothered her she'd chase it away, but nothing had the power to disturb her. Nothing could get that far into her. It was like the mosquitoes that bit Swan out in the fields—he would watch anxiously as the little white swellings formed, sometimes in strange shapes, but after a while they just flattened out and disappeared. Things touched his mother like that, just on the outside of her skin. That was why she could move so quickly from place to place and why she had time to comb out her long hair, slowly and fondly, while other women always worked. Swan knew a few boys from school and he knew that their mothers worked all the time. His mother had her own car and drove it anywhere she wanted, to town or anywhere. She had nice clothes and she liked to stand in front of the mirror and look at herself. Her hair was pale, almost white, and sometimes it lay down on her shoulders and past, straight and fine; but sometimes she had it twisted up somehow on her head in a way Swan did not like. He liked her careless and easy, running barefoot through the house, swearing at him for doing something wrong or muttering to herself about work she had to do; he liked her hands gesturing and arguing in silence, and her face screwed up into an expression of bewilderment as she tried to decide something— with her tongue prodding her cheeks and circling around to the front of her teeth, hard, as if Swan were not there watching her. Swan felt that he could spend his life hurrying after his mother, picking up things she had dropped and setting right things that she almost knocked over, and catching from her little grunted remarks that he must remember because she might forget. Now, sitting on this strange couch in a dim, airless parlor, she stared past Swan to Revere with that look of vacuity—her blond hair thick about her head, pulled up in a great swelling mass and fastened with innumerable pins, her neat, arched eyebrows rigid with thought, her eyelashes thick and confused—and Swan had a moment of terror in which he thought that she would not remember this man's name and that she would lose everything she had almost won.

But of course she would not lose. She began to smile, slowly. "Yes. After today it will be different. I'm really going to be your wife, and when I think of that nothing else matters."

Revere smiled nervously, laughed a short, breathless laugh. He was staring at Clara.

Swan looked down at Revere's shoes. He resented them not thinking of him, not even remembering he was there. He was getting big now. He noticed things more than ever. That strange straight look of Revere's, directed right toward Clara—he noticed that look and it made him want to close his own eyes.

"You hear that, Swan? Nothing else matters," Clara said. She leaned forward to embrace him. "Your father will take care of you and will change your life—my little Swan will grow up just like his father and be big and strong and rich—"

"Why do you call him that, Clara?"

"I like that name, that's my name for him."

"What's wrong with Steven?"

"Steven is his name on the paper, but I call him something else. So what?" Clara said. "I saw in this magazine a man named Robin, he was a movie star, so handsome, so much money—that was when I was pregnant—and I thought of what I would call the baby if it was a boy. I would call him Swan because I saw some swans once in a picture, those big white birds that swim around—they look real cold, they're not afraid of anything, their eyes are hard like glass. On a sign it said they were dangerous sometimes. So that's better than calling a kid Robin, I thought, because a swan is better than a robin. So I call him that."

"They call him Steven at school."

"Sure—what do I care what they call him?" Clara said. "I call him Swan. Nobody else can call him that."

There was a moment of silence. "The kids call me Steve," Swan said.

"Steve. Steven. I like that name," Revere said. "That's the name I picked. God, it's been a long time, hasn't it? All those years—"

"He's seven years old. Yes, it was a long time."

"I didn't think it would ever happen—you coming here finally—"

"You mean her dying. It took her so long to die," Clara said. She rubbed her cheek against Swan's and it was so strange: that she could feel and smell so soft but be so blunt. Swan closed his eyes and smelled her perfume, wishing they were both back in their house, safe, alone, just the two of them. Only she and Swan really lived there, not Revere. That house wasn't much, and sometimes animals crawled under it to die—but Swan liked it better than this big dark house with the rock on the outside. What if lightning struck it and all those rocks fell in on them while they slept . . . ? "It was a hell of a thing. After we're married we won't say anything about it, huh?" Clara whispered. "Because then I'll be in her place and it would be bad luck. In her bed. But right now I can say that it was a hell of a thing. I wanted her to die, but—but I wouldn't really want anybody to die, you know? I just wanted to be with you. I couldn't stop thinking about it even if it was bad, in my dreams I thought of her gone off somewhere and me with you in this house—and Swan with us, like now—with his own father like a boy should be. I couldn't help that. Is that my fault, that I dreamt those things? Is that bad of me?"

He took her hands as if to comfort her. "We both wanted the same thing," he said.

"But look, I don't like anybody to die!" Clara said. "I don't want to be married with that behind me, I'm not like that. It was love that got me into this. I fell in love with you. I didn't ask for that, did I? Did I want somebody else's husband? And your poor wife, what could she do? None of us asked for this, it just happened. She had to die thinking of me all the time, and when you came home to her from me, what did she think? Christ, that's awful! I'd kill any man that did that to me.... What could I do to make it any easier for her? I fell in love and that was that...."

She was staring up into Revere's face. She was both passionate and submissive and there was something urgent, something straining in her voice. They sat in silence for a while. Then Revere muttered, "I know, I know...." He looked at Swan and seemed just now to remember him. A slight coloring came to his cheeks. He said nervously, "It's getting time. Esther must be ready by now, and ..."

"Where are your kids?" Clara said.

"Outside."

"Outside all this time? Why don't they come in and wait?"

"They'll be all right, Clara. Don't worry about it."

They took Swan upstairs, the two of them walking on ahead and talking about something in their new rapid, hushed voices. Clara, in this house, had already taken on the characteristic of walking with her back very straight and her head bowed, nodding in agreement with whatever Revere said, whether she really agreed with it or not. "I spent my nights in here when I was home," Swan heard Revere say to Clara. "She was sick then.... Steven," he said, turning, "this is going to be your room. Come here." He came. He looked into the room and his mouth went dry at the thought of it, a room of his own in this house, with its smooth empty walls and the window at the end with a curtain on it. After today he would be alone. He would sleep here alone and the door would be closed on him. If he had a bad dream he could not run in to Clara; she already belonged to someone else.

"What's this, one of the kids' rooms?" Clara said, opening a door. She looked inside briefly, as if all rooms now were hers to look into. Revere walked along the hall just ahead of her. He tapped at another door and said that that was Clark's room. At the end of the hall he opened a door and Swan's legs worked fast to get him to the door before Revere forgot about him and closed it again, leaving Swan alone out in the hall. "Is that—where we're going to stay?" Clara said, pleased. She looked in and seemed to hesitate, her back very stiff. Revere was saying that all "her" things had been taken out and the room had been painted; it was all new, all clean. Clara nodded. Swan stood a few feet behind them, unable to see past them. He did not care. This was to be the room they would live in and the door would close on it, and he would not be able to run in if he was frightened. He did not care about it. As Revere talked, Swan saw behind this tall dark-haired man another man, vague and remote but somehow more vivid than Revere, whose presence seemed to be descending over this house like a bird circling slowly to the earth, its wings outstretched in a lazy threat. Revere talked, Clara talked. They spoke in quick, low voices, as if someone might still be in that room listening to them. Swan half shut his eyes and could almost hear the voice of that other man, that man who was a secret from Revere and who had gone away and had never come back. . . .

A woman was waiting for them at the stairs. Swan had never seen her before. His eyes shied away from adults, as the eyes of animals sometimes refuse to focus upon human eyes, out of a strange uneasy fear; he felt that this woman's eyes also shied away from him and Clara both. She was introduced to Clara and the two women touched hands. She was an old woman, much older than Clara, so old that just looking at Clara must be awful for her. They talked fast. Both women nodded, and Revere nodded.

"—your aunt Esther," Revere was saying to him.

Everyone smiled. Swan smiled too. He wanted to like this woman, this Esther, because she had the look of a woman nobody else liked. She was tall and gaunt with a face like Revere's, but older, narrowed, and her hair was white and thin so that Swan could see the stark white line of her scalp where her hair had been parted. This white line and the way her gaze dropped, nervously, made Swan understand that she had no power. She was an adult but she did not have any power.

"—Judd should be here, and the boys—the boys are outside," she said breathlessly.

"Don't tire yourself out, Esther," Revere said.

The old woman's hands were like leaves stirred restlessly by the wind. You would think they were at last going to lie still, they were so limp, but then they would begin to move again in jerks and surges they could not control.

"Let me go in the room for a minute," Clara said. "Are they outside already? Are they here? I have to fix my hair—"

"Clara, you look fine—"

"No, I have to fix it," she said nervously. She turned, and Swan was afraid for a second that she would forget and leave him here with these strangers. But she glanced back and said, "Come with me, kid. We'll both be downstairs in a minute." She took his hand and they hurried down the hall together. They left Revere and the old woman behind, and outside a dog was barking, which meant someone was driving up, but when Clara pulled him away he was all alone with her and they were like conspirators together. "You got something on your face—what the hell is that?" she whispered. "Christ, what a dirty kid!"

She opened the door to that room and went right inside. She went right in, pulling Swan with her, and closed the door behind her as if she had been doing this all her life. A big, sunny room. The walls had been covered with light green paper and there were silver streaks in it that dazzled Swan's eyes. "Silk wallpaper, what do you think of that," Clara said. There were four great windows with filmy white curtains that distorted the land outside and made it dreamy and vague; the curtains moved gently in the wind. Clara stood for a moment in the middle of the room, breathing quickly.

Then she said, "Where's that hairbrush? Goddamn it—" She picked up a little suitcase that had been set inside the door and let it fall onto the bed and opened it. Swan wandered around the room, staring. He went to the windows first. His own window, back home, looked out on the backyard and that was all—everything ran back to a scrawny field and ended. He could not see the horizon. Here, so high in the air, he could see the fields and a big woods far away. He was not high enough to see the borderline of mountains, but, in this house, he knew they were there and for the first time he felt pleasure in this knowledge. He leaned against the window and looked down. An automobile had driven up. People were getting out. Two dogs ran at them, barking with joy.

"Oh, here it is," Clara said angrily.

Swan did not turn to look at her. He touched the windowsill; it had warped a little from rain. When you looked closely at the room you saw things like that. There were a few brown water stains in the ceiling, like clouds—nothing anyone else would bother to look at, only Swan. And the big bureau that looked fine and polished, that had some scratches on it; he saw them too.

"Come over here, will you? You want to fall out that window?" Clara said. That showed she hadn't been watching him—he could not fall out the window, Swan thought with disgust. "I got to fix you up. You want to look better than his kids, don't you?"

She wet her finger and rubbed his forehead. Swan submitted without struggle. This room was fresh and sunny, not like the corridor outside and the parlor downstairs; and he had caught a glimpse of the big kitchen with its iron stove and wooden table—that had looked gloomy too. But up here, in this room that would belong to his mother and Revere, everything was fresh. There were even yellow flowers in a vase on the bureau.

"Did somebody die in here?" Swan said.

"His wife died in here a month ago," Clara said. "So here we are." She smiled a half-angry ironic smile at him. "Now, don't worry about anything. Do what I tell you. If they make trouble for you, tell me about it first, don't tell *him*—men don't like that. Tell me if your 'brothers' bother you. I know what kids are like, I had brothers of my own." Clara paused, her eyelids tremulous. For a moment Swan thought she might say more: but she did not. It was like an opaque window was opened at such times, and you could see through—almost!—and in that instant the window slammed shut again, and you saw only your own reflection. "I know, they'll make it hard on you. That's only natural. But someday—well, it will be different. Someday you will have everything—you will be the son he loves best."

"I don't want to be," Swan said sullenly.

"Hell you don't." Clara laughed, yanking at his hair. In an instant she was playful, laughing. Making a game of it: "Do what I say, Swan. Why d'you think I'm here, this place I can hardly breathe, except for *you*." It wasn't a question. Swan stared at his mother, fearful she would say something she wouldn't be able to take back. He felt panic for her, suddenly. How could she make her way among these people who knew so much more than she did? What if she lost everything, after coming so far? "Swan, what the hell are you looking at? Like some damn ol' retard, I swear. Sometimes." Clara stood at the bureau mirror primping the back of her hair the way you'd pet a cat. The image in the mirror leaned toward her as if for a kiss. Ashy-blond hair, smooth healthy skin, a blur of pale blue eyes and parted lips about to whisper—what? Swan's heart began to beat in terror for his mother, and of her.

"Well. We got here, hon. After all these years." She paused, her eyes suddenly sharp through the mirror. "What's wrong? You look like you're going to be sick. . . ."

"I . . . I don't like it here, I guess."

"Oh, yes! You'll like it here. You'll love it."

Clara threw the hairbrush down onto the floor. A nerve in Swan's eye twitched. Swan had seen his mother cry many times—she began to cry now. It wasn't a sad helpless crying like a child's crying but a hard angry baffled crying. It seemed to Swan that Clara must be crying because of what he'd said, for of course he'd said the wrong thing, but he knew it wasn't only just that; with Clara, it would be more. When she cried like this it wasn't for him. She cried only for herself.

Someone knocked at the door, quietly. Clara called in her bright happy voice, "Come in!"

He entered the room, almost shyly. His stooped shoulders, his uplifted hands, his stiff-legged walk and the expression on his face as if he were in the presence of something sacred—these made Swan love him and hate him at the same time.

Clara cried, over Revere's shoulder, "Swan, go away. Outside!"

Quickly, not looking back, he left.

Walking fast and blind along the hall. Colliding with chairs, kicking at them. "Goddamn." It was Clara's voice in him, frustrated yet laughing, too. "Goddamn goddamn damn *damn*." He would not hear anything behind him in that room, they had shut him out of.

At a high window oddly shaped like an egg, the sun was blazing. Seen from Revere's windows even the sun looked different. This should have surprised Swan, yet did not. *From now on. Someday. You will have everything.* He felt the excitement, yet the weight of it. He was jamming fingers into his ears, not just to blot out sound but to hurt. Now he wouldn't be able to come to Clara in the night, she wouldn't be alone ever again. That man, his "father," would be with her. They would shut the door behind them as they'd shut it at the other house but now it would never really open again. His "brothers" would be waiting for him. . . .

It was true, Swan thought. All that Clara predicted. For he had no choice, if Clara had so predicted. *The son he loves best.* It would happen because he, Swan, knew; and his "brothers" did not know. And Revere did not know. He would wait, and he would grow up. Already in his heart he was grown: he was not a child. He was older than Clark, even.

He smiled, thinking this. Removed his fingers from his throbbing ears: had Clara called *Swan?* But there was nothing.

And he knew the adult he would grow into: not Revere, that kindly man, but someone else. Someone else not kind, but sharp-eyed as Clara. That other man had a face Swan could almost see and in his dreams maybe he would see it. There was no haste, it would happen as it must. He would grow into what he would be, without choosing. Revere was his father, and he would love his father yet his real father was someone else. That was his and Clara's secret: he would die with that secret. Now he understood something of the blind dazzling sun. No words, no logic. Only the heat, the terrible blinding light.

2

The morning of the funeral.

Swan had awakened before dawn. His sleep was feathery-light, never strong enough to hold him for long. And then he lay in bed listening to the crows in the tall elms outside the windows. Their cries that were harsh, jubilant; cries of early morning, predators having gotten through the night, and hungry now for their prey. Swan thought *We are going to a funeral today. All the way to the city.*

In the two years he and Clara had lived in this house there had been funerals in the Revere family, but Swan had not needed to attend. "You're spared, sweetie. This time." Clara kissed him, as if they were conspirators. Taut-faced, cinching a shiny black belt around her waist to make her bust and hips more shapely in a black dress of some brocaded fabric purchased for just this occasion: death. Clark had had to go to these funerals: he was seventeen now, a big boy. Jonathan had gone to one funeral. Robert and Swan had stayed home with the housekeeper and had become allies and friends, almost; but when the family returned, Robert had immediately forgotten him. Tagging after his bigger brothers, whom he adored.

Today, Swan would be taken with the others. He'd nudged his head against Clara hoping to be absolved, but no.

"It won't kill you, sweetie. It has to be done."

Almost Swan didn't mind so much, being allowed to sit up front in the car between Clara and Revere. He could stare out the windshield at the landscape, that never ceased to fascinate. His three brothers would ride in the roomy backseat, close-faced, sullen.

Aunt Esther asked to be "forgiven," another time. Couldn't ride in the car because the motion made her heart flutter.

The crows had wakened him, and he carried their shrillness in his head, downstairs to breakfast. There was no escape: every morning they ate breakfast together in the big kitchen. (Revere rose very early, before dawn. But he drank only coffee at that time. He did not "sit down to eat" until seven A.M. with his family and this was a principle of his.) At one end of the table Revere sat leaning forward onto his elbows and at the other end Clara sat and when

Aunt Esther was feeling strong enough to join them she sat between them. Clark, Jonathan, and Robert had their places at the table, that could not be varied. This morning the brothers were edgy, silent. Yet their silence had the look of dogs that had been snarling and yipping at one another a minute before.

When Swan sat quietly at his place, he glanced nervously at Revere, who was mournful-eyed and distracted, and did not return Swan's glance. Often the two smiled at each other, when Swan took his place; but this morning Revere's eyes were glazed over like a scrim of ice on water.

Clark was rubbing his shaved jaws ruefully. He'd cut himself more than once: he was the only one of the brothers who had to shave. Robert was mumbling something to Jonathan about a missing muskrat trap of his, and Jonathan laughed behind his hand, disguising the sound as a cough. Jonathan was fourteen now, narrow-faced, with dark pinched-together features and a blemished skin and not enough flesh on his arms and legs. Seated across from Swan, he never looked at Swan; his eyes were hooded, secretive. Clark, closest to the stove, was watching Clara with a small smile. She was looking sleepily pretty this morning with her hair loose on her shoulders, in a pink quilted robe Revere had bought for his sons to give her on Christmas morning. In all that household, Swan thought, there was nowhere to look so shining as Clara.

"I'll take something up to Esther," Clara told Revere. She was waiting for the eggs to fry; a cautious cook, since her instinct was to be hurried and slapdash. "I feel sorry for her. . . ."

Clark said quickly, "Aunt Esther wasn't ever well. Even . . . a long time ago." Conscious of having said something wrong, as Clark often did, he continued, clumsily flirting with Clara, "How come you aren't like that, Clara? Sick-like, I mean."

Clara laughed, as if she'd been complimented.

"That's not my nature, I guess. I'm healthy as a horse."

Revere said to Clark, "That's enough, now. This isn't a happy occasion."

Clark's face reddened. He was a big thick-shouldered boy, almost his father's size. There was something heavy and swerving in him yet good-natured, the same idle lumbering gait you see in bulls that have been castrated, safe inside their pens. "I didn't mean any-thing disrespectful, Pa." The word *disrespectful* hung conspicuously in the kitchen air amid a sound of sizzling bacon and sausage.

Revere seemed not to hear, however. He was sitting with his el-bows on the table in a way he forbade his sons. Already he was dressed for the drive, in a starched white shirt and dark necktie and darker coat that fitted him tight across the chest. Swan had heard Clara complain to him half-seriously that his expensive clothes never fit him exactly, so they didn't look like what they cost: that, to Clara, was a shame.

Clara spoke in her light glimmering way about the upcoming drive: she was looking forward to meeting her kinfolk, as she called them. "And Swan. I mean, Steven. It will be good for him, too."

Revere murmured a vague assent. Clark, Jonathan, Robert stared moodily at Clara. Was she saying something wrong? Swan guessed that she was, without knowing it. In this household, so much was unsaid; it was like running in a marshy place, where you could sink your foot in quicksand and fall flat on your stomach. Swan under-stood that the boys were thinking of their mother who was dead. *Whoever the woman was, we didn't know her. We don't have to miss her. Only just respect her memory.* Clara had advised Swan, as if instucting her-self.

Swan knew that Revere and the boys went to visit the cemetery every other week or so. They made their plans quietly, maybe se-cretly. The boys' mother had been dead now for two years, Swan knew. In his and Clara's presence they never spoke of her.

Clara served them breakfast—"My men. All of you so hand-some." She made a playful ceremony of it, placing strips of bacon and tiny sausages on napkins to soak up the excess grease. The fried eggs were slightly scorched at the edges, and some of the yolks were cooked hard, but otherwise delicious. Swan liked it that Clara served Revere first, acknowledging how special he was; then she served the others, beginning with Clark. But, serving Swan, she touched the back of his head lightly to signal *Hey! I love you best.*

In this Revere household, they had such small secret signals be-tween them. Sometimes only just a glance was enough.

Now Clara smiled at them all. Urging them to eat while they could. "We're going on a long trip, remember!"

It was a happy time, Swan thought. Or would have been except for the *funeral*. The *wake*. He had no idea what these words meant except he wished he could stay home.

Sunlight flooded the kitchen and lit up the shining copper pans Clara had bought from a mail-order catalogue. Also Clara had ordered fluffy yellow curtains with tiny red flowers on them for the kitchen windows. For the parlor that was so dark and somber even by day she'd ordered similar curtains, of a gauzy white material with tiny red dots in it, curtains that came to only the windowsills, and seeing these in the parlor Aunt Esther had protested, "Clara, no. I'm afraid, dear—*no*."

Clara had torn the curtains down, her face flushed and angry. *Goddamn old bitch. Why doesn't she die, the old bag.*

Swan couldn't understand what was wrong with the curtains, he'd thought they were pretty. Like Clara he felt pushed and herded around by the old woman, you could feel Aunt Esther's power in the house, that Clara had to back down. Still, Clara had the boys carry most of the old furniture upstairs to the attic. By mail order from a Port Oriskany furniture store she'd purchased a handsome living room "suite"—oversized leather sofa and chairs, brass floor lamps, sunburst-framed mirrors and a shaggy wine-colored carpet.

Clara was asking Robert would he like another piece of raisin toast? The piece he'd taken had a burnt crust. Robert seemed about to say yes then changed his mind and said no, what he had was all right.

Swan dreaded Clara addressing Jonathan that way, but Clara knew better. After Swan, Robert was Clara's favorite son.

Robert had clear skin and eyes that were flecked with hazel; he was the nicest-looking of the Revere boys, with a sweet, flushed face and a habit of smiling nervously; something about him made Swan think of a rabbit fattened in a cage. Jonathan was lean, snaky-quick and unpredictable; if it hadn't been for Jonathan, Robert would have been Swan's friend. The week before, Jonathan had pelted a squirrel to death with heavy stones just to make Swan cry, and Robert had begged for him to stop. "I hate you! You always want to kill things."

"Lucky you, you're not a goddamned squirrel," Jonathan had sneered.

If Revere had known, Jonathan would have been punished. But Robert would never have told. Swan would never have told.

Clara, finally sitting down, lifted her fork to her mouth and tried to eat; she sipped at coffee eagerly, and burnt her mouth; seeing Revere's eyes on her, she said edgily, "Oh, honey. I wish we didn't have to go. A funeral makes me . . ." Her voice trailed off weakly.

"If you don't want to accompany us, Clara, you really don't have to. My family would understand."

"No! They wouldn't. They would judge me, and not like me."

"Clara, no."

Swan stared at his plate. The mess of broken eggs and congealing grease. He and the Revere boys squirmed in embarrassment when Revere and Clara spoke like this, in a quick intimate exchange as if they were alone. Clara, calling that old man *honey*! You could hear the tremor in Revere's voice; you could see the sick helpless love in the man's face. And Clara, exasperated, laughing in her edgy brittle way, fluffing out her hair with her hands like a willful child.

Revere said quietly, "Clara, nobody likes funerals."

Mandy had arrived, to clean up in the kitchen. A short heavy woman older than Revere; prim and prune-faced, Swan thought. Always her suety gray eyes were trailing onto Clara, disliking her. And when Clara spoke to Mandy, the older woman stiffened and never met her eye. Mandy behaved as if Revere was God, with exaggerated solicitude and deference; of the boys, she favored Robert because he was the youngest. Swan was invisible to her, she seemed scarcely aware of him. Now she busied herself at the sink, while casting a sidelong look at Clara who was wiping her eyes with a napkin. Swan would have liked to shout at the old woman *You're ugly! You're old! You were never like my mother!*

The five-hour drive to Hamilton, near Lake Ontario.

Swan would remember not wanting it to end. For there was Death waiting, amid strangers Revere called *my family*.

Yet Revere drove well, steadily and with concentration. He was an excellent driver, Swan thought. Behind the wheel of his stately new Packard sedan, silvery-green with a chrome-edged hood and fenders like arched wings. White sidewalls. A low sonorous horn, Revere demonstrated for them as they drove along the highway. Clara spoke repeatedly of what a good driver Revere was. She seemed excited, anxious. Lighting cigarettes and exhaling smoke out the partly opened window. From time to time Revere passed hitchhikers along the road—most were adult men, shabbily dressed, but a few were boys no older than Jonathan. "*I* wouldn't give dirty old bums like that a ride," Clark said righteously. "They'd smell up the car."

Revere said, "They're out of work, Clark. They're homeless. They don't have your advantages, son. 'Judge not lest ye be judged.' "

Swan was seated in the front between Revere and Clara; Clark, Jonathan, and Robert were in the backseat. Yet Swan, Jonathan and Robert shivered with unconscious pleasure that Clark, the eldest, had been rebuked. Only Clara protested, "Oh, he's right! I wouldn't give them a ride, either."

Revere said, bemused, "Of course not, dear. I hope not."

They talked of bums—"vagabonds," Revere called them—for a while. Swan felt his mother stiffen; she seemed twitchy, restless. In the backseat, Jonathan was saying to Clark, "Could be, you'll be a bum yourself someday. Then what?" and Clark muttered, "I'm not going to be any bum!" and Jonathan said, "None of them ever thought they'd be, either."

By the time they reached Hamilton they were groggy from the drive. Clara had several times nodded off, her head lolling against Swan's; at a signal from Revere, he'd removed her cigarette from her fingers, and gave it to Revere to toss out the window. "Your mother is tired," Revere said to Swan, gently, "she didn't sleep very well last night." This intimate fact, so bluntly stated, made Swan blush. Yet he felt singled out for a confidence that excluded his brothers in the backseat, out of earshot.

Hamilton was a real city, as Clark had predicted, not a mill town like Tintern. There was so much to see, entering it, that Swan didn't know where to look. Revere pointed out to him something he'd never seen before—a "railroad bridge." Here, the Eden River had widened and appeared to be faster-moving, a steely grayish hue approaching Lake Ontario—"One of the 'Great Lakes,' Steven. Look at the map." But when Swan studied the map, he became confused and lost a sense of where they were. For the map was paper-flat, and nothing like the world. Swan was staring through the rain-washed railings of a bridge and down into a sudden valley at railroad tracks—so many! Then they were above the river that was moss-gray, a lusterless no-color, swiftly flowing through channels that seemed to have been formed from raised outcroppings of rock. Revere pointed out a dam—"It holds the water back, for electrical power." Swan wondered if he was meant to understand this. He stared at the ragged-looking frothy rapids. Everything here was rushing, impatient. There was more traffic, streams of traffic, cars and trucks pressing forward, impatient. Yet Revere continued to drive with his usual composure, pointing out landmarks to Swan—a tall spire that was the Cathedral of St. Peter, another bridge in the distance, factory smokestacks rimmed with flame. There was an eagerness in his voice that suggested pride, as if in some way he owned these things.

"Is that your factory, darling? That one?" Clara spoke naively, as a girl might speak. Revere smiled, saying, "There's no factory that's 'mine,' Clara. I've told you that my family has invested in Hamilton Steel. But we are only investors." Swan was sitting forward in his seat, staring. It was a confused, jumbled scene made up of patches of open space and enormous tin-colored "oil drums" as Revere called them and ugly buildings behind wire fences with smokestacks silhouetted against the gloomy sky. Halos of light glowed about the tops of these smokestacks. "Are they are on fire?" Swan asked.

Clara laughed lightly. "You can see them burning, silly! Sure they are."

But Revere said, reprovingly, "The smokestacks are not on fire.

They appear to be burning, but it's a combustion caused by fuels. It's self-consuming—the smokestacks won't burn."

Swan felt the importance of being told this fact by the man who was his father; he knew that Clara was the silly one, Clara had been rebuked, and that his brothers in the backseat would be smiling, in secret. He did not look at her.

After a while they came to a large intersection, and turned onto a strange wide road with a divider in its center in which grass and shrubs grew. Immediately it seemed to Swan that the air was clearer, the sky less mottled with cloud. Revere said, "This is Lakeshore Boulevard, Steven. Lake Ontario is just ahead." Swan was staring hard, not wanting to miss the lake. In the backseat the boys were talking excitedly. Clark said, " 'Ontario'—it's the biggest lake in the U.S." Jon said, sneering, "Is not." Clark said, "What is, then?" Jon said, "Lake Superior, stupid." Clark said, annoyed, "There's Hudson Bay, in Canada. *That's* big." Jon said, "That's a 'bay,' not a 'lake.' " Robert intervened, "What's the difference?"

They were passing blocks of stores. Small shops with glittering glass. A jewelry store—a "furrier's"—women's clothing stores. Clara said, "Oh! Look at that dress. So pretty." There was a faint furtive pleading in her voice, that embarrassed Swan. For Revere was sure to say, a little later, that Clara could buy that dress if she wanted it—and it would come as a surprise to her, because she would have forgotten. So much came to Clara like that, as surprises.

Now they were in a residential neighborhood where the houses were as large as Revere's farmhouse. And some were larger. No driveways were quite so long as Revere's driveway in the Eden Valley, but the lush beautiful lawns went far back from the boulevard, and there were shrubs of a kind, ornamental and elaborately pruned, Swan had never seen before even in photographs. He thought how strange it was, they were traveling through all these sights to get to a funeral, to a dead man.

There at last was the lake: so big you couldn't see any horizon. Nor could you see, to the left or to the right, any edge. Revere said approvingly, "Big as an inland sea, Steven. Imagine how it looked to the first explorers." Swan saw that the boulevard here was made of brick, washed clean the way nothing could be clean out in the country; and all the houses had been built to face the water, on little hills. The facades of the houses were blank and impassive as the faces of strangers. Clara nudged Swan, saying, with a kind of gloating triumph, "See, Swan! How d'you like 'Lakeshore Boulevard'?"

"Please call him by his proper name," Revere said.

"'Steven.'" Clara spoke quickly, with childlike obedience; but nudged Swan to indicate that this was a joke. In a formal voice she said, "Steven, how d'you like where your father's people live?"

Swan murmured a vague embarrassed reply.

They turned onto one of the bricked drives leading up from the roadway. Swan was staring at a large foursquare house made of nickel-colored stone. There was a tall flagpole in the front lawn and at its top an American flag—rippling red and white stripes—blew in the wind like a living thing. A flag, for just a private house. There was a steep roof on the stone house made of some heavy-looking material—slate. There were more windows than Swan could count, somewhere beyond twelve. And tall wide chimneys. And columns at the front of the house that made it look like a public building, not somebody's home. Clara seemed frightened suddenly. She took out her compact and dabbed powder on her face, muttering to herself. "Oh, God. I look like hell." She clamped her hat—a small black cloche with a dusky veil with black dots, that Clara complained made everything look like it had pimples—on her head, groping with nervous fingers. Her nails were carefully polished a deep peach-pink, and filed; Swan had seen her that morning, bent over her task with a small bottle and brush.

"These people, these 'Reveres.' They hate my guts."

Several times Clara had told Swan these enigmatic words. *Hate my guts.* But why? And why *guts*?

A middle-aged man, old as Revere, hurried down the front steps of the nickel-colored mansion. He came to Revere, who'd rolled down the car window; the men gripped hands, for a moment wordless. Then the man told Revere he should park in back, so many cars would soon be arriving. Swan noted how well dressed this man was: a dark suit, tightly buttoned; a white shirt with a curiously stiff collar; a necktie that looked as if it were made of gunmetal. Revere drove the Packard to the rear of the house, slowly. He seemed distracted. Swan saw that the house had three full floors, unlike the farmhouse. He saw a garden with people standing in it, in odd postures, that turned out to be statues, gray and startling. Autumn flowers, zinnias and asters and marigolds, were blooming, but there was a left-behind look to the garden, as if something had happened to make it irrelevant. Swan whispered to Clara, so no one could hear, he wished he could stay outside—he could wait in the garden.

Clara ignored him. He saw that her face was bright, taut, tense, and that she was smiling her special smile, stretching her lipsticked lips across her teeth without revealing her teeth. Swan knew that Clara hated her teeth that were discolored and slightly uneven, white-trash teeth she called them, shamed.

They entered the house through a side door. Into a vestibule, and into a hallway that smelled not unlike Revere's house in the Eden Valley: furniture polish, and something dank and musty like mold. It was a rich person's smell, Swan supposed. They were taken into a "parlor" with furniture even heavier and more old-fashioned than Revere's; there was a table so massive, so intricately and senselessly carved, you would think it deserved to be stared at, yet no one took the slightest notice. On this table were tall vases of flowers, mostly white lilies that gave off a sweet-sickish odor.

"Oh, calla lilies. That's what those are?"

Clara spoke tentatively, adjusting her hat. The black-dotted veil gave her a moribund look, as if she were a very old woman peering out at the world with half-blind eyes.

Clara tried to grasp his hand but he shoved her hand away.

"Steven. Come."

It was Revere speaking, quietly. No one would shove away Curt Revere's hand.

Swan was being led forward blindly. Behind him he heard, or believed he heard, Jonathan mimicking his father's voice. *Steven, come! Little bastard.* The other boys giggled.

Now they were in a larger room, that might have been another parlor. Here there was a great shining piano, its keyboard shut. More flowers, and that sweet-sickly odor mingled with the more pungent odor of tobacco smoke. At the windows were curtains flimsy as ghosts. A woman in a dark shimmering dress hurried to embrace Revere; the two were nearly of a height, and might have been brother and sister, except they were so old, Swan thought, confused. Could you be brother and sister, and so old? The woman had gray hair caught back in a tight coil, and her skin looked tight, too. Elaborately, she came to embrace Clara. "Claire. My dear. I mean—Clara. So very good to see you, dear. On this sorrowful occasion." Swan had a sudden terrible impulse to laugh; if he laughed, his brothers would admire him. But he stood unresisting as the woman with the tight-coiled hair frowned over him. "Oh. Is this— Steven?" With jerky movements, she bent to embrace him; Swan neither resisted nor allowed himself to be embraced. Clara poked him meaning he should say hello, should say something, but Swan stood mute. This woman was—who? Someone's great-aunt? Revere's aunt? And not his sister after all? Swan made an effort to listen, initially. But there were too many people arriving, and all of them strangers. Some resembled Curt Revere, and others did not. Many were his age, and even older. Though there were younger people, too—a surprise to Swan. He had come to believe that all Reveres were old, except for his brothers.

"My wife, Clara—"

"My son, Steven—"

Once introduced, Swan was then ignored. His brothers, too, though older, and known to these people, were mostly ignored. Swan overheard a white-haired man say to Revere, gripping his arm at the elbow with startling intimacy, "Curt. He spoke of you often. At the end." Swan was shocked to see Revere's face crease suddenly, as if he were holding back tears.

He glanced around, hoping to catch Jonathan's eye.

If they exchanged a glance, it would be a wink. A man Revere's age, almost crying!

But Jonathan, frowning, was staring at the floor. Shuffling slowly along beside Clark who was licking his lips nervously. Like a steer on its hind legs, Clara said of her eldest stepson, but fondly. And there was Robert, dazed-looking, glancing about as if for help. *Looking for his mother* Swan thought.

Swan felt a stab of satisfaction: he had Clara, and his stepbrothers had no mother.

They were at the front of the second parlor, which was like a hall, where chairs were set up. A wake. Swan had been told: We are going to a wake. He hadn't wanted to ask what it meant: *wake.* It was strange, because death was *sleep* and not *wake.* But he hadn't wanted to ask because he was always asking the wrong questions. And now he was the youngest child in this room, and he'd confused the gleaming mahogany piano with the gleaming black coffin, cylindrical-shaped, at the front of the room. Robert was whimpering to Clara, "Do we have to look, Clara? Do we?" Clara said, "Honey, no. I don't think so," but Revere overheard and said sternly, "Quiet. Follow me. All of you."

Swan's heart was beating hard. Yet he was not afraid. For he knew—he told himself—that the dead man inside the coffin could not hurt *him,* could not touch *him.* It was a fact that *deadness* could not hurt you the way *livingness* sometimes could. Clara was often saying she'd had brothers, goddamned brats they'd been always pulling her hair, pinching and poking her, hurting her, so she wanted Swan to tell her if his brothers hurt him; but of course Swan never did. Swan never would. That was *tattling,* you were a *tattletale* if you did such things though possibly it was *tattletail,* meaning you had a tail like a rat's. Swan was more fearful of Jonathan than of any dead man yet still his heart was beating so it almost hurt, and he hated how Clara kept touching her hair, her hat, her ridiculous black stippled veil so you could see that she was nervous, too. Swan was embarrassed that his mother was different from the other women in the room: even the younger women. Her hair was too pale, and too beautiful. Her face had a kind of glow and wasn't sallow and tired-looking like the others' faces. Seeing Clara, Curt Revere's young wife, you wanted to look nowhere else. She was trying to walk stiffly like the others, yet still her hips moved, her shoulders and arms moved in a way to draw the eye to her. Her shapely legs were encased in silky dark stockings, and she wore high-heeled black patent leather shoes.

"Yes, Clara. The boy should see. He's of age."

"Of age? Goddamn he's *seven*."

"Seven is the age of reason. Calm yourself, Clara."

This exchange was in an undertone. No one overheard except Swan.

There'd been indecision, and therefore hope, but now Swan's left hand was gripped, hard. By Clara. She was all but dragging him forward. She had the tight-jawed look of a woman hiking up a steep incline, damned if she would be daunted. A kind of sick excitement stirred in Swan, in his bowels, the way you felt sometimes when you were about to be sick but didn't yet realize what it meant, that sensation.

He would think, afterward: Because a stranger had died, and was in a gleaming black box at a *wake*, in a stone mansion on Lakeshore Boulevard, Hamilton, New York, and that stranger was related to Curt Revere who was Swan's father, Swan had had to be brought here, and had to look upon *deadness*. Not the many miles of countryside between Lakeshore Boulevard and REVERE FARM in the Eden Valley had been enough to protect Swan, once it was decided. And so he was in this high-ceilinged room banked with flowers that smelled of death.

Swan found himself staring at an elderly man, a stranger, with pale parchment skin, and tightly pursed lips, who was lying on his back inside the gleaming cylindrical box, his eyes closed. Yet how waxy his eyelids looked. How waxy his face, though his cheeks were dabbed with rouge like a woman's cheeks. If you were dead, Swan thought, you lay on your back and everyone else had to stand, and file past to stare at you.

Clara nudged Swan. Whispered for him to shut his eyes, to pray. Pray?

At home, Clara laughed at "pray"—"prayer." But Swan knew he could not laugh here. He was staring at the elderly man, who resembled Curt Revere. Soft white hairs on his head, a thin, sunken face, and though his mouth was meant to suggest a smile yet there was something ironic and bitter about it. Swan shut his eyes tight and hid his face with his hands in the "prayer" gesture he knew, and could mimic like a monkey.

"Son." Revere's hand was gentle on his shoulders.

Swan glanced upward, and in that instant he had a glimpse of his other father: the man with the pale blond hair, the man with the blurred smile and easy laughter.

The vacant blue sky, beyond that man's head. The blue of his eyes. The smell of the outdoors. The wind. What had that man said to him? He'd called him "Swan." He knew him: "Swan." He'd said something about "death"—dying, and the dead—but Swan could not remember.

Why did *dead* mean more in a man, than in a squirrel, a dog, a chicken? At the farm, chickens were killed by hand: their heads torn off in a sharp twisting motion, no more fuss than if you were shucking corn. Why was a man different? Was a man different? *A rich man is different* Swan thought.

"Steven, come away now." Revere spoke gently.

"Oh, Swan! Come away."

Clara was pulling him beside her. Almost, Clara was hugging him against her side, clumsily. He wanted to shove away from her, for he was no baby, he was seven years old which is *the age of reason* and he didn't need his damn mother. Sidelong he watched her, and the others. They were all going to die like the elderly man in the gleaming black box: but they didn't know it. Or didn't believe it. The way a chicken, in the instant before human hands reached out to grab it, and twisted its head from its neck, would not believe it was going to die.

Swan eased free of Clara's clutching hands, and walked away. As if he knew where he was going, in this strange place. But no one stopped him. There was something sweet and rotted on his tongue, he could not spit it out with everyone watching.

He found a bathroom, that smelled strongly of toilet cleanser. Then he found a room with shelves of books. He pulled out several tall heavy books with *Encyclopaedia Britannica* stamped in gilt letters on their spines. He was turning pages, looking at pictures, trying to read in the dim lighting, of a faraway place called Egypt, that was in Africa. Someday, he thought, he would go there: he would never return here.

3

At dawn of that day when Clara had her miscarriage—she had been about three months pregnant—she woke to see her husband dressing in the dark. He stood off to one side, dressing stealthily, and she lay very still, as if he were an intruder who had not yet noticed her. Her eyes were vague and gritty with sleep, her hair lay tangled over the pillow, and her heavy inert peace contrasted with Revere's quick movements. She saw as he turned to pick something up that his chest had grown heavy; his waist was thick. She could hear his breathing. The air was a little chilly—it was September and beginning to get cold at night—and the window behind him glared silently with light, everything slowed down as in a dream and having that strange elasticity of a dream, so that it could belong to any time.

She remembered him without those lard-pale ridges of fat: a younger man undressing before her, trembling with excitement for her.

She thought of Lowry, his face passing in and out of her mind as it always did, not upsetting her and not even blotting out Revere's kindly, hardened face, the look of precise concentration he was giving now to buttoning his shirt. The pregnancy with Lowry's baby had been uncertain, she hadn't known exactly what was going to happen; but this time everything was certain. There was nothing for her to worry about or even think about, except that she wanted a girl. So she looked at Revere in the half-dark and thought that he was a good man and that she did love him, she loved him somehow.

"Were you going to leave without saying goodbye?" Clara said.

He glanced around, startled like a thief. "Did I wake you up?" he said.

"I don't know, it's all right." Clara stretched her arms and yawned. "When are you coming back, I can't remember. . . ."

"Tuesday."

She remembered then that he'd told her this.

"Are you going to miss me, darling?" Clara asked.

He'd been buttoning his shirt. She saw how his fingers hesitated—he had thick, strong fingers. He was not a man who worked very much with his hands for he hired "farmhands" for this purpose; and yet, he was strong, he bore a taciturn authority Clara associated with maleness. It occurred to her that Revere's fingers and everything that was his belonged to her, who had nothing of her own; and had belonged to her for ten years now. Never did she see the tall black letters on the barn REVERE FARM without feeling a stab of elation, pride.

Bitches don't love nobody Carleton had accused her. Drunk, and his face contorted. *Run off. Dirty filthy bitch like all of them.*

She'd proven him wrong. Her drunk-father. White-trash Carleton Walpole left behind in, where was it. Migrant workers' camp in godforsaken Florida.

Revere was looking at her tenderly. In that way, Clara recalled, he'd looked at the instant photo of Clara as a girl, preening seductively for the camera. "Clara, dear, I wish you'd come with me." He sat on the edge of the bed, careful to retain most of his weight on his feet. "I thought you liked train rides. . . ."

He stroked her hair. Clara liked to be touched; lazily she closed her eyes. One of the farm dogs was barking in the near distance. "Your relatives don't like me, Curt. I try, but I can't talk to them. . . ." It wasn't true, exactly: Clara knew better than to try. She saw their eyes on her, judging. *They hate my guts* she dared not tell Revere who would defend them, hurt. "They're so different from you. And that time I went to buy that pretty dress, with the lace collar . . ."

"Clara, haven't you forgotten that yet?"

Revere's flashes of anger came vertically upon Clara, out of nowhere, never addressed to her exactly (for he loved his young blond wife, he adored his Clara) but to attitudes of hers he considered unworthy of a Revere wife. She understood that she had power over this man's anger as long ago she'd had power over Carleton Walpole's anger but that it was not a power she could control: it was like lightning, that could be swift and lethal.

"In the city I could go to a—a museum, maybe?—but not alone. I'd be so lonely by myself. And you're busy. And anyway . . . there are the boys here." Clara didn't want to say *There is Swan* for of course Swan was not her only son now. "And I want to work in my garden, it makes me happy. . . ." One of Revere's farmhands helped

Clara with the garden, a kitchen garden it was called, where she'd planted tomatoes, pole beans, fast-growing cucumbers, zucchini, acorn squash; but also zinnias, marigolds, petunias, and hollyhocks, her favorite flower. At Revere's great-aunt's house in Hamilton Clara had seen what a formal garden was, such precision, symmetry, the way colors were repeated and related, but her garden was nothing like that. Clara's garden was one that Pearl would have liked, Clara thought. Just to walk around in it, maybe to sit in it, in a chair. Sit, and dream. Where it wasn't just kneeling and stooping and picking desperate to fill baskets for a few pennies each. And you the owner of the garden, with a farmhand to help *you*.

"My garden," Clara said. "You like the flowers I bring in, don't you? The zinnias . . ."

Revere seemed scarcely to be listening to Clara. He leaned over her and pressed his face against the side of her face, and her hair that wasn't yet combed out. She felt his warm breath; it was a little stale yet from sleep and she wanted to move away, but did not. His hand had dropped onto her stomach, familiar and heavy. Warm, comforting. Clara put her own hand over his and smiled at him thinking he would be leaving in a minute, in just another minute.

She loved him. He was her husband, he adored her. He was a good father to her son. He was a good man, she knew. Decent, fair-minded, if sometimes impatient with others who didn't live up to his standards. He was a well-to-do man: "rich." Yet he wasn't arrogant, bossy. Not to her, anyway.

Yet it was easier to love Curt Revere when other people were around, and seeing him. Through others' eyes, Clara could admire him. A large man, not tall, but wiry, solid, walking with little grace or a sense of what grace might be; he got most of what he wanted, without exactly demanding it. His torso, even part of his back, was covered with matted graying-dark hair, and on his thick arms and the backs of his hands were softer, finer hairs. Aging, these hairs were turning lighter, like a kind of metal. Clara recalled from the migrant camps those older men, whose muscled bodies were softening, turning to fat; how their bodies must have astonished them, betraying them; and Revere was of that *maleness*. His face was already creased and leathery, his eyesight weakening; often he was short of breath. When at last his muscles did turn to fat he would look sad, puffy, discarded. Clara could think of this with a remote, impersonal regret, the way one mourns over the death of former presidents and generals, men of public life who reveal their private degeneration all at once and die at that moment—up until then they require no sympathy. She could hold him in her arms and look past him, as if looking from the present time into a vortex of no time at all—the Clara who had always been at the center of herself, whether she was nine or eighteen or twenty-eight, as she was now. Whatever else happened, that Clara never changed.

"Are you warm enough? How do you feel?" he said. He kissed her throat. She turned her face so that he could kiss her mouth, not because she wanted him to but because it had to be done. His other wife must have been dog-sick with pregnancies, she thought, the way he fussed over her; he did not seem to believe in her strength, which she took for granted. Nothing bothered her. If she had cramps occasionally it was nothing to keep her in bed, she liked to be up and doing something, anxious not to miss whatever was going on. She hated to be sick and idle, mooning around a sickroom—she had never been sick a day in her life, she told people. She would be healthy until the day she died. But most of all she liked to know what was going on, even if she could not always understand it. Now that Revere had these new interests there was much happening, but it was a man's business—complexities of partnerships she liked to be told about even if she could not grasp their meaning. She could understand money, however, and Revere had enough of that. She believed vaguely that he had much more money than he had had in the old days when he had pursued her, but it was difficult to tell, and certainly it would be difficult to make it clear to people in the neighborhood: what could you buy, past a certain point? She had magazines that showed enormous startling houses and her own house would imitate these (she was having a back porch added) but it took time, time; she had good clothes but nowhere to wear them, and what did people in the country know about these things? All they could understand was something flashy, like her car; Clark's little foreign car, which had cost more money than Clara's, probably was lost on them and looked like a toy. They knew nothing, what could you do with such people?

"When I'm away I miss you very much. I'm afraid you might not be here when I get back," Revere said. Anything lured out of him by her softness or by their intimacy was something he would regret later; he was not that kind of man. Judd was a talker, but not Revere. So she felt uncomfortable when he confessed these things, not because they meant anything in particular to her but because she had no real interest in the private side of this public man's life. She touched his arm, the clean stiff material of the shirt Mandy had fussed over, and felt his warmth inside, a warmth that was alive and pleading but nothing she could respond to as a woman. She loved him about as much as she loved Clark and Robert—she did really like them—and a little further behind was Jonathan, who seemed to resist her but who had such fine eyes, who was almost as smart as her own son. What she felt for Revere was confused on one side with his boys and this house, and on the other side with the man whose name was so well known and who could never be a private, intimate human being, but only a person committed eternally to fulfilling his name.

When she opened her eyes he was still leaning over her, staring hard, and something in his face discomforted her. "You're too serious, don't worry about me," she said. She lifted herself up on one elbow and seemed by this to be getting free of him. He moved aside. "We're going to have a little girl and she'll be as healthy as I am. Don't worry, all right? Now, you don't want to be late."

"I have enough time."

She did not like his talk but she didn't like his silence either. "Well, what do you want?" she said. The weight of his love was sometimes burdensome. She did not like having to walk about inside the circle of his infatuation for her, which was nothing she could understand or admire. To Clara, a man's love was no sign of his strength but rather of his weakness, something you wanted from him but then had to feel a little sorry about taking. "I'm not mad about the other night, that hunting business," she said. "If that's what you mean."

"I hope you aren't still angry. . . ."

"You're right, it's good for Swan to go hunting. Fine. That's fine. I agree." She brushed her hair back and in that instant wanted almost to cry out for something—for escape, for someone to help her. But the impulse subsided at once. She was at home here, warm beneath the covers, safe and protected by Revere and his world. He might seem to be a stranger at times but he was at least a stranger she could handle. "I asked him why he didn't want that gun—that's a real nice gun you bought him—and he told me something, but it didn't make sense. He likes dogs and cats and things, you know, and he doesn't want to shoot rabbits either. He doesn't like the loud noise, he said."

"He has never tried to go hunting," Revere said quietly.

They were tugging over something. Clara felt this, understood it perfectly, and knew enough to give in. "Well, I told him what you said and he said he'd go with Robert, he likes Robert. Robert's nice to him sometimes," she said, wondering a moment later why she had said that "sometimes," which didn't sound good. "He said he'd go today if it was nice. Him and Robert—he and Robert, they get along real well together if they're alone." She paused. All these jagged edges had been covered many times in the last few years, many times. She could run over them smoothly without really drawing his attention to them. "He'd tell you, but he's afraid."

"Afraid of his father?"

"He loves you but he's afraid. A boy should be afraid of his father a little," Clara said cunningly. She tried to remember her own father. Had she been afraid of him? What had he been like? He stood there, at one end of her life, as if at the opening of a tunnel, silhouetted against the light, barring her way back to her childhood: a tall lean man with a narrow face, blond hair, squinting suspicious eyes, a mean mouth. Thank God, she thought, that Revere did not swear in front of women—not much, anyway; that he did not paw and grunt like an animal, the way Carleton had with her mother and then Nancy and who knows how many other women; that he did not drink too much. She awoke from this to hear Revere speaking quietly and she touched his smooth-shaven cheek, feeling a surge of tenderness for him, wishing there was something more of herself that she could give. "He's younger than the other boys, remember," she said. "He's afraid of them, you know how kids are. They don't bother him or anything," she said carefully, knowing of course that Jonathan hated Swan and bothered him all the time, "but you know how kids are. Give him time to grow up."

"Yes," he said.

Clara kissed him. "He'll use the gun. I promise he'll shoot something."

"And, Clara, you should let him alone more. You shouldn't fuss over him."

"O.K., fine. I agree with that."

"My boys never got much attention from their mother because she wasn't well. They aren't used to it—I don't mean they don't like it but they don't know what to do with it. You confuse them. And Steven needs to be let loose more. He needs more freedom."

"You don't know what it's like for a kid to run loose," Clara said. "I do."

"He has to learn to take care of himself."

"But that's what I don't want," she said. She rubbed her cheek against his, wondering how much longer he would stay. She listened to him always and agreed with him in words, and then went on to do whatever she wanted to anyway. She had learned this technique from Nancy, years back. "I want him to be different from other kids. I want him different, I don't want him like—the way I was."

After he left she tried to sleep again, thinking mainly of Swan and of Lowry behind him, another figure silhouetted at the end of another tunnel, Swan's tunnel; but he could not really remember Lowry. He had been too small to remember anything. And it seemed to her that the relationships between people and their fathers were like thin, nearly invisible wires . . . you might forget they were there but you never got rid of them. She was sure that her own father was still alive somewhere: maybe he had finally gotten a real job, settled down somewhere with Nancy and the beginning of a new family, and there he was right now if she wanted to look him up. With her money, she would look him up someday. She could help him out, maybe, if he'd let her; but he might not let her. For Esther, who had grown old and helpless so fast, she felt almost nothing—she was just a stranger who hadn't liked Clara and had gone to pieces when Clara had moved in. It was good she was out of the way. But for her own father, who would be getting old by now, she felt a confused, generous sympathy, blocked up because she had no way of freeing it. In a few years, maybe. There was no need to hurry.

When she woke again it was lighter. The sun was out, the air smelled good. She went downstairs and Swan and Robert were about to go outside. Swan was standing in the doorway to the side shed. "He's fixing up the guns," he said. Clara saw tiny flakes in the corners of his eyes but did not rub them out for him. He didn't like her to do that when anyone else was around.

"Did you both eat?" she said.

"Yeah, we ate." Behind Swan, Robert was cleaning his rifle. He looked up at Clara, frowning. The gun in his hands made him look older. He was thirteen on his last birthday and a handsome, solid boy, with slow eyes and hands. Swan waited in the doorway, pretending to be at ease. He was still a little slight, though she thought he would be growing fast one of these days. He had Lowry's pale, clear blue eyes and something remote and unfathomable in his face, like Lowry, but his silence he had gotten from neither Lowry nor Clara. He had the air of a child perpetually listening to voices around him and voices inside him. Clara wanted to slide her arms around his neck but she knew this would just embarrass him.

"You kids be careful, huh?" she said.

"I'm used to it. I go out all the time," Robert said.

"What about Swan here?"

"I might not shoot anything," Swan said nervously. He did not look at her. "I might just go with him."

"He don't need to shoot anything the first time," Robert said.

Clara had the idea that there was some tension between the boys, that maybe Robert had been talked into this—but from Robert's polite, slow face you could tell nothing. He was really polite, this thirteen-year-old, and Clara was always surprised by it. He handed

Swan his heavy gun and the boy took it, his shoulders drooping just a little in surprise—he didn't remember how heavy the gun was—then he turned away, ready to go out into the shed.

Clara said uncertainly, not knowing if she should say it or not, "Your father never meant to holler at you, Swan." She was speaking past Robert as if he didn't exist, to Swan's back. Swan did not turn. "If you don't want to shoot the goddamn thing you don't have to."

The words were so clearly Clara's—they could never have been condoned by Revere—that Robert lifted his eyes to her. He did not quite smile. "He's gonna be all right," Robert said.

—

"Mornin, Clara."

It was a jovial greeting, a mock-country drawl. Judd Revere was not one to naturally call out "Mornin!" with a lopsided grin so you knew you were meant to laugh at him, and with him.

Judd dropped by in the late morning, when Clara was in her garden. She knew the sound of his car: she straightened, and smiled. Judd came around back whistling, hands in his pockets. They were always happy to see each other, a kind of light flashed between them, like a mirror catching sunshine. A quick flash, others might not note.

On his way into town Judd often dropped by the Revere house. He was a landowner, as he called himself, not a worker, the result being that he had no visible work yet worked continually, in his head. From grudging remarks made by Revere, Clara understood that Judd was very smart. *Eyes in back of his head.*

Clara dabbed at perspiration on her forehead, and brushed at her hair. She was wearing a stiff green straw hat—in fact, a hat Judd had bought for her, on a whim—to shade her eyes. "Well. Looks like he got off to an early start this morning," Judd said, giving *he* a faint intonation you could interpret as admiring, or bemused. Judd was a smiler, Clara thought: so much smiling, and his eyes cautious and watchful, tricky. It was said that you would not want to play poker with Judd Revere but if you needed advice, needed help, Judd Revere was the man to come to, for he would not judge you as other men might. He was a tall, loose-jointed man, not at all like Revere. You could tease him and laugh at him and it wouldn't lodge deeply in him as it would with Curt, where any stray word, any unintended and inadvertent insult, would be lodged forever. Clara thought what a shame it was, Judd wasn't good-looking; for he had the ease of a man meant to be good-looking, like Lowry. And it was a worse shame, it filled her with hurt, rage, resentment, that his snobbish bitch of a wife hadn't once called Clara to invite her to visit, though the women lived hardly five miles apart.

When Judd dropped by like this he would always protest he couldn't stay long, he had errands in town, but eventually he would sit with Clara in her new mail-order "lounge" lawn chairs under the willows and Clara fetched him orange juice. "Fresh-squeezed, I did it myself." Judd would take a big swallow, roll his eyes in a comical yet serious way, and say, "Clara! Delicious." Then he talked. Judd always had news, whether the news meant much to Clara or not. He could talk about politics and things in the newspaper Clara knew nothing of and he could make them interesting, almost. Beyond his voice she was listening for rifle shots, trying not to be distracted. Trying not to worry. Goddamn she was not going to worry, not one of those mothers who wear themselves out worrying. *Needs to be let loose more. Needs more freedom.* Clara hoped those tiny little lines she'd been seeing in her forehead had faded, she'd been rubbing at with cold cream. Judd's forehead was crisscrossed with thin lines like cobwebs but that was all right in a man, even Lowry's face had had lines.

"Judd, I like your hair a little long like that. A man looks nice with kind of long hair." Clara spoke half-teasing and half-serious. He brushed his hair back from his forehead as she said this. She talked at Judd in this fashion, enjoying his company but not worried about it, because he so obviously admired her but would never do anything about it. "How's your little girl?" she said, thinking at once of her little boy who was not so little anymore. "When are you going to bring her over? I like little girls . . . this next one is going to be a girl." And she touched her stomach. Judd looked away, strangely fastidious. He said something about his daughter, whose name was Deborah. She was five years old. Clara took little interest in children who were not immediate to her. She could not quite believe in them. So she listened vaguely, inclining her head toward

Judd. Her gaze moved on to her legs, which were stretched out in the sunshine, and she saw that Judd looked at them now and then too, as if accidentally, bemusedly. They fell silent. Clara sighed. Then Judd began to talk again, about a problem of his. Revere accused him of being slow and lazy and too kind, but what could he do? It had something to do with business and Clara did not respond. Then he asked her about the porch and she brightened. "Clark is going to do it for me. I made all the plans. Now that my husband owns the lumberyard, all of it, I can get anything I want. . . ."

"That's very convenient."

"Clark likes to help me. He's a good boy. Then, next, we might have a swimming pool."

Judd nodded affably.

"They swim in that lake," Clara said, making a face. "There are snakes and bloodsuckers there. Garbage fish—carp. What if they cut their feet and get lockjaw?" Though she was thinking of Swan, her Swan; yet she made herself think of the others, too—her stepsons. "So, don't you think—a swimming pool is best?"

"I suppose so, Clara. Sure."

Like Revere, he seemed scarcely to be listening to her words.

Looking at her. Listening to her voice, and smiling.

Clara said, with an air of pride, "Swan is out hunting now. With his brother Robert."

"Hunting?"

"I think it's good for a boy to go hunting."

Judd shrugged. "I never cared for hunting."

"You didn't?"

"Hell, no. Shooting rabbits, defenseless birds—deer—even if you eat the meat. There's plenty of other things to eat." Judd wasn't smiling now. "Frankly, I don't like spilling blood. For 'sport.' Hunters should be on the receiving end of their own bullets, see what it's like."

Clara thought this over. She liked a man to speak emphatically, and she liked Judd when he seemed to be criticizing, however indirectly, Revere. "Swan talks to you sometimes, doesn't he? Has he ever said anything about hunting? Or—food he eats?"

"What d'you mean?"

"Oh, that Swan! He's so smart, I tell him he's too smart for his own good. Too smart for Eden Valley." Clara paused, smiling without parting her lips. She liked Judd watching her, listening to her. And he was listening now, she could see. "Swan thinks that eating meat is 'wrong.' He eats meat, because he has to, in this house; but he feels sickish, he says, sometimes. 'When you pull the meat from the bone you can see how it was put together.' 'When you chew beef it's the muscles you feel with your tongue.' "

"Well. You can't say that your son is mistaken, can you?"

Clara heard, or thought she heard, another gunshot. But when she listened there was only a sound of starlings, raucous and excited in the trees outside the window. "I'm worried sometimes, Swan has such ideas. Like nobody else. Nobody else here. His teacher says he's 'highly intelligent'—'with an analytic mind'—or maybe it was 'analytical mind'? He's more intelligent now than Jonathan, I think. And Jonathan is almost sixteen. See, it used to be that Jonathan was the one who read a lot, adventure books about places like Alaska, Africa, he was interested in Indians, but now it's Swan who likes to read. I'm proud of him, I want him to know things." Clara spoke dreamily, reaching out to touch Judd's arm with a blade of grass; it was one of her gestures that were seemingly unconscious, unpremeditated. "I want him to read but not if it makes him . . . strange. Too quiet. Different from the other boys. He's only ten, yet he acts older. When I was ten, I wasn't a child any longer, I had to grow up fast, and I don't want that for my son, goddamn I don't."

Clara had been speaking urgently. Judd said, "Why are you so worried, Clara? Has something happened?"

"No. And I don't want anything to happen. Like I don't want Swan to remember about me, how I was living when he was little. Before I came here."

Judd was lighting a cigarette, and he offered her one. Clara guessed that he was thinking of her living alone, Curt Revere's girl-mistress; but really she was thinking of Lowry.

"I want to understand my son when he talks. I don't want to be some damn stupid old woman, that her own son is embarrassed of. Here's a book Swan was reading, I brought out to read for myself." She pointed, and Judd picked it up.

"*A Natural History of Animals.* Sounds like something a boy should be reading."

"Here's another one, I had trouble with—*Descent into a*—" Clara paused, unwilling to attempt the word. "This Edgar Allan Poe, I heard of. He's famous, huh?"

Judd took up this book as well, thumbing through it. He smiled, but the smile was puzzled, Clara saw.

"*A Descent into the Maelstrom and Other Stories.* This is tougher going. Not for a ten-year-old, I wouldn't think."

"You've read it?"

"Some of the stories. But not the 'Maelstrom.'"

"What's it about?"

Clara spoke with such childlike eagerness, Judd regretted he could only shrug. "A typical Poe adventure, I guess. Descending into some region like the bottom of the sea, or maybe hell. 'Hades.'"

Hades? Clara smiled, not knowing what this was.

She was thinking how in the speckled sunshine Judd didn't look homely as she sometimes thought him. Only just awkward, and worn; not by time, for he was much younger than Revere, but by something like thoughtfulness, thinking. Clara would have liked to slide her warm bare arms around his neck, making a gift of herself to any man, wanting nothing from the exchange except to give pleasure, to make someone happy with no consequences. "I hate it that I don't understand my own son, sometimes."

Judd smoked his cigarette, exhaling smoke through his nostrils, somberly. "Don't feel bad about it, Clara. It's the same way with us all. We want to understand the people close to us, but we don't want them to understand us. Right?"

Clara laughed, startled. She'd thought that only she, Clara Walpole, was so secret to herself, impenetrable to others.

Judd said, "Having children doesn't change things. It doesn't change you, much."

"I think it does change you."

"No. Not really."

Having children killed my mother Clara wanted to say. Instead she smiled, teasing. "A man, maybe. A man can be a father and hardly know it. But a woman, that's different."

Judd laughed. "Well, look: my own experience has been that nothing changes essentially, in our souls. Except we become older, and our souls wear thin. I know a hell of a lot more now than I did just a few years ago but I don't know anything that's essential; I have more information, more facts, that's all. I have more money, too. But I'm not a wiser person. It seems to me that nature runs one way, like an hourglass. For most people, everything has been accomplished already—we can't invent, we can't discover, we can't create. We can imitate, that's all. We can fail." He paused, smoking. Clara had lighted a cigarette when he had, but was too distracted to smoke. "I don't have your husband's legendary energy, I wish to Christ I did. I used to think I'd like to clarify one thing, set one thing in order: I'd like to write one book, get everything into it. Truth, beauty—everything." He'd dropped Swan's books beside his chair, and poked now at *A Descent into the Maelstrom* with his foot, with a look of regret. "But I haven't even begun."

"Write a book?" Clara narrowed her eyes.

"One book. And I'd like to travel, too."

"To Egypt?"

"Why Egypt? What makes you say that?"

"Oh, Swan has some idea. . . . There's 'pyramids' there? Ancient ruins?" Clara smiled hesitantly. "Maybe we could all go, Judd? Sometime?"

Judd shrugged. "Maybe."

"I've seen pictures of places in Europe, too. Paris. You don't need to speak French, do you? They wouldn't laugh at me, would they?— I mean, my accent."

Judd shifted uncomfortably. "You don't have an accent, Clara. You speak just fine."

"Bullshit. I talk like white trash. Soon as I open my mouth in some fancy store in Hamilton, the bitch salesclerks look at me like I'm a bad smell. Even the money I spend, Curt Revere's checking account, doesn't make any difference."

Judd said vaguely, as if this were a subject he didn't care to pursue, "My wife, now. She hates to travel."

"So leave her home."

"Well . . ."

"My husband is so goddamned busy, he only travels for business. More and more now, it's land he's buying, or selling, or—what's it called—leasing. It used to be farming he did, he says, now it's 'business.' So he can stay in the U.S. You and I could go, and take Swan."

"You're teasing, Clara? I guess?"

Judd stared at her, exhaling smoke. For a long awkward moment he seemed unable to speak, as Clara remained silent, stubborn. Let him think what he wanted to think, Clara thought. Unconsciously she was gripping her belly; with this pregnancy she'd hardly gained any weight, yet she felt burdened; not the way she'd felt when she was pregnant with Swan, and in love with Lowry.

"Sure, I'm teasing. Try me."

"Clara, aren't you—happy here? With—him?"

"Why don't you make me happy, damn you, instead of asking about it? You're always asking, with your eyes. I can feel you asking."

Judd's face darkened with blood. In his confusion he shook ash from his cigarette, so vigorously the cigarette itself fell into the grass.

"You sound angry, Clara. I don't understand why."

"Bullshit! You know."

"*You* know that he loves you very much. Your husband."

"So what? What can I do with it, what does it mean to me? And you," Clara said, contemptuously, "all that time I was living in that house you'd come around and you wanted to make love to me but you didn't—didn't dare! Think I don't know it? Didn't know it? And you could have married me, if you'd wanted to. Revere was married to that wife of his he had to 'respect,' like he didn't 'respect' me. And now every day almost you come here and look at me, but the hell with you—"

"Clara, for God's sake. What are you saying?"

They sat in silence. They were both excited, aroused. Clara could not have said if she was happy or deeply unhappy; hopeful, as a wayward child is hopeful, or sullen and defeated and without hope. If Judd had touched her, she might have slapped him. Or she might have gripped him around the neck with her strong, slender arms. Judd was sitting with his face turned from her, shocked and still listening to what she'd said. And at that moment the shot rang out.

A rifle shot, too close to the house.

A moment of silence followed, like the silence after a thunderclap. Then they heard the screaming begin.

4

It was a Springfield "thirty-caliber" rifle Revere had given him. With a gleaming wooden stock, and most of the long barrel was wood, with polished metal at the tip. The trigger was like a hook, shaped to fit your finger. Swan had stared at the rifle shocked by its size and frightened of it but Revere had said, an edge of annoyance in his voice, that he was old enough, it was time.

He'd made himself smile, as he did when Clara was watching. He'd murmured *Thank you, Pa* as he knew he should.

He would remember afterward: that was the first false thing.

———

So many false things, he gave up counting. He hadn't enough fingers on both his hands. Hadn't enough toes! When he'd been smaller, a little boy, he and Clara could giggle over such things, counting fingers and toes. But he wasn't a little boy any longer.

Here was a false thing: the way he had to follow Robert along the tramped-down path through the back field and the birchwoods that he'd walked countless times, as if Robert alone knew the way. As if Robert was Clark, or Jonathan. Or Revere himself. Bossy, important. Commanding Swan over his shoulder, "C'mon. This way. And keep your eyes open."

Swan did as Robert said. For here he was *hunting*. Carrying his heavy rifle the way Robert carried his, barrel slanted toward the ground. As Revere had taught them.

Hunting: it was playing at being a man, mostly. *Hunting* was what men did, older boys and men. Swan tried to think that this was something he wanted, this was good; Clara was always pleased, when one of his brothers invited him to come along with them, or even spoke kindly to him.

Little bastard. Pisspot. Mamma's baby Swan-Swan were words of Jonathan's muttered out of the side of his mouth that Clara did not hear. Swan tried not to hear them, either.

Now Robert was saying, in an undertone, "C'mon, Steve! You're so damn slow, I'm gonna piss my pants." It was a senseless remark, like most remarks uttered by the boys. Yet you had to smile, sometimes you had to laugh. It was what you did.

Robert was keeping up a fast pace, it seemed just to make Swan stumble. If Clark and Jonathan had been there, Robert would have fallen behind, too. It was all a game, Swan hated it. It was boring. But it was dangerous, too. He dreaded the rifle going off. Robert could raise his rifle barrel at any time, and shoot. Revere had said that no firearm ever caused injury to any hunter, only careless *huntsmanship*. Swan shaped that word with his mouth, cautiously: *huntsmanship*. You walked with the barrel lowered, and your head raised. A hunter is always alert. A hunter doesn't talk any more than he needs to talk. A hunter keeps his eyes open.

Revere had taken Swan out target shooting three times. He'd never taken Swan hunting for he had no time now for hunting, he said with regret. Revere had positioned the rifle in Swan's arms, the stock against Swan's thin shoulder. The barrel was so heavy, Swan had trouble keeping it erect. And the stock against his shoulder was loose. Revere warned him only once that the kick would "hurt like hell" if the stock wasn't snug against his shoulder but he had not repeated the warning and so when Swan pulled the trigger, the recoil felt like a horse's kick, making him cry out in pain.

Revere had said, See what I told you, son.

For there was never anything that Revere told Swan that was not crucial for him to know. Even if Revere told Swan only just once.

How to position the rifle, and how to sight along the barrel, through the scope; how to bring his trembling finger against the trigger; how to breathe, in and out and in and out and on the expulsion of breath to press the trigger.

Press, not jerk.

And don't shut your eyes.

"Steven. Open your eyes."

That was childish behavior, shutting your eyes. Stupid behavior. Swan knew, and was ashamed.

Hours of tramping in the back fields, in the woods. In the marshy soil by the creek. Gnats had gathered on Swan's sticky face, his eyelids and lips. He was out of breath, trying to keep up with Robert. "C'mon! There's some damn old vultures by the creek," Robert was saying, over his shoulder to Swan, crouched, like the two were in a war movie, "I like to puked seeing them picking apart I guess it was a raccoon or something, that'd died, a few days ago."

Swan remembered that Revere had told them not to shoot vultures, only just hawks. Chicken hawks. Weren't vultures *scavengers*, and necessary? A *scavenger* was a creature that fed upon the dead, and helped keep the earth clean.

Homo sapiens was the name of man. Mankind. In the book about animals Swan was reading, there was little mention of *Homo sapiens*. If there was a reason for *Homo species* on Earth, it was not stated.

Swan wished that Robert would decide to stop hunting and turn back. So far they had sighted nothing except perching birds, and not pheasants. But Swan could not be the one to suggest that they quit. If he did, Robert would tease him. Robert would tell Jonathan, and Jonathan would tease him. *Baby Swan-Swan oh how's Mamma's big baby!*

He would hide away in the hay barn reading for the rest of the day. When he finished one book, he began another; when he finished that book, he began another; but when he finished that book, he returned to the first, not wanting to forget it. So he was always reading, and rereading. It was a comfort to him. The book he was reading now was *A Connecticut Yankee in King Arthur's Court* which he could not decide was real, or made up. Also he was reading *The Call of the Wild* and *Klondike Tales* by Jack London, his favorite books. The pages were bent and soiled from Jonathan, who'd read these books before Swan. Jon had a nervous habit of picking his nose and wiping it on his hands, or on the pages of books, soiling them. Swan was disgusted by such a habit yet hadn't any choice except to read the books.

Now Robert was saying, over his shoulder, "Your ma was teasing Clark about that Siefried girl, how come your ma doesn't get mad—doesn't she care?" Swan hadn't been paying much attention to Robert when he talked like this, rambling, vaguely complaining, or bemused; when they were alone together, Robert confided in Swan, as he would not have otherwise. Swan's silence, his way of turning things over carefully in his mind, drew Robert out. "Our ma was lots different. She'd tell us there was something bad about it. But your ma—"

Lately, when they were alone together, Robert had begun to talk to Swan about his mother. Swan thought of this vanished woman as the *mother-who-was-dead*. Mostly, no one spoke of her in his and Clara's hearing, ever. When Robert got in such a mood, Swan said very little. Robert sometimes talked, too, about their father: his words for Revere were *he, him*. Always when Robert's tone became aggrieved and wondering, the subject was Revere.

"See, he never hit you yet. He's hit me lots of times. Not to hurt, just to—" Robert wiped his face, frowning. Then he grinned. "Jon's got it worse, lots of times. Before you and your ma came here. 'Cause of Jon's 'smart mouth,' he calls it. And Clark! Yeah, he's hit Clark. Once I saw Clark *bawl*." Robert laughed, and Swan saw the flash of the boy's front teeth: a rodent's teeth, a squirrel or a rabbit, some creature they might be going to shoot this morning.

Robert seemed to be asking Swan something, but what? He hated tramping like this, dragging this heavy gun. Wished to Christ he could toss it into the creek and be done with it. Run back home to the hay barn, to his hideaway.

Robert said, wistfully, "You're real lucky, Steve. I seen him sometimes, the way he looks at you."

Swan knew: all that Revere wished for him to learn was important, and he would learn it. For it was just the beginning of what would make him different. Clara was always saying *Learn from him, from all of them. All that you can, learn.*

When Swan had said he didn't want to kill anything, not pheasants, not rabbits, not deer, he hated even target practice in the pasture behind the barns, Clara had pressed her forefinger hard over his lips. She'd shaken her head, sternly.

So Swan knew: he must learn *hunting,* if only to move beyond it.

He would learn, and he would grow up as quickly as possible so that he wasn't weak, and his brothers couldn't boss him around. He would be a man like Revere. He would learn more than his brothers would learn for he would work harder, and he was smarter. Clara laughed with him in secret, yes he was smarter.

Smarter than the lot of them. "Reveres."

One day, you will surpass them.

It was one of Clara's new words: *surpass.* Where she'd gotten it from, a radio program, an article in the Sunday newspaper, or Judd, Swan did not know. But he felt the thrill of it: *surpass.*

Tramping through the pasture, at the edge of the woods, Robert led the way yet spoke to Swan over his shoulder, constantly turning around in his crouch, as no serious hunter would do; as no adult man would do. More and more he was talking, in that way of bafflement and bemusement as if he were thinking aloud. Swan hoped that Robert would talk loud enough to scare away game. Turkey vultures, that were not shy birds, could be scared away by loud-enough voices.

"D'you like them? Those Fluvey girls? 'Lynette Fluvey'—that's her name? On the bus, she's always sittin up by the driver like she's flirting with him—"

Swan, swatting at gnats and mosquitoes, made no reply.

Damn he hated this! Trying not to think about shot birds, shot "game." That mess of bass the boys brought back from the river, perfectly round wide-open staring eyes your own face could be reflected in, if you got that close—something you would not want to do. And the white paper-thin flesh at the mouth torn by the hook . . . And the pheasants and the chickens, their own chickens, dead and ready to be picked of their feathers, with that warm sickening odor rising about them as Mandy worked, whistling. The guts in the bucket. They put the chickens in the oven and browned them some and there they were, right on the Sunday table with its white tablecloth and the candlesticks Clara had bought in Hamilton, everything clean and fancy—and in the middle of it the dead chicken, roasted. Out came their guts, which were changed for stuffing now and spiced up, and their hearts and liver and gizzard and whatnot, and everyone's mouth watered.

Swan spat sideways, like a man. He tasted something ugly in his mouth.

And sometimes it wasn't all the way roasted but would be red and run red, thin trickles of watery blood that got into your potatoes. When they had steaks it did that sometimes. Revere ate that blood, picked the soft helpless meat up on a fork and ate it, and so did Clara, whose teeth could eat anything, and all the boys, who were always hungry, and anyone who was a guest. Only Swan sat there alone and stared and felt his stomach turning over, getting itself ready for what was coming. In his mouth the strands of meat were each vivid and clear; the patches of gristle, fat, muscle, stray flecks of bone. It was all real and all alive. Clara had said, shivering, "What if the heart comes alive and starts beating in your mouth?" and they had all laughed, even Revere had laughed a little. Only Swan had sat there staring as Clark ate the heart. Of course he might be crazy and he had better shut up about it. Clara had told him that.

But . . .

But if he had to kill something he would do it and get it over with. He was ready. He would never be more ready. If a bird flew up he might as well shoot, he could close his eyes at the last moment. He would let Robert tell him what to do. And Revere had already told him. So when he pulled the trigger it would not really be he himself who did it, but his father or Robert, someone else.

"You think it hurts them awful much, to get shot?" Swan said.

"They don't feel nothing."

"Should you shoot more than once?"

"I'll tell you everything to do," Robert said, embarrassed. He was maybe unused to all this—this questioning and talk about what he had done for years without thinking about. He kept glancing over his shoulder, back into the woods, as if he hoped Jonathan or someone was running to catch up with them. At first they had walked stiffly, alertly, but as time went on they began to relax. Swan thought that maybe nothing would happen after all. It could be put off to another day. Around them everything was quiet except for the high invisible birds and the insects, invisible all around them. Swan liked the woods. He liked the sunlight falling sideways, breaking up into patches, showing the moss and the mossy fallen logs as if picking them out just to be shown—things you might miss if you didn't look carefully. Robert walked right through some wood violets. His feet left marks on the humps of moss and broke down weed flowers, and he did not bother to notice how everything smelled: the end of summer, the beginning of fall, with hot winds coming up from the lower valley, rushing up the slopes toward the mountains and unloading on them the rich complex odors of sun-blasted weeds and clover and sweet peas. Swan liked all this. When they came out to the edge of the woods they could look back and down, they could almost see the house and the barns off there in the distance a few miles away—but maybe they weren't seeing them at all, only imagining. It was hot now, outside the cool of the woods. "Christ," Robert said, wiping his forehead. "Everything is sleeping and hid. They know enough to stay out of sight when it's hot." He whispered. Swan liked that; he liked the thought of the birds and animals sleeping, hidden, smart enough to stay out of sight.

Suddenly there was a sharp *crack!*—Robert had raised his rifle, and fired. The shock of the sound reverberated through Swan, he felt it like pain.

"Damn dirty old vulture. Lookit the bastard!"

The enormous black-winged bird had fallen from the crook of a tree about twenty feet away, and was now flapping and struggling in the underbrush. It was emitting high-pitched bleats like those of a car, a lamb, a human baby. "How d'ya like it! Nasty old thing!" Robert was pushing through the underbrush to get a second shot. Swan backed off, feeling sick. He was hoping he wouldn't vomit. Robert fired again, chortling, "Holy Christ lookit the mess. *Guts.*" A wildness seemed to have come into Robert, of a kind Swan had never seen in his brother before.

Swan turned to run blindly away. He crouched in the woods beneath tall evergreens, on a grassless needle-strewn earth out of which numerous toadstools had grown. He forced himself to stare at these: cool pale gray perfectly shaped toadstools. These, too, were living things. Poisonous, he'd been warned. You could break off a small piece of a toadstool, chew and swallow. And then?

Robert was calling him. "Steve? Hey—"

Swan remained crouching, hidden. Not far away in the under-brush there was a crashing sound. White-tailed deer fleeing in panic.

"Don't let him shoot the deer. Please, God."

Robert caught up with Swan, breathing quickly. Swan cringed as if expecting Robert to shoot him.

But Robert said, almost somberly, "Hey. We don't need to tell him about this, O.K.? That it was a vulture."

Swan nodded quickly. Though he knew who *him* was, and guessed that *him* knew everything his sons did, somehow.

Robert said, "He ain't gonna find it, he'd never come here. Any-way it's some old garbage bird. Who cares!"

Overhead in the trees smaller birds were calling frantically to one another. Jays, starlings. Cardinals. Possibly they understood that something had been killed, shot out of the air. One of their own, though a gigantic creature with a wingspread of seventy inches.

Swan said shyly, "You picked it off real good. The first shot."

"Yeah! Guess I did." Robert wiped his face on his sleeve, pleased. The thrill of the hunt, the thrill of shooting a defenseless creature, was still in his face that glowed, Swan was thinking, like a balloon face. "Fucker's so big, it'd be hard to miss. Hate 'em!"

Robert spat sideways, like a man.

Swan wanted to ask could they stop now? But Robert was fussing with his rifle. That look in his face, Swan knew there was more hunting to come. The turkey vulture was just the beginning.

"Next time, you take the first shot, Steve. You got to, sometime."

This was intended as a kindness. The way boys poked one an-other in the arm, not to hurt but to make contact.

They walked on. Swan's head had begun to ache. The rifle was damn heavy, no matter it was a handsome gleaming weapon of which Swan should have been proud. His arms pulled at their sock-ets. Gnats, mosquitoes. Crossing a meadow and the sun blasted them. Swan's eyes ached as a flurry of dragonflies sped before them gleaming and glittering like bullets, and he was sleepy in his feet drifting into that certain mood of his thinking it would be best to hide here in this wild heat-drenched place where except for Robert no one knew who he was. If he could hide here, like a wild creature in the woods. If nobody knew his name. He would surrender even his books that he loved, if he could escape those adults who knew him as *Swan*, and as *Steven*. As soon as they left the woods, there were foothills in the near distance, and beyond these hills the mountains, covered in dense evergreens with stands of white birches here and there. The vast sweep of land was a comfort. Even hunters' loud voices and gunfire could make little impact. Any sudden noise, it was immediately forgotten. Swan smiled to think that the land was something that could hide you, if you wanted to be hidden. The dead white of winter, snow drifting high beneath the trees, could hide you, and nobody would know to put a grave marker up to keep your name remembered because there would be no name to be re-membered. Like the turkey vulture, you would come to an end.

"Steve? See the hawk?"

A hawk, circling above. Another hawk. And still another.

Often you saw them, chicken hawks like these, circling in slow lazy sweeps, not one but several. The hawks were hunting, so maybe it wasn't wrong to hunt them.

Sometimes they killed barnyard fowl. They'd been known to at-tack barn kittens. Any small creature, hawks could prey upon. So maybe it was a right thing, a rational thing, to shoot them out of the sky.

Robert was urging, "C'mon, try! That one's an easy shot."

Swan lifted the rifle blindly. He hardly sighted along the barrel, sweat was making his eyes sting. His finger groped for the trigger and as Robert urged him on, excited, impatient, he breathed deeply but pulled the trigger on the intake of breath, and the *crack!* of the rifle tore at his head, and the stock of the rifle kicked his damn shoulder hard as a horse. Swan whimpered in pain, opening his eyes to see the hawks still circling, unperturbed.

Now Robert tried, but missed. Running after the hawks, not watching where he was going, rifle barrel uplifted, he fired another shot, and still another. "Shit! Goddamn fuckers."

The hawks were gone. No more lazy swooping, they'd disappeared from view within seconds.

Swan said hesitantly, "We can try again, Robert. Tomorrow."

"Fuck tomorrow! You fucked up. You made us miss."

Sullenly Swan murmured, "I did not."

"You *did*! Fucking baby." Robert shouted at him, red-faced with an adult, mysterious fury. Swan stared at his brother thinking that Robert hated him, and he'd always thought that Robert had liked him.

At least, hunting seemed to be finished for the day.

Robert stomped off in disgust. Letting his rifle drag through the tall grasses. Not troubling to put on the safety lock, as Revere had instructed they must do. Swan put on his safety lock and followed his brother at a discreet distance. He could hear Robert muttering and cursing to himself like an adult man. Robert took no more heed of Swan in his wake than he'd take of a trotting dog.

Yet Swan smiled. It was over: he'd fired his rifle once, he hadn't killed any living thing, and he had not thrown up. *That* had not happened, at least.

———

In the lane behind the hay barn there came Jonathan on his horse O'Grady. Galloping the three-year-old chestnut gelding so the horse's sides and powerful chest gleamed with sweat. Swan moved to stand behind Robert. "He ain't s'posed to be fooling around like that," Robert said. Yet you could hear the admiration in his voice. Both boys were wary of Jonathan these days; even when Revere was home, Jonathan could be unpredictable. And today, Revere wasn't home.

Robert waved. "Gimme a ride, Jon?"

"Like hell. Fatso."

Jonathan tried to rein in O'Grady, who was a skittish young horse with ideas of his own. Not a horse to be ridden except by a skilled rider. Swan stared at the horse, always a horse is so much bigger than you expect. This horse's sides were shuddering with restless energy, impatience. None of the boys were supposed to overexcite or overheat the horses, especially on a hot dry day, but Jonathan imagined himself a horseman, with a natural touch. His sharp nervous eyes resembled O'Grady's eyes, showing a rim of white above the iris. As O'Grady hoofed the ground, Jonathan tried to keep him under control.

Robert said, "Hey there, O'Grady. Good boy—"

With a hot expulsion of breath O'Grady snapped at Robert as he reached up to stroke the horse's nose. Robert jumped back, and Jonathan laughed. "You don't fool around with O'Grady, kid. He's half-mustang."

Jonathan read *Deerslayer* comics. *The Huntsman, The Lone Ranger, Red Wolf Indian Tales, Scalphunter.* He used to read books, but Swan believed he didn't any longer, much. There were ragged old copies of *Scalphunter* comics around the house that, if Revere discovered them, he tore into pieces and tossed onto the floor in contempt.

Swan wanted to duck away and return to the house, but Jonathan and O'Grady were blocking his way. And it seemed necessary for him to remain there, in the lane with Robert, something you would naturally do, brothers talking together. Jonathan was asking where they'd been hunting and if they'd shot anything and Robert said hesitantly they'd shot two chicken hawks, down by the creek. "Like hell you did," Jonathan sneered. "Where are they, then? S'posed to nail them onto the barn. *You*," he said, with particular emphasis, to Swan cowering behind Robert, "—you sure didn't shoot nothing. Don't give me that bullshit."

Robert said, faltering, "We did O.K., Jon. We—"

Jonathan cut off Robert's weak whining voice. He was staring at Swan. "*You*, with a rifle. That's a laugh! A Springfield thirty-caliber, *you*. You'd need your ma to pull the trigger, *you*."

Robert laughed, not looking at Swan.

O'Grady broke away from Jonathan, hoofing the ground with such violence, Swan cringed behind Robert. Jonathan cursed the horse and sawed at the reins. The horse's spittle flew. The horse's muscular haunches quivered, its long tail switched. In the hot dry sun there were horseflies, Swan brushed from his face. These flies were the size of bumblebees and their sting was nearly as painful as bees' stings.

Jonathan managed to bring O'Grady under control. Barely. He was sweaty, agitated. In an instant, he and O'Grady might have trampled the younger boys, yet Robert tried to hold his ground as if he wasn't afraid. Jonathan said to Swan, "Swan-Swan, think you could hit the side of a barn? Think you could hit a *horse*?"

Swan backed off, meaning to ignore him. He was holding his rifle against his shoulder, soldier-style. The safety lock was on. His face burned with shame. For Jonathan knew he hadn't shot any hawk, the lie was obvious.

"Think you could shoot a horse? Betcha can't shoot a horse from ten feet."

What happened next was confused. Swan would not recall the sequence of events. He'd turned to walk away intending to cross through a pasture, to get to the house, but somebody was pulling at his arm—it was Robert. Telling him, "Come on"—meaning that Swan and he would continue along the lane, and not be bullied by Jonathan. Except Swan did not want to follow Robert, with Jonathan and O'Grady so close. Swan knew how dangerous horses could be, even the seemingly tamed ones; even mares, and foals. Their hooves, their big yellow teeth, their terrible weight. Still, Swan followed after Robert, skirting O'Grady. Swan could feel the horse's hot shuddering breath on the side of his face. Then he was past, and half-running. He heard the horse behind him, urged on by Jonathan who was laughing. "Hey little Swan-Swan! Mamma's Swan-Swan! Afraid to fire a gun without your ma? *Bas-tid*."

Bas-tid was uttered in a high-pitched yodeling way. Just the sound, hilarious.

Swan grimaced, not looking back. He heard the horse's hooves close behind him. He was bathed in sweat: Jonathan was going to run the horse over him and there was nothing he could do about it. Worse than dying would be to be crippled. Revere had warned them of being thrown by a horse, kicked in the head. What can happen if you're kicked in the head, a *living vegetable* in an iron lung. But Jonathan and O'Grady galloped past the younger boys, Jonathan hooting with laughter. They stood in the lane watching horse and rider in their raggedy gallop along the lane. As if in that instant Jonathan had forgotten them, as no longer worthy of his attention.

Disgusted, Robert muttered to Swan, "Don't be so scared, dummy. He was only kidding."

Swan wiped at his face that was slick with sweat. A horsefly was circling his head, darting and swooping with manic intent.

Robert was walking away from Swan, approaching the pasture fence. This was a barbed-wire fence of about four feet in height, with three taut strips of barbed wire; the boys would cut through the pasture instead of going the long way around, to the house. At the far end of the pasture a small herd of dairy cows were grazing. The pasture at this end was spiky with crudely mowed grass and thistles; it hurt Swan's ankles, where his sneakers didn't protect them. This wasn't a way Swan wanted to go. But it was the way Robert was going, and damned if Swan would not accompany him. He was walking doggedly now, his eyes on Robert's back. He saw how Robert was dragging his rifle, as Revere had told the boys never to do. At the fence, Swan had no choice but to catch up with Robert. Unbidden the words came from him—"Why does Jon hate me?"

These were words you did not say. These were words of shame, and beyond shame.

"Jesus Christ." Robert rolled his eyes. "Forget it."

"Why do you all hate me, Robert?"

"Nobody hates you! Shut up."

"And call me names, why do you call me names?" Swan was speaking calmly, he believed. Yet something hot and stinging moved up into his throat. "I'm not a 'bastard.' Nobody's going to call me that."

"I said shut up."

In the confusion of the moment it seemed to Swan that he and his brother were still *hunting*. Yet, as soon as Robert climbed the fence, and trotted across the field, they would be *home;* they would be within sight of the farmhands in the barns, almost in sight of the house, and of Clara's garden behind the house. Clumsily then, not knowing what he meant to do, he struck Robert between his shoulders with the butt of the Springfield rifle; it wasn't a hard blow, but it was unexpected, and Robert, climbing the fence, lost his balance on the barbed wire, and fell, and his rifle went off. This *crack!* was so close and so deafening, Swan scarcely heard it. And he could scarcely see.

Then he saw: Robert thrashing against the barbed wire, the way the vulture had thrashed in the underbrush. There was an ugly bleeding hole in the underside of his jaw, in his throat. Robert was trying to scream, but could not. Sound issued from him in a high thin shriek that faded almost immediately while Swan stood paralyzed staring at him in a sun-drenched vacuum he could not comprehend.

He would say *I'm sorry, I didn't mean. Robert I'm sorry. I didn't mean.* But he could not draw breath to speak.

Robert had fallen to the ground, and his rifle fell with him, useless now. Swan saw blood streaming out from the terrible hole torn in Robert's throat and running into the prickly grass where it floated lifting chaff with it. Swan was gripping his own rifle, his fingers so frozen onto it they would have to be pried off. He was thinking *If it had not happened yet.* Someone was shouting. Jonathan was on foot now, running toward them. And there came Clara and a man—it must have been Judd—more hesitantly along the lane. Swan was thinking before he lost consciousness that his mother and Judd now calling to him were losing time coming that way, the way adults would come, along the lane when they might have cut through the pasture.

5

"You didn't, did you? Shoot Robert."

This question, calm and determined, Clara would put to Swan only when they were alone together. Sometimes she came to him, to stroke his hair or his hot throbbing face; sometimes she merely looked at him, unsmiling, alert and curious as you might observe a creature whose behavior is unpredictable.

Swan shook his head. Not meeting Clara's eyes.

"*Did* you?"

No. No he had not shot his brother. It could not be a serious question, it was Robert's rifle that had gone off when he'd slipped on the barbed wire.

Still, Clara asked. Her new manner with Swan was brooding, no longer playful. She had *lost the baby* it was said. Not in Swan's presence and not in response to any question of Swan's yet still he knew that Clara had *lost the baby* that was to have been a little girl, a sister of his. And that he was to blame for this death, too.

Though blameless, Swan was to blame.

Robert had bled to death in the car, Clara's car. Jonathan was driving, and Clara was with Robert in the backseat where they'd laid him, and he'd died not five minutes from the doctor's office in Tintern; Judd had stayed behind, and called the doctor to prepare him for the emergency. But no country doctor with an office in Tintern could have saved Robert. Nothing could have saved Robert. He'd bled to death within minutes, an artery in his throat torn to pieces.

Afterward Clara insisted that Revere get rid of the car. It was no good to replace the backseat, the floor. She hated that car!

No, she could not bear thinking about it. That day, what had happened that day.

"That poor boy. Oh, God."

And she would say, "Robert—he was the sweetest one. He loved me, too."

The little girl Clara lost, she had given no name. Not an actual baby but a thing so small, Clara wished not to think about it. Some things are not meant to be, Clara believed.

It was her time they'd said about—who? Pearl. A long time ago.

So with the baby-not-yet-born, the little sister Swan would not have, you could say *It was her time.*

Robert had bled to death. And Clara, beginning to hemorrhage several hours later, had almost bled to death, too.

For years Clara would speak of that desperate drive to Tintern that had failed. For years, in Swan's hearing, Clara would speak of it in a way that puzzled him: for Clara's fury seemed to be directed toward Judd, who hadn't responded adequately to the emergency. He'd been a "coward"—a "big sissy." He'd been paralyzed with fear, evidently.

Just Jonathan and Clara, driving to Tintern with Robert. That wild drive. "It was hopeless. We knew, but we had to try."

With Swan, Clara showed no anger. This too was strange to him, a fearful thing.

If she had slapped him, screamed into his face . . .

Instead he saw her watching him, from a distance. Where in the past Clara would have winked and smiled at him, maybe come to him to fluff his hair or kiss him, now she simply gazed at him as if she were observing him through one-way glass. When she smiled, her smile was slow, tentative.

Finally she said, "Whatever you did to him, keep your mouth shut about it. You understand me?"

She embraced him at last, stiffly. So that they need not see each other's face.

6

He understood her. For a long time he thought of what had happened to Robert continually, as if the *crack!* of the rifle were still reverberating, echoing in his skull. Then by degrees it began to fade. In the years that stretched out between his brother's death and his own, the memory was to return to him unpredictably, often in that twilit dimension between wakefulness and sleep, but sometimes in the presence of others. The *crack!* of the rifle and Robert's desperate struggle not to die, at Swan's feet.

"You don't need to touch that gun ever again." Revere's hand was heavy on Swan's shoulder, Swan had to resist the impulse to shrug it off. He knew it hadn't been his gun but Robert's gun that had killed his brother, yet that made no difference. Revere himself had a repugnance for firearms now, and kept his rifles and shotguns locked away; he would allow no hunting on his property of many acres, not even by men whose fathers and grandfathers had hunted on the Revere property for decades. Robert's rifle, as well as Swan's, Revere locked away with the others. Clark and Jonathan no longer hunted, nor even fished. There was no talk of guns in Revere's presence at any time. "No more. No more. Enough."

Revere had a habit of murmuring to himself even in the presence of others. Sometimes at meals he drifted off in the middle of a remark, and forgot completely that he was speaking. Clark and Jonathan were mostly silent in his company. Swan was uneasy, yet tried to speak whenever Revere addressed him, like an alert, dutiful son. They were aware of the way Revere fell to watching Clara with his strange, heavy stare, with an air of possession that excluded any actual interest or even awareness of what Clara was saying.

On Sunday evenings, Revere began reading the Bible to them. He told them that his own father had done this, when Revere was a boy.

In the winters those evenings were long and uncomfortably warm, because Revere insisted upon his family sitting by the fireplace in the parlor. This was a massive fireplace made of stone that had been dug up on the property, great chunks of fieldstone in the interstices of which spiders dwelled, that species of spider that spins funnels and not cobwebs, like cotton candy. Dreamily Swan watched these spiders dart about, frantic to escape from the fire. Revere favored birch fires, which required careful preparation and stoking at the outset; Clark usually volunteered. Often if wind descended the chimney sparks leapt out onto the rug and Clara had an excuse to jump up and rub a smoldering spot with her foot, muttering, "God!" under her breath. At such times Swan saw in his mother's eyes the trapped glistening look of a desperate creature.

Revere sat hunched by a hurricane lamp, glasses on his nose. He had resisted bifocal glasses for years. Now he read from the Bible in a halting yet authoritative voice, and the rest of the family sat and listened, or held their heads in an attitude of listening, until it was their turn to read.

Except Clara. Clara was "exempted."

No one asked why. Swan supposed it was because Clara had refused, out of a dread of stumbling over words. And Revere would never force Clara to do anything against her will.

Swan, who was a good reader, always a bright, forceful student at school, did not mind the Bible evenings. He would far rather have read his own books but the Bible was an adventure book, of a kind. The Old Testament especially. Nothing made much sense in that long-ago time and things were yet to be decided and defined. At the outset of the Bible evenings, Swan had dared to ask Revere if there might have been dinosaurs in the Garden of Eden, and Revere had stared at him for a long moment before saying, simply, and humbly, that he did not know. "If it was millions of years ago," Swan said. "Before asteroids hit the Earth." Revere nodded as if this remark made perfect sense to him, and continued with his slow halting ponderous reading. The story of Moses and the Chosen People and the Promised Land. The story of plagues, and curses, and terrible punishments meted upon the cities of Sodom and Gomorrah. When Revere read of the wrath of God the Father, his voice thickened; he seemed to be drawing strength out of the grotesque violence itself. Like one of Jonathan's comic books, it was. For there was a curious logic behind the wild illogic. There was good, and there was evil; there were the Chosen People, and there were their enemies. Swan listened dreamily as Revere read, seeing in his father's blunt graying head a shadow of God Himself. *Thou shalt have no other God but Jehovah.* He felt a gathering excitement in Revere's words, knowing that within a few lines the tale would end with death or reward, it hardly mattered which. Lurking over the land was the wide-winged spirit of God, restless and ever-vigilant; at any moment it might swoop down like a great bird of prey, and seize someone in its beak. Swan understood that he and Clara—yawning behind her hand, turning her loose-fitting wedding band around her finger—would be one of those seized by the throat if the world in which they lived now belonged to that God, which of course it did not. *God* was a word in a book, like many words in many books.

Swan knew that the New Testament awaited them, as they made their plodding way through the sandy terrain of the Old, but he was in no hurry for the New Testament: the Gospels. When Jesus came along things were different. It wasn't a comic book exactly. If you were not saved it was your own fault. It was your own choice.

When they were alone Swan asked Clara, "Did you ever talk to God or see Him or anything?"

Clara laughed.

"How come *he* cares so much about it then?"

Revere was *he* to Clara and Swan now, as well as to Swan's brothers; an impersonal pronoun that remained impersonal. It was true that Revere spoke more of religion now, and his "church-going" was more serious. The boys were embarrassed to hear their father utter the word "God"—even "Jesus"—in the way he might be speaking of weather or a neighbor's behavior. Clara simply shut her face up like a fist at such times and made no comment.

Swan asked, "But why do people take time to believe it?"

"They just do. They always have."

"In other books, like the encyclopedia, or science books, nobody talks about God. Wouldn't they, if God was real?"

Clara laughed again, not an angry but a light laugh. The kind that made you want to laugh with her. "How the hell should I know?" She was turning catalogue pages, staring at glossy, colorful photographs. Much of Clara's shopping was mail order: she was never so happy as when the mailman drove up the lane to the house, with packages C.O.D. for "Mrs. Curt Revere." She subscribed to women's magazines as well including fashion magazines, these she studied even more closely. Her hair was "styled" in a fashionable cut, a smooth pageboy that fell just below her ears, and her teeth were now "capped"—her smile wasn't just happy, but whitely gleaming like ivory, and triumphant.

"People have a right to their religion, I guess," Clara said, turning a page. "He wants to believe Robert is in heaven, maybe."

"How can Robert be in heaven?" Swan asked softly.

"Why not? Just as well him, as anybody else."

"There's no 'heaven' in the astronomy books. In the encyclopedia—"

"*He* thinks it's there. That's his right."

Strange how young Clara looked, though Swan knew that she wasn't. Her new teeth—as she called them—made her look younger, and very pretty. If they were in Tintern, or another town where people could see Clara on the street, Swan noticed how they looked at her; not just men but women, too. Swan was in the sixth grade now and sometimes he thought that Clara could almost be one of the girls at the high school: those glowing-faced pretty girls everybody stared at, and envied, and admired. In another year Swan would be attending Tintern Junior-Senior Consolidated High School, with Jonathan—a newly built beige-brick building that looked like a factory except its smokestack wasn't rimmed with flame. Seventh grade through twelfth. Swan could imagine Clara laughing among those kids but he could never imagine Revere that young.

Swan persisted, "You don't think He's watching us?"

"Who's 'He'?" Clara spoke vaguely, staring at a full-page photograph of a model wearing a long red cloth coat with a fur collar.

When Revere had Swan read from the Bible on Sunday evenings, Swan rarely thought of how crazy it all was. Once you began to read, you believed. And he read well, and he knew that Revere was pleased; and Clara was proud of him. And when Jonathan read, Jonathan stumbled and lost his way, and Revere asked him to begin again; sometimes Jonathan had to read a verse several times, before Revere allowed him to continue.

Quietly they sat by the fire—Clark, Clara, Swan—wishing that they were somewhere else. As Jonathan stammered on, his voice low and sullen. Sometimes Jonathan so forgot himself, he picked at his nose, and Revere chastised him.

"Stop that. Use a handkerchief."

Clark, deeply embarrassed, sat with his elbows on his knees, in a pretense of piety and concentration. His forehead was slightly blemished. He was well over six feet tall, with muscled shoulders and upper arms and a hard, wide jaw; if Clark didn't shave every morning a dark stubble emerged on his jaws, giving him a furtive animal look. Yet he was handsome, manly; girls were attracted to him. Swan watched Clark closely when Clark read hoping to determine what Clark was thinking, but Clark read slowly and ponderously, and if he hesitated at a word he simply pronounced it as it struck him, and continued on. As soon as the Bible ordeal ended he was free to drive his car to "see a friend" and he'd come in late that night; Swan supposed he was thinking about that.

Strange how Jonathan blundered, in his reading. Only a few years ago Jonathan had sometimes read lessons aloud, and he'd read without making mistakes. Something must have happened to him: his eyes? The last book he'd read outside of school assignments was *Twenty Thousand Leagues Under the Sea* by Jules Verne; Swan had read it after Jonathan, and saw that only about half the pages were bent and soiled, which suggested that Jonathan had not finished the book. He was fifteen, and had some of the mannerisms of an adult man, a habit of sidelong, suspicious glances and a tight pursing of his lips. When his turn at reading was over, Jonathan sat sullen and unmoving while someone else read; if he glanced up to see Swan watching him, his eyes brimmed with loathing.

Those were the Revere family's Sunday evenings.

———

The Reveres and their in-laws were numerous in the Eden Valley. Swan had many cousins—a dozen? fifteen?—but he was shy around most of them, and sensed their dislike of him. No one muttered *Bas-tid* in his wake any longer, not even Jonathan, yet he imagined he heard this contemptuous word, and smarted at its sound. Clara told him they were only just jealous of him—"Because you're smarter than they are, and better-looking, too." Though Clara now disliked Judd, Swan had always liked his youngish uncle; and there were some others among the relatives he liked, or anyway did not dislike. He felt safest with adults because they mostly left him alone.

Among the adults, especially the men, Swan began to note that certain things were uttered in code. Remarks that had to do with the "property"—with "business." There was a network of names and relationships and these had to do with people who lived in Hamilton and elsewhere. These individuals "in the city" were admired but not liked; when they were mentioned, it was likely to be with cynical smiles. Their world consisted of ownerships, not people. Unless there were cousins who were "engaged to be married" and their marriages were impressive, and worthy of comment. As Swan sat listening, shy-seeming, unobtrusive, unnaturally patient for a boy of his age, his need to be one of these Reveres and to share that name rose in him like a poisonous blossom. *I am a Revere, too! I am one of you.*

After Robert's death, Swan was no longer teased by his young cousins. After Robert's death, these cousins mostly left him alone.

Except: there was Swan's cousin Deborah, Judd's daughter. She was two or three years younger than Swan yet she, too, often sat with the adults, with the women; like Swan, she read books, and she did crossword puzzles; but it did not seem so strange that a girl would do these things, especially since Deborah was considered "sensitive"—"high-strung." She seemed often to have a cold, or to be "just recovering" from the flu; her long crackling-fine fair-brown hair hung down lank about her small doll's face. She was pretty, though often her features were peevish, pinched. Swan became aware of his young cousin when she first demanded to know what he was reading, and when he showed her—a high school geometry text, that had belonged to Clark—she'd made a face and pushed it aside. Other books of Swan's had been more to her liking, and sometimes the two did crossword puzzles together. On her thin shoulders loose fair-brown hairs lay glittering.

Outside the window their Revere cousins ran, shouting. These children were wild and energetic as young dogs. Swan knew that Revere would have liked him to play with them—"play" was the adult term, uttered in innocence and ignorance—but he much preferred to be with Deborah. When he asked her, "Why don't you want to play with—" naming certain of their cousins, Deborah looked at him with faint incredulity that he would ask so stupid a question. "Because I don't want to." At once she turned back to her book, or crossword puzzle; she would never explain herself, and seemed oblivious of Swan's presence. He had an impulse sometimes to tug at her hair, or pinch her pale, perfect little cheek. *Little princess* Clara said of Judd's daughter, meaning criticism, but also admiration. Swan wasn't sure if Deborah liked him or had no feeling for him at all. She was the most self-sufficient of children. Only once she'd said to him, unexpectedly, with a small, curious smile, "Something bad happened to—" (pausing, not recalling Robert's name) "—and you were there? Something bad, with a gun?"

Swan shrugged. Deborah turned back to her book.

—

One day, Clark offered to drive Clara to Tintern. Why? Clara usually drove herself.

"I can be your 'chaf-fer'—like in the movies."

Clara laughed. Between her and Revere's oldest son there had always been an easiness she didn't feel with Jonathan, or with Revere himself. Of all the Reveres, Clark was the most like some kid or young guy you'd meet in a migrant camp. Or, one of the younger bus drivers. He was simple, direct, maybe a little crude. When he spoke with Clara, she could see his eyelids quiver, as if he was want-ing to stare at her hard, but knew he'd better not. Now, in the car, he said in an unexpectedly serious voice, "The way Jon's been acting, I don't want to tell Pa. See, it'd just worry him? Maybe you—"

Clark's voice trailed off. He would rely upon Clara to know what he was saying, and what he meant by what he was saying.

Clara knew that Jonathan was often away from the farm. She guessed that he was paying the hired men to do his chores for him, without Revere knowing. He hated the farm, hated living so far out in the country. He missed meals, and more than once he'd missed the Sunday evening Bible sessions.

Clark said, "Jon's been hanging around with these guys, one of them's Jimmy Dorr, he was ahead of me in school and enlisted in the Navy and got discharged 'dishonorable'—nobody knows why. Him, and some other guys. I heard some things about them."

"What things, Clark?"

"Just things." Clark spoke vaguely and sadly. Yet it comforted him, you could see, that Clara had called him by name. When Clara had first come to live at the farm, as Revere's wife and his "step-mother," he'd said how close their names were: *Clara, Clark.* He'd said it was a nice thing, wasn't it? He had seemed to think it was on purpose.

Now Clark said, shifting his broad shoulders inside his shirt, "I think maybe, I guess it might be—because of Steven."

"Steven." Clara had come to prefer "Steven" to "Swan," at about the time she'd had her hair styled, and her teeth capped. At about the time she'd overheard several Revere women laughing at the name "Swan" at a Christmas gathering.

Goddamn, the name *Swan* embarrassed the hell out of her, now. It was white trash, so clearly. Worse than no name at all.

"Yeah, Steven." Clark's face had become ruddy, his eyelids had begun to quiver. He was driving Clara's new car, a canary-colored Buick coupe, with both his big hands on the steering wheel, near the top. "See, at school Steven gets along better than Jon does. The teachers like him, he's so smart and works hard. It used to be, Jon was one of the smartest kids, he hadn't even had to work. And now—"

"Whose fault is that?" Clara spoke sharply, then paused as if realizing how she sounded. She went on, "It's too bad. Jonathan is what you call 'sensitive'—'high-strung.'"

Clark laughed. "He's got a hell of a temper, is how I see it."

"Jon gets along with me all right." Clara spoke stubbornly, she wasn't accustomed to meeting opposition in Clark.

"Maybe."

"Yes, he does! He was the one, the only one, to help me with Robert. That time," Clara said, faltering. "You know. . . ."

Clark drove in silence, frowning.

"He likes me, Jonathan does. I try to talk to him when I can."

"Well—"

"What do you know, that I don't know? I don't believe you."

"Sometimes Jon tells me how he hates Pa. Hates the farm, and hates Pa. But he don't want to walk away, see: he belongs here, and he's thinking about what the, you know, the property is worth. You can't blame him, see—"

"Why would I blame him? Has somebody said I blame him?"

Clara spoke so sharply, Clark had to mollify her.

"Jon was like this a few years ago, I mean he acted weird when our ma was sick. I mean, his temper. He'd get in fights with me despite I could beat him up, one hand behind my back. Then he'd spend all his time reading. Books about Indians, history and stuff like that, that's so boring at school you want to puke, Jon would read, on purpose. And Pa would find him, and tell him to go outside, do his chores, not act like a baby." Clark shook his head wryly. You could see Clark's ambivalence, recalling these days: he felt sorry for his brother, yet took satisfaction in Jonathan being scolded by their father, who rarely scolded him. "That was before you came to live with us. . . . When Ma was still alive, see? Back then. But we knew about you, kind of. And Swan—Steven. I mean, people knew. They wouldn't tell us openly but we knew. At school, and like that. I got into some real fights," Clark said, smiling, "and beat some bastids pretty bad. Some assholes asking for it. Then Uncle Judd told me about it, and how I should be 'sympathetic' with Pa, and not get into fights. So I tried. But Jon, he wasn't like that. He's weak, like. He can't control a horse, and the horse knows it, see? O'Grady, any time he wants to O'Grady can run with Jon, he's gonna knock him off his back one day and kill him. Those days when Ma was dying, Jon would sleep out with the horses. He'd sneak away, nobody knew where. He started drinking then, just a kid, and he's drinking now I guess, and not eating right. Ever seen how skinny he is? His chest, ribs . . ." Clark glanced sidelong at Clara, who was listening attentively; the two were such healthy specimens, with good appetites, and good-looking, it made sense that they were kin, and Jonathan was excluded.

Clara said, tapping at her teeth with a fingernail, "I'm sorry to hear this, Clark. I . . . like Jonathan."

"He's O.K."

"I think he likes me. . . ."

Clark shrugged.

Clara said, in a sudden flight of fancy, "All of you like me—don't you? You Reveres. Because I sure like *you*."

Clark laughed, as if his stylish blond stepmother had leaned over to tickle him. "Listen, anybody doesn't like you, Clara, is jealous. Assholes."

"Well, why shouldn't they like me? Why shouldn't Jonathan like me?" Clara was speaking lightly, yet there was a tremor in her voice. Clark gripped the steering wheel harder, and concentrated upon his driving. Now he'd told Clara what he meant to tell her, he could relax, some. He could let her stew with it. He wasn't all that comfortable around Clara when she was serious, when there was something melancholy and heavy-hearted about her, flat-footed, like you'd expect of an ordinary woman of her age.

The last thing you wanted to feel for Clara Walpole was *sorry*.

———

During Christmas recess, Clara took Swan with her to Hamilton to visit for a week. She was often on the phone making arrangements, and she spent two days packing, excited as a young girl. Swan lay on the bed watching her. He too was excited about the trip, though anxious about staying in a strange place for so many nights. Could he bring enough books to keep him occupied? Who would he talk with, apart from Clara? His Hamilton cousins were all older. He scarcely knew them. And he felt guilty about leaving his father out here at the farm, when he sensed that Revere didn't want him to go.

Jonathan was behaving so nastily lately, Swan was glad to be free of him.

"By train. 'By train and by airplane'—'all around the world.'"

Clara sang, happily. If sometimes Swan was between her and a mirror he saw how her eyes lifted from him, to focus upon her smiling reflection. Her teeth were so perfect now, and her hair; sometimes she laughed just to see herself. And when Clara was happy, Swan was happy, too.

Part of the excitement was taking a train to Hamilton: just Clara and Swan. Revere had arranged for them to have a *private compartment*.

"Because we can afford it, that's why. Other people, they sit in 'coach.' But not us. Not 'Reveres.'"

At the station in Hamilton, Clara took a cab. Her face glowed as her suitcases were placed in the trunk of the cab, and a door was opened for her to slip inside. She wore her new coat, red cashmere wool with a squirrel-fur collar. When Revere's great-aunt greeted her she had no choice but to exclaim, "Why, Clara! How that color becomes you."

They were guests at the big house on Lakeshore Boulevard. Swan remembered some of the faces but not the names: and hearing them again, he made more of an attempt to retain them. These were the "city people" of whom the Eden County Reveres spoke with both awe and distrust. They were "money people" and not "farm people." But in his presence, which was of course Clara's presence, conversation was less interesting to Swan: about family, mostly. About the farm, and the health of family members. So boring! When talk turned to him, Steven, he felt acutely awkward, self-conscious. Yes he had "grown." Yes he was eleven now. He was tall—"five-one." Blushing to hear himself described as "good-looking" and Christ he hated it when Clara boasted of him, his grades at school. He wanted to laugh angrily at her *I can't help it if I'm smart. It's all I have.*

Cocktail time, and Swan was allowed to slip away. Reading upstairs in the room that was "his." There was dinner here in Hamilton and not supper and it was served two hours later than the Reveres ate at home: eight o'clock in the evening, pitch-black outside and Swan was starving.

He was anxious to see that Clara, with these Reveres, seemed a little uncomfortable; she spoke less frequently than she did at home, and her laughter was quieter, restrained. Swan saw how his mother's eyes darted about, assessing. There were eight people at the dinner table in addition to Clara and Swan and several were intimidating individuals. A "boy" cousin in his mid-twenties with a fat serious face, who had earned something called a MBA from Harvard University; a middle-aged woman with fluffy dyed-looking hair, who was a "trustee" of the Hamilton Art Museum; a man who looked to be in his mid-thirties, snaky-lean, handsome in a smudged, sullen way, whose relationship with the others wasn't clear to Swan—somebody's "attorney"?

This man, brooding, yet quick to smile and even to laugh, had a habit of tapping his fingers on the tablecloth. He seemed not to know what he was doing, and possibly no one else noticed except Swan. How annoyed Revere was, when Jonathan tapped his fingers at the table! And when Robert had been restless, shifting in his chair. Clumsy with his knife and fork. Chewing with his mouth open.

Nobody would speak of Robert here. His was a name no longer spoken. Outside the dining room windows snow was falling, and Swan thought of how cold and lonely it was in the cemetery where Robert was buried, and how desperate Robert would be, so alone; he hadn't ever liked being alone for five minutes. Clara had taken Swan to visit the cemetery only a few times. Out behind the Lutheran church. Close by Robert's grave marker was another, larger, with the name REVERE chiseled into the stone. And, beside that, another REVERE stone. When you looked around, you saw REVERE everywhere—a garden of them. Swan whispered his name to himself, Steven Revere, and then a quieter voice said his true name, which was Swan Walpole. When it came time, he wanted Swan Walpole on his grave marker.

He'd learned that his true name was Swan Walpole because one day he'd looked through Clara's things in a bureau drawer. He'd found a marriage license. Clara Walpole. Curt Revere. Some dates and information. And a photograph he'd never seen, his mother and Revere on their wedding day, Clara smiling broadly yet with her lips closed so that her cheeks bunched out, and her eyes narrowed and squinting, Revere smiling gravely, with an almost boyish anticipation. Swan wondered if the people at this table, the Hamilton Reveres, knew anything of Clara Walpole?

Clara said suddenly to the tapping-fingers man, the way you'd snatch something light and fluttering like a butterfly out of the air, "My son has this book about 'archaeology.' Egyptian things, really old. Like pyramids, 'sphinxes'? D'you know anything about that?"

The tapping-fingers man stared at Clara as if, for a moment, he hadn't understood a single of her words. Then he said, with a smile that included Swan, "Not much. But a little. I'll take you to the museum tomorrow, how's that? Both of you?"

Clara beamed upon Swan. "Steven, how would you like that?"

And for the first time at dinner, Swan smiled.

———

It was the Hamilton Art Museum, and Swan had never entered so large and austere a building. In the high-domed foyer, their voices echoed. The tapping-fingers man, whose name was Ransom, first name or last Swan was never to know, spoke quietly to Clara and to Steven, taking Clara by the elbow of her red cashmere coat as they walked through the chilly, near-deserted rooms. Swan was sharply disappointed: there was no sphinx statue, only just photographs in a dim-lit display case. There were many photographs and drawings, of pyramids, scenes along the Nile River, "phases of the moon." There was a single dwarf-mummy, from the "Middle Kingdom." Ransom peered at a plaque on the wall and read it, as if Swan couldn't read for himself—" 'Egyptian rulers built extraordinary tombs for themselves in which their mummified remains would be preserved, ideally forever. It was believed that if the pharaoh lived forever in the underworld, the nation of Egypt would also flourish.' " Clara admired a display case of crude stone trinkets and tarnished-looking jewelry. "So long ago, you wonder why people bothered."

Ransom laughed at this remark. He might have thought that Clara was being witty.

Clara said, seriously, her hand on Ransom's wrist for emphasis, "It's damn hard to believe people like us lived then. But I guess they'd have to be, the Egyptians, wouldn't they?"

Ransom smiled. "Wouldn't they what?"

"Have to be like us? I mean, human beings."

"Like *you*? I doubt it."

The adults laughed. Swan, staring gloomily into a display case at daggers and "grave artifacts," tried not to overhear.

Ransom treated them to "tea" in the museum's dining room. Wine for Clara and him, and a Coke for Swan. All three ate pastries called hot-buttered scones. Clara licked her fingers, and laughed for very happiness, and Swan supposed he should be happy, too.

—

Next day, Clara told her Revere hosts she was "going shopping."

Two hours in the morning in shops along Lakeshore Boulevard, including an antique store where Clara insisted upon buying a small iron animal for Swan—"For your room, at home. For the windowsill. Like one of the statues in the museum, isn't it?" Swan stared at the hand-sized little creature, an antelope with horns. Its legs were slender, and its tail was upright. A beautiful thing, but Swan felt sad stroking it, he didn't know why. He wasn't thinking that it was not "real"—that some man had made it, with the purpose of selling it—but that somehow there was an actual animal trapped inside it, in the heavy iron. A real animal, that something had happened to. "Well, d'you want it or not? C'mon, sweetie."

Clara touched his hair. After so many months of not seeming to love him, she was beginning to love him again.

In a cab, hailed for Clara by the admiring proprietor of the antique store, Swan held the heavy little antelope on his lap, wrapped in paper. He had the idea that he and Clara were returning to the house on Lakeshore Boulevard, but Clara instructed the driver to take them somewhere else—another large, imposing building that was the Hamilton Public Library.

Clara said quickly, "I have more shopping to do, honey. It would just be boring for you. Here's five dollars, you can buy yourself lunch like a big boy. I'll meet you at around four o'clock, out here on the steps."

Swan was stunned. All by himself, he was expected to be in that building? And buy lunch for himself? He had never done such a thing in his life. Clara said, nudging him gently, "Steven, it's just books in there. Out in the country where we live, there's nothing like this, is there? Go on. My little bookworm." And she nudged him again, less gently.

Blindly, Swan climbed out of the taxi.

He ascended the snowy stone steps without glancing back. He'd left the little iron antelope in the taxi, half-hoping that Clara would forget it.

Inside the library, Swan wandered into a large room with a fireplace in which no fire was burning. There were shelves of books to the ceiling, and an elderly man dozing in a leather chair. Swan pulled out the first volume of the *World Book of Wonders* and began to read before removing his coat. His eyes were glazed with moisture.

A middle-aged woman librarian approached to tell him that the children's library was downstairs.

"I'm not a child. I'm in seventh grade."

This remark surprised Swan, in the tone of Clara's new friend Ransom. Matter-of-fact and unhurried. In fact, Swan was not in seventh grade but sixth.

The librarian relented. Swan remained in the fireplace room, for several hours. Leafing through the *Book of Wonders*, and later *A History of American Aviation* and a handsome book of photographs of Indians by someone named Edward S. Curtis. The Indians in the photographs were very different from those in Jonathan's *Scalphunter* and *Lone Ranger* comics, and Swan wished he could show them to Jonathan.

By one o'clock Swan's stomach began to growl but he told himself sternly he wasn't hungry. He drank from a water fountain in the hallway, and used the men's rest room, and returned to his seat in the reference room. Library patrons came and went, and at last even the elderly man roused himself and departed. At ten minutes to four, Swan left the library to sit outside on the steps, shivering in the wind from the lake. By four-thirty, when Clara had not come, he went inside again to get warm, peering anxiously from a leaded window beside the door. At five o'clock the library was closed, so he had no choice but to leave, this time sitting at the top of the steps with his back against the wall, in a corner. It was December; the sun set early. Harsh little snow-pellets were blown into his face. He thought of the cemetery behind the Lutheran church, and of Robert. He was shivering convulsively. He made himself think of his cousin Deborah, how impressed she would be when he told her about the big-city library.

At last, after about twenty minutes, Clara arrived in a taxi. She opened the door to signal for him impatiently. "Swan! Come *on*."

Annoyed at him, she seemed. For rising from the steps stiffly, like an old man.

"God! Look at you. I hope you don't get pneumonia."

Clara fussed over him, kissing his cold cheek, chattering as they were driven back to the house on Lakeshore Drive. Swan sat silent, sullen. He would say nothing about the little antelope: of course, it was gone. Clara had given it no more thought than she'd given him. But she remembered to ask if he'd had lunch, and if there was change from the five-dollar bill.

Swan told her no. No change.

At the Reveres' house, Swan fell asleep on the bed in his room without undressing. Sometime later Clara came in. "Swan! Are you sick?" He woke confused, not knowing if it was very late; or not so late, and another protracted dinner awaited him downstairs. Clara was wearing a velvety purple dress with a skirt that fell to mid-calf; her windblown hair had been brushed, and fixed into what she called a *chig-non*. "So, sweetheart, you're mad at me? Your mamma?" Swan lay very still smelling her perfume and something else—the wine or liquor the adults drank here, or the scent of her secret life, whatever it was that made Clara so happy. She kicked off her shoes, she sat heavily on the bed beside him. "Don't be mad at me, honey, I'm so happy . . . so happy. I'm happy in this place and I'm happy at home." Shockingly, Clara began to cry. Swan could not recall his mother crying in years. "I can't help it, honey, I'm just so happy—I feel so good. I deserve it, don't I? Don't I?"

For the first time in his life Swan did not share Clara's mood. She'd switched on the overhead light in his room not caring if it hurt his eyes, he shielded his face with his arm. *I hate you. You are a bitch*. He would have liked to punish her, and that name was a punishment, even if she couldn't hear it. Even if she would never know.

7

Two months into seventh grade at the junior high in Tintern, Swan was skipped into eighth grade. This only meant crossing the hall and being assigned to another homeroom. The kids here were older of course, and most of the boys were taller than Swan; there was a long-legged boy related to the Reveres though lacking the Revere name, and this boy observed Swan with unusual interest, though he kept his distance and was not friendly.

Acting like he's afraid of me Swan thought.

In eighth grade, his teachers were polite with him, and often praised him. The teachers seemed to know exactly who he was: Curt Revere's son, Jonathan Revere's younger brother. They gave him A's and called upon him in class when he raised his hand, but not otherwise. As always Swan did extracredit assignments in math, English, history, he read books on an extracredit reading list, and spoke to his teachers respectfully. In each class there was but one adult among thirty or more children and Swan knew that this adult, whether intelligent or not, attractive or not, was the only individual of value in the room, whose opinion of him mattered.

Jonathan was seventeen now, a junior, and had his driver's license and his own, secondhand Chevrolet. Clara insisted that Jonathan drive Swan to school and when he balked, she spoke with Revere. "It makes no sense, son. For you to drive to school and your brother, attending the same school, to take the bus." Revere spoke quietly, and Jonathan mumbled, "Yes, sir."

Swan, riding in Jonathan's car, so close in the passenger's seat to his brother, tried to think of things to say to him. Things to make him laugh, or to impress him. Things to make Jonathan like him. For Jonathan was silent in Swan's presence, withdrawn and ironic in manner; he chain-smoked, tossing Old Gold packages onto the floor, that Swan cleared away. There were dark bruises beneath Jonathan's eyes, his skin was pimpled and sallow. It was difficult to believe that Jonathan had ever done well in school, his grades were never more than C's now, and sometimes D's. Half the time he cut afternoon classes to hang out with his beer-drinking buddies at the Sunoco station where one of them worked, but he had to return to the school to pick up Swan, his brother whom he loathed.

Swan knew: Jonathan loathed him. It was no secret. Jonathan never spoke to him if he could avoid it, and when Swan chattered in the car, Jonathan grunted in derision and switched on the radio, high.

Why do you hate me? was not a question Swan had ever put to Jonathan, only to Robert. There had not been any answer to the question, that he could recall.

One January afternoon when the boys were driving home, Swan took out of his pocket something he meant to impress Jonathan with: a fishing knife.

He'd found it in some trash behind the school. A battered old double-edged knife with a serrated blade, and a plastic handle that had been mended with adhesive tape. The blade was rusted and dull, but it was about eight inches long, and looked wicked. It looked like an Indian dagger in one of Jon's comic books.

"See what I found? Out behind the school."

Jonathan glanced at him, indifferent. But when he saw the knife in Swan's hand he clutched at the steering wheel, and made a whimpering noise. The car skidded briefly on the asphalt pavement.

Swan said quickly, "I found it out back of the school. Somebody didn't want it, I guess." Swan was aware of his brother's surprise, and his brother's moment of fear. It had been only a moment, and Jonathan had recovered, but both he and Swan were aware of it. Forcing himself to laugh Swan said, "Can a knife be sharpened, if it's rusty? Would you like it?"

Jonathan mumbled he didn't want anybody's shitty old knife.

Swan wound down the window and threw the knife out, just to

show Jonathan how little it meant to him. How the hell could Jonathan think that he, Swan, meant harm? He was only twelve and Jonathan was seventeen. . . .

Next morning, Swan told Clara that he'd rather take the school bus after all. Clara, who'd cared so much about this issue only recently, now seemed hardly to care. She seemed to know about Jonathan cutting classes, and drinking with his school dropout friends; but she never spoke of it. "All right, honey. It's probably better, you can make friends on the bus, and get to know some girls," she said vaguely. Her kitchen was being done over and everywhere canvas lay harsh and gritty underfoot.

———

Once he was freed from Swan, Jonathan drove off and spent the day any way he liked: the hell with school. He was still a junior, he hadn't been passed on. So he drove a few miles down the valley and picked up two other kids and they went fishing or inspected motorcycles and used cars in a big slummy lot out on the highway, or, after a while, they got to certain corners before the school bus arrived and drove certain girls to school, though the girls didn't always have time for school.

If Revere was out of town, Jonathan wouldn't bother coming home for supper. They ate in a diner out on the highway, fifteen miles away. He knew that Clara would not tell on him. When the notices started arriving from school asking about why he was absent so much, Clara talked seriously with him and he said that he hated school, he hated the teachers and kids. He was defiant and on the verge of tears. But Clara touched him and said, after a moment, "I know how it is." So she did not tell Revere. He could trust her.

"She's a goddamn filthy bitch," he would say to his friends. "I'd like to slit her up and down and hang her out to drain." And he spat onto the ground, his face contorted with disgust. One of his friends was over twenty, in and out of the Navy already (he had been let go), and he always asked about Clara: did Jon ever see her undressed? Did she walk around without all her clothes on, ever? Jonathan flushed at his questions, embarrassed and angry. Clara ran around the house any way she liked, barefoot and with her hair wet and loose down her back, dripping onto her blouse, and at night she made popcorn for herself and Swan, wearing one of her many robes and not always bothering to see that it was buttoned—but he was not going to tell anyone about this. It was nobody's business what Revere's wife did.

"Why the hell do you want to know?" he sneered. Skinny as he was, no match for this guy, he had no care for how arrogantly he talked—it might have seemed he was asking for a punch in the mouth. "You wouldn't ever have no chance with her, so forget it."

"Wouldn't be too sure of that," his friend said.

So Jonathan laughed scornfully and nastily.

The girls they drove around were the same girls who had been on the school bus for years with them. Now, suddenly, everyone was older. Some girls had already quit school, were married and had babies. It went so fast—the years went so fast, Jonathan thought. He drank more than anyone else because he had more to push out of his mind. They drank for fun but he drank for serious reasons; then, after a certain point, he forgot the reasons and was able to have fun. They drove twenty, thirty miles to get beer and liquor, knowing in mysterious ways just where a certain roadhouse was, what its prices were, what its manager was like. They knew everything, yet no one could have said how they knew; it was mysterious knowledge, breathed in with the air around them.

They went to all the outings and charity picnics. But when the Lutheran church had its outing Jonathan stayed home alone, he didn't say why. While Clara and Revere and Swan and Clark went, he stayed around the house, acting strange. The idea that just a few yards back in the cemetery his mother and brother were buried made him sick: how could people wolf down hot beef sandwiches and all that beer, those barrels and barrels of beer, when out back bodies were rotting and stinking in the soil? Didn't anyone know that?

So he stayed home, feeling shaky, and played poker with the few hired men who hadn't enough money to go out. When Revere and the others came home that evening, he was sitting on the porch steps as if waiting for them. He knew Revere liked that. Or he had liked it, in the days when he still liked Jonathan. It was after dark, so he had taken down Revere's flag and folded it up right.

Clara had talked Revere into buying that flag. She had said that she was proud of being an American, and didn't he want a flag? So they bought one and were American. When Jonathan wandered back from the woods with his gun, he had the desire to shoot the flag into tatters, he didn't know why. What would happen then? What would his father do to him?

He didn't sleep well at night but not because of dreams. He had the idea he never dreamed. He had nothing to dream about.

Clark had warned him about the girls he went out with: "They're pigs, so be careful. You know what I mean."

Clark knew everything, he knew about all the girls. Twenty miles away they'd heard of Clark and were surprised that Jonathan was his brother. But any girl so sluttish that Clark would have nothing to do with her was just right for Jonathan, he thought; she would have to like him. Who else could she get? They weren't ugly, exactly, he and his friends, but there must have been something wrong with them—the prettiest girls ignored them. They had enough money, or at least Jonathan did and he could lend money to the other boys, but still the best-looking girls avoided them and they were always crowded by a certain kind of heavy, lipsticked, sly girl who liked them well enough and laughed uproariously at their jokes. These girls were always impressed by Jonathan's car and the remote prickly excitement of knowing he was a Revere—even if he himself was a disappointment, too thin, and with skin that was never clear. Wasn't he a Revere, might there not be a chance of catching him? Clark went out with a pretty, long-haired girl from Tintern who worked in the drugstore, and this girl certainly wasn't good enough for Revere—he would never let Clark marry her—so the girls Jonathan was able to get were so low that Revere would not even have spat on them, and he felt satisfaction in this.

Maybe he would bring one of them right into the house some-day and announce he was marrying her: she was pregnant and that was that. He would stare into his father's face to see what he thought. "You're not the only one in the family that can marry a whore," he would say to his father.

And what would his father do? Whip him again?

The most he could do would be to kill Jonathan.

He thought about getting a job, since his friends had "jobs." They worked part-time in a service station. By now, his father would have given him a job somewhere if he was ever going to; he had given Clark a job when Clark had been only sixteen. So that was out. He was not going to ask his father about it because it was evidently settled that he wanted no part of Jonathan. Or he might be waiting for Jonathan to straighten out. But it came to the same thing. So he thought vaguely about finding a job somewhere, but he had no skills, knew nothing, could hardly change a tire. He hated the smell of gas, so how could he work in a filling station?

He thought, the hell with getting a job. He didn't want one anyway.

He had a year and a half of school yet to go but he did not go back in the fall. As far as he was concerned, he was finished with it forever. Since he was stupid, there was no point in bothering—he might as well be dead. "Did you ever wish you were dead?" he asked Clark. But Clark, running off to his girlfriend, had no time for him. "Did you ever wish you were dead?" he said to his uncle Judd, whom he resembled closely; but questions like this made Judd nervous. Since that time in the back meadow—the accident with Robert's shotgun—Judd had seemed more nervous. Or was Jonathan just imagining it? Sometimes he himself could hear that blast, then the screaming. . . .

(He had jumped off his horse and run back, and at first he hadn't seen anything at all. Then he saw it. He saw what the shot had done to Robert and how what had been Robert was shattered forever. Just like that. It did not matter that he died later, because he was dead right then. You couldn't fix up anyone who looked like that. . . . A few feet away Swan had been standing.)

"Did you ever wish you were dead?" he said to one of his father's men during harvest. The men all worked hard and were paid well, so they had to like Revere. They saw him rarely enough, so it was easy to like him. Jonathan supposed that they did not like him but he was so scrawny, so punky, that they couldn't be jealous, at least, because he was a Revere. The men thought he was crazy and all they asked him about was Clara—when he told them to shut up they lost interest.

The night he ran away and disappeared, he was out with a girl from a small farm some miles away. She was only fourteen but she looked older: she had a big, sturdy body and long bleached hair that fell past her shoulders. She wore pink lipstick and her fingernails were painted to match. They got beer from a roadhouse and drank it for a while on the back porch of that place until the manager said they'd better leave, some state troopers were probably going to drop in, so they drove around for a while in the dark drinking it while the girl complained about her mother, and finally they parked and finished what was left of it. In the backseat of the car Jonathan wrestled around with her and she teased him, giggling drunkenly, and when she finally gave in he felt that something dangerous was approaching him. He could feel it coming as if he were standing on a railroad track and it had begun to vibrate. For years he had fooled around with girls like this, it meant nothing to him, it was nothing more than going to the bathroom—almost the same thing—but now he felt icy with fear. He tried to make love to the girl but something was wrong. He went cold, dead. Then, when she tried to get up, he began hitting her. He screamed into her face.

"Slut! Filthy bitch!"

He bloodied her face and punched her in the stomach and breasts. He wept with the ferocity of his hatred. Then he pushed her out of the car and left her, his tires kicking up pebbles and dust behind him as he pulled away—and that was that.

8

Outside the high school building it was a cold, clear November day. Many boys had skipped school to go hunting; that was against the "law," but the principal was a cheerful manly man who would not expel anyone. So there was a strange sense of holiday or half-holiday in the air—the usual girls had come to school but only about half the boys had showed up. Swan liked the relative peace in the corridor around his locker. The girls chattered and giggled the way they always did, but it was not quite so high-pitched, so self-conscious. There were no boys nearby to hear them except Swan, who did not count.

He was only sixteen but a senior already, and he must have carried this fact around with him without knowing it like a stamp or tattoo on his forehead that identified him as a freak. In the locker room he could not approach any group of boys and join them, because he didn't know how, nor did he want to know how; out in the corridors or on the stairs or outside in the parking lot, he could not sidle up to any girl and tease her in that certain winning way, because he did not know how and he supposed he did not want to know. Revere had told him about girls and that he should be careful of any situations that might lead to temptation. "Temptation." It was a word out of the Bible and Swan bowed his head in admiration for its holy and ancient uselessness. These days, Revere spoke a little loudly but you had to pretend nothing was unusual. He was hard of hearing, Clara explained; that always happened to men. But she thought it better to let someone else tell Revere about it. So he instructed Swan in a loud, slightly embarrassed voice that he should avoid temptation. He was not yet old enough to understand the complexities of his own body, and when he was old enough, Revere would explain it. For the time being, he should just avoid temptation.

When he'd been only twelve, Clara had told him all about it. He had gotten the idea from her that it was something he would be doing sooner or later, preferably sooner because then he could "grow up better," that it always made the girl happy, but only if she was the right kind of girl. Clara was emphatic about this. "Someone like your cousin Debbie—no. Nobody around here. Nobody on a big farm. But some of those people that live down by the river in those dumps—with all the junk around them—and any time you see a girl standing around a bunch of boys and they're all laughing together—probably she's all right. You understand?"

He respected Revere's standards but he supposed that his mother was right and Revere was wrong. So he stopped thinking about it. He had so much else to think about that he would have to put off anything like that for a while—when he got older, and when Revere had explained to him everything that he had to know, then he would have time for himself. He would then have the rest of his life for himself.

So he did his homework in free periods at school and at home he did additional work and read books that were related to his courses. He did not let these books interfere with his teachers' teaching, though. He could respect their kindly limitations. And he went with Revere on small errands, to Tintern and to other small towns and once all the way to Hamilton, sitting beside his father in his father's new big black car and inclining his head toward him, listening to what his father had to say about money, taxes, buildings, land, wheat, gypsum, and men that had to be hired for the lowest possible pay. He could feel his head filling up slowly. At times he woke to the fear that his head would burst, that facts and ideas were being squeezed into his brain too fast, before he was able to make room for them. But he kept on studying and working at school and at home, he kept on listening to Revere and to the men Revere talked with. His ears were like holes in his head that sucked in information and stored it away, useless as it might seem to be at the moment. Everything he heard was sucked in. He never forgot anything. Along with the important equations he memorized in physics and chemistry were jumbled conversations he had overheard between his mother and someone's new wife she was trying to befriend, or vicious oaths spat out on the cramped little gym floor when the boys were playing basketball, or the sweetly sickish popular songs the girls hummed to themselves out in the corridor. He never forgot anything.

That day he felt a sense of holiday too, but it made him apprehensive. He did not trust unusual feelings. In English class, half the desks were vacant and it was easy to figure out that the toughest boys weren't present: just Swan and two or three boys who would never succeed at anything, especially not at being boys, and a dozen girls. Swan despised this English teacher because she was so like himself, so uncertain. She was a new teacher, just graduated from college the spring before, and he had to turn his pencil round and round in his fingers as she spoke, to find some outlet for his own nervousness. She looked around the room, fearful of seeing something out of place, and finally, ten minutes after each class began, her gaze would come to rest timidly on Swan's face; she could sense that he was different, like herself, he was quiet and that maybe meant he was shy; at least he was intelligent and the rest of the students were stupid. Stupid. Of course they were all stupid, who would expect anything else? Swan did not dislike them for being stupid, he was grateful to them. Whoever was stupid was beneath worry or thought; you did not have to figure them out. This eliminated hundreds of people. In this life you had time only for a certain amount of thinking, and there was no need to waste any of it on people who were not threatening.

Swan sat in the outer row near the windows. A few feet away the window was open a crack, slanted downward, so that the fresh hard air eased onto the side of his face. With one part of his mind he listened to the teacher and with another part of his mind he thought about what he was going to do. Clara talked more and more about living permanently in Hamilton, and he would have to help her with that. It would take them a few years to convince Revere. His father spoke vaguely of how Swan and Clark were to take over everything of his someday, when he got "old and worn out," as he put it—with a special forlorn grin that meant he was joking, he'd never get old and worn out. Swan thought about that. Clark was twenty-four and that meant he was eight years older than Swan. He talked to Swan only the way you'd talk to a child. He would always talk to Swan that way, he would never be able to accept Swan as an equal. . . .

"Steven?" the teacher was saying.

Swan answered the question. He felt the girls looking at him, then back up to the teacher to see if he was right. But of course he was right—they were tired of him. They sighed, they exchanged glances. Swan wanted to snarl across at them, "I didn't ask to be smart." But he sat still, turning his pencil round and round. It had got to be that whenever he was sitting or standing still he had to keep some part of him moving, usually his fingers. He didn't know why. Sometimes he jerked his toes around, hidden safe inside his shoes, so that no one could see; sometimes he tapped his fingernails lightly on the desk. But he could not sit perfectly still. He had the idea that his brain would burst if he did not direct energy away from it.

The bell rang and they filed out. Swan came to the front of his aisle in order to cross over to the door, lowering his gaze. He avoided his teacher's eyes. It was not that he was really shy, as they thought, but that he hadn't time to worry about his relationship with them. He hadn't time to assess and catalogue anyone else. So when he saw the English teacher hurriedly put some papers together, he supposed she wanted to talk with him—about college again—and he walked with shoulders hunched forward out into the corridor where he would be safe.

But he was just outside the door when he heard her say, "Steven?" So he had to wait. She caught up with him, a tall ungainly woman in thick-heeled shoes, with a voice always gentle when she wasn't teaching. "Have you talked to your parents any more about college? What did they say?"

Swan had talked to no one. He wasn't going, he couldn't leave home. He said, "They want me home for a year. My pa is sick."

"But—"

She had nothing to say. Swan waited politely for her to let him go.

"I'm sorry to hear that," she said finally. She sounded bewildered. Swan nodded, made a clicking sound with his teeth that indicated he knew nothing, he was confused, that was the way life was. Before turning to leave he let his gaze rise up to flick across hers, which was only polite. Then he was safe.

Study hall was his next period. It was held in the school's dingy little library, which was just another classroom. The walls were lined with ragged old books and there were two long tables for students to sit at. It looked quite empty today. In this room the cheap fluorescent lights were always flickering; Swan saw with disgust that they hadn't been fixed yet, and they had been broken for a week. He sat by himself at the very end of one of the tables, with his back to the window. A few girls filed in and let their books fall at the other end of the table, sighing and whispering. They looked down at him with their bright, penciled little eyes, then looked away. One leaned across to whisper to another and her black hair fell across her face. Swan narrowed his eyes and watched her secretly. He was prodding the soft flesh about his thumbnail with the nail of his forefinger.

He thought of how nice it would be to be alone with that girl, to hold her in his arms. He thought about kissing her. But she sat back, flicking her hair back, and he saw she was chewing gum. Her name was Loretta Stanley and she lived in Tintern. As soon as she sat back, she looked vulgar and cheap; just to be with her and to touch her would be cheap. It was only the thought of her that fascinated him. . . . He opened his math book and looked at the problems. There were additional problems at the back of the book that he always worked out and might or might not hand in to his teacher. He began to work the first problem, leaning over his paper. The fluorescent lights flickered. A girl on the far side of the room giggled. The teacher in charge of study hall got to her feet; there was a sense of daring and danger. Swan kept on working. When he finished the problem he turned to look out the window, as if this were his reward. Fresh, clear air, not air sullied by the odor of gum and cheap cosmetics and hair spray . . . But the sky beyond the gritty window had turned gray, the color of slate. In this land the sky changed rapidly and violently. If it was spring he would worry about a tornado, but it was only November, early winter, so they were safe. Because this room was on the second floor of the building, he could see nothing out the window except the sky and an ugly black smokestack that rose from the part of the school building that had only one floor. Out past this, miles away, the land rose to ridges and hills and then, at the horizon, dissolved upward into that higher ground that was called mountains. Somewhere between the mountains and this building lived the Reveres. He felt as if he were an alien in this room, waiting patiently for the time to come when he could return to his proper place. He had nothing to do with the smell of chalk dust and wet leather, the whisking sounds of girls hurrying by in the hall, the louder sounds of teachers' heavy heels on the old wood floor. His head ached and he pressed his hands against his eyes.

All I want, he thought, is to get things straight. Put things in order. Then, after that—

He took his hands away and blinked dazedly. After that? He could envision no future beyond the long years that awaited him, of struggle with Clark and then with other Reveres, probably his uncles, and after that the many-faceted struggles Revere had always taken on with such energy in the past: with men like himself in other cities, with workingmen, with unions, with builders, carpenters, merchants, trucking concerns, trains, and on and on out to the furthermost limits of Revere's world, which stretched out endlessly and was a universe of its own. The only way out of it was the way Robert had gone, by accident, or Jonathan had taken on purpose. Swan understood that and perhaps that was why his head ached and he feared his brain might burst.

He put down his pencil and went to the front of the room. The teacher was an old, mannish woman with a sour mouth; she taught history. "May I go to the rest room?" he said. No one here said "may" but Swan said it anyhow, to show that he knew he was different, but what the hell? Out in the corridor he walked with his head drooping. He could smell all the familiar odors of the school—his eye took in the streaks of pale light reflected off the dented lockers that stretched out before him. All this was old, familiar. He saw someone's lost mitten and that too was familiar. He had lived a hundred years here. He felt that his mind could take it all in—the teachers as well as the students, the seldom-used closets and corners no one else ever glanced at—but that his mind could do nothing with it. It remained ugly and inert and confident, a building that had been already overcrowded and outdated as soon as the last fixture was screwed into place. He could take in his classmates and the students in lower grades, those his own age, and he believed he could predict for them all unsurprising and unpromising lives, but he had no power over them to help or befriend them, to answer any questions they might have. They had no questions and they had no idea what questions they might have.

He went across into the annex where the junior high rooms were. This period was study hall and there were no classes. He went to Deborah's homeroom and looked in, making sure the teacher could not see him. Deborah was sitting up at the front, just as Swan always had, these strange and perhaps frightening children one never knew what to do with except to keep them in clear sight—protected from the healthy coarseness of the other students. Deborah was writing in a notebook. The notebook was twisted at quite an angle; she had this queer stilted handwriting that slanted far to the left. Swan watched her and was happy that she was sitting so close to the door, that she hadn't seen him and knew nothing, did not suspect she was being watched. He would have liked her to sit straighter, not to let her shoulders hunch over the desk like that. Sit up, Deborah. Sit back. But of course that was the way Swan sat too—as if pressing against the desktop and the book that lay opened on it, trying to get closer, a little further ahead. She'd been sick with pleurisy last spring and had missed weeks of school; Swan had felt a rush of possession toward her, as if, kept home with her ugly mother and her weak father, she would be safe from all "temptations" and could truly belong to him. She had the look of a child who would never be quite well. Her skin was smooth and pale, but the paleness was underlaid with an olive hue. Her eyes were big but a little too big, too intense. Her small lips were pursed together with concentration; other mouths hung half-open, in the aftermath of slack grins. Swan fitted the edge of his thumbnail into the crack between two of his lower teeth and worried it up and down for a few seconds, watching her. She was his cousin and he thought he might love her. Of all the Reveres and the families married into them, she was the only one he liked—even though she did not return his friendship.

She wore a blue wool jumper with a gray kitten made of felt for a pocket. Swan thought he had never seen anything so beautiful.

When he returned to the study hall, however, he felt depressed. He came in and the air seemed to suck at him, eyes lifted to take him in with a mysterious female interest, assessing, pondering— the eyes of girls who bided their time in the public school until they were old enough to quit (at sixteen) or old enough to marry (often at an age younger than sixteen). As he passed her, Loretta gazed at him and he returned her look with a heavy, contemptuous droop of his eyes. Then he was at his seat. Why here, what was he doing? At such times he believed himself an individual in a dream not his own like one of those hapless voyagers of Edgar Allan Poe who made no decisions, were paralyzed to act, as catastrophes erupted around them. The floorboards of this place were worn smooth from generations of footsteps and the cracks between them seemed to be widening every day. Ugly black cracks through which one might slip, fall, never be seen again.

Briefly, the sun appeared. Swan crumpled up a piece of paper and let it fall to the floor into the patch of sunlight.

Stop. You will have to.

It struck him then: he must stop reading, and he must stop thinking. He could lose himself in a female body: Deborah, or Loretta. Though better yet Loretta, who did not know him as a Revere. He was seized with panic as, lifting his eyes, he saw shelves of books he had not read and would never read; the infinity of books he'd seen in the library in Hamilton, in the reference room where he'd dreamed away an afternoon and in other rooms in that building only glimpsed, at a distance. A library is a mausoleum: books of the dead. And so many. And so many secrets lost to him forever. Hadn't time for it all and if he couldn't do it all then there was no point in doing any of it. For such an effort would be like drawing a single breath in the knowledge that you would not draw another. You were fated to suffocate, to die. You were fated to become extinct. His teachers spoke to him enthusiastically of college—"You will want to apply to the very best universities, Steven"—but he knew he could not, he would not. He was fearful of leaving Eden Valley and of leaving REVERE FARM. He was fearful of relinquishing all that he'd won in Revere. And he was fearful he would forget the powerful, potent air of Revere's world, those hundreds of acres—no: there were thousands—that were identified as *Revere land*. If he should relinquish this claim, if he should forget all he'd learned since Clara had brought him here, what then? If he kept reading his mind would burst but if he pushed his books aside, as Jonathan had done, if he rejected the works of the mind, he would never learn all that he needed to learn—for knowledge is power, and he needed power. He remembered Revere pointing out casually the frothy rippling rapids of the Eden River, as they'd crossed the bridge at Hamilton. *Power. Dammed-up, to supply power.* He smiled, he was not going to be frightened. Yet he felt, between the two impulses, his muscles tense as if preparing him for danger. Unconsciously he dug the tender flesh about his thumbnail until it bled.

At that moment Loretta turned, to smile at him. A flame passing between them.

After class Loretta lingered by her desk until he came by. She lifted her sooty eyes to him and smiled again, insinuatingly. "*You* don't like to hunt, Steven, do you?"

"No."

"Not for animals anyway. Right?"

Her sly smile. Her tongue wetting her lips. Swan swallowed hard, understanding that this was the kind of girl Deborah could never be, and the kind of girl he required. That oval, hard, knowing prettiness that could be wiped off with a thumb, smeared. The pale freckled forearms exposed by pushed-up sleeves in a way that was both glamorous and prim. Swan saw his hand reach out and with a startling authority not his he saw his forefinger tap a mother-of-pearl cross the girl wore on a fake-gold chain around her neck.

"Right."

———

A few days later Swan crossed the street from the school and entered the diner to buy cigarettes. Did he dare to ask for Old Golds, or would the salesclerk laugh at him? He'd begun smoking to give his nervous hands something to do, but he never smoked at home. Clara would not have cared and Revere would probably not have noticed, but he wanted to keep it secret just the same. He thought that if he was growing up, changing, he would keep it to himself for as long as he could.

The kids who ate in the diner were of a different crowd from those who stayed safe in the close, milky-smelling cafeteria room at school; they were not necessarily older but they were louder, more sure of themselves. Swan liked the crowded smoky atmosphere into which he stepped bringing a flurry of snow in with him. The pneumatic device above the door hissed and the door closed very slowly, so that he had the impulse to pull it shut behind him. A group of high school students stood around the counter, making noise, and all the booths that ran along the front of the diner were filled. There was a floor-stomping, shrieking anonymity here that Swan never felt back in school, where everyone was still named as precisely as they were on the teachers' seating charts; here the country music from the jukebox filled in any gaps there might be in conversations or thought. Swan went to the counter and asked for a package of cigarettes, any brand. He was confused and lonely in this place and would not have been surprised if his classmates—these brassy adults who, in the world of the diner, clearly knew everything important about life—turned to stare contemptuously at him. No one looked.

When he turned, opening the cellophane wrapper, he let his gaze run along the row of booths. Those faces and even the backs of those heads were familiar to him, yet at the same time strange. Was it possible that Swan, who supposed he knew so much and had never had any choice about it, really knew very little? He had always been aware of his classmates but he had never thought seriously about them. Even back in the country school, the boys who tormented him had existed on the periphery of his real life, which was his life at home. He was on a kind of voyage with them but their destinations were far different; when the voyage ended he would get off to go his way and they would go theirs. He had not hated them because he had not thought that much about them. There had been the whole Revere family to keep in his mind: uncles, aunts, cousins, new babies, new wives, the legends of older men now senile or crippled or dead, his own father, his father's father, the table-thumping accounts of spectacular successes that were legal, but not so legal they had no sensational surprise to them. And all that land, so much land, tended and tortured into a garden so complex one might need a lifetime to comprehend it . . . His classmates had seemed to Swan to whirl about in their own trivial little world that had to do with the friendships and hatreds of one another; that was all. As soon as he had come into Tintern in eighth grade he had been aware of a central group in his class—an amorphous but unmistakable unit of boys and girls who seemed omnipotent in their power. They had only the power to give or deny friendship, to include or exclude, and Swan had not cared about that. He had not cared. Though he had no interest in them he had been overhearing for years the tales of their weekend and after-school exploits, their parties and hayrides and wild night-riding out on the highway, and, as time went on, their romantic alliances and feuds that marked them as adult, mysterious. He thought their bright clothes and loud voices drab enough, trivial as the high school classes they all disliked, but he could not help admiring something about them—their blindness, maybe? Their complacence?

He was crossing the street and heading back toward school when he heard someone behind him. "Steven?" she said. Loretta was hurrying toward him, her head ducked. She wore a bright blue kerchief to protect her hair from the snow. Swan saw how her hair bunched out and made the kerchief puffed and bouncy; a lot of work had gone into that hair. The windows of the diner behind her were steamy; above her head a big sign ran the length of the building, cracked and peeling. CROSSROADS LUNCHEONETTE—TRUCK STOP—DRINK COCA-COLA. Swan had never looked at that sign before.

"If you're going back I'll walk with you," she said.

They walked along. Swan lit his cigarette and then offered her one. He thought: If she takes it that will mean something. She took it and he lit a match for her, the two of them pausing in the snow. Flakes had dampened her hair on top, on her thick puffy bangs. She had a hard, smooth, carefully made-up face. She could have been any age until you saw her eyes; then you knew she was young.

"I s'pose they're laughing at us back there," she said, alluding casually and with brittle humor to something Swan was expected to know about. "But I really have to get back early. I really do." They walked along self-consciously. Loretta wore drab little boots with gray fur on top that looked like cotton; it was thick and had separated into bunches. Her coat was plaid, blue and yellow. Cheap. Everything about her was cheap. Swan felt sorry for her but at the same time knew that in the high school world he had to enter every day she was superior to him—not only a year older, but superior because she "knew" things he didn't; she ran around with the right people while Swan, Steven Revere from up the valley, ran around with no one. He shivered, thinking of her as she had been that day in the library, her dark glossy hair falling over her shoulder and swinging free.... He had always been aware of Loretta but had not bothered to truly look at her, just as he had been aware of all his classmates. Somewhere inside his brain, stored away with other useless, foolish knowledge, were faithful records of all their alliances and loves, going back to the eighth grade passions that were expressed by scribbled notes and inked initials on the backs of hands.

"I didn't see you in there when I went in," Swan said, as if he had been looking for her.

"Well, I saw you come in. I didn't know you smoked."

He had no answer to that. They were walking up the driveway to the school—cracked pavement with crumpled-up papers and junk in its gutters. The air was very wet and not cold. Neither Swan nor Loretta dared to look at each other, but were fascinated by everything around them. Swan said, pointing to one of the orange-yellow buses parked forlornly out in the lot, "That's the bus I take." Loretta nodded with interest. He was aware of her beside him, the silhouette of her head. She was several inches shorter than he. The girls who were loudest, most confident, who had bright red lips that might say any word and show no shame, always turned out to be short and modestly proportioned. Swan shivered again and was so nervous he had to keep wiping snowflakes out of his eyes just for something to do. They were so vivid and real, he and this girl. It was not a bright day, but the sullen air glared about them, setting them apart and dissolving everything else back from them—the school building with its gray concrete blocks, the withered evergreens at the corners of the school. Even their voices sounded harsh and loud. A whisper would have carried everywhere, to every corner of the school, Swan thought. He had no idea what to do with this girl, who seemed to be pushing against him—even when she was several discreet feet away—and offering her face up to him, her big penciled eyes and face caked with pink-toned makeup. He did not know the style of language and behavior the other boys knew instinctively. He did not know what to say or do and the knowledge of his stupidity depressed him.

After they had been having lunch together in the diner for a few weeks, they idled by her locker one day—the old locker tumbling and crowded with books, papers, old scarves, tissues, a mirror with a yellow plastic frame, and her sweater and coat—he tried to talk with her as he would have talked with Deborah. He told her of his nervousness, his need to smoke. As he talked with her, leaning in with one arm up over her head in the classic pose all his classmates used and which he was consciously imitating, he tapped lightly on the thin metal of the locker with his fingertips. Loretta smiled as if he had begun to tell a joke or a complicated story. He went on, uncertainly, to say that he did not think his father would like her because he didn't like Clark's girl Rosemary, and she was something like Rosemary; and at last she began to listen, her eyes getting keen and sharp. He thought the irises were like tiny pebbles, like pellets. "So what are you saying?" she said, standing back flat on her heels. The sockets of her eyes were fiercely shadowed by the dimness of the hall. Swan understood then that he could not talk to her and if he tried he would only disturb her. He could not talk to his mother either, and of course not to his father, and never to Clark and never to his teachers, and it made sense that he could not now talk to Loretta, who walked so close to him and smiled dazzlingly up into his face as if these gestures of intimacy had nothing at all to do with Swan himself and his problems, but were just conventional gestures everyone used. As soon as he understood this he was all right. He was even relieved. When he encountered Deborah he could say things to her, certain things, and she understood, even if she offered him no friendliness and certainly no intimacy. But Loretta was another person.

"Nothing, I'm sorry," he said.

"I know your father's a big deal, so what? You trying to tell me something?"

"I said it was nothing. Forget it."

He had caught on to something arch but at the same time pliant in her—her edginess could always be caressed into softness if the caress had a harsh enough sound to it.

Loretta lived half a mile away and he could never walk her home because he had to catch the school bus. He felt juvenile and degraded by this fact, but Loretta did not seem to mind. She stood out back with him in the crowd of kids from the "country"—which could mean anything from the scrubby lower section where families lived fifteen to a shanty, to the vast rich farms of the Reveres off to the north of Tintern—and she cradled her books against her chest, standing with her back straight and her shoulders ready to shrug up in a coquettish gesture, while Swan smiled down into her pretty, ordinary little face and felt somehow illuminated by her presence, made special, important. He could not understand why she liked him. He could not understand why she had singled him out, abandoning some other boy or boys in favor of him, and he had abdicated to her the complete privilege of choice—it would never have occurred to him to turn to another, more intelligent girl. He would never be able to approach his cousin Deborah with the casualness he approached this Loretta, whom he scarcely knew even after weeks of lunches and huddled talks, though he felt that he knew Deborah thoroughly and that knowing her was like coming across a splinter of himself. But he could touch Loretta and slide his arm around her; in the precarious safety of an emptied stairway he could kiss her; he could bump his nervous forehead against hers secure with the knowledge that she knew how to do this: she was smiling and conspiratorial, she was never embarrassed.

They met out in the corridor during classes, each asking to be excused at the same time and exhilarated with the idea of such fraud, such daring—seeing her come shyly out of a classroom down the hall made Swan wonder dizzily who he was to have such power. He led her down the back stairway past the double doors to the cafeteria and past the first floor (there were no classrooms at the rear of the first floor) and down the basement, the last flight of stairs absolutely forbidden to all students and generally of no interest to them—where, in a dim alcove under the stairs, surrounded by the mysterious comforting hum of machinery and the permanent odor of food from the cafeteria, they could stand pressing against each other, kissing, and Swan felt so strongly how nice she was—he could think of no other word—that he had to keep telling her, telling her. He felt that they drifted out from themselves, from Swan and Loretta, into a sweet mild anonymous world where there was only the gentleness and kindliness of affection, simple affection. He felt how easy it was to be good and how intoxicating this girl's warmth, which was never a threat to him, asked nothing of him but only wanted to give; he wondered if the men who had come to Clara's arms had discovered this sweet entrancing silence and if all men discovered it sooner or later.

Some months later, when Clara tried to talk to Swan about her, he was uneasy and avoided her eyes.

"But why, what's wrong?" she said. He thought her too eager, too simple. What business was it of hers that he had a girlfriend? That he had turned out to be less freakish than everyone suspected should not have surprised her. "Why don't you want to talk about her? Clark says she's cute, he knows both of her brothers—"

"I'm not interested in Clark's opinion of her," Swan said.

"But Clark says she's nice. Why don't you look at me? There's nothing to be ashamed about."

He flinched as if she had struck him.

"A boy your age should have a girlfriend, there's nothing wrong with it. Why don't you want me to tell your father? Clark always went out with lots of girls, even Jonathan did—I guess—and it didn't mean they were going to marry them. All your father is afraid of is you or Clark marrying someone below you, that's all, but he knows how it—"

"He doesn't know anything about it," Swan said.

"There's nothing wrong with her—is there?" Clara said.

Swan tapped his fingers impatiently on his desk. Since his mother had come in his room he couldn't leave; that would be a mistake, it would be admitting defeat. She sat on the edge of his bed, her legs crossed at the ankles, as if she owned everything in here, including him. After a moment Swan said, beginning quietly, "You think it's all so simple. You think it's just two animals together and that's that—no, don't interrupt me. I know what you think. But it isn't like that. I don't act with Loretta the way you think and there's nothing wrong with her. I don't do what you think."

Clara stared at him. "What the hell are you talking about?"

"When I was thirteen you told me about girls . . . and how it would be all right if I, if I . . ."

"I did?" Clara laughed. "Why did I do that?"

He saw that she did not remember. How had he been able to remember every word and gesture of that conversation while she had forgotten?

"Tell me what I said. I must have made you mad, right?"

"No, you didn't make me mad."

"But you're mad now? Because you have a girlfriend you have to turn against your mother?"

"I haven't turned against you," Swan said.

"Look around at me, then. Why do you look so sad? What's wrong?"

"I don't know what's wrong," Swan said helplessly.

She brushed his hair back from his forehead as if she wanted to see him more clearly. Her fingers were cool and deft. He thought that if she stayed by him, this close, or if Loretta pushed up so perfumy-close against him, he could escape the sense of alarm and depression that was like a puddle of dark water moving steadily toward his feet.

9

But Clark ended up marrying his Rosemary, that birdlike, short little girl with plucked eyebrows and hair dyed black to set off her white, white face, white as flour and just as softly smooth to the touch. To escape Revere's anger he moved out the day he announced his plans, and he and the girl were married a week later. The Revere women and women in Tintern generally began counting months and weeks, staring at Rosemary's trim little stomach whenever they saw her, but nothing happened. Their first baby wasn't born until a year later and by then it was all forgotten and Clark's place with his father was settled: Revere was speaking to him again and he was given a good job, in a few years he might be managing the lumberyard if he did well, but he had been lost forever to the vastness of Revere's schemes and fortunes. He and Rosemary lived in town upstairs in a two-story white frame house, on one of Tintern's better streets.

He began putting on weight along with his wife when she was pregnant, a plump, serious worried young husband. In a year or two he would be able to bring her out to the house, maybe, but in the meantime her family took them in and crowded about them and loved them dearly, as proud of their son-in-law as if he had come down from the mountains to wed Rosemary and had been able to take her back up again.

—

A week and a day before that wedding, Clark had driven to the railroad depot to pick up a package for Clara. It was a long, heavy thing—another rug from an Eastern import store. He had taken off from work at the lumberyard to get the rug before the depot closed, and he had just enough time to drive by the drugstore to say hello to Rosemary; then he was off on the drive home. It was early April now. He felt a sense of elation that had nothing to do with spring or with Rosemary, whom he loved sweetly and simply and whose petite body seemed to him vastly exciting, but with this package he was bringing home. It was a present, a gift. He was proud of bringing it to Clara, who showed such gratitude and such surprise over everything, though her attention did not last long.

When he got home the old dining room rug had been dragged out. Clara wore jeans and an old shirt; she was barefoot. "God, it looks big," she said. "You think it's the wrong size?" The dining room furniture had been pushed out into the other room and Clark was a little surprised that Clara had done it all herself. "I want to get it all fixed up for your father. I want to surprise him," she said.

They struggled with the wrapping around the rug, grunting and sweating. "If Swan was home he could help," Clara said. But Swan had his own car now and took his time about coming home; and anyway Clark was glad he wasn't around. He felt a sense of possession toward this rock-heavy rug in its awkward packaging, as if it were something he had picked out for Clara himself.

When it was unrolled finally, the rug astonished them with its colors. They felt a little shy before it. "My hands are dirty, I shouldn't touch it," Clark said. Clara was bent over the rug, staring at it. She bit her lower lip thoughtfully. But Clark, who was embarrassed by beautiful things as if they were an affront to his manhood, broke the silence by saying: "Guess I'll drag all this junk back in." The "junk" was the old, good furniture that had belonged to Revere's first wife, reclaimed from the attic by Clara. She had discovered that its graceful lines and mellow wood were exactly the kind of thing she had been seeing in her magazines.

Afterward they sat at the dining room table but with their chairs turned around, so that they could look at the rug. They drank beer and talked quietly, aimlessly. Clara sat with her knees hunched up and her bare heels just on the edge of the chair; she kept staring at her new rug and as she did, her lips would turn up slowly into a smile. Clark was oddly pleased. "When you get married I'll help you with your house," Clara said. "I can tell if things are quality or not."

"Who says I'm getting married?" Clark said.

"Oh, you. You're a nuisance," Clara said, waving at him.

After supper Clark drove down the road to a tavern just for fun. Usually he did not go out alone but tonight he felt like doing something different; he was restless. In the tavern he stood at the bar and talked loudly and seriously about politics with the farmers who came in. He could tell that they liked him. He warmed at once to anyone who liked him and his magnanimity sometimes puzzled them; they were not accustomed to such friendliness from a Revere. But they did like him. At about eleven, one of his friends came in, a young man who had been married for maybe five years now, who wasn't doing well and had been avoiding Clark. But in ten minutes they had made everything up, Clark had won the man's friendship again, it was all right. They were both the same age, twenty-five. Tears came into Clark's eyes at the thought of them knowing each other so long. The young man said he had to call his wife to say why he was staying out so late, and Clark went over to the telephone with him. They were both quite drunk. After the man hung up Clark called Rosemary's house. Her mother answered and said she was in bed, was it important? Clark said yes, it was important. When Rosemary came to the phone he told her that he loved her, how was she? Tears had come into his eyes again. When the roadhouse closed he had to drive his friend all the way home because the man had passed out, then he had to drive home by himself, taking the turns as precisely as possible. Sometimes he drove fast, sometimes slow. He did not seem to know what he was doing except when he tried to make a turn then he could tell by a weak queasy sensation in his stomach if he was going too fast. When he got home it was quite late and the house was dark except for the back porch light. He turned off the ignition and sat smiling toward the house. He was too lazy and content to move.

He must have fallen asleep, because he woke up to Clara shaking his head. She had hold of his hair. "Wake up, come on," she said. She was whispering. "You want your father to know how drunk you are? Drunk like a pig?"

He felt a surge of nausea, then forgot it. He was very sleepy and peaceful. A long gap of time seemed to pass and then Clara jerked him awake again, bent low to hiss something into his face. "I'm O.K.," Clark muttered. "I can sleep here. . . ."

"Come on, please. Wake up. You don't want trouble."

Her hair was loose. She shook him again and strands of her hair flew into his face, stinging and tickling him. Clark did not remember her opening the car door, but it was open. He tried to step out but it was like stepping out over a chasm; everything was dark and strange.

"Clark, please—come on," Clara said.

She took hold of his head and shook it hard. Clark seemed to be working his way up through a heavy, warm pressure of water. He woke suddenly to see Clara bent over him. Behind her was the clear night sky and the moon, just a chunk of the moon, and he wondered why she looked so worried. He reached out and his elbow just brushed the horn—it almost made a sound—and he took hold of her. "Don't be so mad," he said sleepily. He pressed his face against her. Clara made a noise that might have been a surprised laugh, then she pushed against his forehead with her hand. "You're real nice," Clark muttered. "Wait—don't—"

He shut his eyes tight and held her. His mind stumbled backward away from this woman standing here in her half-open bathrobe and her bare feet to that earlier, younger Clara who had come home one day with his father. Just a girl. For years he had heard about her and one crazy time he had even gone all the way over to her house, risking everything, that whip of his father's or worse, just to stand by her windows and try to look in. . . . Now he had hold of her and dreamily, dizzily, he thought that he would never give her up. It seemed to him that he had struggled a long way to get to her.

"You're crazy, let go," she whispered. Clark pulled her down and tried to kiss her. He felt her hesitating—he was sure of that—and then she dug into his neck with her fingernails. "You son of a bitch, let go! Let go!" she said. Clark fell backward but did not really fall: he was still sitting in the car.

The next morning, before Mandy made up breakfast, Clara called him out into her "garden room." She was already dressed. Her hair had been pulled back, skinned back, and fastened with pins. On her right hand was the old purple ring she hadn't worn for years. Clark started to tell her how sorry he was, how miserable he was. "Yes," Clara said. She did not seem to be listening. Nor did she seem to be looking at him, exactly. "What you have to do is get out of here. You know that. You can't stay in the same house with me now."

"All right," Clark said.

"You just can't," she said, and her face, caught in the morning light that flooded the windows, was not the face he had loved and wanted the night before—there were fine feathery lines on her forehead and by her mouth. She was still a beautiful woman but the woman he had wanted was gone now anyway: that young girl Revere had brought home to marry.

"Do you understand?" she said. Her gaze was flattened and remote, like a cat's gaze. Then it sharpened upon him and he could see that she was a little frightened. She tapped at his arm and then let her fingers rest. "I'm sorry you did it. I didn't know—I never— But you can't stay here now. Go and marry her and that's that."

Clark bent to hear her better. "Marry who?" he said politely.

10

On Swan's eighteenth birthday he rode in with his father to Hamilton, where they met Clara and had dinner at a hotel restaurant. Clara visited the city often, usually staying in a hotel, but this time she was at a relative's house. When Revere asked her what she did she was pleased and vague, explaining she had to shop, had to check out stores, had to see people. It was not clear whom she saw, but Revere did not ask. He distrusted his city relatives; he thought they looked down on him.

Revere had come in for important business—his aunt's estate was being settled. Swan was disturbed by his father's tired, haggard look. The waiters looked at him as if he were an impressive kind of ruin, a man they ought to know but could not quite place. Revere mistook his waiter's solicitousness for something else. "Do they want to hurry us out of here, and we just came in?" he asked Clara.

Swan had no appetite. He had been listening to relatives arguing all day. But he opened his menu and looked at the words, which he tried not to translate into images of food. Clara said, just as he knew she would, "They're having Judd and his wife out to dinner, but not us. I know it." Swan expelled his breath to show how foolish this idea was; he wanted to stop Clara before she aroused Revere's anger. "They knew it was Steven's birthday but what the hell? Anything they can do to hurt me, they do it."

"They're busy, it's a lot of work," Revere said.

He closed his menu. He was over sixty now: a heavy, slack man with sharp bruiselike furrows on either side of his nose. He had a fixed, rather indifferent stare when he did not wear his glasses. Opening his napkin, shaking it out, he glanced down at it as if he had no idea what it was. Then he put it in his lap. They watched him, Swan and Clara, their eyes drawn heavily to him. For a while he said nothing, his face was hard and austere as a mask; then his lips began to tremble. He said, "Don't worry, they'll be sorry. I know how to get back at them."

"Yes, but you won't," Clara said.

He shook his head slowly, gravely. Swan felt cold. All afternoon he had had to sit by his father and hear his father's slowed-down, groping voice, his meandering off onto obscure and foolish problems, and he felt exhausted.

He was exhausted all the time now and never could he locate the core of his trouble. When he had still been seeing Loretta he had had these moments of unaccountable, terrifying exhaustion, as if a pair of great wings were pounding against the walls of his brain and had been pounding for so long that everything was going numb, dying. Unfolding his napkin, moving his silverware nervously and needlessly around, he thought of Loretta and wondered what she was doing. What he had last heard about her was nothing surprising—marriage, a baby. Loretta. He kept mixing her up in his mind now with Clark's wife, whom he saw occasionally. But Loretta had been his girl. Narrowing his eyes, he tried to avoid Clara's look and retreated to the secret contemplation of Loretta, who had loved him and had never once been able to talk to him, not once. That last night they had lain together in his car and he had been dizzy with wanting her, a real physical agony he had hardly been able to control, and when she said, "It's all right, Steven," he had prayed in his mind to God, who he understood did not exist and never had, begging: "Let me just be good and kind. I want to be good. I don't want anything else." Loretta had drawn him down to her with her arms and her sweet soft mouth. Never had he said the word "love" to her and he had not said it then—but he had almost thought it—and at the nearness of that thought he recoiled from her, trembling. He was terrified of sinking into that swamp with her. He was not going to drown in her body. Because there was no sweet mild world they shared without consequence: they were Swan and Loretta, two real people, and anything he did to her would not dissolve out and away as if in a dream. It would be real. It would involve them together forever.

"You won't hurt me," she had said.

But it was nothing like what Clara had promised—how strange and simple, how cruel his mother was! You didn't make girls happy in that simple way; they wanted and needed more, and if you couldn't give them anything more?

So he had stayed free of her and he had forced her to become free of him. And Clara had said, hearing it was all over: "Well, I'm just as glad. She was sort of trash anyway, wasn't she?"

Now Clara was shedding the cold haughty look she always wore into stores and restaurants, and as she read the menu a childish, cunning look came onto her face. Swan watched her in fascination. "Oh, this looks good. It isn't too expensive, is it?" she said. She pointed to something and showed it to Revere; he shook his head no, it wasn't too expensive. Swan smiled. He did not know what his smile meant: just the reaction of witnessing rituals, ceremonies that have been repeated many times. Clara always did this. He wondered if she did it with the other men she met here in the city—if she met other men; she was secretive now, in a vague sloppy way— and if they shook their heads, no, in the same way Revere did. When Clara moved her head, slivers of light darted off her diamond earrings. Yes, they were diamond. They weren't rhinestone. But how could most people tell the difference?

That was one of the things that bothered her these days.

"Have anything you want, Clara," Revere said.

They could relax in the shadow of this man and what he had done for them. Swan tried to think of Revere as his father, his *father*, and though the idea of Clara being his mother should have been harder for him to accept, still he could not quite understand what it meant to have a father. What did it mean, exactly? How was he to behave toward this man? He imitated any models he came across— he had been imitating and improving upon Clark's style for years— but at the very heart of their relationship was a sense of dry and forlorn emptiness across which father and son might contemplate each other forever. As Swan was more and more able to understand Revere's problems, his role was becoming simpler in one direction and more complex in another. He was turning into a kind of clerk or secretary. Or a kind of lawyer. Already he had spent time with one of his father's new men—his tax accountant—trying to explain to the man why Revere refused to pay certain things and agreeing yes, yes, it was irrational, but how were they going to get it paid without Revere knowing? The older Revere got, the more crucial it was that the game he played not be violated. He demanded to be fooled, lied to, misled. Swan believed that the people who worked with and for him knew this, but if they didn't, he, Swan, knew it and they would have to listen to him. There were certain things one could tell the old man, certain reports one gave him and others one did not. This was getting simpler because all he had to do was transform himself into a kind of machine to master it. But being Revere's only remaining son was getting more difficult. Robert was never mentioned, Jonathan had vanished out of their lives, and Clark was discussed in the way Revere had always discussed obscure relatives who had failed . . . so that left Swan—Steven—and it wasn't enough just to play chess with the old man and let him win; the old man was getting bored with winning chess. It was becoming necessary to nudge him a little to correct him, before he made a catastrophic blunder and lost everything. Swan thought of how simple everything might be if only his father would die, but the thought was a shameful one.

His father ordered drinks for himself and Clara. Back over Clara's shoulder was a wall mirror framed by a tacky red velvet drape, and Swan tried to avoid seeing himself in it. His mother's hair had been cut the other day, apparently, radically cut so that it hugged her head and crept in alarming bunches of curls up to the crown of her head, urged up there by some kind of trickery. Swan could not decide if she looked good or ludicrous. She could be both at the same time, maybe.

"Steven, you should have ordered a drink too. It's your birthday," Revere said.

"I don't like to drink."

Revere considered this as if he had never heard it before. There were wedges beneath his eyes—dark, tired pouches. He looked like a man who is thinking constantly, thinking painfully. Swan and his mother were light-skinned, light-haired, and curiously supple and casual beside this impressive old man; to a passerby the relationship among the three of them would be quite obscure. Swan thought: God knows I don't like to drink. If I got started drinking I might not ever stop. He wished that he could tell this to his father and throw all the blame for it onto that man's lap.

"Bessie looks sort of old," Clara said.

"Does she!" Revere said. "Well."

"I thought so. Ronald is in Europe, did you hear? Studying in Copenhagen—neurology."

The way Clara enunciated "Copenhagen"—"neurology"—you would think she said them every day. Swan smiled. "Ah, Steven," she said, a little sharply, seeing that smile, "you should have kept on with school. Why let them get ahead of you? He isn't much older than you are."

Swan shrugged. A negligent and self-derisive movement of his shoulders perfected by Jonathan in those days of the drive to school, and back. "I had enough of studying. Books."

"But why?" It was Clara's saddest disappointment: Swan's indifference about going to college. Valedictorian of his graduating class, and he hadn't gotten around to completing applications to any university until it was too late for the year. Vaguely Swan said he could go to college in a few years, maybe.

"Steven, you always loved to read so. . . ."

"Well, I don't any longer. My brain is burnt out."

Swan laughed, and Clara stared at him. How strange her son was becoming to her! She was growing fearful of him, almost. He was reminding her of someone, Swan sensed. "If I had the chance to learn things, and wasn't so stupid," Clara said, tapping at her teeth with her fingernails, "I would be so proud. I would! All my life there have been people around me—like in the newspapers, and on the radio—the Reveres in Hamilton—who are smarter than I am, and can talk better. I always wished I could see into the past like some people. Like at that museum, remember? 'Ancient Egypt.' 'Pharaohs.' History, things that have happened for a reason. And these people, they can understand life. But me, I . . . I never could." Clara faltered and Swan felt a stab of something like pity, sorrow, wonder: What was his mother trying to say, whom was she thinking about?

"Well, I don't have time for books now. Like I said, my brain is like a lightbulb, burnt out." Swan thought with satisfaction that he was safe from the massive crammed shelves of libraries and the high-ceilinged rooms of museums, so much demanding to be read, known, stared at, absorbed—that vast garden of men's minds that seemed to him to have been toiled into its complex existence by a sinister and inhuman spirit.

Revere said, "I never went to college. None of us did. Why? You need a 'moneyman'—you buy him. Same thing with a lawyer."

Swan smiled across the table and into his mother's occluded gaze. So? You see? That's wisdom. You didn't really want for me to get past him, did you? Wasn't it enough for me to be equal to him? And so much younger?

—

That night, lying in the strange hotel room, he cast his mind about for something that would let him sleep. He thought of his cousin Deborah, whom he had last seen at Christmas—a big Christmas party at Clara's. Not a successful party, not quite, but maybe the relatives had eaten more than in other years, stayed later, maybe they had been more friendly, and Clara was obviously willing to wait any number of Christmases to bring them around to the point at which they would embrace both her and Swan—she could wait forever, this Clara Walpole! Deborah had come but probably she had wanted to stay home. He watched her all during the meal, sitting next to her father but not even talking to him, a thin, shy, haughty girl with long brown hair and brown eyes. She looked as if she might be stupid until her eyes moved upon you, then you felt something strange. . . . After the long, loud dinner Swan sat by her and talked. They were alongside the Christmas tree, almost behind it by the window, and outside it had been snowing; he remembered all this. The snow was gentle and peaceful, but inside children were running, shouting—he hated them. Swan told her about going to the city with his father, trying to make her feel some of his confusion, his worry, without exactly telling her.

But she interrupted to say, "I hate your mother, do you know that?"

Swan was stunned. "You what?"

"I hate my own mother too. So it's all right."

She looked up at him and smiled. There was something unreal about her gaze: she was too young to be staring at him like that.

"Tell the truth, Steven! You hate both of them yourself."

"No."

Slyly she poked him. "Come on."

"I hardly know your mother. And why should I hate my own mother?"

Deborah's face shifted into an expression of contempt. "You know the truth but you don't speak it, so why should I talk to you? If you loved me and respected me . . ." Swan was embarrassed, and said nothing; they lapsed into silence. After a moment Deborah said meanly, "You're what is called a 'bastard.' 'Illegitimate.' Your mother and father weren't married when you were born. So why should you tell lies like everybody else, all these hypocrites? You're from the outside, everyone knows it. *You* can speak the truth."

"No. I'm not from the outside," Swan said. "I'm Curt Revere's son."

He had an impulse to take hold of Deborah, to hurt her. But the impulse passed quickly. He could not hurt her, he loved her; and if he didn't love her, he could not love anyone else. She was his sister-self. Yet with her, he had to pretend. "What you say isn't true, Deborah. So shut up."

Thinking now of that girl, on the verge of sleep, and wondering why, like him, she was so unhappy, and undefined; so like himself, but a Revere. Even her clothes looked old, of a bygone era, and they never seemed quite to fit her slender body, as if they'd belonged to someone else. *We could leave here. Live somewhere else. Europe. Alaska. Mexico. Deborah!* In his half-sleep he imagined making love to Deborah but before he could kiss her mouth, before he could enter her body, she faded and was gone.

—

On his twentieth birthday Swan was also away from home: in Chicago with Revere to meet with "moneymen." And that summer he spent weeks in Hamilton, staying in a hotel; meeting with his father's people, and quarreling; threatening them with actions Revere himself had not thought of, yet were belligerent enough to be an old man's ideas. Selling property. Selling investments. "Pulling out." Reinvesting. The Eden County Reveres were making a good deal of money on wheat, corn, soybeans because of government tariffs on imports, and what did Revere care if other interests weren't yielding nearly so much? Swan wanted to think it wasn't just the federal government, laws passed by Congress as a result of lobbying, bribery. The future was automated farming, like factories; except the products were to be eaten. Except, if you were smart, your workers weren't unionized, and could be fired with a few days' pay. The biggest U.S. companies could be broken by strikes, but not Revere-owned farms. Not yet.

When Swan was twenty-two he took his father up on the threat of buying out the partners.

"What are you waiting for, Pa? They're just laughing at you."

"Like hell they are. They'll change their minds when . . ."

Swan closed his eyes. "You've been talking about this for ten years."

His brain swerved and plunged past his father's. He was a young horse cruelly yoked to an aging horse. Forced to hobble his pace to match the other's. He had his own ideas, he knew what he wanted to do. In his mind was a land surveyor's map of the countryside from the Eden Valley north into Hamilton. Clearly he could see it intersected by a new highway; an interstate highway larger than any road that had yet been built in upstate New York. This was the future, he knew. He would purchase more land, always more land, and he would rebuild and expand the barns; tear down the old-style silos and build new ones, weatherproof. He would buy into a frozen foods company for that too was the future. He was feverish thinking of all he might do; the thought of so much power lying latent in the mute, brute land, waiting for someone to seize it. Clara was right: you needed to know what the past was. But you needed to know only to plunge into the future.

Swan had overseen the sale of the gypsum plant. He'd have liked to bail out on the Tintern lumberyard but Clark, damn dumb slow-witted Clark who hadn't had an idea in his head in his life, ran it.

Swan told Revere that the only one of the relatives he trusted was Judd. He spoke slowly and clearly so that Revere, frowning, turning his bifocal glasses in his hands, would not misunderstand. "It's taken me five years to realize that you distrust them but you continue to work with them—why? Uncle Judd can maneuver them out. We'll buy them out, and the hell with them. And if Uncle Judd doesn't want to do it, I'll convince him. I think I know how."

Revere's stern little line of a mouth smiled slightly.

———

"How strange you are now. Sometimes I don't know you."

Yet Clara spoke half-admiringly. She knew to keep her distance.

Swan laughed, his mother was so fanciful. Yet it was true, maybe.

Even when shaving, he avoided seeing his face. Without know-ing it he'd perfected a means of shaving that involved gazing only at his jaws, through part-shut eyes. Seeing no more of himself than he needed.

———

It became a time then when Swan was intoxicated with all he'd inherited—he could sit at the window of the third-floor room he'd commandeered as his office, and stare at nothing; not even out the window at the land that had once so enthralled him, foot-hills, mountains, much of it Revere property. Figures, speculations danced in his head. They lived at the center of activity, and pro-duction: REVERE FARM had become a model farm of the New Era: barns rebuilt and humming with efficiency, like factories; dairy cows milked by machines and not fumbling human fingers; hun-dreds of acres of wheat ripening toward harvest. Swan could feel his heart the beating heart of the farm, and the range of his desire, scanning the horizon as far as he could see, was the measure of what they would someday attain. "They." He liked to think that he was lifting them all with him, all the Reveres; those long-deceased men and women who'd loved and hated one another so fiercely, bound together by a single name and committed to living out the drama of that name. The lush, fertile countryside through which the Eden River coursed north to Lake Ontario had first been settled in the early 1700s, and by the time of the Revolution, the first Reveres had arrived. And now—

Then Swan would wake from his trance and think, What am I doing?

He was not one of them. He cared nothing for them.

He could leave it all, even now. Walk away.

But his mind flooded with figures, speculations, rumors, theo-ries. Steven Revere was not the only young Revere with ambition and plans. There were others in his generation, and one of them the fat-faced cousin with the Harvard degree: Swan's rival, you could say.

They spoke by telephone, solely. They never met.

The telephone was Swan's instrument, sparing him face-to-face meetings with people he disliked. There was still a residue of shy-ness in him: Clara's towheaded son. Now he rarely read anything except newspapers and financial news; if he listened to the radio, it was to financial news. Rarely did he walk out onto the farm as Revere still did, and yet more rarely did he enter the barns, the stables. He scarcely knew the horses' names, and which foals belonged to which mares. There was a farm manager, and the manager had assistants. Swan was spared, and would be spared. He'd long ago realized in himself an unnerving weakness—a mystical sort of love—for this inherited land, that was almost a terror in his blood. "The land"—a fine gauzelike scrim occluded his vision, the way the information packed into print, into books, had once threatened to invade his brain and leave him powerless. All knowledge is a drug, Swan believed. And all drugs can be addictive.

He would fight it. He knew how. He'd isolated it—this sensation, as of imminent helplessness—as the way in which a fetus grows in its mother's belly: tiny head taking form, tiny arms, legs, torso, fish-body becoming human; sucking its energy from the encasing flesh and growing, always growing. Mysteriously growing. If he knew where this demonic energy came from, he would know the secret to all things.

———

It was about this time that he bought a pistol and carried it with him when he drove into the city. When he walked about the city streets alone he liked to let his hand rest on it, in his pocket, knowing that it possessed a power that he did not. Thinking *I am armed now, I am ready.* Swan smiled at the strangeness of such comfort: his heart beat with less strain.

The only time Swan left the handgun in his car, locked in the glove compartment, was when he picked up a woman somewhere and took her back to his hotel: one of those young women sitting conspicuously alone in bars, positioned so that winking neon lights, reflected from the street outside, softened and made their faces alluring. They might have been salesclerks, office workers, nurse's aides and not prostitutes, or anyway not exclusively prostitutes, available without the intervention of a pimp. If Swan sensed a male presence, Swan retreated. He was filled with a moral repugnance for such a transaction, he could not bear it. The women he encountered were friendly-seeming, hopeful that he would "like" them. He knew, and he paid them money in excess of anything they might have asked, because money was the means by which he kept them from him.

What he feared, if he'd been drinking: that, overcome with passion or anguish, exhausted as if he'd run a great distance to their anonymous and malleable bodies, he might confess to them that he did not know what his life was, what he was doing, where he'd come from, or why his brain pounded with desires he could not comprehend. Always he was *running-toward*, yet at the same time *running-away* as in a dream gone bad. "I hurt my brother once. One of my brothers. It was an accident. Yet I did it on purpose." He was fearful of uttering such words in the lulling intimacy of sex; in the false intimacy of sex; in the brainless aftermath of sex. He was fearful of uttering words he could not retract. And of plunging onward saying he was a killer who had not completed his work and was waiting for his final deed to rise up within him.

He was frightened of these women yet returned repeatedly to them whenever he was in the city. Away from the valley, Steven Revere was not Curt Revere's son. Nor Clara Walpole's son: how furious Clara would be, to know of Swan's secret, sexual life! He smiled to think of the revenge he was taking, even if it was revenge upon himself, too. Saying, one night, to a girl he'd met in a Hamilton cocktail lounge and with whom he spent several hours: "How do you keep going with your life? I mean, how do you keep living?" It was a serious question and the girl considered it seriously yet finally she laughed and said, "It's how I am."

He was astonished at this reply. At the simplicity and sincerity of this reply. He thought of the long afternoon in the Hamilton library, and of waiting for his mother outside on the stone steps in the wind. A bitch she was. A whore. Even a child knows. And recalling Clara later that evening as Swan lay listless on his bed, how his mother had spoken to him in her rapid soft dazed voice of how happy she was, and how she deserved happiness; and he had believed that this was so, Clara deserved happiness, yet at the same time he knew she must be punished, and he alone was the instrument of punishment.

"Is something wrong? Did I say something wrong?" the girl asked, seeing Swan's face.

Female pleading. You were meant to respond protectively, yet you wanted to lash out, to hit and to hurt.

He left her abruptly, shaking with an anger he did not understand. In his car unlocking the glove compartment and seeing, yes to his relief the pistol was there, that mute and not-heavy object that fitted with such ease and logic in the grip of a man's hand.

Explain to that girl what he'd done, and had not yet completed. What he and Clara had done. Explain, and she would not have cared. *It's how you are. We are.* How close he'd come to hurting her, she could not have known.

11

In Hamilton, in a hotel into which he'd checked under the name *Walpole,* he ran his finger idly along the listings of Physicians & Surgeons in the local directory. The name *Piggott* struck him. He called to make an appointment.

The Hamilton Reveres had their physicians and surgeons, you could be sure. Their favored hospital. When one of them was stricken by illness, they purchased the very best medical attention.

If *Piggott, E. H., practice limited to internal medicine,* had an opening late that afternoon, Swan guessed that *Piggott, E. H.,* was not likely to be one of the Reveres' physicians. He was grateful that, as the breathy receptionist informed him, she could "fit him into" the doctor's schedule.

An office on the eleventh floor of one of the older downtown buildings, a few blocks from the lake that was choppy and no-color beneath a glazed-looking sky. Swan had had one of his blanked-out nights, the previous day. Was it the weekend? He guessed not, since Piggott had office hours. And others in this building had office hours.

In Piggott's waiting room were several other patients. Swan was disconcerted: somehow, he hadn't imagined other people. He hadn't imagined waiting.

He gave his Walpole name to the receptionist. He was ten minutes early for his five-fifteen appointment. He sat, restless and edgy.

Picked up an old *Time* to leaf through, without interest. The financial news would be not new, and so without value. Other features—politics, films, books—were of no interest to him. "Mister?"—the child was perhaps four years old. His mother was a woman of about Swan's age, maybe older, with a sad, hardened face; she wore a dress of slovenly glamour, and oddly dressy high-heeled shoes. Swan had only glanced at her when he'd entered the waiting room, and he had not noticed her child at all. "Mister? Hiya."

The greeting—"Hiya"—was uttered in a solemn tone. Swan smiled, and said, "Hiya" in return. He was surprised that the little boy was so soft-spoken, and so beautiful: his skin was pale and smooth as a doll's rubber skin, poreless, perfect; his lips reminded Swan of the lips of children in classical paintings, children who weren't meant to be human but of divine origin. Baby Christs, cherubs. "Want one?" The boy held out a roll of Life Savers to Swan, opened at one end. Across the room, seated uncomfortably in a plastic hard-backed chair, the boy's mother was smiling at Swan.

She's got her kid to pimp for her.

"No thanks," Swan said.

The child backed away, disappointed.

"He's just like that, he's a friendly kid," the mother called over, apologetically. Her voice was younger and softer than Swan might have anticipated. But Swan wanted nothing to do with them, with her. He would be seeing a woman that evening.

Others in the waiting room were observing him. Judging him as out of place in Piggott's office, maybe. His good clothes, his air of impatience, disdain. The way in which he flipped the pages of magazines, and tossed them down. As if none of the magazines could tell him anything he didn't already know.

At the Hamilton Statler, Swan was staying in a suite on the top, twenty-fifth floor; this was by far the tallest hotel in the city. He never drew the drapes. He believed he could feel the building sway, just perceptibly, in the wind off the lake. Scattered across a table were papers, most of them legal documents, he'd been going through with Revere lawyers earlier that day. In the other room, the bedroom, was the so-called king-sized bed in which he would lie that night; he would lie with a woman, that night; and above the bureau was an ornate-framed mirror that would record indifferently whatever occurred in that room, in darkness or in light.

Swan had left his pistol in the room, of course. Hadn't wanted to carry it into Piggott's office. A small-caliber, twenty-two semiautomatic six-shot Remington; not an impressive firearm, made of ordinary stainless steel with plastic grips. It was second- or thirdhand, he'd paid less than two hundred dollars for it. If Revere knew that Swan had bought such a gun, and carried it on his person, the old man would have been astonished. Swan smiled to think of him stammering *There's only one use for a handgun. . . .*

Swan wasn't so sure about that. He had yet to decide.

At five-thirty-five, the name "Walpole" was called. Swan rose at once and followed a middle-aged nurse into an inner office, that smelled of varnish and disinfectant. There was Dr. Piggott frowning at him, as if trying to place him. A new patient? New to Hamilton? Swan had not realized, he would have to answer so many idiotic questions.

Piggott was not a young man. He wore bifocals with flesh-colored nose pads. His teeth were obviously dentures. Yet his hands were graceful and his fingernails shone with cleanliness. His voice was paternal if somewhat mechanical—"What did you want to see me about, Mr. Walpole?"

Never in his life had Swan been called *Mr. Walpole*! He smiled, confused.

"I'm sure it's trivial. This symptom . . ." Swan paused, not liking that word, "symptom." It sounded clinical, as if he were trying to usurp a medical term. "During the night I can't seem to sleep and during the day I seem to want to sleep. Only to sleep. Like there's a dark well drawing me down, the water is sweet, delicious . . ." Swan listened to these words, fascinated. He had never spoken such words aloud before. What he said was true, and yet: until he'd spoken the words, he had not understood, entirely. "Sometimes when I'm driving I feel my—I guess it's my brain?—my 'consciousness'?—start to go out. Like a candle flame. I want only to close my eyes. The yearning is so strong. . . ."

Piggott asked how long had he felt like this, how long had he been experiencing this symptom, and Swan said he didn't know, maybe a year.

All my life.

"I'm not sure, Doctor. I don't want to exaggerate it. I'm healthy otherwise, I think. I'm sure."

Piggott was examining him, his body. Listening to his heart and asking him to open his mouth, and to cough; staring into his eyes and ears with instruments; tightening a band of rubber around his upper arm. He'd begun to perspire. He felt that he was a body, a vessel that might have contained anyone, presented to this man, a stranger, as you might drive a car into a service station and have it "serviced." What was Swan resided in his brain, inaccessible.

Piggott was asking again how old Swan was, and Swan told him another time: "Twenty-five. No, twenty-six." He wondered if the doctor believed him to be older. Had he an older heart, was his blood pressure that of an older man? Piggott asked, "Occupation, Mr. Walpole?" and Swan had to think. At the core of his icy perspiring there was something warm, peaceful, delicious: sleep. He wanted to sleep more than anything, just as he'd confessed to Piggott; but confessing had not erased his desire, as perhaps he'd thought it might.

Yet, if he returned to the hotel, and lay down on the absurdly large bed, he wouldn't be able to sleep.

"There's something wrong with me, isn't there? You can tell me, Doctor. My heart . . ."

"No. Your heartbeat, your blood pressure, appear to be normal. I would guess that, ordinarily, your blood pressure is even lower than my reading, and my reading is low," Piggott said. " 'Low' is good."

"Is it!" Swan smiled. "I guess I knew that. Of course. 'Low' is the opposite of 'high.' . . . High blood pressure."

He was speaking wildly. He sounded drunk. What had the doctor asked him? A question he had not answered.

"I help my father on his farm. He owns a farm south of here. In the Eden Valley."

"And is this a large farm, Mr. Walpole?"

"No. Not large."

Craftily he would not tell a stranger the truth. He was wanting to leave now, to put his shirt back on, escape. But Piggott was observing him closely. "You've said you have 'no history' of illness. Not even childhood illnesses? Chicken pox, measles . . ." Piggott was jotting notes on a clipboard; Swan knew that no one would ever look at those notes again, this was a waste of time. He made brief answers, that sounded plausible. Piggott asked, "How about your mother? Your father?"

"My mother has always been healthy. She's never been in a hospital that I know of." Though she'd been hospitalized at the time of the miscarriage. "My father, he's an older man." Swan gnawed at his lower lip, not liking what he'd said. *An older man.* He loved Revere, it was unfair to speak of him in such a way. Always the man had been *an older man.* Clara had married him because he had money, and he was older, and would die.

Piggott said, in a careful, kindly voice, "Mr. Walpole, you seem to be rather nervous. Are you always so nervous?"

"Nervous! I'm not nervous."

"You give that impression. Increasingly, now."

When Swan caught sight of himself in mirrors or store windows he was struck by his casual, rangy reflection—hair so blond it could only grow on the head of an idiot. His face was movie-actor bland, a face of mere surfaces. Why did this fool say that he was nervous?

"I'm the opposite of nervous, Doctor. Like I told you, I keep wanting to fall asleep."

"I will refer you to a neurologist, to arrange for more thorough testing. But, first, will you tell me who is your regular physician, Mr. Walpole?"

Neurologist! Possibly he had a brain tumor.

"No one. I don't remember."

Piggott frowned at this obvious lie.

"But where have you gone for medical examinations? Somewhere in the Eden Valley?"

"What about the Eden Valley?"

Swan spoke agitatedly. How did Piggott know where he lived?

Piggott said, quickly, "I only meant, Mr. Walpole: surely someone in your family sees a doctor?"

Swan shook his head, as if not understanding.

The awkward moment passed. Piggott said, "I will need to take a blood sample, if you don't mind."

"Why should I mind? I have plenty of blood."

Swan thought that actual pain would be good for him. It would distract him. He was disappointed that Piggott called in the middle-aged nurse to take his blood, while Piggott left the room.

Deftly the woman wrapped a strip of rubber around Swan's upper arm and tapped at his veins. She selected one, and began to slide the needle in, and Swan jerked his arm, knocking the needle away. It had felt like an insect's stinger. "Sorry! Did it hurt?" the nurse asked, and Swan muttered no, and they tried again; and another time his forearm jerked, involuntarily. A rivulet of sweat was running down his forehead. "Maybe your other arm. I'm sure I will have better luck." The nurse meant to be good-natured, confiding. Swan had no intention of resisting like a child or a neurotic female; yet when the nurse began to sink the needle into a vein at the crook of his right arm, the arm jerked another time. "Maybe Dr. Piggott would have better luck...."

"The hell with Dr. Piggott. The hell with this."

Swan spoke calmly, almost pleasantly. He grabbed for his shirt, walked out of the room buttoning it. He passed by an office in which the old doctor was standing, but too quickly for either to make eye contact with the other. In the outer office, where the breathy receptionist was on the telephone, Swan remembered to take out his wallet and toss onto the counter several twenty-dollar bills.

———

He returned to the hotel, where both doors to his suite were marked DO NOT DISTURB. He believed that, in fact, nothing had been disturbed in his absence, though lights flashed on the telephones meaning that someone had called. He checked the lining of his suitcase, where he'd hidden the pistol. He took it out, checked to see that the safety was on, and replaced it. *Keep the safety on, son. Until you mean to use your firearm.*

Descending then twenty-five vertiginous floors to the swanky cocktail lounge where he ordered a scotch neat and drank it swiftly like medicine: the prescription Piggott had failed to write for him.

"All I want is sleep, doctor. Barbiturates." He sounded maudlin and self-pitying and yet: the sexy young cocktail waitress hovered near, with a sly smile. "No more, honey. I've had it." He was through with women, or almost. Tipped the waitress a twenty-dollar bill, as compensation.

At eight-thirty he met Deborah in the hotel lobby. She wore a stylish coat of black cashmere and carried a black leather purse. Her fair, fine hair was cut unnervingly short, as if to mock Swan: to mock any man who believed her female, womanly. Because this was the Hamilton Statler, Deborah had entered the lobby shyly; she was glancing about in dread of seeing someone she knew.

"We're cousins. We have a right to see each other. It isn't fucking incest, is it?"

Swan spoke quietly, pleasantly. Deborah frowned at him.

"You're drunk."

"No. I'm waiting."

"Up in your room, you might have waited. Why down here? I feel so exposed. . . ."

"Didn't you want to have dinner? I made a reservation."

"I never said dinner. I don't want dinner. I'm not hungry, for God's sake."

They were close to quarreling. Deborah had the tight-wound look of a cat about to claw. In the elevator, Swan kissed her. He kissed her mouth hard, hungrily. Deborah slid her arms around his neck and kissed him in return, then pushed him away, breathing quickly. "You do these things on purpose. You don't respect me."

Deborah was pulling off her gloves, impatiently. Swan liked to see her rings: the pretentious yellow diamond ringed by smaller diamonds, and the equally pretentious white-gold band. It was a ritual both seemed to enjoy, Deborah yanking off her gloves, Swan smiling at her rings. She'd been a married woman for how many years, Swan kept forgetting. Every night sleeping with a man not-Swan, and somehow that, too, was gratifying.

When the door opened at the twenty-fifth floor, Swan pushed her out before him. Inside his room, Swan switched on lights and shut the door and bolted it. "I don't love you, I think I hate you. I hate myself with you, that's certain," Deborah said. She tossed her gloves and purse down. The color was up in her normally sallow face; her eyes were moist. "Strange. I can come up to your room with you, but I don't think I could eat with you. Any normal thing. Any normal act. No."

Swan was unbuttoning the cashmere coat. He smiled at the woman's peevish, pinched face. She was close to him as a sister: though of course he'd never had a sister, what did he know? "What does all that mean, Deborah? Your preamble."

"Don't make me angry, Steven. Don't hurt me any more than you've already done."

"Deborah. I didn't know I'd hurt you at all. . . ."

He was struck by her words. Even if she were fabricating, he was struck, for a moment faint with love for her.

Earlier, Swan had ordered bourbon sent to the room. They each had a drink, standing. Swan kissed Deborah several times, in a way of greeting. Then she turned, went into the adjoining room and Swan followed her, and turned off all the lights except the bedside lamp. They were more comfortable with each other now, if still guarded. Swan was dizzy with the scent of Deborah's hair; so excited he had to hold himself back, and not overwhelm her. In the somewhat cold, unfamiliar bed, large as a football field Deborah remarked, she pressed her face against his beating throat, hid her face, and whispered that he was her only friend, even if she could not trust him he was her only friend on earth. "I think about you all the time, Steven. It isn't even that I love you, you are necessary for me. When we were children, I hadn't known. I took you for granted. You were always there, the 'bas-tid.' Now I need you. I'm ashamed to say how I need you. I can say anything to you, can't I. I can do anything with you. You can't make me ashamed. You can hurt me, but you can't make me ashamed."

Deborah had slender, hard arms and legs. Her body was eel-like, warm and wiry and slender, yet with a muscular rigidity that seemed to Swan sexless. In the half-light Swan saw her large, dilated eyes, the eyes he'd been seeing for most of his life. It always surprised him that his young cousin had turned into a beautiful woman.

"What did he say when you told him you were going out?"

He meant Deborah's husband. Like Clara's husband, a well-to-do older man. But a city dweller, with two children from a previous marriage.

"Never mind about him."

"Doesn't he wonder? This time of evening . . ."

"I said keep quiet."

They made love ardently but haphazardly, like inexperienced children; Swan knew he was overexcited, overly forceful, yet couldn't hold himself back. Deborah liked to be hurt, but only to a degree. Afterward she kissed him, saying, "Something is happening with you, isn't it," though not in a voice of inquiry; and Swan debated telling her about his desperation that day, making an appointment with a doctor whose name he'd found in the Yellow Pages. "I'm nervous, is all. Insomniac." Deborah laughed, pinching the flesh at his waist. "You! I'm the one who's nervous and insomniac. You're healthy as a—steer."

Swan had only a vague idea of what time it was. How rapidly time was passing. He held Deborah, thinking *I don't need anything else. Only just this.* Yet he waited for something more to happen, some powerful passing-over of his love into her, or hers into him. Almost, it had happened the last time they'd been together. He had felt her body quickening beneath him, straining to be with him, so that she was left bathed with a dewy perspiration. Her skin burned, her eyes were widened and staring. This time, they were more conscious of each other, and edgy.

The way a woman responds to sexual intercourse: such violence, such helpless passion, you want to think it means something more than it does. Swan guessed it must be so with women, witnessing a man's passion. Imagining themselves its origin, its cause.

Deborah said, stroking Swan's forehead, "I'm thinking of going to Italy, in September. Venice, Rome."

"Is he going with you?"

She stiffened, as if Swan had said something hurtful.

"Well. I'll miss you."

They were silent. They drifted toward sleep. Somewhere far below on the street a siren wailed. Swan felt a rivulet of sweat running down his naked side, light as tickling fingers. Deborah was awake, and speaking in that way she did at such times, when they were faceless to each other. "D'you remember, Steven, when we were kids? It seemed to go on so long! You used to stay in the house, away from our noisy cousins. I used to watch you, in secret: reading your books. I loved you then, I think. And you—you'd never done a crossword puzzle, before me. . . ." Deborah stirred, and fluffed out her short damp spiky hair. The bedside lamp had a silken rosy shade that softened Deborah's features. "You didn't have dinner, then?" she asked. "I wasn't hungry," Swan said. "Except for you." He was feeling weightless, unreal. He guessed that Deborah had asked him to take her from her husband, to travel to Italy with her, and he'd pretended not to understand.

"When I want to sleep, I can't. I'd thought I was, just now. But no. You woke me, talking."

"Oh, Steven. It isn't like you to be so self-absorbed."

Deborah was sitting up, not minding if her small pale breasts were exposed. She was capable of sudden vehement motions, near the end of a meeting with him. Swan said, alarmed, "Deborah, don't leave yet—"

"Yes. I should."

"Honey . . ."

Honey always sounded pleading. Close to begging.

"It seems to mean so little, when I'm with you. Only at the moment. Then, afterward, there's no memory. Like an hourglass, making love with you. The sand runs down." Deborah spoke thoughtfully, not accusingly. "I married him to leave home. And now I live in a large, beautiful house, I have a beautiful life, I know, and yet—none of it means much to me. I'm busy constantly yet I have nothing to do. There are books I try to read, but I can't seem to read them. I don't do crossword puzzles any longer, so it's as if my life is the crossword puzzle, I can't solve. I don't know what I want, darling. Except for you I have everything. And yet—"

"Go to Italy. Don't wait until September."

"You'd let me go, I suppose? Yes."

"I can't very well stop you, can I?"

"You used to talk of traveling to Egypt. And India. Remember your map books? We pretended we were 'homesteaders' in Alaska."

Alaska! He remembered, but vaguely.

Suddenly Deborah was saying in a low, hurtful voice, "Look at your mother and my uncle Curt. They loved—they love—each other, so much. For years she was his mistress, just a girl who couldn't have known whether he'd marry her, or care for her really; she had his child, she had faith in him. And he adored her . . . he adores her. That's why people hate them, out of jealousy."

Swan rubbed his hands against his eyes. "Deborah, you're talking about my mother."

"I know it, so what? I admire Clara, too."

"You hate my mother. You've said."

"She dislikes *me*. She sees through me, my pretensions. She's the only genuine Revere, because she isn't a Revere."

Swan lay very still, thinking. Sleepless for so many hours he felt that thinking, the activity of his brain, was a kind of gluey fluid through which he had to propel himself, with an effort like swimming. If you cease that effort, you drown.

"I used to dream I would break free to some other country, and I'd be myself, there. I would know when I arrived, I would be so happy. Now it's different. I'm like a bulb that's burning out. Except for you I just keep going. I'm not even unhappy about it, any longer."

"Steven, please—"

"It's like everything was decided when I was born. Like in a book, or a map. I was never able to see it."

"Do you mean God?"

"God? What about God?"

"Seeing you. Seeing us. From some perspective we can't have."

Swan felt the insult, that Deborah should interpret his predicament in a theological way. There was that limitation to her, the country-girl's failure of imagination, he despised.

To amuse her he told of seeing Piggott. A doctor out of the Yellow Pages. "And he couldn't draw blood out of me. My veins are all dried up."

"What doctor? Why?"

Swan shrugged.

"Is something really wrong with you? Steven."

It excited him to be called by that name; it might have been that he was being mistaken for another man. Swan pulled Deborah down beside him, wanting to hide himself in her body; to get through to her what he knew he must tell her: that there was a great love dammed up in him but it could not be loosed. The more rigid that love lay inside him, frozen hard, the more frantic his body was to convince both her and himself that he really did love her. She was saying, half-sobbing, "Steven, I love you—I love you. Please."

At the very end, when he felt his backbone arching, his body dissolving in a spasm that sucked the breath out of him, he shut his eyes upon the flux of light only to see Clara's young adoring face melt in and out of his vision.

By train and by airplane. All around the world.

———

After she left, he dressed and went downstairs. He asked for his car. He must have looked strange because the man at the desk stared at him; when Swan returned his stare he looked away. Music was coming from somewhere behind them. Sentimental dance music, love music. Swan waited for the car to come and now it seemed that time was drawn out: there was a gilt clock over the elevator whose minute hand jumped with the passage of each minute, but very slowly, very frigidly did it move so long as Swan watched it. Some people came in, laughing. The telephone rang at the desk. Swan watched the clock. He thought it might be broken, then the minute hand jumped. At this rate it would take him a week to get there, he thought. In his imagination the highway between here and Tintern stretched out for thousands of miles, not marked on any map, a secret distortion more relentless and sterile than the great wide deserts of the Southwest, marked so blankly on the maps he had tacked up in his room at home.

Finally the car was brought around. Swan gave the man a dollar. When he drove off it seemed to him there was a slight shove, as if he were pushing off to sea and someone had given him a helpful shove with his foot. Swan squinted to get his vision clear and saw a policeman rubbing at his nose with a professional look, not three yards away. The city lights were confusing but he knew enough not to think about them. No matter how the night lights shone and wavered before him, he would drive right through them and think nothing of it. He drove slowly. He could not quite believe in the reality of his big automobile, so he had no reason to believe he might crash into someone else. Everyone else was floating by. Then he saw that it had begun to rain: was that why he had thought he was going to sea? At once the rain turned into sleet. The streets would be dangerous. It was late March, struggling into spring.

That morning Clara had said, "It's sure trying to get sunny."

For several hours he drove straight into the sleet. No one else on the highway except trucks flashing and dimming their lights to greet him. Swan felt absurdly touched, that strangers should signal to him as if they knew him. He had to wonder: was there a secret alliance of individuals, to which unknowingly he belonged, and was it wrong of him to feel such indifference for it? Outside, shapes and ghostly lights floated by in the night, part-lighted service stations, roadside restaurants, houses, rising up and falling away in silence. He drove on. His foot became numb from the constant pressure, he was afraid to slow his speed. He had become one of those fated actors in the movie he'd seen, speeding into the dark unthinking, in the knowledge that a final scene awaited, words and actions had been scripted for him to fulfill.

He arrived at Revere Farm before morning.

Clara kept a back porch light burning, who knows why! Swan hurried from his car without troubling to shut the door, and ran to the porch. Its white wrought-iron railings were slick with ice. With the childish panic of one who'd been locked out of his house, Swan pounded on the door. He was panting, his breath steamed. Then he thought to take out his key. His fingers were trembling so from the cold, he could hardly jam the key into the lock. Overhead he heard a sound. Someone was calling. He swore and turned the key in the lock and managed to get the door open.

Clara was approaching, cautiously. She had no idea who he was: he saw his mother, Swan thought, as a stranger might see her, and was struck by her wild, astonished-looking ashy hair, her youthfulness. A silky pale-orange kimono-robe flapped around her, he was aware of her breasts encased in the bodice of a matching nightgown. Recognizing him, Clara became at once frightened, and angry.

"You! For God's sake, what are you doing? Are you drunk?"

"Is he awake? Tell him to come downstairs." Swan was pleased with himself, he spoke so calmly.

"He thinks it's somebody trying to break in. He'll get the gun." Clara went to call up the stairs, "It's just Steven! Your son!" There was silence upstairs. Then Swan heard Revere's slow, heavy footsteps. "Never mind, Curt, it's all right!" Clara called.

Curt. Swan still resented that name, somehow.

"No, let him come down. I want to talk with him."

Clara stared at him. "You what?"

"I want to talk to him. You and him." Swan could not stop shivering. There was a roaring in his ears like a distant waterfall. "We can sit in the kitchen here. Please."

"Steven, what? Are you drunk?"

"Go sit down, I said please."

"Your father will—"

"Shut up, Clara."

"Look, who are you talking to?"

"I said, shut up."

Still he was calm. He would remain calm. He dared to push his mother before him, dared actually to touch her, the silky kimono she'd purchased for herself in a Hamilton store, the fleshy heat that exuded from her. She stared at him, swallowing; she was frightened, and yet would hide it; her eyes narrowed like a cat's, yet she sat at the table where Swan had pulled out a chair, in the dark. Fumbling for the switch, Swan turned on the light and saw that the kitchen was gleaming with smart new lime-green tile and glass cupboards. Fine polished cherrywood paneling hid the old, ordinary walls.

It came to him in a flash: the Reveres, and Clara and himself, seated at the old rectangular woodtop table. He could rememeber Curt Revere's seat at the table and he could remember Clark's but he wasn't sure where Jonathan had sat, or Robert. And where he'd sat, the youngest.

"Is he coming down, or what?" Swan asked. Now he was becoming impatient, listening for Revere's footsteps on the back stairs.

"He's an old man. What the hell do you want with him, like this?

Can't it wait till morning? Are you in trouble, is it something that happened in the city? You didn't hurt anyone, did you?"

"Where is he?"

"If you want him, go get him yourself."

They waited. Clara was breathing harshly, looking at Swan and then away, wiping at her eyes, as if she saw something in his face she wasn't yet ready to absorb. She was frightened, Clara was frightened at last. Long ago he had known she must be punished, she had sent him away with five dollars to buy his own lunch, she'd left his miniature antelope in the back of a taxi, she cared nothing for *him*. It was this judgment she saw in his face, yet could not believe.

Swan glanced down and saw that he'd tracked up the tile, his wet feet were leaving small puddles. And still he was shivering.

"Yes, look at you, you'll be sick in the morning," Clara chided. But her words didn't quite convince either of them. Then she said, in a softer voice, "Swan—"

"Don't call me that!"

"What are you going to do?"

Revere descended the stairs slowly, one of his knees was stiff with arthritis. An old farm dog, your heart was wrenched with pity for such dogs, their baffled eyes snatching at your own. Swan half-shut his eyes. Damn he did not want to feel pity. When Revere stood in the doorway Swan saw that he'd hastily put on overalls—old work pants that were faded and soiled. His voice was hoarse, baffled.

"Steven? What are you doing here?"

Swan said, louder than he wished, "Come in here! Sit down!"

He took out his pistol and lay it on the counter, so that they could see it. His hands were shaking badly.

"What are you—"

"Stop! I can't stand you talking!" he shouted at Revere. "Come in here, sit down with her, be quiet."

Revere came in, haltingly. He was staring at Swan's pistol. He had never seen it before, he did not approve of handguns. Since Robert's accident he did not approve of firearms on his property. Clara was sitting limply, hugging herself. She too stared at the gun, and then at Swan, startled, assessing. Her face was clammy-pale. Swan had never seen her so *respectful*. In the vestibule she'd looked young but in the bright overhead light you could see she was not young, fine white lines in her forehead, at the corners of her eyes, bracketing her mouth. Her skin was sallow, it was skin that now required make-up. It was not a skin to be examined closely.

Swan was trying to articulate what he wanted. He began to speak but his words ended in a gasp for breath. Dr. Piggott had not pre-scribed medicine for him, you could say it was Piggott's fault. He must sleep, and he would sleep. He covered the pistol with the flat of his hand as if embarrassed. "I don't want to . . . I mean, I want to . . ." He stared at them, his parents. The clock and the new re-frigerator hummed, ". . . explain something to you." Yet, as he stood, waiting, no words came to him. Finally he had no choice but to pick up the pistol, and check the safety.

"Swan—" Clara cried.

"I said, don't call me that! I can't stand it!"

They were calculating could they take the gun from him, he knew.

Revere, an old man suffering from high blood pressure yet canny, shrewd. And Clara.

"I came back here to explain to him, Clara. What needs to be done. To us. Before it's too late, and something happens to him."

"Steven, no . . ."

Clara's bare toes were curling on the tile floor. It was preposter-ous, he saw what he believed to be remnants of red polish on her toenails. He said, "I want him to hear, to be a witness. Then he can explain, later."

Sharply Clara asked, "Later—when?"

"What is he saying?" Revere asked.

"Nothing! He's crazy!" Clara got to her feet, suddenly. Swan was forced to step back against the counter. He held the gun pointed at her, not very steadily. Yet he held it, he was determined. Clara said hotly, "You, what are you doing? With your brains, how stupid you are! Never went to college, why? Look at you now, behaving like a crazy man waking us up like this. They will come and lock you up and you know what I will say?—I will say 'The hell with him, he had all the advantages and threw them away.'" But Clara's face seemed to break. She paused, with the look of a drowning woman. "Swan, everything I did was for you—you know that. Everything—"

"No. Not for me."

"For *you*."

"I can't stand you talking—"

"But what did I do wrong? Tell me! All my life was for you—all of it." She was trembling, preparing to jump at him. She would use her nails. She would claw him, pummel him. She was taunting him as crude children would taunt one another. "No, you're not going to shoot. Not me, not anybody. You think you can kill your own mother? You can't, you can't pull the trigger. You're weak, you're nothing like your father, or your grandfather, that's my secret knowledge of you—'Steven Revere.'"

Swan raised the pistol, blindly. The roaring in his ears was deafening and yet he would remain calm, he was determined.

Revere was on his feet, moving to interfere. Clara pushed back at him, to keep him away. She taunted Swan, "Think you can pull the trigger—well, you can't! You can't!"

At the last instant Swan's hand swerved. His finger jerked on the trigger, it was the old man he struck. Revere cried out, stumbling back against the counter. He would fall, a bullet wound would blossom red in his chest, but Swan did not see him fall. Already he had lifted the gun to his own head.

12

When she was only in her mid-forties she had this strange trouble with her nerves. Sometimes the right side of her body would fall numb, as if asleep, paralyzed. She stayed at the Lakeshore Nursing Home, where she was the youngest patient: at forty-five she looked years younger and the pretty little nurses stared at her with pity. She went on trips "home"—that meant to distant and uninterested relatives—but she was never well there or anywhere, and she could not return to Revere Farm because the property had been sold, so after a while she remained at the Lakeshore Home permanently and in a few years she was not even the youngest resident any longer, though she would remain the most attractive for some time.

Clark came to visit her. Every week or two. On Sundays in good weather he took his stepmother out to dinner at the White House, a showy inn with a Negro doorman in coat and tails. Clara would be vague and distracted; she had the air of an invalid anticipating pain. If, with her tremulous hand, she overturned a glass, she sat staring at the water soaking into the white linen tablecloth as if it were a catastrophe she might as well see through to the end.

In his car that was showy too, in the way of mid-century America, Clark drove the mostly silent woman along the lakeshore. Sometimes he brushed tears from his eyes, while driving. He wasn't an alcoholic: he could control his drinking. Still, a few shots could trigger his emotions. He talked to Clara about his children, about his wife, the damned lumberyard he hated and wished to hell would burn down. He talked about how things were changing in the valley, how Tintern was expanding; there was a West Tintern now, with a shopping center, fast-food restaurants. On land his brother Steven had bought cheap.

He was crude, head-on as a flummoxed farm animal. Saying "Steven"—"Steve"—as if not knowing how the name, the mere sound of that word, would make Clara stiffen.

Or if he knew, not giving a damn.

"You're the only one who knows. You were there. The only one who remembers, Clara."

With the passage of years, Clark came to see Clara less frequently. Every month, every two months. But he telephoned her, and he never forgot Christmas, Easter, Mother's Day. At the Home, Clara was Clark's mother: though he looked hardly younger than Clara, the nurses would call out to Mrs. Revere, "Your son is here, Clara. Here he is." A hefty man, inclined to wheezing. His stomach hung over his straining belt. His face was beefy, the ruins of a good-looking boy's face. There was something fierce and tender in his manner, as he stood at the doorway of "Mrs. Revere's" room, turning his panama hat in his hands.

Clark pretended not to notice how annoyed Clara could be when he interrupted her television programs. She was in her early fifties now: she'd begun to gain weight at last. The Home was a private establishment, and expensive. From her husband she'd inherited far more money than even the Home would devour, though she wasn't much aware of it, or grateful for it. It was Judd Revere who oversaw the finances, with Clark's approval. Clark said repeatedly, "She could get well if she wanted to. She could live with us." But at the door of his stepmother's room, peering in at her, he wasn't so sure. On either side of her mouth there were sharp lines. Her once-beautiful eyes were bloodshot and clouded and ringed with soft puffy tissue. Her once-beautiful ashy hair, now thinning at the crown, dry and brittle. Clark might have been waiting for the younger Clara to return, as if it were a matter of his showing up at the right time.

He was a suitor. He was a long-lost son, confusing her with his own mother whom he scarcely recalled. He insisted upon taking her from her room, out into a garden area where goldfinches hovered about feeders, and some of the more active residents trimmed roses. Clark steered Clara to their usual bench, where he could brood and mourn the past, seated with his fleshy thighs outspread and his elbows on his knees. When he asked Clara how she felt, she would answer reluctantly, as if the effort wearied her, or bored her.

"I can breathe. I can walk. I'm not like the others, yet. I can still bathe by myself, but somebody has to be right outside the door. I'm afraid at night, that's when the . . ." She paused, searching for the word: *paralysis*. ". . . when it begins. Through my legs and my spine and if I can't reach the bell, nobody will come till morning. In the night, sometimes I die. It's so quiet then. I could be at peace then. It happened like that to my mother. She fainted in a field—tomatoes. She died there. Her head was in the dirt. Her pretty hair. I brought water for her to drink but she couldn't drink. I said, 'Oh, Ma!' and she said, 'Go away, Clara. I'm not your ma.'"

On her better days they walked, after a meal at the White House. Sometimes they walked along the river, without speaking. The staff at the Home encouraged Clark to take his mother out: "Her heart is strong, she can live a long time yet. You seem to be her only visitor." One balmy spring day when they were walking along the river, Clara somewhat slowly, stiffly, two girls in their early teens pedaled up on bicycles, suddenly close behind them. Both girls had wild, dirty, ferret-faces. One yelled, "Watch out, you old hag!" because Clara had not moved aside for her.

She was even quieter than usual for the remainder of that day. Sitting with her limp hands in her lap, still and silent and aggrieved. When Clark spoke to her she made no pretense of listening. He felt his throat ache with a grief of his own—his wife couldn't understand what this grief was, why he drove so far to visit his stepmother whom she, the wife, so violently disliked; why he could not explain himself to her. Clark was to continue visiting Clara for the rest of Clara's life, for many years, though after her first stroke she would scarcely seem to know him, or look away from her television set when he appeared.

"Clara? It's me, Clark. . . ."

She seemed to prefer action programs: men fighting, swinging from ropes, riding horses and driving fast cars and shooting guns, killing the enemy repeatedly until the dying gasps of evil men were but a heartbeat away from the familiar rhythms of the commercials, the opening blasts of their singsong lyrics, that changed with comforting slowness over the years.

Afterword

Joyce Carol Oates

"Dare you see a soul *at the White Heat*?"—this striking opening of one of Emily Dickinson's most enigmatic, and perhaps most personal poems (#365), has always seemed to me an ideal metaphor for the passion of writing. To experience the *White Heat* is not at all the same as comprehending it, still less controlling it. One is "inspired"—but what does that mean, exactly? One is empowered, thrilled, fascinated, exhilarated and, in time, exhausted; yet one can't be at all certain of the value of what has been created for others, or even for oneself. Especially, a writer's early white-heat-driven works come to seem to the writer, over the passage of years, mysterious in their origins, brimming with the energy of a youth not yet discouraged or daunted or even much aware of how any ambitious work of art might be received by others. All writers look back upon their early creations with envy, if not always unalloyed admiration: how much strength infused us then, for our having lived so briefly!

A Garden of Earthly Delights was originally written in 1965–66, published in 1967, and has remained in print more or less continuously, as a mass-market paperback in the United States and more recently as a Virago "Classic" in England. Yet, in rereading it, in preparation for the Modern Library edition, which seems, in some quarters, a kind of canonization of a text, I was dissatisfied by it, and undertook a new edition in the summer of 2002. As a composer can hear music he can't himself play on any instrument, so a young writer may have a vision he or she can't quite execute; to feel something, however deeply, is not the same as possessing the power—the craft, the skill, the stubborn patience—to translate it into formal terms. In preparing *them* (1969) for a similar Modern Library edition in 2000, I rewrote some sections of that novel, revised others, and trimmed here and there, but did not feel the need to rewrite approximately three quarters of the novel, as I have done here. In reexamining *Garden,* I saw that the original narrative voice had not been adequate to suggest, still less to evoke, the complexity of the novel's principal characters. The more complexity we acknowledge in others, the more dignity we grant them. The Walpoles—Carleton, Clara, Swan—were in fact far more than fictitious characters to me in 1965–66, yet I failed to allow their singular voices to infuse the text sufficiently; the narrative voice, a version of the author's voice, too frequently summarized and analyzed, and did not dramatize scenes that were as vivid to me as episodes in my own life. The Walpoles are strong-willed individuals not unlike those with whom I'd grown up, or had known about as a child in an economically distressed farm community in western New York in the 1940s and '50s; they are quirky, unpredictable, wayward, self-aggrandizing and self-destructive, with distinct and idiosyncratic voices of their own, and would be resentful of their stories being "told" by another. Though a social analyst might diagnose the Walpoles as victims of a kind, the Walpoles certainly would not see themselves in this reductive way, and as their chronicler, I have no wish to portray them as purely victims either.

Composing the original version of *A Garden of Earthly Delights* in 1965–66 was very like my experience in composing *Expensive People* a year later: as if I had poured gasoline on my surroundings and lit a match to them and the flames that leapt madly up were somehow both the fuel of the novel and the novel itself. These "white heat" experiences are like waking dreams, consuming one's imagination, utterly fascinating, exhausting. The novel-to-be springs into a visionary sort of life like something glimpsed: an immense mosaic, a film moving at a swift pace. You "see"—but you can't keep up with that pace. The novel opens before you like a dream, drawing you into it, yet it's a dream in which you are somehow participating, and not merely a passive observer. So swift and obsessive was the original composition of *A Garden of Earthly Delights* for the young writer in her mid-twenties that it didn't dawn upon me, preposterous as it must sound, that "Carleton Walpole" might have been partially modeled upon my paternal grandfather, Carlton Oates; it did not occur to me that my grandfather, whom I had never met, an apparently violent and often abusive alcoholic who had abandoned his young family to destitution in Lockport, New York, in the early 1920s, and whose name was never spoken in our household, might have acquired a mythic significance in my unconscious, if one believes in "the unconscious" as a putative wellspring of creativity. If I had been asked why I'd named my character "Carleton" I would have had no answer except that it had sounded appropriate. (Readers have told me over the years that "Carleton" is a likely name for a man born in the Kentucky hills, whose ancestors emigrated from England in the previous century.) Only when I read biographical material about my family, in Greg Johnson's 1998 biography of my life titled *Invisible Writer,* did the connection seem obvious, like the similarity between "Clara" and "Carolina" (my mother's name). How opaque we are to ourselves sometimes, while transparent as crystal to another!

Of course, a literary work is a kind of nest: an elaborately and painstakingly woven nest of words incorporating chunks and fragments of the writer's life in an imagined structure, as a bird's nest incorporates all manner of items from the world outside our windows, ingeniously woven together in an original design. For many of us, writing is an intense way of assuaging, though perhaps also stoking, homesickness. We write most avidly to memorialize what is past, what is passing, and what will soon vanish from the earth. No more poignant words have been uttered than William Carlos Williams's lines *With each, dies a piece of the old life, which he carries . . . ;* if I had to suggest a motive for metaphor, certainly for my own decades-long effort in the creation of metaphor, it would be something like this. A novel is so capacious, elastic, and experimental a genre, there is virtually nothing that it can't contain, however small and seemingly inconsequential. *A Garden of Earthly Delights*, my second novel, and my third book, is, like my first novel, *With Shuddering Fall* (1964), crammed with "real" life, landscapes and incidents, only slightly altered.

Migrant farmworkers were often seen in western New York when I was growing up, especially in Niagara County, which is mostly orchards and farmland. Seeing these impassive-looking men, women, adolescents and children being driven along our country roads in battered buses, I wondered at their lives; I could imagine myself among them, a sister to the young girls. (The migrant workers I saw were predominantly Caucasian.) I grew up on a small family farm in Millersport, where the crops required picking by hand: pears, apples, cherries, tomatoes, strawberries. (Eggs, too, another sort of hand-picking.) Months of our lives were given up to "harvesting"—if we were lucky and had something to harvest—and I can attest that little romance accrues to such farmwork, still less to sitting self-consciously by the side of the road at an improvised produce stand hoping that someone will stop and buy a pint, a quart, a peck, a bushel basket of your produce. (Early conditioning for the writer's solitary yet cruelly exposed position in a capitalist-consumer society!) In rereading *A Garden of Earthly Delights* I was surprised that relatively little of this firsthand picking experience is included; entirely missing is the kind of picking I did most, from ladders positioned in fruit trees, that could be treacherous. (Not just that your shoulders, arms, neck and legs were strained, and not just that you might fall, but also you were easy game for stinging insects like bees and flies.)

My early editors at Vanguard Press were offended by the frequent profanities and crudeness of speech of the characters of *A Garden of Earthly Delights*, objecting particularly to Clara's speech. For even as a girl, Clara can be forcefully crude. Yet to me, such speech was more or less commonplace; not so much within the home (though my father, Frederic Oates, sharing some of the characteristics of the fictitious Carleton, was not what one would describe as a speaker of genteel middle-class English) as outside, overheard as adult and adolescent speech. Strange to admit, the crude language of the characters in much of my fiction strikes a nostalgic chord with me; even the sudden flaring-up of bad temper and violence common to a world of the economically deprived doesn't seem to me ugly or morally disagreeable, only just authentic. In such worlds, men in particular speak and behave in certain "manly"—"macho"—ways. (How different—very different!—from the seemingly civilized world in which I have dwelled since 1978, in Princeton, New Jersey, where such mild profanities as "hell" and "damn" strike the ear as strident; as out of place as sloppily guzzling hard cider from a jug would be, in the way of Carleton Walpole.) Can one be nostalgic for a world in which, in fact, one would not wish to live, as for incidents one would not wish to relive? The stab of emotion I feel at recalling my one-room schoolhouse in Millersport, so very like the schoolhouse Clara Walpole briefly attends, is difficult to analyze. I would not wish any child I know to endure such experiences, yet I could not imagine my own life without them; and I think I would be a lesser, certainly a less complex person, if I had been educated in a middle-class community, or had grown up in a supremely civilized community like Princeton. (It was in the schoolhouse and its desultory "playground" that I first grasped the principles of what Darwin might have meant by the strife of species, the strife of individuals within species, and the phenomenon of "survival by natural selection.") I did not live in a family so haphazard and impoverished as Carleton Walpole's, but I knew girls who did, among whom was the closest friend of my childhood and early adolescence. Though such terms as "victims of abuse"—"abuse survivors"—are clichés at the present time, they did not exist in the era of *A Garden of Earthly Delights*. On the contrary, it was not uncommon in certain quarters for men to beat their families and remain morally as well as legally blameless; though sexual harassment, sexual molestation, and rape may have been commonplace, the vocabulary to define them was not, and it would have been a rare case reported, and a yet rarer case taken seriously by police. *A Garden of Earthly Delights* is a wholly realistic portrayal of that world, but it isn't so much a novel about victims as it is about the ways in which individuals define themselves and make of themselves "Americans"—which is to say, resolutely not victims.

A Garden of Earthly Delights was imagined as the first of an informal trilogy of novels dealing with disparate social classes, focusing upon young Americans confronting their destinies. Though in my short fiction of the 1960s I rarely explored social and political themes in depth, focusing instead upon intimate emotional and psychological experiences, in my novels I hoped to evoke much larger, more grandly ambitious landscapes. My models were Balzac, Stendhal, Dickens, Flaubert, Mann, and Faulkner. When I moved to Detroit, Michigan, in the early 1960s—I would live there through the July 1967 riots, and beyond through months of exquisite civic tension—I was galvanized to believe that the writing of a novel should be more than purely private, domestic, or even, contrary to the reigning Nabokovian imperatives of the day, apolitical and aesthetic; I wanted my novels to be realistic portrayals of individuals unique in themselves and yet representative of numerous others of their generations and social classes. (Strange, that I had not read Dreiser! Not until decades later would I read *An American Tragedy* and the more capably executed *Sister Carrie*, whose resilient protagonist might have been an older cousin of Clara Walpole.) My early fiction had been set in a somewhat surreal/lyrically rendered rural America ("Eden County") suggested by my own background in western New York ("Erie County"); after moving to Detroit, I began to write about individuals in cities, though their ties, like my own, might be rural. I seem to have made an early, curious identification with Swan Walpole, since an incarnation of this Hamlet-like character ("Hamlet-like," I mean, in my then-young writer's imagination) appears in one of my first-published stories, "In the Old World," a co-winner of the *Mademoiselle* short-story competition while I was an undergraduate at Syracuse University in 1959. In reliving Swan Walpole's life, through my rewriting of much of *A Garden of Earthly Delights*, I see him as a kind of alter ego for whom the life of the imagination (he's a bookish child, in a world in which books are devalued) is finally repudiated, as it was not, of course, for me, for whom it was more a salvation, if "salvation" isn't too melodramatic a term. Swan is burnt-out, self-loathing, and finally a suicide because his truest self has been denied, and that "true self" would have been a writer-self, an explorer of cultural and spiritual worlds. I would not have known in 1965–66 how this young man's experience would parallel the ways in which America itself would seem to have repudiated, in the 1970s, '80s, and '90s, even into the morally debased and economically ravaged twenty-first century, a further loss of innocence of this nation at such odds with its own ideals and grandiloquent visions: *Swan, c'est moi!* (But only in fantasy.)

In this new edition, which is slightly longer than the original, the principal characters, Carleton, Clara, and Swan, are more directly presented. My intention is not to narrate their stories so much as to allow the reader to experience them intimately, from the inside. Though there are no first-person passages or experimental sleights of hand, of a kind I would employ in *Expensive People* and *them*, the Walpoles speak more frequently; we are more frequently in their heads; lengthy expository passages have been condensed, or eliminated. Very little in the plot has been altered, and no new characters are introduced or old characters dropped. Clara and Swan move in their original zigzag courses to their inevitable and unalterable fates; Carleton moves more swiftly to his, a self-determined fate that more befits the man's character. In the new *A Garden of Earthly Delights* Carleton is acknowledged as more heroic than I had seen him originally, when I was so young. Clara is more sympathetic, and Swan more subtle and capricious in his spiritual malaise. (Swan and I share a predilection for insomnia, but not much else.) I knew little of nursing homes in 1965–66, and now in 2002 I know all too much about them, since my elderly, ailing parents' experiences over the past several years, which makes the conclusion of *A Garden of Earthly Delights* particularly poignant to me. How chilling, a young writer's prophecies seem in retrospect! If we write enough, and live long enough, our lives will be largely déjà vu, and we ourselves the ghost-characters we believed we had created.

The effort of the rewriting was not to alter *A Garden of Earthly Delights* but to present its original characters more clearly, unoccluded by an eager young writer's prose. They seem to me now like figures in a "restored" film or figures seen through a lens that required polishing and sharper focusing. What remains unchanged is the chronicle of the Walpoles, my initial attempt at an "American epic." The trajectory of social ambition and social tragedy dramatized by the Walpoles seems to me as relevant to the twenty-first century as it had seemed in the late 1960s, not dated but bitterly enhanced by our current widening disparity between social classes in America. *Haves and have-nots* is too crude a formula to describe this great subject, for as Swan Walpole discovers, to *have,* and not to *be,* is to have lost one's soul.

PRINCETON, AUGUST 2002

A Note on the Type

The principal text of this Modern Library edition
was set in a digitized version of Janson, a typeface that
dates from about 1690 and was cut by Nicholas Kis,
a Hungarian working in Amsterdam. The original matrices have
survived and are held by the Stempel foundry in Germany.
Hermann Zapf redesigned some of the weights and sizes for
Stempel, basing his revisions on the original design.